The Consulting Detective Trilogy
Part I: University

Darlene A. Cypser

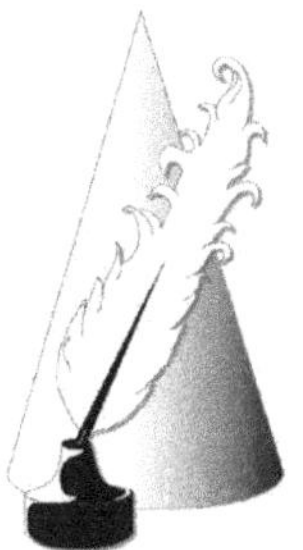

Foolscap & Quill

The Consulting Detective Trilogy
Part I: University
© 2012 Darlene A. Cypser

Set in Baskerville Classico & Times New Roman

www.theconsultingdetective.com

ISBN 978-1-938143-47-2

Foolscap & Quill, LLC
151 Summer Street #1018
Morrison, CO 80465-1018
www.foolscap-quill.com

Contents

Chapter 1

Simple Steps

"Even his iron constitution, however, had broken down under the strain...."
Dr Watson, The Reigate Squires

It was some time before Sherlock Holmes recovered from the events of late 1871. Physically, it took many months; mentally, it took many years. He was bound by both a promise to the living and a commitment to honour the dead, and being so bound he set the full force of his will to rebuilding the shattered pieces of his life. Yet sometimes will alone is not enough.

The morning after Sherlock had given up his deadly fast, Jonathan Beckwith sat at his usual post upon the hearth in Sherlock's room. Sherlock had eaten his breakfast and the tray had been sent back to the kitchen empty, no doubt to the delight of Tessy, the cook. Now as Jonathan watched, Sherlock pulled back the quilts and pushed himself to the edge of the bed. He was still very weak, Jonathan could tell. The long illness followed by the two day fast had taken their toll upon him. Jonathan stood and walked quietly to the side of the bed where Sherlock sat.

"May I help you, sir?" Jonathan asked.

Sherlock looked at him.

"Help me stand," Sherlock said, reaching up to place his hand upon the boy's shoulder.

Sherlock leaned upon Jonathan's shoulder as he shifted his weight on to his trembling legs. He was uncertain they would hold him. Slowly step-by-step they walked to the small table across the room. Sherlock sat gratefully in one of the chairs next to the table and rested. He was so very weak, and yet he must do it. He must be strong. He stood shakily again and walked back to the bed with Jonathan's assistance. He fell upon the bed exhausted, breathing heavily.

"Are you all right?" Jonathan asked.

"Yes," Sherlock replied between breaths.

In a few minutes, when he had caught his breath, Sherlock insisted on doing it again.

In the past week, Jonathan had seen frightening dark sides of Sherlock that he had never known existed. Now he was impressed by his young master's determination. Jonathan could see how difficult even walking was for Sherlock right now. Yet he insisted on pushing himself to the limits of his endurance. If determination alone were enough then Sherlock would go far. That is not to say he would be happy, for these days Sherlock was solemn and silent for the most part. He lacked the youthful spark of the year before and was driven solely by his promise to his brother Mycroft and his commitment to honour the memory of the lost Violet. For now that was enough.

Sherlock repeated the journey from the bed to the table and back numerous times each day thereafter, soon without Jonathan's assistance. When that became easy for him he began circling the table and walking back to his bed without stopping. He insisted on taking his meals at the table and ate with purpose. He took little pleasure in it. It was fuel he required to accomplish his task. He continued to lengthen his route about his room as he gained strength. He knew he had a longer journey to make very soon.

A week later Jonathan was helping Sherlock dress.

"Art thou—Are you sure you can do this?" Jonathan asked, slipping for an instant into his native broad Yorkshire, as he sometimes did when he was nervous.

"I must do it," Sherlock responded as he put on his coat. "Now go and do as I asked."

Sherlock sat fully clothed upon his bed gathering his wits and his strength for the task before him. A moment later the door to his room opened silently and a furtive Jonathan entered and closed the door behind him.

"Yes, sir. He's there," Jonathan said.

"Good. Now come with me down the stairs, but if he should come out get back quickly. I can't have him see you helping me, understand?" Sherlock insisted.

"Y-yes, sir" Jonathan responded.

Soon Sherlock stood before the door to his father's study. He waved Jonathan back, braced himself, drew himself up straight and knocked firmly upon the door. He entered when the call came. After closing the door behind him, Sherlock said, "Father, I would like a word with you."

Squire Holmes did not show his surprise that his youngest son now stood before him when he had been at death's door barely a week before, but Sherlock knew it was there. He knew that his father admired strength and determination in a man, and Sherlock intended to use that knowledge to get what he needed. What he needed was a career so he could leave this place, and for that he needed to attend the university.

Siger Holmes told Sherlock to be seated. Sherlock sat slowly, trying not to show how glad he was to be sitting down. They spoke for a long time, but there were many things they did not speak of. They did not speak of their last interview in the study or what came after, or Siger's doubts of his son's sanity. They spoke of the future, not of the past.

Jonathan waited anxiously outside the door of the study. Thomas, the butler, scowled at him once, but Jonathan ignored him. He was under orders to be where he was and doing what he was. At last the door opened and Sherlock came out, erect as before, but quite a bit paler. As the door shut behind him Sherlock leaned heavily on Jonathan's shoulder for a moment then straightened up again.

Jonathan started to speak, "Are you—."

But Sherlock waved him to silence.

"Upstairs," Sherlock whispered.

But as they reached the staircase, Sherlock's head was spinning and he reached out for the banister to keep himself from falling. He hung on to it for a moment. Just then his brother Sherrinford came down the hall.

"Sherlock!" he exclaimed, but Sherlock motioned him to silence as well.

"Help me upstairs—quickly now!" Sherlock whispered, fearing his father would appear at any moment and all his efforts would be undone.

Sherrinford and Jonathan helped Sherlock up the stairs between them. As they approached the door to Sherlock's room, Mycroft appeared in the hall.

"Sherlock?" Mycroft inquired, asking a thousand questions with one word.

Sherlock turned to him.

"I spoke to Father," he said.

"Ah!" Mycroft said, and followed the three of them into Sherlock's room. Sherlock lay down upon his bed breathing heavily.

"Should I send for the doctor?" Sherrinford asked.

"No, I'll be fine. I just don't have my strength back yet," Sherlock said.

"You shouldn't exert yourself so," Sherrinford said.

"I had to speak to Father," Sherlock said.

"To what end?" asked Sherrinford.

Sherlock leaned back and drew a deep breath. Then he looked up and caught Mycroft's eye.

"He said that he will seek a new tutor for me," Sherlock said.

"Oh, Sherlock, that is indeed good news," Sherrinford responded joyfully. "I don't know how you accomplished it, but I am happy for you, just the same. That is all the more reason to rest and gather your strength. Now, Jonathan, don't you let this brother of mine talk you into any more jaunts around the house until he is strong enough."

"Yes, sir," Jonathan agreed.

"I shall go and tell Amanda this wonderful news," Sherrinford said, giving Sherlock a firm pat on the shoulder and leaving the room.

Mycroft offered his huge hand to Sherlock.

"Congratulations, Sherlock. I know it wasn't easy, but the road ahead of you isn't any easier," Mycroft said.

"Nor was the road easy for her..." Sherlock said, looking away from his brother for a moment. His mind recalled for an instant the last dim image of Violet before he lost her in the snowstorm. He pushed the memory away and looked back at Mycroft. "But I will try to honour her memory the best I can, and match her strength—if I can," he concluded, returning his brother's grip.

"I must return to London in a few days," Mycroft said. "Don't forget your promise while I'm gone."

"I won't."

Sherlock continued his therapeutic walks about his room.

"You are growing much stronger, Sherlock," Dr Thompkins said two weeks later as he examined Sherlock.

"Yes," Sherlock agreed.

"I understand that you have requested a new tutor."

"Yes. I would like to begin lessons as soon as possible. Here in my room, if necessary," Sherlock said.

"Don't push yourself too hard, Sherlock. You don't want to have a relapse."

Sherlock looked away.

"Doctor, I think it is far more likely that I will have a 'relapse' if I lie in bed and do nothing," Sherlock said.

"You are still having nightmares, aren't you?" Dr Thompkins asked.

"Yes," Sherlock admitted.

Sherlock did not tell the doctor of the other attacks that occurred while he was awake. Suddenly his mind would be overwhelmed and he would be reliving that awful day. These attacks would appear unbidden in the midst of whatever he was doing. Afterwards he would be haunted by visions of Violet or – or his prior tutor. He had told no one of them.

"The nightmares will go away eventually," the doctor said.

"I hope so," Sherlock said.

Dr Thompkins looked thoughtful for a moment. She had asked more than once recently if she could visit, but Dr Thompkins hesitated to bring the subject up. He was still very careful about what he said to Sherlock. He was afraid that any word or deed could cause him to slip back into the depths in which they had nearly lost him. Dr Thompkins proceeded cautiously.

"Sherlock, you must come out of your isolation eventually," he said.

"I know," Sherlock responded. "I-I need time."

"Your own parents have not seen you for nearly a month," the doctor said.

"I spoke to my father two weeks ago," Sherlock countered.

"Well, yes, I heard about that little jaunt and I didn't exactly approve. But you seem to have survived it. If you start lessons soon, it will be all the more difficult to make excuses for your seclusion."

"Make excuses to whom?" Sherlock asked.

"To your mother," Dr Thompkins said. "She wishes to see you."

Sherlock closed his eyes for a moment and inhaled deeply.

"It is not an unreasonable request," Dr Thompkins continued. "Any mother would want to verify with her own eyes and ears that her son still lived. But if you are not ready—"

Sherlock opened his eyes.

"I will see her," he said.

"When?" asked the doctor.

"Now, if convenient," Sherlock said.

The doctor started to leave, but stopped and turned back toward where Sherlock sat at the table.

"She doesn't know about the — the knife incident. Sherrinford and I never told anyone about that. Your father did not want her told about the attack on the maid. She does know that you were refusing to eat," he said.

Sherlock nodded his head in acknowledgment. He could not change the past.

Dr Thompkins returned in a few minutes with Sherlock's mother. Mrs Holmes had last seen her youngest son weeks before, pale and gaunt, unconscious and barely drawing breath. It had shocked her. She had waited in fear, expecting the announcement of his death at any moment. Suddenly the running of the household had seemed a trivial distraction from what mattered. The cancellation of the Squire's Ball and the pall over the Christmas holidays was irrelevant. She prayed but for one gift, and she had been greatly relieved when they told her Sherlock would live.

He looked so much better now as he sat there at the table in his dressing gown. He was still quite pale and still thinner than usual even for Sherlock. He was nearly eighteen now, but he seemed to have aged much more than a year in the past twelve months. She was heartened when he rose and walked towards her. Suddenly overwhelmed by relief that he had not died she came forward with her arms extended.

Sherlock had not been expecting this. They were not close. He could not remember his mother ever having embraced him. He stepped back a step. The sudden change in his expression combined with his back step made her think he was about to faint. She grabbed his hands in hers and called his name. The doctor interceded.

"There, there, Mrs Holmes, I think you have just overwhelmed him a bit. Have a seat, Sherlock," he said.

"I'm fine, Mother," Sherlock assured her, but sat back down.

She gave his hands a squeeze before releasing them and sitting across the table from him.

"There, now," said the doctor. "Let's just take things slowly and not exhaust him."

"I'm sorry, Mother, to have frightened you," Sherlock said.

"You've had a difficult time. You look so much better," she said.

"Thank you. I am stronger."

"We must guard against a relapse," said Dr Thompkins.

"He is quite right, Sherlock. You should listen to the doctor," she said.

"Yes," Sherlock agreed.

"I understand that you have a new tutor coming soon. Do you think that you will be well enough to study?" his mother asked.

"Yes, Mother," Sherlock said.

"It seems rather dark in here," Mrs Holmes said, noting that the heavy curtains were pulled over the windows.

"The sun on the snow," Sherlock said hesitantly. "It-it hurts...m-my eyes."

He did not tell her that the bright sunlight on the snow seemed to bring on the attacks. No one knew that was why Sherlock insisted that the curtains remained closed.

"Well, we can't have that, can we? What are you reading?" she asked indicating the book on the table that he had set down when she entered.

He told her, and they talked for a few minutes about books and then the conversation wandered to family matters.

"And we are redoing the nursery for when the child arrives," she said.

Sherlock blanched. Too late the doctor realized that he should have warned her not to speak of that.

"Wh-what child?" Sherlock stammered.

His mother reached for his hand.

"Are you sure you are feeling well?" she asked.

"Yes. What child?" Sherlock repeated.

His mother looked up at the doctor.

"He doesn't know," Dr Thompkins said.

"Sherrinford and Amanda's child, dear. I'm sorry. I thought Sherrinford would have told you," she said.

"No, he hasn't. When is it expected?" Sherlock asked.

"A few months, doctor?" she said looking towards Dr Thompkins.

"In early April," the doctor responded.

"Of course, the Squire is hoping for a boy to assure the succession of the estate," she said and prattled on about interviewing nursemaids, but Sherlock did not hear most of it.

Dr Thompkins saw Sherlock's attention lag and decided to end the interview.

"Madam, I'm afraid he's tiring," Dr Thompkins said.

"Dear me, I should let you rest," she said patting Sherlock's hand before she stood.

Sherlock blinked at his mother and seemed to mentally return from some distant place. He stood and thanked her for visiting somewhat distractedly. The doctor saw her out the door and closed it behind her. As he did, Sherlock crossed the room and lay down upon his bed.

"Jonathan?" Sherlock said without looking up.

"Yes, sir," Jonathan responded.

"Please ask my brother Sherrinford to step in," Sherlock said.

Quietly Jonathan left the room.

"I am sorry," Dr Thompkins began.

"No need to apologize, doctor," Sherlock said with his eyes now closed.

Jonathan returned with Sherrinford.

"You wished to speak to me?" Sherrinford asked Sherlock, somewhat concerned by the tableau of Sherlock lying back on the bed and the doctor standing next to it.

But Sherlock opened his eyes, sat up cross-legged on the bed, and looked at his brother.

"Yes," Sherlock said in a very business-like fashion. "I wished to congratulate you on your impending fatherhood."

Sherrinford closed his own eyes for an instant and drew a breath.

"Your mother told him," the doctor said.

Sherrinford looked back at Sherlock.

"I'm sorry. Under the circumstances I was afraid—" Sherrinford began.

"It is quite understandable," Sherlock said icily. "I appreciate your concern. It's just as well I know now because otherwise if I had heard the cry of an infant I would have thought I was hallucinating. Are there any other secrets that you are keeping from me?"

Sherrinford tried to gauge his brother's mood. Sherlock did not seem angry or upset. His words were just very cold and formal. It was not like the old Sherlock, but it was very much like the new one.

"No, none," Sherrinford responded.

"Please don't keep anything else from me," Sherlock said.

"I'm sorry. I won't," Sherrinford said.

"I think you will be an excellent father," Sherlock said. He left unsaid the fact that his own child would have been born around the same time if not for the tragedy.

"Thank you," Sherrinford said. "How was the visit with

Mother?"

"Awkward and exhausting, but I think it pleased her," Sherlock responded.

"And you?" Sherrinford asked.

"It is my duty as a son to please my mother," Sherlock responded. "But as I said, it was exhausting. So I believe I will rest now."

"Then I shall leave you to it," Sherrinford said, taking the hint and leaving the room.

After he was gone the doctor stared at Sherlock for a moment.

"I am fine, just tired," Sherlock said.

"Then I will be going as well," Dr Thompkins said, but before he left the room he caught Jonathan's eye. Jonathan knew what the look meant. It meant "watch him." There had been no need for it. Jonathan knew that his job was to watch Sherlock. Sherlock saw the look exchanged between them and also knew what it meant. Sherlock lay down again and closed his eyes.

"Relax, Jonathan," Sherlock said. "I merely wish to sleep."

Chapter 2

Restoring Order

"The incident left a most unpleasant impression upon my mind."
Dr Watson, The Dying Detective

Sherlock's mother began visiting him for a few minutes each morning. The visits were much shorter than the first. She enquired about his health and they engaged in polite conversation. Otherwise Sherlock had very little interaction with the rest of the household.

One morning his mother said, "It is your birthday today, Sherlock."

"I had lost track of the days," he responded.

"The doctor warned me that a celebration might be too stressful for you but your father was wondering if you were fit enough to join us for supper. It is just the two of us these days. Sherrinford has been taking his meals with Amanda in their rooms. We won't be entertaining any guests for a while."

"I hadn't really thought of it. But yes, I think I could do that," Sherlock said.

As the supper hour approached Jonathan helped Sherlock dress, but Sherlock made his way down the stairs and to the dining room alone. His parents met him at the door to the dining room and his mother took his hand. Sherlock nodded to his father.

"Good evening, Father."

"Good evening. You are looking much stronger."

Sherlock thanked him and they entered and sat down.

As supper was served Sherlock did not look up. He concentrated on his glass, on the liquid within it and on his hand holding it not shaking. He knew the maids would be here, including Michelle. It had been her resemblance to Violet in the dark bedroom that had caused him to react as he had. He knew that now, yet still the encounter, as he had perceived it at the time, was etched painfully in his memory. He tried to shut that memory out of his mind. He knew his father was aware of the incident and was watching him now as she served him. Sherlock shut that out of his mind as well. He shut Michelle out of his mind. He shut everything out but the glass on the table and his hand around its stem, and he concentrated on keeping that hand from shaking. Then the maids withdrew and he relaxed and ate in silence. His parents did not disturb his silence, satisfied for the moment that he had joined them at the table.

Sherlock's body grew stronger, but the nightmares continued. Jonathan no longer sat up with Sherlock at night as he had when he first came to work at Holmes Hall. But he was never far away. A storage closet next to Sherlock's room had been converted to sleeping quarters for Jonathan so he could be close at hand. Sherlock would wake gasping and shaking from a nightmare to find Jonathan standing next to his bed holding a candle, with his straw-coloured hair in his sleepy eyes. Sherlock would send him back to bed and try valiantly to return to sleep himself. But often he tossed and turned for hours, tormented by fragments of the dream before he finally fell into an exhausted sleep.

Far worse, however, were the waking dreams that tore Sherlock out of space and time and threw him back to the awful day that Violet had disappeared. He would come out of these attacks weak and trembling and unable to fully concentrate for hours or days afterwards. Sherlock tried to hide them, but they seemed to be increasing in intensity and frequency. That terrified him. What if he had one before his parents? He knew he must gain control of his own mind. He must concentrate. The violin helped. While he was playing it all other thoughts ceased. It was the only true peace he had.

The violin still vibrated as Sherlock lifted the bow from it one evening in early January. He set first the bow and then the violin down upon his bed and leaned back for a moment against the pillows. He shut his eyes and savoured the afterglow of the piece. There was a knock upon the bedroom door. Sherlock looked up as Jonathan opened the door. Sherlock was surprised to see his father at the threshold with Andrew Goble, the deacon who had visited the previous summer, behind him.

"May we come in?" asked the squire.

"Yes, of course. I am sorry, but I was not expecting visitors," Sherlock said as he sat up on his bed and pulled his dressing gown tighter about him.

"We are the ones who are intruding," Andrew Goble said. "In fact, when I heard you playing, I asked your father to wait before knocking. I did not wish to interrupt and I am glad that we did not. It was beautifully done. Bach's Sonata no. 1, was it not?"

"Yes, thank you," Sherlock said.

"Sherlock, you remember Andrew Goble, don't you?" the squire asked.

"Yes, sir," Sherlock responded.

"He has taken the position of curate at the village church. I have proposed that he also act as your tutor," his father said.

"The squire told me of your illness and I understand that in spite of it you wish to recommence your studies as soon as possible?"

"Yes, sir," Sherlock confirmed.

"I would be happy to tutor you, Sherlock, but I want to be certain that you would be comfortable with me as your tutor before I accept the position," Andrew Goble said.

"Yes, sir, I think that would be fine," Sherlock said.

"Then we have an agreement, sir?" the squire asked.

"Yes, sir," Andrew Goble responded, and the two men shook hands.

"We will start tomorrow, if Dr Thompkins approves."

"Thank you, sir," Sherlock said.

Andrew Goble returned the following day. He had decided that the best way to begin would be to test Sherlock as the college would. They spread the exam over two days. Sherlock did the best he could, though he was frustrated by the limits of his concentration. So much of the exam covered subjects that he had studied with — with his prior tutor — and that sparked distracting and unpleasant memories. Repeatedly he had to force himself to focus on the exam before him, but somehow he managed to get through it. When

Andrew returned on Friday with the corrected papers, he shook his head and Sherlock's heart raced.

"It is astounding," Andrew said.

"Tell me," Sherlock said.

"The Professor told your father that he had doubts that you would be accepted. Is that correct?" Andrew asked.

"Yes," Sherlock said.

"You have been ill and you were given no time to cram before I tested you. That leads me to wonder how you would have done under other circumstances because you did exceptionally well!"

"What?" Sherlock asked.

"My dear Sherlock, you know more about the exam subjects than I did when I matriculated. I have no doubt whatsoever that you would be accepted today."

"Then he was lying about that as well," Sherlock said with great relief.

"Well, I shall leave judgments of your former tutor up to higher powers, but you don't really need tutoring at all," Andrew Goble said.

"Don't abandon me yet," Sherlock begged him. "When is the next time I can sit for the exams?"

"They are normally given in January for the Michaelmas Term."

At Sherlock's request, Andrew Goble and Dr Thompkins met with the Squire the next day.

"Your son is very intelligent and knows more of the required subjects than is necessary to be admitted to Sidney Sussex College," Andrew Goble said

"Is he physically strong enough to sit for the exams?" Squire Holmes asked the doctor.

Dr Thompkins shook his head. Sherlock started to protest, but held his tongue.

"It is too soon," Dr Thompkins said. "He is much stronger than he was, but it is a full day's journey to Cambridge. It would be too tiring for him."

"Father, please allow me to try," Sherlock pleaded.

"Sherlock," Dr Thompkins said turning to him, "You would be so exhausted by the time you arrived that even if the journey did not make you ill, you would be in no condition to write any exams. I'm sorry."

Andrew Goble spoke up again.

"Squire Holmes, I would be happy to go to Cambridge with you and present my recommendation. I have the practice exam that I administered your son. Perhaps we can secure some special arrangement due to Sherlock's illness."

"I appreciate your offer, Mr Goble, and gladly accept it," the squire said. "I will wire the Master at once. Please advise me when you will be available to travel."

"I shall consult with the vicar, but I should be able to leave as soon as Monday," Andrew Goble said.

"I will provide a letter giving my professional opinion that Sherlock is still too weak to make the journey now, but if his progress continues at the current rate he should be sufficiently recovered to attend the Michaelmas Term," Dr Thompkins told the Squire.

"Thank you, doctor," Squire Holmes said.

Sherlock thanked them all before returning to his room. Sherlock knew the doctor was right. He still had far to go. He must work harder.

When his parents had taken him to France for his health three years before, his father had hired an instructor to teach Sherlock to fence. It had helped him build strength and endurance. He expected it would again. But this time he had months, not years, to get into training. Back in his room he sent Jonathan to retrieve his epees from Sherrinford.

"Hand one to me, Jonathan," Sherlock said when Jonathan returned with them.

Jonathan did as he was asked. Sherlock wrapped his fingers around the hilt and felt the weight of it. The epee was heavier than the violin, but he felt he was strong enough to work with it.

Sherlock began his training that afternoon by stepping through the fencing positions in his room with the epee. He repeated the fencing exercises in his room again after supper. The bedroom was not large enough to wield the epee aggressively without endangering the furnishings, but he could repeat the salute and the en garde position, and change between each of the eight guard positions over and over. He concentrated on form and gained strength merely from the repetition.

When Squire Holmes returned from Cambridge he sent for Sherlock and told him that the College Master had been impressed with the work Mr Goble had shown him and was willing to make allowances for Sherlock's illness. The Senior Tutor of the college would be coming in two weeks to examine Sherlock in person.

Sherlock Holmes and Andrew Goble discussed this visit.

"What is my weakest subject?" Sherlock asked.

"You are weakest in your Greek, but you might benefit more from reading it in context than simply working out assignments. A general review of mathematics would not hurt. They place a great emphasis on mathematics at Cambridge."

So Sherlock divided his time over the next two weeks between reading the Greek texts that Mr Goble recommended, reviewing geometry, trigonometry and calculus, and repeating his fencing exercises in his room. At Sherlock's request Andrew drilled him every few days even though Andrew himself was certain of Sherlock's success.

When the sleigh returned from the railway station on the 30th of January it delivered to Holmes Hall a bearded man of about forty years with keen eyes, an angular nose, and a high forehead. He was ushered into the Squire's study and introduced himself as Reverend John Clowe, the Senior Tutor from Sidney Sussex College at the University of Cambridge. After a brief discussion with the Squire, Sherlock and Rev. Clowe retired to another room. To Sherlock's surprise Rev. Clowe did not give him any passages to translate or problems to work out. They merely talked. Rev. Clowe spoke of Cambridge University and Sidney Sussex College, and the Fellows and undergraduates and what they studied. He and

Sherlock talked about mathematics and classical literature, but also about mechanics, electronics, chemistry, agriculture, history and mountaineering. They spoke for hours before joining the family for supper.

Sherrinford came down for supper that night. He greeted the Senior Tutor warmly and begged him excuse his wife's absence. Sherrinford had studied at Sidney under Rev. Clowe's guidance seven years before and he enjoyed meeting the Senior Tutor once again on more even footing. Andrew Goble also came for supper and the conversation was lively. Sherrinford was heartened to see Sherlock keeping up his end of it though he could tell that his younger brother was tiring from the stress of the day. After supper the gentlemen assembled briefly in the squire's study.

"I thank you for your hospitality, Squire Holmes," Rev. Clowe said. "I have had a very pleasant visit. Your son is very intelligent and knowledgeable. When I return to Cambridge tomorrow, I will recommend that he be admitted to Sidney Sussex College. You should receive an official notice by letter shortly."

Sherlock was relieved by this announcement and the squire was pleased. Andrew and Sherrinford offered their congratulations.

"Thank you very much, Reverend Clowe," the squire said. "I appreciate the extraordinary efforts that you have made in this matter."

"You are quite welcome. I believe your son will be a great asset to our college. Now if you will excuse me, I shall retire early. I have a long journey tomorrow," Rev. Clowe said and bid them all good night.

Sherlock continued to train hard. In his room with no one watching but Jonathan, Sherlock Holmes pushed himself to the point of exhaustion each morning. Then he would tumble onto his bed and sleep until lunch came. After eating he would repeat the process.

But sometimes Sherlock would be torn from the present. Suddenly he would be reliving the day of the snowstorm in his mind and come out of the vision shaking. Then he would stay in bed for the rest of day, and maybe longer, with his face buried in his hands trying not to think of it. He would send word downstairs that he was too tired to attend supper in the dining room. Each attack was a set-back to his plans.

One afternoon in early spring when a breeze was pushing at the curtains, Sherlock set aside his epee as he finished his exercises.

"Jonathan, is there still snow upon the moor?" he asked.

"No, sir. Most is green now."

"Open the curtains then. Do it slowly."

Jonathan did so. Slowly the big blue sky appeared and beneath it the wild green of the moor. Sherlock blinked at the light. The sun was on the other side of the house. The yard and the outbuildings were partially in shadow, but the moor was brightly lit.

Sherlock walked over to the window seat and sat down. He had not sat there in months. He looked out the window. It was a glorious day, a day like the one when he had first met Violet on the moor. That was almost a year ago, he thought. So much had happened in that year....

A hand gripped his arm and broke his thoughts. Sherlock looked up at Jonathan who stood next to him and then down at Jonathan's hand upon his arm.

"I'm sorry, sir," Jonathan said removing his hand. "I was concerned when you didn't answer. Do you wish me to close the curtains again?"

Jonathan's touch had broken the train of thought which probably would have led to another attack. Sherlock looked up at the boy standing next to him.

"You know, don't you?" Sherlock asked.

"Know what, sir?" Jonathan asked.

"Of these attacks I have," Sherlock said.

"Yes, sir," Jonathan admitted.

"You touched my arm on purpose to stave one off?" Sherlock said.

"Yes, sir," Jonathan admitted.

"You were successful. How can you tell when I am about to have one?" Sherlock asked.

"Well, sir, you seem very far away. Your eyes just stare at nothing and see nothing, and you don't respond to sounds. If you are deep into it, you don't even notice if I touch you."

"But if you touch me earlier it breaks my train of thought and prevents the attack from occurring," Sherlock said thoughtfully.

"It seems so, sir," Jonathan said.

Sherlock remembered other times when his mind had wandered and a touch had jarred him back to reality. Sherlock was suddenly grateful to have an outside observer to help him understand the phenomenon.

"You have been studying me for sometime, haven't you?" he asked Jonathan.

"Nearly five months now, day and night. I'm sorry, sir, but I was instructed to watch you carefully," Jonathan said.

"That's quite all right. I understand your position," Sherlock acknowledged. "This wasn't the first time you've tried to bring me out of this state by touching me, was it?" Sherlock asked.

"No, sir, I've tried before," Jonathan admitted. "I've sorry, sir, if I offended you."

"No, no, Jonathan," Sherlock said waving his hand. "Pull up a chair and sit down. I am tired of looking up at you. I am trying to learn from your observations."

"I will tell you anything I can. But I don't know much. I know that you are quite shaken by these attacks. You seem to do better when they don't happen. So I've tried to stop them. This is the first time it worked."

"I was totally unaware of your attempts," Sherlock said. "I appreciate your efforts. Continue them."

"I know about the nightmares and the headaches, too, sir," Jonathan said.

"Have you told the doctor or my brother about the attacks?" Sherlock asked.

"No, sir," Jonathan said.

"Why not?" Sherlock asked knowing that Jonathan's position required him to report on his condition and behaviour.

"I only tell them things when your life is in danger," Jonathan said.

Sherlock looked at Jonathan intently.

"I had not realized that before," Sherlock said.

Sherlock turned and gazed thoughtfully out the window. There had been times when he had questioned Jonathan's loyalty to him.

"There is another reason," Jonathan said.

Sherlock looked back at him.

"And that is?" Sherlock asked.

Jonathan looked down.

"Perhaps I should have told this to you months ago. I was afraid—" Jonathan broke off.

"Please tell me now," Sherlock urged the boy.

"In December I heard Thomas talking to another member of the household staff. He was telling her something he overheard the squire say the night before I came to stay at the Hall."

"What did my father say?" Sherlock asked with some trepidation.

Jonathan hesitated.

"Go on," Sherlock urged.

"The squire asked the doctor if you were suffering from some form of insanity," Jonathan said.

Sherlock closed his eyes.

"H-he said if twas true, he'd - he'd—," Jonathan tried to continue.

"He'd what?" Sherlock asked, his heart pounding.

"He'd 'ave thee put away in an asylum," Jonathan concluded.

"Who else was in the study?" Sherlock asked.

"The doctor and your brother, Mr Sherrinford," Jonathan said.

"After that my brother hired you?" Sherlock said.

"He sent a note to me that evening," Jonathan confirmed.

Sherlock rose thoughtfully from the window seat. He realized now that Sherrinford had hired Jonathan to protect him, not just from himself, as he had long known, but from his own father. That was so much like his eldest brother, always the guardian, the protector. When Sherrinford had not been able to fulfil the role himself, he had found a surrogate in Jonathan. Sherlock knew he had been harsh with Sherrinford over the last few months. He did not entirely know why. Sherrinford had searched for Sherlock after the blizzard and brought him back half frozen. Undoubtedly he had saved Sherlock's life. But Sherrinford had also hidden from Sherlock how long Violet had been missing until her horse returned lame, starved, and alone. Sherrinford had held Sherlock down when they took his knife from him for fear he would harm himself. In the dark, twisted recesses of his mind Sherlock had blamed his eldest brother for these things. Sherlock now understood why his brother had done them and yet he still kept Sherrinford at a distance as if his brother's affection for him was itself dangerous.

Jonathan stood and replaced the chair next to the table. He was heartened by the conversation. It was the longest talk he had had with Sherlock since he had come to work at the manor house. But he returned to his original question.

"Would you like me to close the curtains, sir?"

Sherlock turned and looked back out the window.

"No," Sherlock said. "Leave them open. You may return the epee to the wall," he told Jonathan. "I'm finished with it for today."

Sherlock retreated to his bed and lifted his violin to his chin and played. When he looked up again the sky and the moor were still there beyond the window. It seemed a strange sight. It was the view he had grown up with, but now it seemed different. His thoughts were interrupted by a knock at the door. Sherrinford entered when Jonathan opened it. Sherrinford immediately looked up at the window.

"Trying something new?" Sherrinford asked as he crossed over toward the window and looked out.

"Yes, it is an experiment. It does improve both the lighting and the ventilation," Sherlock said as he watched his brother more carefully than he had in months.

"And how is it working otherwise?" Sherrinford asked.

"It will take some adjustment," Sherlock said.

Sherrinford walked across the room.

"I see the epees are back up," he said.

"Yes. We are attempting to restore order," Sherlock said as Sherrinford wandered to the other side of the room.

"Sit down, Sherrinford. Amanda's having the baby, isn't she?"

Sherlock said.

Sherrinford smiled at Sherlock and sat down on a chair next to the bed.

"Yes," Sherrinford said without bothering to ask how he knew. He was pleased to have Sherlock reading his thoughts from his actions again as he did in the past.

"You are worried about Amanda?" Sherlock said.

"Yes."

"Did the doctor indicate that there was any difficulty?"

"No," Sherrinford said. "He said mother and child were doing fine and that I should find something else to do for the next eight hours or so."

"So you came here? This is not a very cheery place," Sherlock said.

"It seems more so now with the curtains open," Sherrinford said.

"Perhaps," Sherlock said. "Don't you have some planting to oversee or some such?"

"They don't need me for any of that. Eston can manage it. The fields are being ploughed. The ewes are lambing; the cows are calving and the horses are dropping foals. None of which will distract me from the birth of my own child."

"I suppose not," Sherlock admitted.

"I don't mean to remind you—," Sherrinford began.

"Don't speak of it," Sherlock insisted sharply.

"Perhaps I should go," Sherrinford said afraid that he had upset his brother.

"Sherrinford, please wait," Sherlock said softening his tone. "At the moment I am inclined to play my violin. If you would like to sit and listen, you are welcome to."

"If you wouldn't mind, I would like that very much," Sherrinford responded.

Sherlock picked up the violin and bow again and played. Sherrinford sat and listened in silence. In a corner of the room Jonathan listened and watched them both and hope rose within him that order would be restored.

Chapter 3

Growing Stronger

"I think our quiet rest in the country has been a distinct success..."
Sherlock Holmes, The Reigate Squires

At Sherlock's request Andrew Goble continued to visit him regularly. Sherlock had learned something from Rev. Clowe's visit. He did not ask Andrew to lecture him. Instead the two young men began taking walks about the gardens of the estate. The walks were not social occasions for them, but rather a peripatetic form of study. It was not truly Aristotelian, for as they walked, it was Sherlock who questioned Andrew and Andrew who would answer the best he could. Sometimes Andrew would loan Sherlock books for further study.

The walks helped Sherlock further gain in physical strength and they forced him to look outward. After the inner darkness of the winter the world seemed new to him. Yet he was surrounded by familiar objects that stirred memories, dangerous memories that brought forth troubling emotions. He tried to block out those memories and banish the emotions. He attempted to observe each object through a scientific and logical filter and analyse the object's connections with its surroundings and the wider world, but not its connection to him. He endeavoured to remove himself as a factor in the equation. He was merely an instrument to observe and analyse. It took effort to establish this habit of thought and he was not always able to maintain the necessary level of concentration to avoid such distractions.

Early one morning in late April Sherlock said to Jonathan, "Come, gather up the fencing gear. We shall move our training outside."

They went down to the yard behind the manor house where Sherlock had taught Jonathan to fence the previous summer. The first day they performed just a few exercises before returning to

Sherlock's room. Over the next week they progressed to longer exercises until at last Sherlock proposed that they attempt a bout. They took up their positions and engaged on Sherlock's call. Jonathan could tell that Sherlock was still much weaker than he had been the previous summer. But Sherlock made up for the lack of strength in skill and raw determination. Hard-pressed, Jonathan backed away from Sherlock repeatedly until he stood in the space between the out-buildings.

From where Sherlock stood he could see the spot where he had given Violet the locket. He remembered how he and Jonathan had contrived to hide her visit with a fencing bout. His concentration began to lapse. Sherlock backed away from Jonathan. Jonathan pressed him. Sherlock fended him off, but backed further away, coming suddenly out of the shadow of the buildings into the bright spring sunlight. As Sherlock was blinded by the light, Jonathan scored. But as he did, Sherlock collapsed to his knees. Distressed, Jonathan dropped his epee, threw off his mask and rushed to Sherlock's side.

"Are you ill, sir?" he asked.

Sherlock did not reply and Jonathan realized that he must be having another attack. Jonathan looked up at the manor house. The squire was probably in his study on the other side of the building. Kneeling beside him, Jonathan gently removed Sherlock's fencing mask. Sherlock neither resisted nor aided him. As the mask came off Sherlock buried his face in his hands. His heart was pounding and his breath came quickly. He was trembling all over. Jonathan waited by his side. After a few minutes Sherlock began to slowly uncoil. He reached out with trembling hands and picked up the mask and epee that lay beside him. He stood up.

"Perhaps we should quit for the day, sir," Jonathan suggested.

Sherlock turned to look at him and for a moment Jonathan saw that distant, haunted look in Sherlock's eyes that he had seen in December. He shivered. Sherlock blinked and his eyes focused.

"No. I-I cannot quit. I must continue," Sherlock said. With trembling fingers he pulled on his mask once more. "En garde!"

Jonathan put his own mask back on and they engaged once

more. Sherlock was obviously still shaken. His lunges were weak and his concentration was poor. Jonathan realized he could easily score. He chose instead to maintain a reasonable defence until Sherlock had scored and he was able to convince him to return to his room. There Sherlock fell upon his bed. Jonathan was careful never to allow that to happen again. From then on he gave up a point rather than back into the shadows of the out-buildings.

The attack did not discourage Sherlock from fencing. He insisted that they practice every day the weather was fair. As Sherlock spent less time worrying about merely maintaining his grip on the epee and keeping his balance, he touched once more the mental discipline that his French fencing master, M. Bencin, had taught him. Suddenly nothing in the world existed but his need to anticipate his opponent's next move. Jonathan had seen Sherlock exhibit this trance-like concentration only once before. The previous summer Sherlock had mostly worked at teaching Jonathan rather than developing his own skills. Now Sherlock strove hungrily for the highest level of mental discipline he had learned in France, and the control and peace of mind it offered him. At such times Jonathan doubted that Sherlock saw him any more as a student, or a servant, or even another human fencer, but rather than as some part of a puzzle, a factor to be analysed and conquered. Jonathan continued to increase in skill, but he rarely ever won a point.

When Sherlock thought he had trained enough, he invited Andrew Goble to fence with him and they began doing so regularly. Andrew was fascinated by Sherlock's level of concentration while fencing and noticed how it began to overflow into other aspects of Sherlock's life.

In late June Mycroft came up from London for his nephew's christening and to see how Sherlock was faring. Sherrinford had written to Mycroft frequently concerning Sherlock's progress, but Mycroft had received no letters from Sherlock himself. Sherrinford met Mycroft at the railway station in Thirsk and spoke to him on the carriage ride back to the manor.

"I am still concerned about Sherlock," Sherrinford said.

"From what you have written, I would say that he has made substantial progress. You must be patient with him," Mycroft said.

"Yes, yes, I am patient with him and I will continue to do so. Things are better than they were. At least he is speaking to me again. But he has changed so much," Sherrinford said shaking his head.

"All people change as they mature, this was just much more sudden than most," Mycroft said.

"And more painful. I hope that I can learn something from all this in raising my own son," Sherrinford said.

"Ah, if each generation were more efficient at learning from the mistakes of the previous, I think that the human race would be happier," Mycroft said.

Sherrinford laughed.

"I've never heard anyone else who could be so pessimistic and amusing at the same time, Mycroft," Sherrinford said as the carriage arrived at the door. "Come, you will see Sherlock for yourself."

They entered by the front door but Sherlock was not in the manor house. They found him around back pinning the curate to a wall with his epee.

"There are times such as this, Sherlock, that I am very glad that is not a real sword you are wielding," Andrew Goble said after Sherlock backed off and they removed their masks.

"Thank you," Sherlock said somewhat breathlessly.

"You should definitely find others to fence with at the university. Perhaps if there are enough you could organize a club," Andrew said.

"I will consider it," Sherlock said turning towards his brothers.

Then Andrew Goble noticed Sherrinford and Mycroft watching them.

"Ah, Sherrinford, so you were observing your brother pinning me like a butterfly?" he said.

"We came just at the end," Sherrinford said. "Andrew, this is our brother, Mycroft. Mycroft, this is Andrew Goble, the new curate."

"Though I confess to not looking very priestly at the moment,"

Andrew said removing his gauntlets.

"—And Sherlock's tutor," Sherrinford finished.

"Not that he needs any tutoring," Andrew said. "My role turned out to be more that of an advocate than a tutor. Now, as you see, I provide Sherlock with a larger, more experienced opponent to defeat than Jonathan here."

Mycroft shook hands with Andrew Goble.

"It is a pleasure to meet you," Mycroft said. "You were in a fencing club at the university?"

"No. They don't have a formal club there yet. Just a few of us who had fenced in school would get together for some bouts. I can testify that your brother's skills far exceed those of anyone I encountered there."

"But since you have just recovered from a spring cold perhaps you are not at your best," Mycroft said.

"Oh, I see, this is a family trait!" Andrew said with a laugh.

"Yes, an inheritance that I missed," Sherrinford said.

"The only one," Mycroft said with a grin at his eldest brother.

"Yes, I had a bit of a cold there for a while. But even at my peak and his worst, your brother Sherlock could put me to shame."

Mycroft turned his attention to Sherlock who had stood silently with his mask under his left arm and his epee in his right hand during this exchange. Sherlock still looked somewhat gaunt and pale and he was breathing heavily at the moment from his exertions during the bout. As Mycroft looked at him, Sherlock saluted him with his epee by way of greeting, but said nothing. He did not smile as the old Sherlock would have. Their eyes met and Sherlock returned Mycroft's gaze steadily. The mischievous twinkle was gone, but so was the deep pain that Mycroft had seen there in December, or at least it was hidden away.

"I trust you are feeling better, Sherlock. What I have seen testifies that you are substantially stronger," Mycroft said.

"Yes. However, if you will excuse me, I should wash and change. I shall see you at supper," Sherlock said. He bowed to Andrew Goble and bid him good evening and headed towards the house. Jonathan trailed behind him silently.

"Andrew, are you joining us for supper?" Sherrinford asked.

"Thank you, no, I should be getting back to the vicarage," Andrew said gathering up his gear.

After supper Mycroft knocked on Sherlock's door. He entered when Jonathan opened the door and found Sherlock sitting at the small table reading a book. Mycroft sat down and observed Sherlock in his introspective fashion. Sherlock returned the gaze.

"You have come to inspect?" Sherlock said.

"I wished to see how you are coming along," Mycroft said. "Physically you are much stronger."

"Yes, but I still have far to go and I have only four more months to accomplish it. I must be ready to attend the Michaelmas Term at Cambridge. I have some questions I would like to ask you about the university," Sherlock said deftly shifting the conversation. "I want to know all about it before I go."

Mycroft answered Sherlock's questions and allowed him to direct the conversation. Mycroft was silently thankful that Sherlock's intellect was reasserting itself and controlling the emotional turmoil that had threatened his sanity and his life. He knew his younger brother had great potential but he must find his own path.

As the months passed, Sherlock drew out the fencing bouts with Andrew Goble. He would forego obvious opportunities to thrust, and instead bait him and slowly draw him into a trap. Jonathan watched with fascination as new levels of Sherlock's skill unfolded and he tried to learn by observing Sherlock's techniques.

Jonathan did not know whether the fencing was the cause, but he knew Sherlock was sleeping better. As spring changed to summer the nightmares were becoming rare and the attacks were growing further and further apart.

By July Sherlock felt certain that he was free of the attacks. He had had none in over six weeks. He had put on weight and muscle and he felt ready to journey beyond the manor. With Dr Thompkins' consent he travelled with his parents to London. They stayed in the family's house in Kensington for four weeks and purchased a new wardrobe for Sherlock.

Despite the significant improvements, Sherrinford and Dr Thompkins argued strenuously that Sherlock was still in danger of a relapse and would fare better with Jonathan attending him in Cambridge. Sherlock himself did not resist these arguments.

While Sherlock was in London with his parents, Sherrinford had the household staff at Holmes Hall teach Jonathan how to prepare and serve meals, how to properly care for a gentleman's clothes, and many other things Jonathan would need to know. Jonathan learned quickly, but he was restless the entire time Sherlock was gone. Even being able to visit his family more often did not make the boy less anxious.

"What's moithering thee, Jonathan?" his mother asked one day.

"Nowt," Jonathan said.

"Tis Mr Sherlock, isn't it?"

"Aye."

"What'is it?"

"Ah've no reason. Ah'm wont to bein' there when 'e needs me."

Mrs Beckwith smiled at her son as he looked up her. He looked like a smaller version of his father. He was thirteen now. He had grown so much in strength and wisdom in the last year, but he was still a boy.

"Och, th'art like a parent when thy child is out of sight."

"Tis 'ow twill be for thee whilst ah'm at Cambridge with him?" Jonathan asked.

"Aye," she said.

He threw his arms around her, and mother and son hugged each other tightly. She knew that she was already losing him. His loyalties had shifted very much to his young master. It was what she had trained him for all his life, and he was fulfilling his duties with far more courage and devotion than she had ever imagined. But that thought didn't make losing him any easier. She savoured the time they had together.

Soon enough the squire and the mistress of the manor returned from London with their son and Jonathan returned to attending

Sherlock around the clock. Jonathan found that his concerns had been groundless. As he heard it, Sherlock had interacted politely with tailors, boot makers and shopkeepers, as well as visitors to the house in London. The squire had been satisfied.

Chapter 4

Cambridge

On a frosty morning before dawn in late September, servants loaded trunks and bags on the carriage as Sherrinford, Sherlock and Jonathan prepared for their journey to Cambridge.

"You will write, Sherlock."

"Yes, Mother," he agreed.

Sherrinford kissed Amanda on her forehead and held his finger out to tiny Arthur in his nurse's arms. Sherlock saw his nephew wrap his hand about Sherrinford's finger and he saw the joy that lit his brother's face. He turned away and climbed aboard the carriage. Sherrinford joined him shortly. Jonathan was already sitting on top next to the driver.

"I think I can give you a few tips while we are in Cambridge," Sherrinford said as they rode toward Thirsk. "Not about studying, of course."

"Did you do any reading while you were there?" Sherlock asked.

"Well, yes, of course. If I hadn't, I would never have squeaked through on the poll degree."

"Ah, the refuge of eldest sons," Sherlock said.

"I know my math and my classics, but I'm not quick like you and Mycroft. Give me a few months rather than a few days and I could do all the papers required for an honours degree. Whether I study much or a little doesn't change that. My brain just plods along. I learned that a long time ago. It is not like Mycroft's! I don't know if you remember it, but even though Mycroft is two years my junior and matriculated at Sidney two years year behind me, he finished a double honours degree in the same year I finished my poll degree."

"That must have been distressing."

"Not really. I was long accustomed to the differences between us and not everyone in Cambridge is obsessed with study. I met some men there who never cracked a book the whole time. After a few years of carousing in Cambridge they merely went somewhere else."

"Seems rather an expensive holiday," Sherlock observed.

"I'm sure their fathers thought so. I didn't run with men quite like that, more of the sporting type, men who are now junior government ministers, or working their way up in business. Once in positions of power they will make appointments and transact deals with other members of the college boat club or the cricket team. For men like them the university was more about making connections than reading. If you were a good sport, whether you took honours or not was irrelevant.

"But Mycroft!" Sherrinford continued, "I never saw anyone so single-minded about the whole thing as he. He calculated exactly what he needed to do get his degrees and proceeded. I think he went for the double because he knew it was rare enough to be additionally impressive and because it was hardly more effort for him. Do you know that he had a position lined up before he took the first Tripos? A few weeks before it he spoke with the visiting father of one of the other men in his college. I don't know what Mycroft said, but he was invited to an interview in London a week later and took up his position shortly after completing his degrees. Oh, yes, Mycroft and I are pretty far apart on the scale of educational accomplishments. I have never understood why Father was so much harder on you about it. Even if you don't reach Mycroft's levels you most assuredly will surpass mine."

"I'd rather not discuss it," Sherlock responded.

Sherrinford paused briefly. He had grasped the idea that Sherlock did not like to discuss certain topics, but he didn't know exactly what they all were. He returned to the subject of Mycroft which seemed to be a safe one.

"I wasn't ever jealous of Mycroft," Sherrinford continued. "It would be like being jealous of the moon. He is a phenomenon to be admired. I think he could have any position he wanted in the whole world. I must confess that I don't understand what he does in the one he has."

"He doesn't talk about it much," Sherlock agreed.

"No, and he is quite deft at shifting conversation away from it. So there is no use trying. But back to my college days. I learned a great many things during my days at the university which weren't in any books."

"Such as?"

"They are not things I can explain easily: things about the way the world works, about people, about myself even."

Sherrinford continued rather unsuccessfully trying to explain what he couldn't explain until they reached the railway station at Thirsk just as the sun was rising.

"Life among the flocks of undergraduates is very different from life in Yorkshire, or any of the other places you have been. You'll see," he said as they descended from the carriage.

Jonathan had never been to a railway station before but he had little chance to look around as he concentrated on keeping up with the Holmes brothers. The luggage was unloaded from the carriage and given over to a porter not long before a metallic monster roared into the station screaming, squealing and spewing smoke and steam. Behind it were some boxes on wheels with windows. Jonathan could see people inside the boxes.

"You're coming along with us in the first-class carriage, Jonathan," Sherrinford said. "I don't want to lose you in the mob in third-class."

"Thank you, sir," the boy said. He hadn't the slightest idea what first or third-class meant but he was glad not to be separated from them.

"Mycroft and I didn't have to take these long rides down from Yorkshire when we were at Sidney," Sherrinford said as he settled into the seat of the first class carriage.

"I remember," Sherlock said. "Those were the years Father, Mother and I lived in the house in Kensington."

"Until you nearly drowned in the Thames."

"Yes."

"Mycroft and I were almost grateful to you for that. It meant

Father was doing less looking over our shoulders towards the end of our time in college. Gave us a bit more freedom."

Sherlock didn't respond. He had closed his eyes and was leaning back against the seat.

"Are you all right?" Sherrinford asked.

"Yes," Sherlock said. "We have a long journey ahead. I thought perhaps I'd take a nap."

"An excellent idea. I think I'll try it myself."

Sherrinford closed his eyes and settled back.

Jonathan looked up for a moment at the Holmes brothers as their talking ceased. He suspected that Sherlock merely wanted a bit of quiet without Sherrinford's chatter. He also suspected that Sherrinford knew it.

The engine's whistle blew and Jonathan's heart leaped. He turned toward the window again as the carriage began to roll forward. He was already the furthest he had ever been from home. He had lived all of his thirteen years within Mycroft Manor, the Holmes family estate, and except for some short excursions upon the moors, he had never been outside the dale. He was miles beyond it now.

With much chugging, creaking, and puffing of smoke the train began to pick up speed heading southeast. Farmlands shorn of their summer crops flashed past his window wrapped in wisps of morning mist. Now and then he could see a farm house or the steeple of some village church. The train stopped briefly a few times at some small stations but no one boarded or left the train. Porters exchanged some bags marked "Royal Mail" and the train moved on again.

The land was flatter here. Sometimes they passed stands of trees naked of their foliage. The pastures and the wild grasslands lay golden, dotted with copper-coloured shrubbery. Sometimes they were broken by a still pond reflecting the autumn sky.

The carriage jostled and swayed. Jonathan turned back to the interior of the carriage but his fellow-passengers seemed unconcerned.

"The points," Sherlock said without opening his eyes, "Where different tracks meet. There will be more."

As Jonathan turned back to the window they crossed a river wider than any beck or gill Jonathan had ever seen before. It meandered along beside them and large buildings rose up in the distance — great blocks and towers and spires and buildings of every kind. But now the whistle was blowing and before he had time to think the train slid under an arch in the wall of the great city of York, and stopped with a brick and stone railway station towered over them.

Sherrinford chuckled as Jonathan craned his neck to see as much as he could out the window.

"You've never seen a city before, have you, Jonathan?"

"No, sir. I wish I could see more of it."

"Perhaps someday you will. Today we are continuing on to Leeds where we will change trains. We will have to change twice more before we reach Cambridge."

"Is Cambridge like York?"

"No, each have their own wonders."

After a while the train began to move again but this time it was moving in reverse, backing through the wall of the city on to a new track, then grinding to a stop and starting forward again, south-westward this time. This track was less straight than that from Thirsk to York, rounding a bend to head almost due south then swinging sharply west. Then there were many points, and many other tracks beside them as the train stopped with a hiss at the station in Leeds.

"Come, Jonathan," Sherrinford said, "Stay close."

Jonathan followed the Holmes brothers as best he could while looking around. While York had seemed to be something out of a fairy tale, Leeds was more rushed and sooty. He spun around staring at the wonder of the buildings and the people all rushing about. He didn't understand how Sherrinford could find his way so easily. Sherlock seem to know the place as well. But Jonathan knew that left to himself he would soon be hopelessly lost. With that thought in his head he looked over to seem the Holmes brothers nearly disappearing out of sight. He ran to catch up.

Sherrinford led them to a little a cafe not far from the railway station where they had some tea and pastries. Then it was back to the station to board another train heading south towards Derby.

As they approached Derby, the elder Holmes brother kept checking his watch. Just outside of town, he stepped out to have a brief discussion with the guard.

"It seems we are in luck, we are ahead of our time and can catch the 12:15 to Ely. That will save us a longer wait here."

At Derby they descended and Sherrinford immediately led them to another train waiting on the tracks that left soon afterwards.

The journey from the North Riding of Yorkshire to Cambridge was a long one and the leg from Derby to Ely was the longest. In time the rocking of the train lulled Jonathan to sleep. A jolt of the train snapped him awake again. He looked about in confusion to Sherrinford's amusement.

"Nothing's amiss lad. It's always a bit rough crossing those points."

But there was something, or rather, someone, missing from the carriage.

"Where is Mr Sherlock, sir?" Jonathan asked.

The last few hours had been something of a holiday for Jonathan. With Sherlock and Sherrinford only a few feet from him in the carriage, he had not had any duties to attend to. For a change he could be just a boy awed by the new sights and sounds but now that his charge was missing from the carriage he felt he had been neglecting his duties.

"Oh, he went to stretch his legs. He was getting a bit restless."

"In the train?"

"Yes."

"Perhaps, I should find him, sir," Jonathan offered.

"No, I am sure he is fine. He knows his way around a train better than you do. I don't want to have to hunt you down."

Jonathan turned back to the window. The autumn sun was low in the sky, piercing the edge of a bank of clouds. It sent rays across the flat land dotted with lakes and marshes that the train was passing. It almost seemed there was more water than land here and sometimes it was difficult to tell where one ended and the other began.

Even though he looked out at the passing scenery, Jonathan could not enjoy the view as well as he had before. Sherlock had been quiet during most of the journey. These days he rarely engaged in idle chatter. But thinking him safe Jonathan had paid little thought to what his master may be thinking or feeling. Now Jonathan's mind began conjuring innumerable disasters that could be overtaking his master while he sat idly looking out the window. All that came to an end when the door to the carriage opened and Sherlock walked in.

"We are approaching Ely," Sherlock said.

"I suspected as much. If our luck holds we will make a good connection there to Cambridge and we will be freshening up in our hotel rooms within the hour."

"I'll be glad of it. I am quite tired of this journey," Sherlock said, sitting down.

They were lucky in their connections and the journey from Ely to Cambridge was quick, but the sun set before they arrived. They descended from the carriage in darkness at the Cambridge railway station where they were directed to a bridge across the railway line.

"The luggage will meet us at the exit from the station," Sherrinford said as they crossed over. "This station is some distance from the college. We need to engage a fly into town."

In front of the station they found a crowd of passengers and drivers shouting and jostling each other as they all tried to strike up deals. Sherrinford stood taller and broader of shoulder than most and he gently but firmly ploughed his way to the fore. Soon he had bargained with a driver and had their luggage transferred to his vehicle. Sherrinford Holmes directed the driver to the hotel where he had engaged rooms in advance.

Jonathan rode up front with the driver and looked about him in the dark. While the distant view of York had spoken to the boy of medieval knights, and Leeds had shouted commerce, Cambridge was different. It was grander than Leeds and yet younger in spirit than York. The University Arms hotel was itself an impressive building, and that night Jonathan dreamed that he had been swept away to foreign lands. When he awoke he found it was still true.

The following morning after breaking their fast Sherrinford and Sherlock left Jonathan at the hotel with the luggage.

"Sydney is less than half a mile from here," Sherrinford began.

"Then let us stroll there on foot," Sherlock agreed to his brother's unfinished thought. "I have had enough sitting for a fortnight."

Sherrinford laughed.

"You will have plenty of more of that at the University. Besides, cabs might come at a premium right now," Sherrinford said as they exited the hotel.

Seeing Cambridge for the first time by the light of day, Sherlock took his brother's meaning. The street was clogged with carriages and wagons and young men dodging in between. Travel on foot might indeed be faster.

Despite Sherlock's impatience the previous afternoon he now seemed in good spirits as they headed up Regent Street. Fifteen minutes later he stood before the gatehouse of Sidney Sussex College. It was an imposing structure, like the entrance to a medieval castle, though lacking the moat and the drawbridge. Thick stone walls stretched right and left of the gatehouse. Sherlock felt it would not have seemed terribly out of place if archers had been stationed upon the walls. There was that defensive, cloistered sense about the place even from the street. 'This was going to be very different from Yorkshire,' he thought.

"Come along," Sherrinford said.

Gowned undergraduates wove their way past the Holmes brothers as they entered the college and made their way to the Senior Tutor's office. The outer room was full and they were forced to wait their turn.

"Mr Holmes, Sherlock, it is good to see you both again," Rev. Clowe said as they entered his office at last.

"We are glad meet you again, sir," Sherrinford said shaking his hand, "I had nearly forgotten the chaos that surrounds the beginning of a new term."

Rev. Clowe smiled.

"There is a bit of a bustle. You are looking much heartier than you did in January, Sherlock," Rev. Clowe said. "I am glad to see it."

"Yes, sir, I am feeling much better. Begging your pardon, you are from the West Riding, are you not? Near Sheffield, perhaps?"

"Good heavens. How do you know that?"

"Just a shadow of it in your speech, undoubtedly worn thin by your years here at the University."

"You have a very sensitive ear, Sherlock. I had no idea anyone could tell."

"I missed it when we met before," Sherlock confessed.

"You were recovering from your illness. Well, to business, I have many people to see today. As we discussed in January, freshmen usually live outside of college in licensed lodgings. Here is a list of the lodgings available. I suggest that you take those in Sidney Street immediately if they suit you. They are quite close and they won't last."

"We shall look at them straight away."

"Here is the Student's Guide to the University. You should read it carefully. Here is a list of the rules of the college. You will need to purchase your academical costume and sundries for your lodgings. Here is list of recommended tradesmen and a letter of introduction to a washerwoman. I understand that you will be reading for the Mathematical Tripos. Rev. Douglas Healy will be your supervisor. You should meet him as soon as possible. He will explain how he wishes to proceed. Here is the list of lectures. Some are at Sidney, but some are in other colleges. You should acquaint yourself with the lay of the land so you can arrive at your lectures on time. If you should have any questions or problems, do not hesitate to come to me."

The Holmes brothers thanked him and made their way out past the students waiting in the outer room. They headed out through the college gates to inspect the licensed lodgings in Sidney Street. The street was bustling with hansoms, four-wheelers and conveyances of every description and students dodging in between. The lodgings were in a four-story building not far from the college.

The landlord, Mr Darley, was happy to show them.

"It's a pretty set of rooms, gentlemen," Mr Darley said as he led them up the stairs. "A little bigger than they have over at Sidney with a bit of a kitchen. You won't get that there."

The lodgings consisted of a generous sitting room, a smaller bedroom, and a kitchen. They were furnished comfortably but simply. The sitting room contained a couch and a couple of chairs before the fireplace, a small table with chairs for dining, and a desk in one corner next to a bookcase. The kitchen off the sitting room was tiny with a block for working and an iron stove, but it had a pantry or gyp's closet attached that was as big as the kitchen itself. The single bedroom contained a bed, a table next to it with a lamp, and a wardrobe.

"Do they suit you?" Sherrinford asked Sherlock.

"They look adequate."

"What do you want for them?"

Mr Darley gave him a figure. Sherrinford frowned.

"Inherited t'building from me uncle," Mr Darley argued to his look. "Keeps a roof over me 'ead and food on the table, but I'm not living 'igh, and some o' the young men can run me and the girl ragged."

"Well, that won't be the case with my brother," Sherrinford said. "He has brought his own servant boy who will see to any meals that he doesn't take in college as well as handle any visitors."

"Ah, the boy will save me quite a few steps. I'll give you some consideration for that," Mr Darley replied and turning to Sherlock he continued, "And you look to be a proper gentleman, sir. Not one for much carousin' or comin' in after curfew."

Mr Darley named a lower figure that they agreed to and they sealed the deal.

"You'll find it a good place for reading. I've had a number of firsts among my men, a Wrangler even," Mr Darley said to Sherlock.

"I suppose that it is quieter at the top of the stairs than down below," Sherlock said.

"That it is, sir. You're from the north, aren't you? A long journey, isn't it?"

"It is indeed," Sherrinford said. "But we still have arrangements to make. We will return shortly."

With the latchkey in hand Sherlock and Sherrinford returned to the University Arms and arranged for Sherlock's trunk and other luggage to be moved to the new lodgings. They chose to walk back and await the porters. This time Jonathan joined them walking a few steps behind, and occasionally stumbling over his own feet as he looked about the city. As soon as they climbed the stairs and unlocked the door Jonathan began inspecting their new quarters. Mr Darley appeared shortly.

"You gentlemen must be famished. If you will allow me, I'll have a cold luncheon brought in while the porters are bringing your things over."

"That sounds excellent," Sherrinford said. "You can take Jonathan along to help."

"I'll do that, sir, and I'll show him where to find the water closet and the coal on the way."

Twenty minutes later Jonathan was helping Mr Darley and his servant girl lay bread and butter and cold fowl, cheeses, fruit and sweets and a jug of ale upon the table.

"Before I forget, here's a list of things you will be needin' to set up housekeeping," Mr Darley said. "It's not like those lists provided by some landladies who fill them full of unnecessary things so they can stock their own stores from your closet. Only the necessities. And you won't ever find anything missing in this house. Iffen you do I'll be the first to want to know who done it. If there is anything else you need, please let me know."

Jonathan followed Mr Darley to the door and closed it behind him.

"They are very fond of lists here," Sherlock said as he looked through the stack of papers they had accumulated while Sherrinford attacked the food.

Sherrinford laughed.

"I suppose they are. There will be time enough to look at them. First you must come here and eat something."

Sherlock obeyed.

"Is thieving by landlords as widespread here as Mr Darley suggests?" Sherlock asked as he chose a bit of bread and cheese.

"At least that's the common wisdom," Sherrinford replied. "In college a lot of thefts are attributed to bedders and gyps, but so many undergraduates leave their doors open to the world that no one can say for sure. You may want to have Jonathan latch the door if he is going out on an errand while you are away. Otherwise upon your return you could find any number of fellow-students have made themselves at home."

"Seems a bit rude."

"Undergraduates don't always follow the social niceties. There are many little precautions that will make life easier here, and cheaper. For example, during the first few weeks of the term you will be visited by a host of supposed 'gentlemen,' some claiming to be fellow-students or friends of your father's, trying to sell subscriptions to encyclopaedias or magazines, or seeking donations to some charity. They're all swindlers. They especially seek out freshmen in their first term. You'll be best off if Jonathan merely turns them away at the door."

"Jonathan?" Sherlock called.

The boy appeared at the threshold of the bedroom.

"Yes, sir?"

"Did you hear that?"

"Yes, sir. Men collecting for charities or selling subscriptions are to be turned away."

"Yes. That's all."

Jonathan disappeared again.

"You have a very attentive servant there."

"I think he notes when I inhale and exhale," Sherlock said.

"With just cause. Does it trouble you?"

"No, but I am very aware of it."

"You should count yourself lucky. Most undergraduates are sharing a gyp and bedder with several others and they have to fight for their ear."

"Do you think anyone will think it odd that I have my own servant?"

"No. In fact, it might improve your standing in their eyes. Only the wealthiest undergraduates, or those from noble families, tend to have their own servants."

After lunch Sherrinford drew forth his pocketbook and extracted some bank notes from it. He separated them into two piles.

"Father entrusted these to me. This is your first month's allowance and this is an additional sum to cover your initial college expenses and to settle you here."

He handed the bank notes to Sherlock.

"The two of you have a lot of unpacking to do, and you should study those lists and guides. I have a few errands to run. I'll come around this evening and we can go out to supper. There are many fine restaurants in this town."

The next morning they visited Mathew & Gents and Swan & Hurrell's which were both crowded with other freshmen. They purchased groceries, crockery, glasses and cutlery, and had them delivered back at the lodgings while they continued on to purchase Sherlock's academical attire.

"A rather absurd outfit," Sherlock commented upon donning the cap and gown.

"Far less gaudy than the undergraduate gowns of some other colleges. Regardless of whether it is fashionable, the cap and gown are required to be worn by undergraduates in Cambridge at all times on Sundays and after sunset on other days, in all university buildings, and at lectures, Hall and Chapel," intoned Sherrinford from memory.

"So they can tell the riff-raff from the locals?" Sherlock asked.

"And vice versa," Sherrinford responded with a twinkle in his eye. "Whether a badge of honour or merely a sorting technique, I doubt the gown leads to less trouble. There always seems to be some youths in town bent on baiting undergraduates, and some undergraduates who find no greater sport than baiting locals. The curfews are supposed to limit such encounters. The college gates are locked at 10 o'clock sharp. Landlords in licensed lodgings will enforce the curfews as well and report violations to the college deans. Ostensibly every undergraduate is to be in by ten o'clock, but the deans take no notice of anyone being out until twelve, except by making them pay a penny fine to the porter for each hour they are out after ten. The university proctors and their bulldogs—"

"Bulldogs?"

"Not really dogs. I believe the proper term is 'beadle' but everyone calls them 'bulldogs.' They are assistants who patrol the streets with the proctors to enforce the university rules. The proctors will collect a fine if they catch you out on the streets after curfew or violating any of the other rules of the university."

"Were you ever caught?"

"Well, no, but we took turns at watch when we would slip out to a local pub. We had a close call a time or two that gave us the fidgets for a while, but we gained courage again. We knew that we were unlikely to be sent down for sneaking a pint after ten."

"Did you ever try anything more daring than that?"

"I didn't, but — well, some tales are best left untold."

After lunch Sherlock and Sherrinford hunted down Sherlock's lecture halls. Some were in Sidney Sussex College, but some were located in St. John's College and Trinity College. As they strolled about the grounds of the three colleges, Sherrinford told Sherlock stories of his own days at the University. Then they meandered down King's Parade past the library and Senate House, then past Pembroke and Downing Colleges before returning to Sidney Street. On the fourth morning Sherrinford stopped by Sherlock's lodgings before heading to the railway station.

"I wish you success with your studies, Sherlock."

"Thank you."

As he stood at the door Sherrinford was suddenly hesitant to go. Sherlock seemed to be doing well enough, but it had only been ten months. Then out of the corner of his eye he saw Jonathan lurking silently in the background. Sherrinford knew the strength of the boy's devotion to his brother and it comforted him. He patted Sherlock on the shoulder, bid him farewell and left.

Chapter 5

University

"Still seeking knowledge at the old university."
Sherlock Holmes, The Red Circle

All undergraduates were required to attend services at the college chapel at least once a day six days a week and twice on Sundays. It was required more as a matter of discipline than one of religion and students could choose morning or evening prayer services. Sherlock normally chose to attend Morning Prayers to be done with it. His day typically began with a cup of coffee and a soft-boiled egg before he donned his cap and gown and headed to Chapel.

Many undergraduates chose to sleep in rather than attend Morning Prayers. Since they were required to be present, but not actually required to listen, there were reasonable suspicions that some chose to do their sleeping in the chapel itself. Sherlock Holmes was not among those.

The Sidney Chapel was small and had neither an organ nor a choir. There was nothing particularly remarkable about the services. During them Sherlock amused himself by observing the congregation. The ordinary rules of 'the game,' as Sherlock Holmes and his brothers had played it, did not apply here. Most of those in view were undergraduates or fellows of the college, and thus determining their occupation was no longer the point. But there were other things to discover. It was more challenging to come to conclusions about these men when their pedestrian clothes were partially covered by the academic gowns. However, undergraduate gowns were short, leaving the all-important knees and cuffs of the trousers visible. The gowns themselves also showed signs of individual wear. Sherlock found the evolution of the gowns fascinating to watch and it told him much about the members of Sidney Sussex College.

The gowns of the freshman declined rapidly from a crisp

freshness to something less attractive, based on the care and habits of their wearer. The gowns on some third year students more concerned with sports or other un-academic pursuits had degraded to hardly more than a worn necktie. But scholars and others with their eye on Fellowships had maintained their gowns with supreme care and dignity.

Cecil Hamley was an intriguing study. He was the third son of the Duke of Wuttset and thus properly "Lord Cecil." His academical gown and his clothing underneath were always of the highest quality and very well-maintained. Lord Cecil did not seem to have aspirations to be a scholar, but he was something of a fop. His neatness of dress allowed Sherlock to be certain that the indications on his collar and sleeves were always quite fresh and that told him something about the frequency with which they were renewed.

When a Sidney undergraduate appeared at Chapel one morning with grey sandstone dust upon the knees of his trousers and a dusty handprint on the back of his gown, Sherlock hypothesized that he had taken up the forbidden sport of night climbing on the university buildings and had grabbed his gown hurriedly the night before when a proctor approached after his descent from a building.

The senior members of the college also attended Morning Prayers. Many of them held Fellowships and thus were officially 'Fellows' but were often called 'Dons' (from the Latin *dominus* meaning master) by the undergraduates. The Fellows were all much more careful about their academic attire. Sherlock knew some of the Fellows by name only and saw them only at Chapel; others gave the lectures he attended.

Sherlock Holmes knew Rev. Clowe, the Senior Tutor, best of all the senior members of the college, since it was he who had come to Yorkshire to interview him. Rev. Clowe oversaw the academic progress of all the graduates and undergraduates of Sidney. He was a very approachable man who frequently invited students to attend breakfast with him and was generally well-liked. Reverend Clowe was himself a man deeply interested in science, and he had been instrumental in encouraging the construction of Sidney Sussex's new laboratory.

The services at the chapel were conducted by Dr James Hoch, the Dean of Sidney Sussex College. Many of the undergraduates cringed at the Dean's approach. This was not because there was anything disagreeable about the thirty-year-old man with a special interest in inorganic chemistry, but because the chief duty of the Dean was supervision of the conduct of the undergraduates. It was his responsibility to discipline any misbehaviour by the undergraduates within or without the walls of the college. Dean Hoch would note any failure of attendance at Chapel or Hall. The university proctors reported to him any students found in town after curfew or in any place from which they were banned. Information filtered to the Dean from Fellows, porters and landlords at licensed lodgings, and occasionally from the police. Stories circulated among the students concerning those the Dean had sent down for gambling, or confined to "gates & walls" for fighting in the courts. The undergraduates feared Dean Hoch more than those who reported to him and would do nearly anything to keep a report from going to the Dean.

But most hated and feared of all was the old Master of Sidney Sussex College. He was rumoured to be a tyrant, and the sixty-year-old Rev. Philip Roberts looked the part with his white beard, hooked nose, and a stern, impatient glare in his eyes. Little leniency was to be expected from him once a matter came into his hands and a student would fare better to plead his case to the Dean or Senior Tutor before it was set before the Master for a final decision. Freshmen had little to do with Master Roberts, and Sherlock Holmes seldom saw him save at Chapel.

After Morning Prayers Sherlock attended lectures until lunchtime. He then returned to his rooms. He was luckier than most undergraduates who lived in college. For lunch they were likely to have only the college common provisions of bread and butter and possibly a spot of jam. However, Jonathan had adapted quickly to his new duties and the ways of life in Cambridge. He spent his mornings at the market and the shops in town and Sherlock's diet improved as a result.

Jonathan continued to refine his command of the Queen's English by careful attention to the speech of the many gentlemen at the University. But at the marketplace, the boy not only discovered which merchants had the best produce for the lowest prices, he learned to speak the Cambridgeshire dialect and put that skill to practical use. He learned that some merchants charged locals less. So he adapted his speech and behaviour while in town and soon was seen as a local boy. It helped him stretch Sherlock's allowance further.

So in the mornings there were eggs and at lunchtime Sherlock often had his choice of fresh fruits and cheeses as well as hot muffins and inches of butter (as butter was traditionally sold in Cambridge). Whether it was the result of his illness and fast, or a life-long habit, Sherlock remained the slightest of eaters. The memory of Sherlock's near-death by starvation was far too fresh in Jonathan's mind and he encouraged his master to eat in any way he could.

Some days Sherlock had more lectures in the afternoon and twice a week he met with his supervisor, Rev. Douglas Healy. Rev. Healy was an acerbic man who seemed to be rather indifferent to the assignment of supervising undergraduates. Both he and Sherlock tolerated their required time together and saw little of each other outside of that.

Each undergraduate was expected to appear at the Sidney Hall at supper time four days a week in addition to Sunday. They were not necessarily required to dine, but they must have their attendance marked. Sherlock usually went directly there from his supervisions or afternoon lectures. As the college clock was striking half-past four each day little knots of undergraduates would form about the steps of the Hall, and Sherlock would join the students streaming across the court in expectation of the dinner-bell. Since Sidney Sussex was one of the smaller colleges, the crowd waiting was not as large as could be found at Trinity or King's but the spirit was the same. The bell would ring, the doors would be thrown open and the crowd would pour into the hall to squabble over and deride the over-priced victuals waiting inside.

Sidney Hall was a large open chamber used for many types of events. Each evening it was set up with a high table cross-ways at one end for the Fellows and lower tables for the Sidney undergraduates running length-wise to fill the rest of the room.

The freshmen had a table to themselves with a second year scholar at its head to maintain order and advise the younger men. At dinner Sherlock mostly ate in silence and used the opportunity to continue his observations of his fellow-students at close range. While they chatted over their supper, he could study their clothing, habits, manners of speech and topics of interest. Matthew Simons seemed to be perpetually off on some other spiritual plane. Wickery was undoubtedly destined for politics, reading law and always espousing some position on something. Blankton, Slackmire and Hackstead were far more concerned with sports than studies. Musgrave was prim and aloof with as much history hanging about him as he was reading. Reserved almost to the extent of coldness, his face rarely gave expression to the thoughts inside. Mickleby was reading for the Natural Sciences Tripos, but was fond of practical jokes as well. He often proposed performing some experiment with their supper, though Sherlock was uncertain whether it was inspired by a spirit of scientific inquiry or the thrill of a stunt. The men at the table usually voted that just consuming supper at Sidney was a daring enough experiment. Ericcson seemed a serious student of the Classics with ever a Greek or Latin quote on his tongue. The other Holmes, Trevor, Smith and a few others were quiet and nondescript. Lord Cecil, of course, as the son of nobility, had the privilege of dining at the high table with the Fellows despite being an undergraduate. He and his friends would pass by the table of others of their year on their way to the high table just to throw a few taunts at them.

One evening as Sherlock was leaving the Hall to return to his lodgings a voice called to him.

"Mr Holmes!"

Sherlock turned to find the Senior Tutor behind him.

"Yes, sir?"

"How are you getting along in your studies?" Rev. Clowe asked.

"Fine, sir."

"Good, good. I'm inviting some members of the college for breakfast tomorrow. You should join us. It is a good opportunity to become acquainted with some of the second & third year men."

"Yes, sir. What time?"

"Oh, about 7 o' clock."

"I'll be there."

Upon Sherlock's return to his rooms he told Jonathan of the appointment before he settled down to reading. In the morning he set off for the rooms of the Senior Tutor. Sherlock recognized a number of other undergraduates as well as some of the graduate fellows.

Conversation over coffee cups and pastries was informal and wide ranging.

"So is it true, Rev. Clowe that you nearly incinerated your rooms in college?" asked Lord Cecil.

Rev. Clowe laughed.

"Not precisely. It is part of the reason that I championed the construction of the Sidney's laboratory so that students would have a safer environment for their experiments."

"Tell us what really happened."

"I am sure that the rumours are far more exciting than the truth. But this is how it happened: Shortly after I became a tutor of the college, two other Fellows and I thought that we would like to take a medical degree, as it might be useful to us. So we went to Professor Humphrey's lectures in anatomy and to Professor Living's in chemistry. We became very interested in chemistry and wished to do some experiments. St. John's College was the only college at that time which had a laboratory. So now and again we tried some simple experiments in our own rooms. Once while we were running an experiment the rubber tube that was conveying hydrogen to our retort caught fire and we saw that the flames were stealing up to the explosive mixture. We all dived under the table as the safest place and waited in agony for the coming explosion to blow the college to atoms. Finding after a while that nothing happened, we recovered from our fright and looked up to find the fire had gone out."

"Cowards," Lord Cecil yawned.

"Yes, we all accused each other of that. But it pressed home to us the need for a more controlled space for chemical experiments and the funds were found to build the laboratory."

Also in attendance at the breakfast were the captains of several of the college athletic clubs bent on recruiting new members and Sherlock happened to wander in their midst.

"Holmes, ever participated in sports?"

"A little fencing and boxing in the past."

"You should join our cricket club," one said.

"Oh, can't you see he's more of a track and field man?" another protested.

"Thank you, no. I think it will to be all I can do to keep up with my studies. I'm hoping to sit for the Little Go this term."

"The exercise will do you good even if you are reading hard."

"I'm sure it would, but I don't think I'm quite up to competition yet."

"Mr Holmes had a serious illness earlier this year," Rev. Clowe interjected.

"Of what nature?"

"I had a very bad case of pneumonia," Sherlock said.

"Nearly killed him, his father said," the Senior Tutor said. "We are lucky he was able to join us this term."

"Yes," Sherlock agreed, but suddenly the room seemed very crowded.

"Goodness! How did that come about?"

"I—" he began but his heart was pounding and he stopped. "The story is rather complex."

Sherlock look away from the young men gazing at him. He felt like he was suffocating.

"Please excuse me," Sherlock said and left the room and hurried down the stairs. When he gained the court, he leaned against the wall. His pulse was racing. As he stood there he heard the bells for

Morning Prayers and realized he had left his cap and gown back at the Senior Tutor's rooms. He reluctantly mounted the staircase to retrieve them. As he did, fellow-students from the breakfast passed him heading down the stairs towards the chapel, donning their academical costumes as they descended. A few gave him sideways glances as they passed.

Back in the rooms, Rev. Clowe was attending to his own gown while his gyp cleaned up the remains from breakfast.

"Mr Holmes, you left rather precipitously. Are you ill?"

"I just needed some air," Sherlock said as he picked up his cap and gown.

"I apologize if I embarrassed you by mention of your illness."

"I don't like to talk about it, sir."

"I shall keep that in mind," Rev. Clowe said laying his hand on Sherlock's shoulder. "But come along or we shall both be late for Chapel."

Sherlock Holmes walked to the chapel with Rev. Clowe. By the time Morning Prayers were over the sensations had faded and he went on to lectures as usual. But the incident had its effects. Sherlock believed he had conquered the mental turmoil which had plagued him earlier in the year, but he still felt some discomfort at mixing with other members of the college and the incident at the breakfast merely made that worse. He knew he had overreacted. He didn't want it to happen again. He was not accustomed to being surrounded by so many men of his own age. He dodged a few other invitations to wines and breakfasts, or to join sports clubs. Soon word got around about the incident at the breakfast. The invitations stopped coming. Sherlock spent most of his free hours studying alone in his rooms. Some men of his year thought him a bit of a swot. Others did not know what to think, but they did not go out of their way to seek his acquaintance or visit his rooms.

Sherlock Holmes spent his first six weeks at Cambridge University concentrating on his reading and his lectures. Except for those observations which were almost instinctive with him after his years of playing 'the game' with Mycroft and Sherrinford,

Sherlock thought of little beyond mathematics. He did not find the subject inspiring, but it was what he was here to do. He would study mathematics. He would obtain his degree. He would find a position far away from Yorkshire— in London, perhaps. He would live a normal life away from his father, away from the memories. That was his plan and the next step in that plan required him to take the Previous Exam this term. The Previous Exam, called the "Little Go" by undergraduates, was a prerequisite to the honours degree exam. Having the Little Go behind him would qualify him to take the Mathematical Tripos as soon as he had fulfilled sufficient terms in residence.

Some undergraduates obviously had other ideas about the purpose of their presence there, as was demonstrated by the ruckus on November 5th. Sidney Street that night became a heaving mass of undergraduates amusing themselves by baiting policemen and making a general disturbance. In time they were all rounded up and the street cleared. The next morning they had to appear in court where they were fined ten shillings each. Sherlock never participated in such antics. Unless necessary he stayed in his rooms. His regular circuit that term was between the colleges and his lodgings. He had no call to wander farther afield in Cambridge. If there was anything he needed, he sent Jonathan out to the market or down to Harry Johnson's shop opposite Christ Church College. He spent as little time outside as was possible to travel between the buildings and he paid little mind to the weather.

54

Chapter 6

Maelstrom

"With a suppressed groan he dropped on his face upon the ground."
Dr Watson, The Reigate Squires

One day in November when Sherlock opened the heavy door of the lecture hall he was hit by a blast of cold air. Some snowflakes swirled in. It was snowing. As this fact pierced his consciousness Sherlock hesitated. His heart was pounding. He hadn't been out in snow since.... He backed up and several other undergraduates passed him. He let the door close behind them. He paced back and forth. He was being foolish, he thought. It was a natural phenomenon. He had seen snow many times in his life. It was crystallized water, nothing more. He opened the door again. He stepped out. The door closed behind him. He walked forward. The wind whipped at his gown. He gripped his books. He merely had to cross the court, go through the gatehouse and walk across the street. He concentrated on the door opposite which was his immediate destination. The cold wind bit at him. Memories nibbled at the edges of his mind.... No! Sherlock tried to separate the cold and snow from his memories of that awful snowstorm that had nearly killed him, but he could not. He tried thinking of other things. He tried to review the mathematical proof the lecturer had been discussing line-by-line in his mind, but it was not engaging enough to keep other thoughts at bay. The cold and the snow teased his senses and brought forth memories that gnawed at him. He tried to push them aside. The snow was falling heavily. The wind wrapped it around him. Suddenly Sherlock was completely surrounded by white and vivid memories swirled about him in the snow, memories of being lost in the snow on the moor. The college buildings, the grass, the trees, everything was gone; everyone was gone; Violet was gone; he had lost her in the storm; she was never coming back. Once again he saw HIM holding her; he saw the frightened look on her face; then she disappeared into the snowstorm. He'd lost her in the storm, and wandered blindly on the moor until he fell....

He tried to catch himself, but hands grabbed his arms and pushed them down.

"Mr Holmes?"

Sherlock heard the crackling of the fire. He opened his eyes slowly. He was lying on one of the couches in the Junior Combination Room. Dean Hoch was leaning over him. Behind him was a tangle of undergraduates.

"There you are, Mr Holmes," Dean Hoch said. "You had us worried. Blankton and Hackstead found you lying out in the snow in the court and carried you in."

Just then Mickleby came running in with Jonathan behind him.

"They sent for me, sir. Are you ill?" Jonathan asked him.

"I-I don't think so. I must-must have fallen. I-I don't remember," Sherlock lied. He did remember. He remembered too well. He remembered too much.

"Well, you seem a bit shaken," Dean Hoch said. "Perhaps you should take the rest of the day off. I will inform the Senior Tutor."

Sherlock returned to his rooms with Jonathan. They didn't speak, but he suspected that Jonathan knew the truth. Sherlock tried to put it out of his mind, but he could not. The snow had unlocked the door he thought he had closed forever. Visions from the past accompanied him home. He gripped Jonathan's shoulder, not to steady his feet on the snow-covered ground, but to lead him through the swirl of snow and images that surrounded him. Back in his rooms Sherlock tried to study. He stared at his books, but the ghosts would not leave him. Jonathan ran out and brought back something for Sherlock's supper. Sherlock picked at his meal. He had no appetite. Finally he pushed it away, tossed the books aside and went to bed. But there was no peace there either.

Jonathan found Sherlock over his books at his desk in the wee hours of the following morning, his head resting in his hands. He looked up as Jonathan entered the room.

"Are you ill, sir?" Jonathan asked.

"No. I couldn't sleep. It seemed a good time to study," Sherlock lied.

A nightmare had awakened him. He had tried to study afterwards, but he had been unable to concentrate on one word of the book before him as thoughts and images from the past plagued him. In and around it all was a growing fear: If this had returned now, would it come back again and again, no matter how he fought it?

"The room is cold," Jonathan said. "Let me build up the fire."

"Yes, do that, but then go back to your bed."

It was after Jonathan had returned to bed that Sherlock's eye fell upon the paper calendar before him and with a start he realized that it was only four days from the anniversary of the day Violet had vanished. He reached out and touched the date with his finger as if it was some palpable connection with her, with the past, as if somehow he could go back to that moment and change everything. Then he heard once more his father's inquiry, "Do you deny that you are the father of the child she carries?" and he saw once more the view out the study window. He saw Violet break free and run to her horse. He followed and lost her in the snowstorm. Eventually the storm in his mind subsided, and trembling, Sherlock lifted his head from his desk horrified by the fact that he'd had two attacks in less than a day. Exhausted he threw himself on his bed, but sleep held no rest for his tortured mind.

The next morning Sherlock was late rising and missed Morning Prayers, but he dragged himself out of bed in time to attend his lectures. As Sherlock was leaving, Jonathan protested.

"But sir, you have not eaten."

"I'm late for a lecture," Sherlock said and left.

It was snowing again. He ran swiftly towards his lecture in St. John's College trying to shut the snow out, but he was haunted by the feeling that Violet was just out of sight and that he should call out to her. He resisted the urge. He had to tell himself over and over that she was gone. He bumped into another undergraduate and his mind snapped back the present and he apologized. In the lecture hall he could not pay attention to the lecturer.

That night his sleep was shattered once more by the old nightmares. When he awoke he was afraid to go back to sleep, but he had no respite when he was awake. Days passed with no relief. He had fought so hard for control and now it was falling through his fingers like sand. He tried to hide his torment, but he could not eat or sleep. He could not concentrate. He knew he could not go on this way.

Jonathan knew something was wrong. He could tell Sherlock was not sleeping well. He heard him up at night. He suspected that Sherlock had an attack in the court, but he dared not ask. Was he ill? Sherlock denied it, but he ate very little. Jonathan's fears drove him to protest, but Sherlock was irritable and they argued.

"Thou mun eat!" Jonathan insisted, once more reverting to broad Yorkshire in his fear and frustration.

Jonathan was a boy here alone at Cambridge with Sherlock. He did not have Sherlock's brother or the village doctor to confide in. He did not know what to do.

Sherlock continued attending lectures though he received no benefit from them. He was too distracted to understand what the lecturers were saying. As he left one lecture at Sidney, he bumped into the caretaker of the building causing him to drop several tools and a tin that spilt some of its contents on the floor. As Sherlock bent down to help him pick up the tin the man stopped him.

"Don't touch that. It's poison."

"Poison?" Sherlock asked.

"Arsenic. A spoonful'll kill a man and a lot less will make 'im awfully sick."

"What are you using it for?" Sherlock asked.

"Rats. This building has rats," the caretaker said.

"There goes one now," Sherlock said pointing across the hall.

The man looked but didn't see anything.

"Where?" he asked.

"He's gone," Sherlock said taking his hand out of his pocket. "I'll let you get back to your work.

Sherlock returned to his rooms early.

"I'm sorry, Jonathan. I have not been well. I'm going to my bed. Please bring my lunch to me there."

Jonathan brought Sherlock's lunch to him on a tray.

"Is there anything else I can do for you?" Jonathan asked.

"No. Go now and close the door behind you," Sherlock said.

"Yes, sir," Jonathan said.

Jonathan obeyed with some hesitation. Sherlock had never asked him to close the bedroom door since they had come to Cambridge. Jonathan stayed near the door and listened. He heard the normal sounds of silver and china. Then silence. A drawer opened and closed. Then he heard footsteps back and forth, back and forth. They stopped. Another drawer opened and closed. He heard more pacing, then a scratching sound, writing? The bed creaked again and there were sounds of eating again. As the sounds continued Jonathan began to relax. At least Sherlock was eating. Suddenly he heard a gasp and a choking sound followed quickly by a crash. Jonathan rushed back into the room. The tray and its contents lay scattered about the floor and Sherlock was bent double on the bed. His arms were pressed to his stomach; his breathing was heavy, punctuated by groans. Jonathan stepped over the remains of Sherlock's lunch and approached him.

"You are ill. I should get a doctor," Jonathan said.

Sherlock looked up at him and shook his head.

"No," he said and reached up his hand as if to grasp Jonathan's arm, but then he was hit by another spasm and doubled in pain again.

Jonathan turned to go for help. Then he saw the note lying on the floor. It must have fallen from the tray. It was addressed to him. Suddenly he understood that this was not merely a case of the gripe. He glanced back at Sherlock for an instant, then he scooped up the note and threw it in the fireplace as he ran through the rooms and out the door. Jonathan sped down the stairs and banged on the landlord's door. Mr Darley opened it immediately.

"Mr Sherlock is ill. He needs a doctor quickly," Jonathan told him breathlessly.

Mr Darley rushed up the stairs with Jonathan and into Sherlock's bedroom. Sherlock was nearly insensible with pain, but still conscious. The landlord grabbed Sherlock and pushed him back against the bed. Jonathan could not see what he was doing, but suddenly Sherlock began retching. The landlord forced Sherlock to lean over the side of the bed. Finally Sherlock stopped vomiting and collapsed upon the bed. Mr Darley lifted the unconscious Sherlock in his arms and carried him down the stairs calling to Jonathan. The horrified boy followed in silence. Out in the street Jonathan frantically hailed a passing cab.

"Quick, driver," Mr Darley cried, "to the hospital!"

Chapter 7

The Hospital

*"The glorious sunshine which was bursting its way through
the hellish cloud of terror which had girt us in."*
Dr Watson, The Devil's Foot

It was bright. Sherlock heard voices. They were all overlapping in his mind: "I could still shoot you....a thief...your father wishes to see you...can't believe you are my son....She's gone." No, no....

Sherlock jumped as a hand picked up his wrist and different voices invaded his consciousness.

"He's coming around," one of the new voices said.

"That'll save someone's neck," another said.

"Not necessarily. We'll have to watch him for several days. Sometimes there can be a delay in the reaction," a gruff voice responded.

Sherlock blinked his eyes open as he struggled to consciousness. It was bright, too bright. He squeezed them shut again.

"Move that light a little. It's blinding him," the gruff voice said.

Sherlock opened his eyes again. He saw a broad, bearded face with ruddy cheeks looking down at him. Beyond was a cluster of other, younger faces.

"Hello, I'm Dr Burton and these are my medical students."

"Where?" Sherlock gasped. His throat was raw.

"You are in hospital in Cambridge. You seem to have ingested a fair amount of arsenic," Dr Burton said.

They knew, Sherlock thought.

"S-something about saving... someone's neck," Sherlock said trying to pierce the fog in his mind to recreate what he had heard while half-conscious. "What d-did he mean?"

"He was referring to your servant," replied Dr Burton. "He came in with you, but later they arrested him for poisoning you." Dr Burton shook his head. "A mere child—"

But Sherlock reached up and grabbed hold of the doctor's coat and struggled to get up.

"No," he tried to shout, but it came out as a croak. "No. He didn't. You must—."

The medical students took hold of Sherlock from all sides and pushed him back down. He struggled against them.

"No, no, no," he kept repeating. "He didn't do it."

"Bind him," Dr Burton said peeling Sherlock's fingers from his jacket. "Jones, go to Fulbourn and ask Dr Mackenzie to visit."

The students bound Sherlock's arms and legs to the bed with wide straps. He resisted but there were too many of them.

"Chloral, Dr Burton?" one of the students asked.

"No. No," Sherlock kept repeating.

"No. We don't know how much arsenic he consumed. I'd rather have him awake for a while," Dr Burton said. "Come on, lad. Calm down."

"Please listen," Sherlock said hoarsely, panting after the exhausting struggle.

"Certainly," Dr Burton responded.

"Alone," Sherlock whispered glancing over at the students.

"Yes, yes," Dr Burton said. "You fellows back off. He can't do anything now. Go check on Mrs Randolph."

"Now we are alone," he told Sherlock.

"You must speak to the police," Sherlock said. "Tell them that Jonathan didn't do it."

"He didn't poison you?" Dr Burton asked.

"No, he didn't," Sherlock said.

"The arsenic was in your lunch that he said he prepared, and he's not denying that he put it in there. When they arrested him, he said absolutely nothing," Dr Burton said.

"You must tell them he didn't do it," Sherlock insisted.

"Then who did?" Dr Burton said squinting at him.

Sherlock closed his eyes.

"I did," he said quietly.

"I see," Dr Burton said.

"Please, you must tell the police the truth. Jonathan should not pay for my mistake. He's saved my life more than once," Sherlock insisted.

"More than once? Do you make a habit of this?" Dr Burton asked.

"No, I-I—" Sherlock stammered.

Just then a smaller man approached.

"You are upsetting him, Dr Burton," the smaller man said.

"Ah, Mac, I did not know any of this when I sent for you. I'm just learning it now," Dr Burton said. "Mr Holmes, Dr George Mackenzie. Dr Mackenzie, Mr Sherlock Holmes."

"You've bound him. You know I don't approve of that," Dr Mackenzie said quietly.

"He was getting a bit out of hand. We can't have that here," Dr Burton said.

"Please, please tell the police to release Jonathan," Sherlock interjected.

"I think he will calm down significantly if you just do as he asks," Dr Mackenzie said.

"I'll send a note over to the constabulary, but they might want to take a statement from you before they release him," Dr Burton said.

"That's fine. That's fine," Sherlock said laying his head down with a sigh. "I'll do anything."

"See, he's much calmer already," Dr Mackenzie said. "You will behave if I unbind you, won't you?"

"Yes," Sherlock agreed.

"With your approval, Dr Burton?"

"Yes. But I'll hold you accountable, Mac," Dr Burton said walking off.

"This is his hospital," Dr Mackenzie said quietly to Sherlock as he released the bonds on Sherlock's arms and legs. "So if you do misbehave he might have them bind you again. But I don't think the human spirit responds well to being bound."

"Thank you," Sherlock said rubbing his arms.

Dr Mackenzie offered Sherlock half a glass of water.

"Sip it slowly," he told him.

"Arsenic poisoning, eh?" Dr Mackenzie asked when Sherlock

was done.

"Yes," Sherlock said.

"Self-inflicted?"

"Yes."

"I hear it does wonderful things for the hair and skin if it doesn't kill you, but I don't recommend it," Dr Mackenzie said.

"You came from Fulbourn?" Sherlock asked.

"Yes."

"From the asylum?"

"Yes. I am the medical superintendent there."

"Do you think I am mad?"

"Not yet. You'll have to work harder if you want to convince me of that," Dr Mackenzie said.

"Why did Dr Burton send for you then?" Sherlock asked.

"Oh, sometimes he sends for me when patients are violent. He thinks I understand better what is going on inside people's heads," Dr Mackenzie said.

"Do you?" Sherlock asked.

"Sometimes," Dr Mackenzie agreed.

Sherlock leaned back against the pillows and shut his eyes.

"You would like it if someone understood what is going on inside your head, wouldn't you?" Dr Mackenzie said.

Sherlock opened his eyes and looked at him.

"Yes, but how did you know that's what I was thinking?"

"Lucky guess," Dr Mackenzie said.

"No, you deduced it," Sherlock Holmes said.

"Well, perhaps a bit of induction and deduction in there. I've been doing this for a while," Dr Mackenzie said with a smile.

Sherlock closed his eyes again.

"You are an undergraduate at the university, aren't you?" Dr Mackenzie asked.

"Yes, Sidney Sussex College," Sherlock said.

"Ah. I teach clinical courses to university medical students. So I interact with a number of people at the university," Dr Mackenzie said.

"Do you want me to tell you why I did it?" Sherlock asked.

"Do you want to tell me?" Dr Mackenzie said.

"I'd rather not talk about it right now," Sherlock said.

"That's fine. The only reason I'm not going away and letting you sleep is that there is a constable approaching us," Dr Mackenzie said.

"Good evening, Dr Mackenzie, is he one of yours?" asked Chief Constable Bevans.

"Oh, no, we're just having a chat," Dr Mackenzie said.

"Mr Sherlock Holmes is it?" Bevans asked Sherlock.

"Yes, sir," he responded.

"I was told that you wanted to make a statement."

"Yes, sir."

"Think he's fit enough, doc?" the Chief Constable asked Dr Mackenzie.

"He seems fairly coherent to me," Dr Mackenzie said.

"I understand that it was arsenic poisoning?"

"Yes, sir," Sherlock said.

"You know this for a fact yourself?"

"That's what the caretaker said he was using to kill the rats. I took some of it when he wasn't looking," Sherlock said.

"The caretaker?" Bevans said.

"At the college, Sidney Sussex, sir," he said.

"Go on," Bevans said.

"I told Jonathan that I was not feeling well and asked him to bring my lunch in the bedroom on a tray. He did so and then I dismissed him and told him to close the door. I put the arsenic in my own food. Jonathan had nothing to do with it. He came in when I was sick. He said he was going for help. Things are rather a blur after that. I-I never thought that anyone would accuse Jonathan."

"Why did you put arsenic in your food?" Bevans asked.

"I don't think you need an answer to that, Chief Constable," Dr Mackenzie interjected.

"I suppose not. But usually if a man tries to kill himself he leaves a note of some kind. We didn't find any note."

"I-I did write a note. I remember - I remember now that Jonathan picked it up as he left the room," Sherlock said.

"He didn't tell us anything about a note. In fact, he's refused to tell us anything about anything. He could have ended up going all the way to the gallows if you had succeeded in killing yourself. I think you and he need to do some thinking about that so I don't hear of either one of you again."

"You will release him?" Sherlock asked.

"Yes. You're alive and say he didn't do it. So I have no reason to hold him. Good evening, Mr Holmes, Dr Mackenzie," the Chief Constable said.

"Good evening,"

"Now you should rest. I'll come by tomorrow," Dr Mackenzie said.

"Good night."

Sherlock shut his eyes. He did not quite understand it, but there was something soothing about Dr Mackenzie. They hadn't spoken much but he felt calmer than he had in over a week. It was something in Mackenzie's manner. But before Sherlock could determine what it was he fell asleep.

Sherlock awoke the next day when Dr Burton was checking his pulse.

"You were starting to worry me," Dr Burton said.

"How so?" Sherlock asked.

"You slept for over thirteen hours," Dr Burton said.

"Is that bad?" Sherlock asked.

"Not if you needed it. I kept checking to make sure you had not passed away on me. Arsenic is tricky stuff. It can cause organ or nerve damage that is not immediately apparent. Some people survive the initial ingestion and suddenly develop paralysis or jaundice and die a week later."

"So you don't know for a fact that the arsenic won't still kill me?" Sherlock asked.

"That's correct. Though since you were trying to kill yourself, I guess that might not matter to you."

"Now, Dr Burton," a quiet voice spoke up, "You know that people don't attempt suicide because they feel life doesn't matter, but rather because life as they are experiencing it has become unbearable."

"I've heard you say that," Dr Burton said.

"Good morning, Sherlock," Dr Mackenzie said.

"Good morning, Dr Mackenzie," Sherlock said.

"How are you feeling this morning, physically, I mean?"

"A bit queasy, but mostly hungry," Sherlock said.

"I've taken the liberty of ordering my own prescription for that," Dr Mackenzie said.

From behind him came a nurse with a tray containing a bowl of oat-meal porridge, some toasted bread and a glass of milk. She set it on the bed before Sherlock and departed.

"A good regimen of oat-meal porridge'll clean out the residual arsenic," Dr Mackenzie said.

"Dr Mackenzie has a peculiar sense of humour," Dr Burton said. "He knows that there is no proof of that."

"But it doesn't hurt," Dr Mackenzie said.

"No, it doesn't," Dr Burton said.

"And it is more comforting than saying that there is nothing we can do," Dr Mackenzie said, "or just hiding the residual risks of arsenic poisoning from the patient."

"True," Dr Burton said. "I think any information that will discourage patients from ingesting arsenic should be given to them."

"I don't think any of them find it a pleasant experience," Dr Mackenzie said.

Sherlock ate as he listened to the banter between the big, gruff Dr Burton and the small, soft-spoken Dr Mackenzie. They were an unusual pair, but he sensed a great deal of respect and admiration between them.

"Do you handle a lot of poisonings here?" Sherlock asked.

"We have a few accidental poisonings, mostly children eating rat poison or fruit stones. Not as many intentional poisonings," Dr Burton said.

"I encountered more attempted suicides at my previous place of employment in Norwich," Dr Mackenzie said.

"I see," Sherlock said.

"Has Dr Burton told you of the visitors?" Dr Mackenzie asked.

"I haven't had a chance. Your landlord and your college dean wish to call upon you. They've been inquiring all morning while you were asleep. I told them that they could visit after you woke and had eaten. I should send word to them soon."

Sherlock looked worried.

"Do they know?" he asked.

"Darley was there in your rooms," Dr Burton said. "He induced vomiting. That probably saved your life. So he knew it was something you ate. Someone told the police. They asked us to confirm that it was arsenic poisoning before they arrested Jonathan."

"Did they release him?" Sherlock asked.

"Yes, and Jonathan would like to visit as well. He brought by some of your clothes. So we can make you presentable for your guests, if you are finished with your breakfast. I'll send a note to them."

A half hour later Sherlock was sitting up propped against pillows wearing his own dressing gown when Mr Darley and Dean Hoch from Sidney Sussex College were led over by Dr Burton.

"Good morning, Dean, Mr Darley," Dr Mackenzie said.

"Good morning, Dr Mackenzie," Dean Hoch said. "We would like to have a few words with Mr Holmes."

"Then proceed, gentlemen," Dr Mackenzie said, but made no effort to withdraw.

The Dean gave him a look, but said nothing. Sherlock observed this exchange with interest. The usually talkative Dr Burton had also been silently watching.

"Mr Holmes, Mr Darley here said that when he saw your condition he suspected arsenic poisoning and knew he had to act quickly," the Dean said.

"My nephew got into the rat poison when I was livin' in London and he looked like you did," Mr Darley said. "The doctor down the street made him puke and said that getting it out of his stomach fast is what saved him. The doctor showed me how to do it. So that's what I done."

"After he left you here, Mr Darley told the police of his suspicions before reporting to me," the Dean said. "The police said that the hospital confirmed it. They arrested your servant for poisoning you, but they released him a few hours later at your request. We spoke to Jonathan this morning, but he would not say anything. He said it was not his place to."

"Rightly so," Dr Mackenzie said.

Dean Hoch looked at Dr Mackenzie curiously.

"Has this -uh- happened before?" the Dean asked.

"Good heavens, man, I've never heard of someone eating arsenic like that twice," Dr Mackenzie said.

Dr Burton cleared his throat.

"No," Sherlock said, taking a cue from Dr Mackenzie.

"Special arrangements were made when you sought admission to the college because you were recovering from an illness," the Dean said attempting a different tact. "What was the nature of that illness?"

"I was caught in a snow storm upon the moors and lost my way. I nearly died of pneumonia. It was months before I regained my strength."

"And your collapse in the court a few days ago?" the Dean said.

"I don't remember what happened. It was snowing—" Sherlock said uncertainly.

"Ah, I see how it could be," Dr Mackenzie interjected. "The snow squall could have provoked memories of your earlier illness. They could have so overwhelmed you that you collapsed."

Sherlock looked searchingly at Dr Mackenzie. How did this man know these things?

"Yes, that could be it," Sherlock responded thoughtfully.

The Dean cleared his throat.

"Well, we have no interest is noising this about, especially if it won't happen again," he said.

Dr Mackenzie gave him no cues this time, but Sherlock knew what answer they wanted.

"No, sir, it won't," Sherlock responded.

"Very well, then—" the Dean concluded.

"You won't mention this to my father, will you?" Sherlock asked.

"I think it is a private matter between you and your father," Dean Hoch responded.

"Thank you, sir," Sherlock said.

After they left, Sherlock turned to Dr Mackenzie.

"What influence do you have over them?" he asked.

"I have a few connexions at the university," Dr Mackenzie said. "It is in their interest to keep it quiet. Neither the college nor the university would like such publicity."

"You told me that Jonathan had saved your life more than once," Dr Burton said changing the subject.

"Yes...," Sherlock said hesitantly.

"But what you said about the snow-storm and the pneumonia was true, wasn't it?" Dr Mackenzie.

"Yes," Sherlock said.

"There is just more to the story than that," Dr Mackenzie suggested.

"Yes, but I don't want to talk about it," Sherlock said.

"Later, perhaps," Dr Mackenzie said.

"Well, I see that I am getting nowhere with that inquiry, especially with Mac backing you up," Dr Burton conceded. "They'll be bringing lunch soon. You should rest until then. I'll allow your servant to visit in the afternoon."

"As much as I'd like to meet Jonathan, I must return to the asylum," Dr Mackenzie said.

"You will come again?" Sherlock asked.

"Would you like that?" Dr Mackenzie asked.

"I'd like to talk some more," Sherlock said.

"Then I shall make a point of visiting again tomorrow," Dr Mackenzie said. "In the meantime, do what Dr Burton says. He may act like a bear, but he means well and he is an excellent physician."

"I will," Sherlock agreed.

Chapter 8

Doctor Mackenzie

"You, a doctor—you are enough to drive a patient into an asylum."
Sherlock Holmes, The Dying Detective

After lunch Sherlock was resting with his eyes closed when he heard a familiar soft step. He opened his eyes. Jonathan approached.

"Good afternoon, sir. You are looking much better," he said.

"Thank you. Jonathan—"

"I know, sir."

"You destroyed the note?" Sherlock asked.

"Yes, sir," Jonathan conceded.

"Don't risk being hanged for my sake," Sherlock insisted.

Jonathan did not respond to this.

"How long will they keep you here?" Jonathan asked.

"A few more days."

"Is there is anything you need, sir?" Jonathan said.

"Bring my books, Jonathan. I'm already behind on my studies. Perhaps I can catch up on my reading here."

"I will bring them, sir," Jonathan said before he took his leave.

Dr Mackenzie appeared again the next morning while Sherlock was eating his breakfast.

"I see that you are continuing to follow my prescription," Dr Mackenzie said.

"Yes. Dr Burton said that if your theory were true that I should eat nothing but oat-meal porridge. However, I've decided to forgo that experiment."

"I think they've actually managed to put a pound or two on you since you've been here. You weren't eating well before that?" Dr Mackenzie asked.

"No," Sherlock said.

"I have heard comments in the past about the food at the Hall at Sidney—"

"It wasn't that."

"No? You have Jonathan. Is Jonathan not a good cook?"

"He's a fine cook. Sometimes I am too distracted to eat," Sherlock said.

"Is that true?" Dr Mackenzie asked of someone out of Sherlock's range of vision.

Jonathan came forward with a box of books.

"Which, sir?" Jonathan asked.

"Sometimes he is too distracted to eat," Dr Mackenzie clarified.

"Yes, sir," Jonathan responded to him, and then he said to Sherlock, "I'm sorry, sir. They didn't tell me that you weren't alone."

"Quite all right, Jonathan," Sherlock said. "Dr Mackenzie said that he wanted to meet you. Dr Mackenzie, this is Jonathan Beckwith."

"I'm glad to meet you, Jonathan."

"Dr Mackenzie," he said with a bow. Then to Sherlock he said, "I brought your books."

"Put the box here next to the bed. I will look at them later."

Jonathan set the box down next to the bed.

"Draw up a stool, Jonathan," Dr Mackenzie said.

Jonathan looked at Sherlock who nodded. Jonathan sat down.

"Interesting. There is a master-servant relationship here, but there is something more. You knew each other before that relationship began," Dr Mackenzie said.

"Yes, but how did you know that?" Sherlock asked.

"You look each other in the eye. Most people don't look their servants in the eye and most would not want their servants to do so."

"Ah," Sherlock said, folding his napkin.

"Allow me to move that," Dr Mackenzie said putting the breakfast tray out of the way.

"Also, I observed how upset you were that Jonathan had been arrested. Few people would be that concerned about a mere servant," Dr Mackenzie said.

"He's saved my life more than once," Sherlock said. "I felt that gaol or worse was a shabby way to repay that."

"Jonathan knows a great deal about you, more than anyone

else, I wager," said Dr Mackenzie.

"Yes," Sherlock admitted.

"But he's not telling," Dr Mackenzie said.

"No, sir," Jonathan replied.

"Even when silence could lead to the gallows?" Dr Mackenzie said.

Jonathan looked down.

"Ah, I see that frightened you, but you still would not break your silence."

"I've told him not to risk the gallows for my sake," Sherlock said. "I don't want any more deaths on my account."

"You have been responsible for deaths?" Dr Mackenzie asked.

"Yes," Sherlock responded darkly, looking down at the bed. He had not meant to let that slip. His guard was down. There was something about Dr Mackenzie which encouraged him to speak his thoughts more freely than he would to others.

"How many?" Dr Mackenzie asked softly.

Jonathan was disturbed with the direction the conversation was going, but said nothing.

"Two," Sherlock said, without looking up. A solitary tear rolled down his cheek.

"Doctor—" Jonathan began, but Sherlock cut him off with a wave of his hand. He was struggling between a desire to tell these things to Dr Mackenzie and a desire to maintain some control. There was something about Dr Mackenzie that made him want to confide in him. His defences were so low that the battle was lost before it was begun.

"When was this?" Dr Mackenzie asked.

"A year ago," Sherlock said.

"At the time of the snowstorm?"

"Yes. She disappeared during the storm and was never found," Sherlock said.

"You were looking for her?"

"Yes."

Dr Mackenzie stood up and turned one of the lights more directly on Sherlock.

"This snowstorm, it came up suddenly, blinding you," Dr Mackenzie said in a soft voice. "Everything was white and you were lost and she was lost, but you kept looking for her and looking for her."

Sherlock began trembling and breathing hard. He seemed to physically retreat from the world, burying his face in his hands.

"Doctor—" Jonathan began.

"Ssh," Dr Mackenzie said.

"He can't hear us anymore," Jonathan said.

"You are familiar with these attacks?" Dr Mackenzie asked as he checked Sherlock's respiration, pulse rate, and muscle tension.

"Yes," Jonathan admitted.

"Are you willing to talk about them?" Dr Mackenzie asked.

"Not without his word, sir," Jonathan said.

Dr Mackenzie turned the light back where it had been and sat down. He held Sherlock's wrist and monitored his pulse. It was very fast. Something was going on. He took notes. Jonathan watched silently as the doctor analysed the physical signs of his master's suffering that he himself had seen many times before.

Sherlock moaned, dropped his hands away, and blinked his eyes open.

"Sherlock?" Dr Mackenzie said

Sherlock looked up at Dr Mackenzie. Sherlock's eyes held a somewhat haunted, pained look. He said nothing.

"Sherlock, I needed to examine you during one of the attacks," Dr Mackenzie said. "You had reached the right state of mind to precipitate one and had given me enough clues to do so."

"H-how did you know?" Sherlock whispered.

"The Dean mentioned one that you had in the court at Sidney. I recognized it for what it was."

"I remember you made a remark about 'provoking memories'" Sherlock said.

"Yes," Dr Mackenzie said. "And the look you gave me suggested I had hit close to the mark."

Sherlock closed his eyes and covered his face with his hands again.

"When you have these attacks you re-live the past, but sometimes it is all jumbled up?" Dr Mackenzie suggested.

Sherlock looked up at him again.

"H-how do you know?" he asked in amazement. He had not described the attacks to anyone.

"I've worked with other people suffering from attacks like these. That's how they've described them," Dr Mackenzie said.

Sherlock stared at Dr Mackenzie.

"Am I going insane?" Sherlock asked.

"You still haven't convinced me of that," Dr Mackenzie said.

"Then what is it?" Sherlock asked.

"It seems to be a nervous reaction to a severe shock. Such attacks are often found in conjunction with other symptoms such as nightmares, headaches, irritability, melancholia, hallucinations, and difficulty concentrating."

Sherlock and Jonathan both stared at Dr Mackenzie as he described the rest of Sherlock's symptoms.

"And sometimes suicide attempts," Dr Mackenzie concluded.

"Is there a cure?" Sherlock asked hopefully.

"If you are asking if there is medicine I can give you to make it stop, the answer is no," Dr Mackenzie said. "However, there are ways of managing the symptoms. I know of some former sufferers who may be completely cured. At least they have shown no symptoms in years."

Sherlock sighed.

"I-I tried to control it, but it came back."

"And then you tried to poison yourself," Dr Mackenzie said.

"Yes," Sherlock agreed. "Will you help me?"

"The most important thing for you to understand is that there is no cause for despair. You are not alone. You are not insane and you can function in society. If I am to help you, you must promise me you will not attempt suicide again and if you feel the urge to do so that you will come to me first. If you make further attempts at suicide, even if you don't succeed, you could cause permanent physical or mental injury."

"Yes, I promise. But don't do that again," Sherlock said.

"I promise I won't induce another attack without your consent."

"Thank you," Sherlock said.

"But I must return and make my rounds at the asylum," Dr Mackenzie said, rising. "I will visit you again tomorrow. Good day, Sherlock."

"Good day, doctor."

Sherlock sighed. The attack had drained him.

The following morning Dr Burton intercepted Dr Mackenzie.

"What did you do to our Mr Sherlock Holmes yesterday? He was very withdrawn after you left. I had a notion to send for you once or twice. In fact, threatening to do so was the only way we convinced him to eat. Then he was up half the night with nightmares. Jonathan is with him now but I don't think there has been a word between them."

Dr Mackenzie looked thoughtful.

"It may be more severe than I thought," he said.

"What may be? You know we aren't set up here to deal with lunatics."

"He's not a lunatic. You spoke to him before. You know he can be rational and intelligent."

"Yes, sometimes. But I've also seen him incoherent and aggressive. Now I have to add melancholy to the list. Seems more like one of your cases than mine."

"Yes, you are right about that. He has a nervous disorder, most likely traumatic neurasthenia, but it is possible that it is being intensified by the arsenic. I don't think the asylum is the best place for him. Besides, you know the asylum is full, but even if we had room...."

"We can't keep him here," Dr Burton said.

"No, no, go ahead with your plans to send him home tomorrow. I'll try to cheer him up today and I'll keep seeing him after he leaves."

Dr Burton squinted at him.

"Well, you're the expert here. I hope you know what you are doing," Dr Burton said.

"Has he eaten yet this morning?" Dr Mackenzie asked.

"No," Dr Burton.

"Have a nurse bring his breakfast."

"I'll do that," Dr Burton said and walked off.

Dr Mackenzie sat down next to Sherlock. Jonathan looked up at him but Sherlock did not move or speak.

"I'm sorry, Sherlock," Dr Mackenzie said. "The residual effect was greater than I anticipated."

Sherlock said nothing.

"You should have let Dr Burton send for me."

"I didn't want to trouble you," Sherlock said without opening his eyes or looking up.

"It is no trouble. I want to help you. Besides it was my doing—"

"It could have happened anyway."

"It is true that you weren't far from the edge, but I pushed you over."

"You meant well."

"Tell me what you see when you have these attacks."

"No," Sherlock said shaking his head. "Thinking about it makes it worse."

"Dr Burton said you had nightmares last night."

"Yes."

"Are they the same?"

"Some are."

"Will you tell me about the nightmares?"

"No."

"A girl lost in a snowstorm..." Dr Mackenzie said, "...and you were lost, too. That's all I have. Sherlock, I need more information. You seem like an intelligent young man to me. Let me explain. This type of nervous disorder is often difficult to diagnose and treat because the symptoms are so variable. They come and go. Different things seem to provoke acute attacks in different people. This type of nervous condition has been found most often in soldiers and victims of train accidents. In both of those cases the sufferers are sensitive to things that remind them of the event. It can be a noise that sounds like gunfire or something more tenuous that reminds them of what happened, even the weather. The more I know the better I will be able to help you."

"I-I can't—."

A nurse appeared with Sherlock's breakfast.

"Come, Sherlock, sit up and eat," Dr Mackenzie said. "We won't talk of it any more. We'll talk of other things."

Reluctantly Sherlock turned over and sat up and the nurse put the tray before him. He began eating without paying much attention to what he was eating. Dr Mackenzie talked about some articles he had been reading recently in medical journals. Sherlock was only half listening, but now and then Dr Mackenzie said something that caught his attention and he would ask a question. Dr Mackenzie would respond to his questions and gradually it evolved into more of a conversation than a lecture. Suddenly Sherlock looked down at the tray.

"Porridge?"

"It was Dr Burton's doing, not mine."

"Dr Burton wants me to go."

"Well, yes, he does, but I don't think the oat-meal porridge has anything to do with it. It is more likely a joke at my expense."

"He likes to tease you," Sherlock observed.

"Yes, he does."

"He thinks I should be in the asylum."

"You heard that?"

"Yes."

"It is not his decision, nor his area of expertise."

After the nurse took the tray away, Dr Mackenzie turned to the box of books that Jonathan had brought the previous day.

"You haven't touched these, have you?"

"No," Sherlock admitted.

"Well, let's see what we have here. Mathematics, mathematics, and more mathematics. You are reading for the Mathematics Tripos?"

"Yes."

"Very popular at the University. I was never terribly fond of mathematics myself."

"It is my father's idea. He wants me to be an engineer."

"Is that what you want to do?"

"I don't know what I want to do. It's as good as anything, I suppose."

"What do you dislike about mathematics?"

"The emphasis on memorizing proofs and standard formulas."

"Do you have trouble memorizing things?" Dr Mackenzie asked.

"No. I can do that easily. Well, at least normally I can—."

"Then why don't you like it?"

"Why clutter your brain with them?" Sherlock asked. "I think it is more important to understand the concepts and work things out logically. If your logic is sound, then the results should follow regardless of whether you followed any conventional method or not."

"That's true, but wouldn't memorizing a formula be a convenience once a method has been established?"

"Perhaps if you don't confine yourself to a standard formula you might find a better method of obtaining the correct results."

"Interesting. What do you enjoy about mathematics?"

"The logical structure of it and working through practical problems with it."

"How have you been doing at your studies?"

"Fairly well until the last few weeks. Since—since I had the attack in the court I haven't been able to concentrate."

"So you are falling behind?"

"Yes."

"Well, perhaps, you should try to tackle these books today. I'd suggest staying away from the parts you find distasteful and concentrating on those that are more engaging."

"I will give it a try."

"Promise me that you will have Dr Burton send for me if you are having any problems."

"Yes, I promise."

"Otherwise I will be back tomorrow morning to accompany you to your rooms."

Dr Mackenzie appeared at the hospital the next morning as Sherlock was being discharged.

"Remember, if you feel any tingling, numbness, paralysis or any other unusual sensations in the next week I need to know of it immediately," Dr Burton was saying.

"Yes, Doctor."

"And stay away from the rat poison," Dr Burton finished. "I leave him in your hands, Mac. I have other patients to see."

"How are you feeling this morning?" Dr Mackenzie asked.

"Better."

"Did you do any studying?"

"A little."

"I have my carriage out front to take you to your rooms, but I would like to propose a detour."

"Where?"

"I suggest that we take a brief tour of the asylum. It isn't on the way at all, but it's only a short drive."

Sherlock looked anxious.

"I'm not taking you to stay," Dr Mackenzie assured him. "This is just a visit. Are you agreeable?"

"Yes," Sherlock said.

The carriage rolled east past Downing College and then southward beyond the railway station. Soon they were surrounded by farms, but Sherlock was not much interested in the scenery or in conversation. He was trusting a man he had met a few days ago, quite possibly with his entire future. All his instincts told him he should trust Dr Mackenzie and yet he was unsure enough of his own judgment to fear he had made a horrible mistake in agreeing to this trip. Silence seemed his best refuge. Dr Mackenzie chose not to break his silence but to listen to it.

Several miles out of town the carriage turned down a lane to what seemed like a private estate with lawns and stands of trees. The man at the gatehouse waved familiarly to the carriage and Dr Mackenzie nodded to him as they passed. They rolled past a comfortable looking house upon the drive then turned and stopped before a large Elizabethan brick building. It could have been a country manor house or a school but it did not fit with what Sherlock imagined an asylum to look like.

"Here we are," Dr Mackenzie said. "Wait here, Henry, we will be back shortly."

As they entered the building it became obvious that this was Dr Mackenzie's domain. Several people greeted him as they passed.

"Oh, Doctor, I was not expecting you back so soon," one attendant said.

"Just a brief tour, then I shall be off again. We will deal with those matters this afternoon," Dr Mackenzie said.

Sherlock was comforted by the doctor's words which were consistent his statement that this was merely a visit and yet.... He continued to listen and observe in silence.

"I took a sabbatical when I was the Assistant Medical Superintendent here and did some travelling," Dr Mackenzie said as he led them down the halls. "I visited asylums throughout England and the Continent. Some are superior to ours and have facilities and programs that I would like to introduce here, but we lack the funding to do so. On the other hand, some of the asylums I visited were absolutely horrifying. I saw some very cruel and unsanitary conditions. What is perhaps most frightening is that there are people managing such institutions who would take anyone handed over to them without questioning their true state of mind, and the conditions in their asylums are bad enough to drive anyone insane. We have laws here in England which are meant to prevent such things, but I wonder how well they are followed when the patient has no ally on the outside.

"While this asylum is much cleaner and kinder than some, most of the patients who come here never leave. We try our best to help people manage themselves and their affairs with the hope that they can move back out into society and make their way in the world. But many who are brought to us are beyond help. Sadly their families often abandon them here and don't even visit. They live out their lives within these walls," Dr Mackenzie said. "We try to provide the best home we can."

As they entered the dining room they heard a raised voice. The words were angry and slurred.

"You took mine!" a great bear of a man yelled at another patient, then turned around and confronted Dr Mackenzie.

He was a muscular man standing on the balls of his feet with his knees slightly bent. His arms were forward in a defensive position. Yet he swayed a bit as if unsure of his balance and his hands trembled. Attendants were moving towards this mighty man from the other side of the room, while the other patients backed away.

"Who are these men? They shouldn't have come!" the man shouted at the Dr Mackenzie.

Dr Mackenzie held up his hand and the attendants held back.

"Joseph, they are merely visitors. They have not come for you."

"No?" Joseph responded. His body visibly relaxed and his face brightened. "I'm sorry, Doctor."

"Quite all right, Joseph, but I think it is time for you to attend your work."

"Yes, Doctor," the man responded and left the room, his former dispute forgotten.

The attendants then began ushering the other patients from the room and urging them on to their work. Some of them seemed quite normal as they walked passed Dr Mackenzie, Sherlock Holmes and Jonathan on their way out the door. A few seemed suspicious or curious about these strangers. Others exhibited some odd behaviour as they passed. One man kept slapping himself in the head; another was having an animated conversation with no one. The other patients seemed accustomed to this behaviour and paid no attention to it. No, the young men with the Medical Superintendent aroused far more curiosity by their presence alone.

"All the patients here work if they are capable of it." Dr Mackenzie told Sherlock. "We attempt to match their skills with work needed here at the asylum. Some do laundry; some clean rooms; the fittest ones work the farm. The asylum produces most of its own food. Joseph there seems to enjoy his work on the farm. We don't know what type of work he did before. He has only been with us a few weeks and we don't know much about him yet.

"Joseph isn't his real name. It is the one we gave him when

he came to us. He didn't know his name or where he came from. Constables picked him up in the midst of a fight in a pub. They thought he was drunk due to his slurred speech, trembling and difficulty balancing. They held him for a day and those symptoms did not improve nor could he tell them who he was. So they brought him here. He has significant vision and hearing problems as well as these bursts of temper and paranoia — though he quickly forgets the outburst. He may have a traumatic brain injury. We know his past life was a hard one due to the number of scars and old healed injuries but we don't know what he did or where he is from."

"I suggest that you consult the local sporting clubs," Sherlock said, finally breaking his silence.

"Why?" Dr Mackenzie enquired.

"He obviously is a former boxer of long standing. Someone in that circle is likely to recognize him even if he has been retired for sometime," Sherlock replied.

"Obviously?" Dr Mackenzie asked with his eyebrows raised.

"His stance, his bulk, his ears, as well as the old injuries that you just mentioned. They all are indicative of the professional or highly-ranked amateur boxer."

"It could be," Dr Mackenzie said, nodding his head thoughtfully. He was fascinated both by Sherlock's theory and the fact that it had prompted him to speak. He was not sure what to make of either one. But there was still one more thing he meant to show them.

"I will look into that possibility. Now come this way," the doctor said leading them to another wing of the building to a closed and locked door. He took out a ring of keys, selected one and turned it in the lock.

"Please stay near the door after we enter. Sometimes Mary Ann is frightened by strangers."

The door opened into a small room. A young girl sat in a corner. Food drooled down her chin. An attendant wiped it off and tried again to feed her.

"Hello, Mary Ann," Dr Mackenzie said.

The girl held up her hands. They were both wrapped in bandages. Dr Mackenzie walked over to her and took her hand

and squatted down next to the attendant.

"Finish your breakfast, Mary Ann. I'll come back to see you again later," Dr Mackenzie said letting go of her hand. He led Sherlock and Jonathan out into the hall.

"Why are her hands bandaged?" Sherlock asked after Dr Mackenzie had closed the door.

"She scratches — herself, other people. She doesn't intend to harm anyone but she flies into rages. She's done some serious damage. We finally determined the only way to stop her short of a straitjacket was to keep her hands wrapped up.

"Mary Ann tried to starve herself to death because she found life unbearable. She did not die but the attempt caused severe brain injury."

"Why did she want to die?"

"She had seen her whole family murdered before her eyes."

Sherlock closed his eyes.

"Her symptoms before the suicide attempt may have been similar to yours. I might have been able to help her if she had been brought to me then. Now there is little we can do but keep her safe," Dr Mackenzie said sadly.

They left the asylum and entered the carriage again. Sherlock was silent during the ride.

Chapter 9

A Look into Hell

*"I broke through that cloud of despair and had a glimpse
of Holmes' face, white, rigid, and drawn with horror."*
Dr Watson, The Devil's Foot

Two days later when Dr Mackenzie visited he found Sherlock curled up in a chair before the fire in his sitting room studying. Dr Mackenzie sat down across from him.

"How are things progressing?"

"It is not as bad as it was, but I'm still having trouble concentrating."

"Any more attacks?"

"No, but I haven't gone anywhere or been exposed to anything that would provoke one."

"Any nightmares?"

"Minor ones."

"But you are sleeping?"

"Yes."

"Is he eating?" Dr Mackenzie asked, turning to the often invisible, but nearly always present, Jonathan.

"Yes, sir."

"Well, right now I think it would be best not to upset things. I think we should wait a few days and see if you continue your progress," Dr Mackenzie said giving Sherlock his card. "Send for me if you need my help."

"Yes. Thank you."

He gave a second copy of his card to Jonathan as he left. Jonathan nodded his understanding.

Dr Mackenzie stopped by a week later. Sherlock Holmes was out.

"How is he?"

"He's doing better. He's gone back to attending lectures."

"That's good."

"I believe he is still having trouble concentrating."

"We can hope his concentration will continue to improve."

"Yes, sir. The Dean is allowing him to miss Morning Prayers and Hall for a while to catch up on his reading."

"I hope that helps. Tell him that I will be in London for a few days."

"Yes, sir."

The following day Jonathan had finished his preparations for Sherlock's supper short of the actual cooking. He glanced at the clock. Sherlock was late coming back from the lecture hall. Jonathan looked out the window. Snow was falling. It fell in large flakes that mostly melted when they hit the ground. A few clumps were beginning to form on the grassy spots on the ground. It was still light, but would be growing dark soon. Jonathan went to the closet and found the lantern. He trimmed the wick and lit it. He shrugged on his coat and muffler, pulled on his gloves and headed down the stairs. Twilight was setting in as he crossed the street and entered the gates of Sidney Sussex College. He found Sherlock easily enough. He was curled up in a chair before the fire in the Junior Combination Room with one of his books. The rest were piled at his feet. He looked up as Jonathan approached.

"Are you coming back to the lodgings for supper?" Jonathan asked.

"Yes, I should," Sherlock said getting up and picking up his overcoat from the chair arm. He took up his armful of books and notes and followed Jonathan out the door. He hesitated just beyond the door. The snow was still falling and the ground was now covered with a light dusting of white. Jonathan looked back at him holding the lantern aloft. Sherlock said nothing but started walking again. Jonathan turned and led the way across the court and through the college gates. They had crossed the street and were nearly to their lodgings when Jonathan heard the books fall, the sound soften to a dull thud by the snow. He looked back. Sherlock was down on one knee. The books lay scattered in the snow. Jonathan backtracked, wrapped his left arm around his master's waist and urged him up.

"Come, sir. I will return for them," Jonathan said.

They stumbled up the front steps together and Jonathan directed Sherlock into a chair before the fireplace in the lobby. He went back out to gather up the books and papers. As he returned he saw Mr Darley approaching the chair where Sherlock sat with his head leaning on his hand. Jonathan dropped the pile of books and they hit the wooden floor with a loud crack that resounded through the old building. Sherlock and the landlord both snapped their heads around to look at him.

"Sorry, sir," Jonathan said blowing out the lantern and clipping it to his belt before once more gathering up the soggy papers and books.

"Are you feeling well, Mr Holmes?" the landlord asked.

"Yes," Sherlock said looking up at him.

"Not meaning t' be forward, but I takes an interest in my young gentlemen here, and with what happened—"

"He is just waiting for me, sir. I have the latchkey," Jonathan interrupted holding up the key as proof.

"If that's it then. I just wanted to make sure nothing's amiss. It all falls to me when things go wrong and the relations come asking questions."

"Good evening, Mr Darley," Sherlock said rising from the chair and heading towards the stairs.

"Good evening, Mr Holmes," Mr Darley said, not sounding completely convinced.

Jonathan set the books down outside the door, unlocked it and held it open for Sherlock to enter. Jonathan picked up the books before closing the heavy door behind him. He set them down near the fire and looked up. Sherlock was not in the sitting room. Jonathan found him lying on his bed with his coat still on. Jonathan helped him out of his coat and his boots.

Two days later Dr Mackenzie knocked on the door.

"I came as soon as I read your note. Where is he?" Dr Mackenzie said.

"He hasn't been out of bed these last two days. He hasn't eaten.

I don't think he's slept either," Jonathan said.

"He had another attack?" Dr Mackenzie asked.

"I believe so, sir."

Dr Mackenzie entered the bedroom. Sherlock lay curled upon the bed with his hands covering his face. He did not move when Dr Mackenzie entered.

"Hello, Sherlock," Dr Mackenzie said.

Sherlock half opened his eyes to look at him.

"Tell me what you saw," Dr Mackenzie said.

Sherlock merely shook his head.

"I need to know," Dr Mackenzie asked.

"I-I can't. I can't," Sherlock said.

"Why not?" Dr Mackenzie asked.

"I can't think about it. If I think of it, I can think of nothing else. I have to shut it out," Sherlock whined, his white-knuckled fists clenched against his forehead.

Dr Mackenzie reached out his hands and began to grasp Sherlock's wrists.

"Sherlock—," Dr Mackenzie began.

"No!" Sherlock snapped and Dr Mackenzie withdrew his hands.

"Sherlock—" he began again.

"I have to shut it out. I have to shut it out," Sherlock repeated.

"You aren't shutting it out," Dr Mackenzie retorted. "You're shutting it in!"

Sherlock flinched at his words, but said nothing.

Dr Mackenzie stood up and walked away from the bed. He was frustrated. He wanted to help this young man, but he lacked the information to do so. He had to know more. But he realized that his frustration was causing his objectivity to slip. Sherlock was very upset and pressure right now was likely to cause him to withdraw further. Dr Mackenzie knew he had to find a way to calm the lad. He could give Sherlock chloral. It would make him sleep, but its effects weren't likely to improve his state of mind. Dr Mackenzie returned to the bedside.

"Sherlock, let's try an experiment. You are rather tense. Perhaps if I gave you a bit of morphia. Just enough to make you relax.

Maybe that would help. Are you willing to give it a try?"

"Yes," Sherlock whispered.

Dr Mackenzie retrieved his medical bag and prepared the syringe. Then he asked Sherlock to turn over on his back and he obeyed.

"It will take a few minutes to reach full effect."

Sherlock said nothing.

Dr Mackenzie plunged the needle into Sherlock's arm and then withdrew it and put it away. He reached for Sherlock's wrist and felt for his pulse. Sherlock opened his eyes slightly and looked at him. Slowly Sherlock's eyelids closed again. Sherlock's pulse and breathing slowed under the influence of the morphia. Then his breathing took on the deep steady rhythm of sleep. Dr Mackenzie walked into the sitting room. Jonathan stood up.

"He's asleep," Dr Mackenzie said.

"Would you like some tea?" Jonathan asked.

"Yes, I would like that," Dr Mackenzie said.

Dr Mackenzie sat down and pulled a copy of *The Lancet* from his bag and began reading. Jonathan returned soon with a tray. He poured the tea and prepared to withdraw.

"Please stay, Jonathan. Sit down," Dr Mackenzie said.

Jonathan sat down.

"I suppose you were listening?" Dr Mackenzie said.

"Yes, sir," Jonathan admitted.

"I did only give him a little morphia. Not enough to make him unconscious. But he was so exhausted that once he relaxed he fell asleep," Dr Mackenzie told him.

"I understand, sir," Jonathan said.

"You've seen him worse than this, haven't you?" Dr Mackenzie asked.

"Yes, sir," Jonathan admitted.

Jonathan seemed about to say more but stopped. He was torn between his confidential relationship with Sherlock Holmes and his fear. Dr Mackenzie sipped his tea and waited.

"Dr Mackenzie," Jonathan said after some thought. "I only break Mr Sherlock's confidence if his life is in danger. I don't think that is true right now. But that could change quickly. I want to tell you my own thoughts."

"Please do," Dr Mackenzie asked.

"It seems to me like he is falling into a hole and he cannot stop himself from falling. I am afraid that if he falls too far down in that hole, no one will be able to reach him to pull him out."

"Was he like this before he took the arsenic?" Dr Mackenzie asked.

"No. He wasn't eating or sleeping well after he fell in the court, but he was still going to lectures. Perhaps he was afraid he would get like this."

"That's why he took the poison?" Dr Mackenzie asked.

"I don't know. He was somewhat better after he returned from the hospital, but-."

Jonathan broke off and seemed to be listening.

"Excuse me, sir," he said rising.

A cry from the other room had them both on their feet. They found Sherlock sitting up in the bed drenched in sweat, his face contorted by a look of horror. He was shaking all over. His hands were grasping at the air.

"No. No. No," he kept repeating in a hopeless voice.

Compassion won out over objectivity. Dr Mackenzie sat next to Sherlock on the bed and wrapped his arms about his shoulders. With a shudder Sherlock went limp in his arms, passively submitting to the embrace that he had not the energy to resist.

"Tell me what you saw, Sherlock," Dr Mackenzie crooned softly. "I can't help you if you don't tell me. You must tell me what you saw."

Sherlock sighed. Perhaps it was the influence of the morphia that caused him to obey this time or perhaps it was the terror of the dream. But between panting breaths Sherlock described his nightmare.

"W-we were on t-the moor," he whispered, "Violet and I. It was s-summer. I w-was holding her."

Dr Mackenzie felt Sherlock's tears running down his arm.

"The sun was rising. A shadow fell over us. I looked up,"

Sherlock continued.

Dr Mackenzie could feel Sherlock's heart beating faster as the story progressed.

"It was-was — him. H-he grabbed her arm. H-he pulled her from me. I reached for her. I could not grasp her. Then he had fangs and-and claws. H-he tore her apart. I c-could not stop him. He ripped her apart. I could not stop him. H-he devoured her - her and the child. I could not stop him."

Dr Mackenzie looked up at Jonathan.

"I could not reach her. I could not stop him. I-I-" Sherlock whispered, his voice fading away at the end.

Sherlock sobbed and fell silent.

"Quiet now. You should sleep some more," Dr Mackenzie said.

Dr Mackenzie pressed Sherlock back down on the bed and pulled the blankets up over him. Sherlock lay there panting with his eyes closed. Gradually his breathing slowed again. Dr Mackenzie signalled to Jonathan and the two of them returned to the sitting room.

"I gather from the look on your face that not all of that was true?" Dr Mackenzie said.

"No, sir," Jonathan said.

"Her name was Violet, correct?" Dr Mackenzie said.

"Yes, sir," Jonathan agreed.

"They met on the moor?" Dr Mackenzie asked.

"Yes, sir," Jonathan confirmed.

"This man with the fangs and claws?" Dr Mackenzie said.

"None that I ever heard of, sir," Jonathan said.

"But there was a man involved?" Dr Mackenzie asked.

"Yes, sir," Jonathan said.

"Who?" Dr Mackenzie asked.

Jonathan shook his head.

"Unless he tells you—" Jonathan said.

Dr Mackenzie waved his hand.

"Was she torn apart and eaten?" he went on.

"I can't answer that," Jonathan said shaking his head.

"In hospital he said that she was lost in the storm on the moors and never found," Dr Mackenzie said. "I can see how a tortured mind could arrive at that. And the child?"

"I can't answer that," Jonathan repeated.

"Can't or won't?" Dr Mackenzie asked.

Jonathan frowned.

"All I know are rumours. I won't repeat them," Jonathan said.

Dr Mackenzie frowned. He stood up and paced the floor.

"So the part about a man with fangs ripping her apart was a hallucination?"

"Yes, sir," Jonathan said.

"Has he ever had nightmares or hallucinations which were that surreal before?" Dr Mackenzie asked.

"I don't know, sir. He has never told them to me," Jonathan said.

"Nor to anyone else?" Dr Mackenzie asked.

"Not to my knowledge, sir," Jonathan said.

"I wonder," Dr Mackenzie said thoughtfully. "Perhaps the morphia caused some distortion of his memories. I need to do some research. Can you take care of him for now?"

"I will do my best," Jonathan replied.

"Tell him I have gone to do some research, but I will return in the morning," Dr Mackenzie said as he pulled on his coat.

"Yes, sir," Jonathan said.

Chapter 10

Fears Revealed

"I found him a prey to the blackest depression."
Dr. Watson, The Reigate Squires

When Dr Mackenzie returned in the morning Jonathan told him that Sherlock was still asleep. Dr Mackenzie looked in the bedroom for a moment before returning to the sitting room.

"Wait half an hour and then begin making his breakfast," he told Jonathan quietly.

Dr Mackenzie entered the bedroom and sat next to the bed.

"I'm surprised you can still fool Jonathan after all this time. He's a bright boy," Dr Mackenzie said. "How long have you been awake?"

Sherlock was silent.

"Sherlock, do you want me to help you?" Dr Mackenzie asked.

"Yes," Sherlock whispered.

"Then you must answer my questions," Dr Mackenzie said.

"I don't know how long I've been awake," Sherlock whispered.

"How do you feel?" Dr Mackenzie said.

"My head aches," Sherlock said.

"That might be an effect of the morphia. Unfortunately, I think it had other undesirable effects," Dr Mackenzie said.

"Like horrific nightmares?" Sherlock asked.

"Yes. Do you remember that?" Dr Mackenzie said.

"Yes," Sherlock said.

"Have you ever had any like that before?" Dr Mackenzie asked.

Sherlock was silent for a while and Dr Mackenzie was afraid he wouldn't answer.

"Once," Sherlock said finally. "I think it was morphia then, too."

"When was that?" Dr Mackenzie asked.

"A year ago," Sherlock said.

"Why were you given morphia then?" Dr Mackenzie asked.

"I-I had a knife. I wouldn't give it up. My brother held me down. The doctor injected something. Everything faded out. They took the knife."

Dr Mackenzie winced. He knew that the use of force often had negative effects on the mental state of patients. But he also knew that sometimes it was necessary.

"It probably was morphia," Dr Mackenzie asked. "But more than I gave you yesterday. Do you remember the hallucination that you had back then?"

"Yes," Sherlock whispered.

"Tell me about it," Dr Mackenzie said.

Sherlock rolled over on his back and turned his face away from Dr Mackenzie.

"You have to trust me, Sherlock," Dr Mackenzie insisted.

"I do," Sherlock whispered.

"Then you need to answer my questions. If we are going to experiment with drugs that might help you, then you must to be willing to describe the effects," Dr Mackenzie said.

Sherlock sighed.

"It was like my brother was still holding me. Then it was-was someone else and he-he ripped my heart out of my chest with his hand," Sherlock said.

"The same man with the fangs?" Dr Mackenzie asked.

"Yes," Sherlock said barely audibly.

Dr Mackenzie paused, then decided not to pursue that subject at the moment.

"I did some research last night," Dr Mackenzie said. "I found several case histories of people experiencing hallucinations while taking morphia. I found one that may be very similar to your situation. It was the case of a soldier who had been wounded in battle. He had a nervous condition similar to yours. They were giving him morphia for his injuries, but he eventually begged them to stop due to the horrific nightmares and hallucinations it caused him to have. They were distorted and surreal versions of the battle. The distortions seem to have been caused by the morphia. He quit having them when they stopped giving him morphia. Based on that information and your own experience, I think that we should not give you any more morphia."

"I agree," Sherlock said.

"But part of what you saw in your nightmare last night was real," Dr Mackenzie said.

"Yes," Sherlock confirmed.

"You met Violet on the moors," Dr Mackenzie said.

Sherlock looked up at him sharply.

"You told me her name last night," Dr Mackenzie said.

"Y-yes, I did," Sherlock admitted, shifting his gaze to the ceiling.

"You met on the moors?" Dr Mackenzie said.

"Yes," Sherlock agreed.

"You loved her?" Dr Mackenzie asked.

"Yes," Sherlock said quietly.

"She was lost in the snowstorm and never found?" Dr Mackenzie continued.

"Yes."

"She is presumed dead?"

"Yes."

"She and your child?"

Sherlock half sat up and turned to Dr Mackenzie.

"I am piecing this together from scraps you have given me. You said the word 'child' last night. I presumed that there was some close connection or you wouldn't have mentioned it. I chose the most obvious one."

Sherlock fell back against the bed.

"Yes," he said.

"And you blame yourself for this?"

"Yes. Yes, I do," Sherlock said with growing heat, "and don't argue with me about the logic of it. You don't know—You don't know anything about it."

"No, I don't. But the logic or illogic of it is irrelevant to me. If that is what you feel, then that is what you feel," Dr Mackenzie said.

Sherlock stared at Dr Mackenzie.

"It is not my intent to make you stop feeling what you feel, but rather to help you control how those feelings manifest themselves,"

Dr Mackenzie continued.

"They should not manifest themselves at all," Sherlock insisted.

"Why not?" Dr Mackenzie asked.

"Because I cannot cope with them!" Sherlock cried.

"If that is true, then that is one possible solution. But you tried merely bottling them up inside and they came back out. That method alone will not work."

"Then what will work?" Sherlock said with mounting anger and frustration.

"We are just beginning to explore that. I need your assistance to continue doing so," Dr Mackenzie continued. He had definitely noticed Sherlock's emotional shift from melancholy to anger.

Sherlock was silent.

"There seems to be another man involved whom you also blame. Who is he?" Dr Mackenzie asked.

Sherlock jumped up out of the bed, exclaiming, "No! I will not talk about him!"

The leap from the bed made him light-headed. He leaned against the wardrobe.

Dr Mackenzie started to rise.

"No, I'm fine," Sherlock said pushing off the wardrobe and walking away from it.

"Why won't you talk about him?" Dr Mackenzie asked.

"I will not sully my brain by even thinking his name," Sherlock spat as he paced the floor.

"But he is obviously in your brain. He is appearing in your dreams and hallucinations," Dr Mackenzie argued.

"That I cannot control, not now, not yet, but I will not consciously — I will not willingly — think of him. He is a demon who must be exorcised. I will not talk of him!" Sherlock insisted.

"Excuse me, sir," Jonathan said from the doorway holding the tray. "I have your breakfast."

Sherlock turned and scowled at him. Then he looked at Dr Mackenzie and back to Jonathan. He saw there was a conspiracy afoot. His look softened. It was a conspiracy to get him up out of bed and eating again. He suddenly realized that he was hungry.

"Bring it in," Sherlock said sitting back down on the bed and allowing Jonathan to position the tray before him.

Dr Mackenzie watched in silence. He was glad to see Sherlock eating. When Sherlock was about halfway through his breakfast he turned to Dr Mackenzie.

"Thank you," Sherlock said. "You have interesting methods."

"I'm not sure I'd call it a 'method,'" Dr Mackenzie replied. "That implies some consistency of results. Sometimes it is just luck that I strike the right chord with a series of questions. You are the one who changes what is going on inside your head, not me. The fact that you can make the change is what distinguishes you from the patients in the asylum. No more questions today. I must be going shortly. I believe you have some studying to do."

"I will try," Sherlock said.

The following day when Dr Mackenzie entered the sitting room it was obvious that something had occurred a short time before. Some of Sherlock's books had been thrown against the fireplace and papers were scattered about the floor. The calendar which had previously hung on the wall also lay among the debris, a ragged hole in the top showing that it had been torn from the wall. In the midst of this circle was Sherlock Holmes, wrapped in his dressing gown and curled up in a chair drawn before the fire.

"What is this?" Dr Mackenzie asked pointing to the floor.

"I was trying to study," Sherlock said.

"It looks more like a physics experiment than mathematics. A study of gravitational effects, perhaps?" Dr Mackenzie said.

"An exercise in futility," Sherlock grumbled. "I can't concentrate. Jonathan's been helping me remember how I managed to get my mind under control before. I hardly left my room for months. The curtains were kept closed against the snow all winter. I saw only a few people for a long time and slowly readapted to dealing with other people. Gradually the attacks and the nightmares became less frequent, and I thought they had gone away for good. But now—"

"Excuse me, sir," Jonathan said. "If I may, there were other things."

"Go on," Sherlock said to Jonathan.

"You spent a lot of time playing your violin and fencing. I believe they both helped you," Jonathan offered.

"I had no idea that you played the violin or fenced," Dr Mackenzie said.

"I do. But I left the violin and my fencing gear behind in Yorkshire," Sherlock said.

"Perhaps you could send for them?" Dr Mackenzie suggested.

"Dr Mackenzie, you don't understand," Sherlock countered. "Even if I had them here, I don't have enough time. I can't concentrate. I can't study. I've missed most of my lectures recently. Even when I go they make no sense. My sleep is disturbed by nightmares. These nervous attacks can fell me at any time and leave me in a funk for days. Before I isolated myself not only to be able concentrate on controlling my own mind, but to hide my condition from my family until I could control it. To come here to the University I had to fool my father into believing that any odd behaviour on my part had been caused by my illness alone and that it was over. If he knew that I tried to poison myself—."

Sherlock reached down and picked up the torn calendar and waved it at Dr Mackenzie.

"I don't have months to pull myself together again," Sherlock continued. "The term ends in ten days. I must go home in ten days for the holiday. If my father sees the state I am in, he won't allow me to come back. He'll have me locked away somewhere. You said that many asylums are not as well-managed or as enlightened as yours. You told me that the families of patients often abandon them after they are there. If I go back like this, that's what will happen to me. I fooled my father before, but it took time. I-I can't do it in ten days. What difference does it make whether I study or not, if I have no future?"

"Why do you think your father would have you locked away?" Dr Mackenzie asked.

"Tell him, Jonathan," Sherlock said.

"Last winter I overheard the butler speaking to another member of the household staff. He said he had heard the squire say that he'd have Mr Sherlock sent to an asylum if he showed any other signs of odd behaviour," Jonathan said.

"He would do it. My father would do it," Sherlock said dropping the calendar to the floor and burying his face in his hands.

Dr Mackenzie had taken Sherlock to visit the asylum to discourage him from further attempts at suicide. Now he realized that the visit had fuelled Sherlock's underlying fear of being confined to an asylum. Sherlock was right. Dr Mackenzie hadn't thought of how close they were to the end of the term. He had not considered the idea of Sherlock leaving so soon. He needed more time to work with him. There must be a way.

"Sherlock, there is a drug that some doctors have experimented with in the treatment of some nervous disorders," he said. "There have been a number of claims made about it, but I have seen relatively little definitive information, just anecdotes. I can't guarantee that it will help or that it won't have some unwanted effect like the morphia, but I could procure some and we could see if it helps."

"I'm willing to try anything," Sherlock said.

Chapter 11

Experimentation

"In order to have an accurate idea of the effects"
Stamford, *A Study in Scarlet*

"Did you bring it?" Sherlock asked anxiously as Dr Mackenzie entered the sitting room.

"Yes," he responded.

"If it doesn't work, if I get worse, or no better, promise me that you won't let me go back to Yorkshire. Put me in your own asylum if you must. Promise!" Sherlock pleaded.

Dr Mackenzie could see now the fear that had driven Sherlock to take the arsenic before. If there had been room in the asylum he would consider it now, but if Sherlock's symptoms grew worse, he'd give him his own bed if necessary.

"Yes, yes, I promise. Now come into the bedroom and lie down," he said.

Sherlock obeyed.

"There is something else I should tell you before we do this," Dr Mackenzie said as he drew out the necessary materials from his bag.

"What?"

"I spoke with Rev. Clowe. He said that you were planning on sitting for the Previous Exam this term."

"Yes."

"He is sending a request to the Vice Chancellor that you be excused from the exam this term, and the Dean has agreed to excuse you from attending Hall and Chapel for the rest of this term."

"What did you say to them? Will they tell my father?" Sherlock asked anxiously.

"I didn't tell them anything that they didn't already know. I merely gave them my opinion that you needed some time to pull yourself together. They have agreed not to notify your father. The conditions for that agreement are that you spend the Christmas holiday at home and that you manage to return to your studies at the commencement of the Lent Term."

Sherlock looked concerned.

"Trust me, Sherlock. It is not the first time I've spoken for an undergraduate, especially in their first term. Some just break down under all the changes and pressures of coming to the university. Your case is different, but they don't need to know that. They can understand that a man has his pride, but there is a limit to how far they will go to hide things from your father. Now roll up your sleeve. Remember that you agreed to describe the effects to me and answer my questions."

"Yes, yes, I will," Sherlock said.

Sherlock watched as Dr Mackenzie inserted the syringe needle under the skin of his left arm, screwed down the plunger, and then carefully pulled the needle out again.

"A slight tingling, numbness in my arm...." Sherlock said closing his eyes.

"Interesting," Dr Mackenzie said, taking notes. "The whole arm or just at the site of the injection?"

"It started there, but has spread," Sherlock said.

Then Sherlock opened his eyes and raised his brows and then relaxed them.

"What is it?" Dr Mackenzie asked.

"A surge of, of exaltation, elation. I've felt it before though much stronger. I think I've been given this before," Sherlock said.

"When and why?" Dr Mackenzie asked.

"When I had pneumonia. I don't remember when the doctor started it. I first remember seeing puncture marks in my arm. But I have no memory of the week or so before then."

"Pneumonia, pneumonia," Dr Mackenzie repeated thoughtfully. "Did you have bleeding in your lungs?"

"I don't know. I remember one morning he said my lungs were clearing and he wasn't going to give me an injection. It was the day before they told me she was gone," Sherlock said.

"Violet?" Dr Mackenzie asked, surprised that Sherlock had

followed the memory of the sensation of the drug to associated memories that he usually avoided.

"Yes. They searched for her while I was ill but never found her," Sherlock said.

"But they had found you?" Dr Mackenzie asked.

"My brother Sherrinford said he found me in the stone hut on the moors. I don't remember that. I don't remember reaching the hut."

"Why was Violet out in the storm?"

"I think she was frightened."

"Of you?" Dr Mackenzie asked.

Sherlock frowned.

"No. I don't think she knew I was following her."

"What frightened her?"

"He did," Sherlock said.

"Who?"

"Moriarty," he said.

"Who was Moriarty?"

"My tutor," Sherlock said.

"The man with the fangs in the nightmare?" Dr Mackenzie asked.

"Yes," Sherlock confirmed.

Dr Mackenzie found that interesting. Two days before Sherlock had become very agitated and refused to give the man's name. But now under the influence of the drug it did not seem to bother him at all.

"How do you feel now, Sherlock?"

"Quite good."

"In control?"

"Yes."

"Intelligent?"

"Yes."

"Energetic?"

"Yes."

"Like you can do anything?"

"Yes."

Dr Mackenzie concluded that this cocaine was a very dangerous drug. He also noted that Sherlock's pulse, temperature, and respiration rate were high. The South American natives chewed the leaves of the wild coca plant that the drug was originally derived from. Reports said that they felt no fatigue, hunger, thirst, or cold while under its influence. But Dr Mackenzie wondered how long they lived that way. A human body running at such a high rate with no sense of fatigue or hunger could burn out like a match. That was besides the purely neurological effects. Somehow the feeling of euphoria produced by the drug seemed to be overwhelming Sherlock's negative emotions related to his memories. Dr Mackenzie wondered how that feeling was produced and what the long term effects would be. Could it be similar to the other physical effects? Was the drug using up some limited resource in the brain with no warning signs? He thought of Hans Christian Anderson's tale of The Little Match Girl and shivered. What were they playing with here? No one had experimented with it long enough to be certain.

"You don't mind talking about Violet?" Dr Mackenzie asked.

"No."

While Dr Mackenzie was curious about this traumatic event in Sherlock's life, he did not want to press the advantage the drug was giving him for fear that there would be some devastating reaction when it wore off.

"Come. Let's go for a walk and see how it affects you physically," Dr Mackenzie said.

They drew on their overcoats and their hats and mufflers and headed out. Sherlock blinked at the daylight and pulled his hat brim down.

"Awfully bright out," he said.

"It's the drug," Dr Mackenzie said quietly. "Your pupils are dilated. They can't react to the sunlight. You have to shade them. It will be especially difficult for your eyes if you go out a sunny day with snow on the ground. You might not be able to see at all. It will also probably make reading more difficult even indoors."

The air was brisk, but Dr Mackenzie soon noticed that Sherlock was perspiring. He removed his glove and touched his hand to the young man's cheek.

"You seem to be a bit too warm," the doctor said.

"I feel fine," Sherlock Holmes responded.

"Well, we don't want you burning up. Just loosening your muffler a bit and unbutton your coat."

"Certainly, doctor," Sherlock said complying.

They wandered through the streets of Cambridge, down Sidney Street, through Pety Cury, up Market Hill, around past the Corn Exchange and through little byways south. Dr Mackenzie watched Sherlock. Under the drug's influence Sherlock was very different from the sluggish, tormented young man who had tried to kill himself hardly more than a week before. He seemed very lively and talkative. He was enthusiastic about much of what he saw. He had spent little time in the town since coming to the University and was excited to be exploring it.

Sherlock had a trick of making comments about passers-by which suggested he knew them, or something about them. When Dr Mackenzie inquired, Sherlock denied knowing the people. Dr Mackenzie's questions about how Sherlock knew these things were brushed off as Sherlock's attention was drawn by something or someone new. Dr Mackenzie found himself having trouble keeping up with Sherlock both mentally and physically. Sherlock's body was functioning at a higher rate. At what cost? Dr Mackenzie wondered.

Dr Mackenzie soon discovered one drawback of Sherlock's induced energy and enthusiasm: Sherlock seemed to have little concern for his personal safety. Once Dr Mackenzie pulled Sherlock back from the path of a moving hansom cab. Sherlock thanked him, but seemed unshaken and went on as before. Dr Mackenzie suggested that they stop for a bite to eat, but Sherlock showed no interest in food or in slowing down. As they reached Trumpington Street, Dr Mackenzie convinced Sherlock that they should turn north and walk past the other colleges of the university. As they did so, Sherlock maintained a running dialogue comparing the architecture of the college buildings with other buildings he had seen in cities on the Continent. Dr Mackenzie had had no idea how well-travelled this young man was. He knew from his own travels that Sherlock was accurately describing buildings in Italy, France and Germany.

They had turned on Green Street not far from Sidney and were only a few blocks from Sherlock's lodgings, when the end came. Dr Mackenzie was surprised by the suddenness of it. Sherlock was staring at a painting in the window of a shop for several minutes in silence. Dr Mackenzie realized later that he should have recognized the silence as a symptom that the drug was wearing off after Sherlock's loquaciousness. Or perhaps he should have noticed that Sherlock was leaning on the frame of the window as he stood there. But Dr Mackenzie hadn't noticed either. He was standing behind Sherlock, watching over his shoulder wondering what he was thinking. Then Sherlock began slipping from in front of him. Dr Mackenzie caught Sherlock under the arms as he fell and guided him to a nearby bench. As Dr Mackenzie examined Sherlock, he saw that his eyes were no longer dilated.

"I'm sorry," Sherlock said. "I am suddenly exhausted. There was something about that painting in the window. I felt as if I were falling into it."

"You nearly did. Did you sleep at all last night?" Dr Mackenzie asked

"No, I was so worried about all of this I couldn't sleep," Sherlock said.

"So you've only had a few hours sleep in the past four days?" Dr Mackenzie said.

"I suppose so," Sherlock said.

"Sherlock, you need to sleep if you are going to pull this off," Dr Mackenzie scolded. "I should have made you stop and have something to eat. This is exactly what will happen if you don't eat and sleep enough. Your body is going to collapse when the drug wears off. It could ruin the impression you are trying to create. If it happens at the wrong time or place you may not be able to inject a new dose. You need to keep your strength up enough to tide you over those gaps without it. It is very important that you remember these things."

"I will," Sherlock said.

"I want you to sleep tonight with the assurance that it did work. You were lively and talkative, perhaps a bit too lively and talkative. I think next time we will try a lower dose. But I do believe it will work. For now though, we should get you home and fed and rested. Should I find a cab?"

Sherlock looked around.

"No, it is only a few blocks. I feel a little better now after sitting here. I think I can walk the rest of the way."

He stood up and they walked on. As they climbed the stairs to his rooms, Sherlock asked, "Do you really think I can do it?"

"Yes. We need to refine the dosage and we don't have a lot of time to experiment. But I think we can narrow it down. I'll come back tomorrow and we can try again," Dr Mackenzie said leaving Sherlock in Jonathan's care with instructions to feed him and put him to bed.

"How do you feel?" Dr Mackenzie asked the next morning.

"Somewhat drowsy," Sherlock said.

"Did you sleep last night?"

"Yes," he said.

"Do you remember what you told me yesterday about who had frightened Violet?"

"Yes."

"Do you mind that you told me?"

Sherlock frowned.

"I do not wish to speak of him."

"Do you object to my asking you questions when you are under the influence of the cocaine? You seem not to be bothered by them then."

"You are asking if I mind you prodding inside my head when I lack the will to stop you?"

"Essentially, yes."

"I don't know."

"To some degree it is like pulling a tooth when the patient

is under chloroform. In that case there could be pain after the chloroform wears off. That could be true in this case, too. I don't know. I've never done this before."

"Dr Mackenzie, you are the first person who has ever understood, even in an academic sense, what I am going through. My parents merely saw it as alien and frightening, and thus something that should go away. My brothers and Dr Thompkins were sympathetic, but I could sense it frightened them as well. They had absolutely no comprehension of what was happening. In two weeks you have given me more help and more hope than anyone in the past year. I would be a fool not to trust you."

"Come, then roll up your sleeve and we shall try again. This is a lower dosage than yesterday."

Dr Mackenzie talked to Sherlock as he had before while the drug took effect. Again Sherlock reported numbness in his arm followed by a wave of elation.

"Yesterday you said that this man Moriarty frightened Violet and she rode off. How did he frighten her?"

Sherlock hesitated.

"I don't know. I saw him holding her arms. There was fear in her eyes. Perhaps it was his manner. Maybe something he said."

"You were there?"

Sherlock did not seem as comfortable with his questions today.

"I saw them through the window."

"Why would he want to frighten her?"

"Because he was an evil man, Dr Mackenzie, and I don't want to talk about him."

Dr Mackenzie noted that the lower dose that they were trying today was not sufficient to overwhelm Sherlock's feelings concerning Moriarty. He checked Sherlock's pulse, respiration and pupils again and then closed his notebook.

"Come, we shall take another walk."

Their walk went well and they returned to Sherlock's rooms without incident.

"Tomorrow I would like to try a still lower dose and I will show you how to inject yourself."

EXPERIMENTATION

The following morning Dr Mackenzie returned for another experiment.

"I think this will be easier to do if you sit up," Dr Mackenzie said holding out the syringe.

Sherlock leaned against the headboard and took the syringe in his right hand. He held it like he had seen Dr Mackenzie do.

"You want the needle to come in just under the skin. Avoid hitting any blood vessels or muscles. Once it is in you have to twist down the plunger, which is a bit harder to do one-handed. Now carefully pull it back out."

Sherlock followed the doctor's instructions and then handed the syringe back. He closed his eyes and felt the tingling and numbness spread in his left arm followed by excitation in his brain. It was definitely weaker this time.

"You said that you had brothers?" Dr Mackenzie asked as he tracked Sherlock's breathing and pulse rate and noted them in his book.

"Yes, I have two. Sherrinford is the eldest. He runs the family estate with my father. My brother Mycroft works in London for the government."

"Will your brother Mycroft be returning to the family estate for the holiday?"

"I presume so," Sherlock said.

"You should write to him and suggest that you travel north together. It might be better if you had a companion you could trust during your journey in addition to Jonathan since this whole process is new to you."

"I will send a wire to him and suggest it," Sherlock said.

"Who else will be there?" Dr Mackenzie continued.

"My mother, my father, Sherrinford's wife, Amanda, and their son, Arthur," Sherlock said. "Perhaps some guests. Normally they hold the Squire's Christmas Ball and invite everyone in the dale."

"Normally?"

"It was cancelled last year due to my illness," Sherlock said.

"I see. How old is your nephew?"

"Less than a year. He was born in April," Sherlock said.

Dr Mackenzie could see that Sherlock was become increasingly uneasy.

"What is it about your nephew that troubles you?" Dr Mackenzie asked.

Sherlock drew his knees up and rested his elbows on them and his forehead on the heels of his hands.

"It is not my nephew. It is when he was born," Sherlock said.

"April?"

"Yes."

"Was that when your own child would have been born?"

"Yes," Sherlock whispered. "And I returned to Yorkshire and met Violet in April."

Sherlock lapsed into silence. Then soft hurried footsteps came into the room from behind Dr Mackenzie. Jonathan approached the bed and firmly grabbed Sherlock by the arm. Sherlock's head snapped up and he blinked at Jonathan. Jonathan released him.

"Thank you," Sherlock said to Jonathan and then turned to Dr Mackenzie. "This dosage isn't working."

"You nearly had another attack?" Dr Mackenzie said.

"Yes," Sherlock said rubbing his hand against his forehead.

"Jonathan stopped it?"

"Yes."

"How did you learn to do that?" Dr Mackenzie asked Jonathan.

"From months of watching and trying to do what I could," Jonathan said. "I failed many times."

"Well, you figured out what many doctors missed, and succeeded where they failed to even try. I have never seen that done before," Dr Mackenzie said with growing respect for Jonathan's intelligence. "I think we have determined that this dosage is too low."

"Yes," Sherlock said.

"I think I now know what dosage would be best," Dr Mackenzie continued. "We only have a few more days. I want to try an experiment. I'll give you enough of the drug at the second dosage that we tried to cover the next three days. I will provide a schedule for the injections which you must follow precisely. I will come around and check on you. I must be certain that you can handle this by yourself. Don't vary the dosage. If it is too high it could cause odd behaviour. It could even kill you."

"I understand," Sherlock said.

"After three days, you will stop for two days so we can see how you react. We will need Jonathan to keep a careful watch over you through both phases. He should go with you if you go out."

"I will stay by his side," Jonathan said.

112

Chapter 12

Holiday in Yorkshire

"It arrived upon Christmas morning, in company with a good fat goose."
Sherlock Holmes, The Blue Carbuncle

The experiments went well and on the day that Sherlock was to begin his journey northward, Dr Mackenzie arrived early with the cocaine and the syringe kit.

"I suggest that you wait until your brother arrives so the first dose lasts as long as possible. I have only provided you with enough of the drug to see you through the days. It is not enough for the nights. Your body needs to rest. You need to keep eating and sleeping or you will wear yourself out," Dr Mackenzie reminded him. "If you vary the dosage or use it at night, you will risk running out before the end of the holiday."

"I won't. I will follow your instructions," Sherlock assured him.

There was a knock at the door. It was the landlord.

"There is a gentleman below who says he is your brother, Mycroft, Mr Sherlock," Mr Darley said, eyeing Dr Mackenzie.

"Thank you," Sherlock said. "Jonathan, start down with the bags. We will follow in a moment."

Under Dr Mackenzie's watchful eye, Sherlock took the syringe out of the box, filled it as he had been taught, and carefully inserted it into the skin of his left arm. He then pulled the needle back out and laid it in its case. Sherlock closed the case and placed it in one of his bags. Then he rolled down his sleeve and fixed his cuffs. Dr Mackenzie handed him his coat and then his overcoat.

"I think I'm ready," Sherlock said.

"Good luck," Dr Mackenzie said.

"If this works, I will be back in two weeks," Sherlock said. "Come down with me now and meet my brother Mycroft."

Sherlock locked the door and he and Dr Mackenzie descended the staircase together. Mycroft was ensconced in one of the large chairs before the fire. He stood as they approached and surveyed them both in his introspective fashion.

"Dr Mackenzie, my brother, Mycroft. Mycroft, this is Dr George Mackenzie," Sherlock introduced them.

"Pleased to meet you," Dr Mackenzie said.

"It is my pleasure, Dr Mackenzie. May I ask if you are an alienist?" Mycroft asked.

Just at that moment some other people entered the building.

"He is," Sherlock said quickly. "I will explain on our journey." Mycroft nodded.

"Merry Christmas, Dr Mackenzie," Sherlock said as they headed out to the cab Mycroft had waiting.

"Merry Christmas," Dr Mackenzie said waving after them as Sherlock, Mycroft and Jonathan entered the cab and the driver loaded the remaining luggage.

At the railway station a porter assisted them with their luggage and they boarded the train which was waiting on the track. Jonathan was grateful that they took him with them into the first-class carriage as Sherrinford and Sherlock had on the trip south. He was grateful not because of any imagined deprivations in the third-class carriage, but rather for the opportunity to observe Mycroft and Sherlock together.

Jonathan had rarely seen Mycroft. When Mycroft had performed the amazing feat of dragging Sherlock mentally back from the brink of the grave, Jonathan had been sent from the room and had not witnessed it. There was some mention later of a promise between them but always in his presence their conversations seemed abbreviated and circumspect as if they were hiding something from his tender ears. As he listened to them talk in the hours afforded by the long train ride he began to understand.

Once the three of them were established in the first-class carriage, Mycroft looked at Sherlock again.

"You had a relapse," Mycroft said. There was no solicitousness in his words or manner. He was stating a fact.

"Yes," Sherlock responded.

"Dr Mackenzie has been helping you recover and you are injecting yourself with some drug," Mycroft continued.

"Yes, but tell me how you know," Sherlock asked.

"Your letters stopped for several weeks then a telegram arrives suggesting that we travel north together for the holiday," Mycroft said.

"A reasonable suggestion," Sherlock said.

"Yes, but the fact that you spent the additional money on a telegram suggests that it was a last minute thought and thus you had other things on your mind earlier. The telegram also contained no information about what had occurred in the interval or how your studies were going. I inferred that since you had last written something had happened that you did not wish to write about and that your studies weren't going well. The alternative hypothesis was that you had been studying too hard to write or think of the holidays before then," Mycroft lectured. "Physically you look better in some ways than you did when you were in London, but you have lost weight again. Undergraduates more often gain weight in their first term than lose it. That suggests an illness of some type and argues against the second hypothesis. If it had been an ordinary illness you wouldn't have hesitated to write about it."

"As for the injections," Mycroft continued, reaching across and taking Sherlock's right hand in his own hands and turning it over, "when you came down there were distinct indentations in the fingers of your right hand. They are fading now. And," he said with a wave of his hand, "your pupils are dilated. That suggests not only a drug, but that you injected it yourself. That further suggests that the doctor instructed you on the use of the syringe so that you could maintain the dosage yourself while you were home. Some stimulant, perhaps?"

"Correct on every count so far. But what of Dr Mackenzie? How did you know he was an alienist?" Sherlock asked.

"You introduced him as a doctor and he carried a bag. However, he lacked many of the accompanying signs of being in active medical practice. That combined with my knowledge and observations of you, and the fact that you did not seem physically ill suggested an alienist," Mycroft concluded.

"Correct," Sherlock said.

"I do have a question, however," Mycroft said. "How did you meet Dr Mackenzie?"

"I met him while I was in hospital," Sherlock said.

"Why were you in hospital?" Mycroft asked.

"Arsenic poisoning," Sherlock said.

Mycroft raised his eyebrows.

"Perhaps you had best start at the beginning," Mycroft said.

Sherlock explained to Mycroft what had occurred over the last few weeks and why he was taking the drug.

"Sherrinford told me of Father's threat, but neither of us knew that you knew," Mycroft said.

"Jonathan told me much later. The version I heard may have been distorted since I heard it third hand, but I think the message is clear enough," Sherlock said.

"Sherrinford thought so. He was frightened by it," Mycroft agreed.

"As was I," Sherlock said

Sherlock's loquaciousness on the trip varied as the influence of the drug varied, fading out as it did. His true nature lay somewhere between the extremes. Jonathan had no doubt that Mycroft observed the variation in his brother's behaviour and mood, but if so he catalogued it without comment. Mycroft conversed when Sherlock wished to converse, and not, when he did not, and after his initial inquiries regarding Sherlock's health Mycroft left the topic of conversation entirely up to his younger brother.

In general, Jonathan learned that Sherlock and Mycroft needed fewer words between them to communicate. At times Sherlock would ask for an explanation from Mycroft and the request would sound like that from a student to a master. In such cases Mycroft would respond at length and Sherlock seemed to study every word. But often times merely a word seemed enough to steer their thoughts along the same path. It was no wonder that Sherrinford had said they were closer, for their minds seem to work in similar ways. Sherlock was obviously the more quick-tempered and emotional of the two. Could Mycroft truly understand the paths Sherlock's mind strayed down as a result of the shocks he had endured, or did he merely comprehend on an intellectual level how best to lead him back? If recent actions on Sherlock's part had breached some promise between the brothers, no word of it was spoken. Perhaps none was necessary, for they each anticipated what the other would say.

Later Sherlock injected himself again while the train was stopped at a station rather than face the challenge of controlling the needle on a moving train. The sleigh from the manor was waiting for them at Thirsk. Sherlock settled down in the fleece and pulled his cap over his face while the luggage was being loaded. The brothers rode in silence and Sherlock fell asleep. Jonathan shook him as they approached the manor gates. Sherlock sat up with a start. He realized that the previous injection had worn off and it was not practical to do another in the sleigh. He would have to do his best without it. Mycroft entered the house first followed by Sherlock who was looking somewhat pale and worn.

"Sherlock, you are looking ill!" his mother cried coming forward to him as he entered.

"I'm just tired from the journey," Sherlock said holding up a hand. "I do think I shall rest a bit before supper, but don't neglect to call me. Come, Jonathan," Sherlock said.

Sherlock headed up the stairs to his room. Jonathan followed with Sherlock's bags.

The squire himself had silently observed the exchange.

After greeting his parents, Mycroft headed for his old room. Sherrinford followed him in and shut the door behind them. The brothers sat down and looked at each other.

"You want to know the truth?" Mycroft asked.

"At least the rest of it," Sherrinford agreed.

"Sherlock had a relapse. It seems after what happened last year he had been suffering from nightmares, headaches, and hallucinations for months. Sherlock believed that he had managed to control them before he went to the university. However, a few weeks ago they began to recur. He feared he was going insane. He took arsenic," Mycroft explained.

"Arsenic? Oh, my God," Sherrinford said.

"Jonathan went for help and Sherlock was taken to the hospital. If Jonathan had not been with him he probably would have died."

Sherrinford looked agitated.

"He broke his promise. How can we be certain he will not do so again?"

"He's been making a valiant effort. We have no way of knowing how difficult it is for him. At least now he has some assistance. The doctor at the medical hospital consulted with an alienist named Dr Mackenzie and he has been helping Sherlock recover," Mycroft continued.

"This alienist, he doesn't think Sherlock is insane, does he?" Sherrinford asked.

"I only met him very briefly and there was no opportunity to discuss the matter with him. Sherlock says Dr Mackenzie believes he is suffering from a type of nervous condition caused by traumatic events. This doctor knows of some people who seem to be cured. Sometimes it just takes time."

"But Father would not have the patience for that," Sherrinford said.

"Sherrinford, Sherlock is aware of Father's threat to put him away," Mycroft continued. "Between that and the bad memories here, he was terrified to come back. But he realized that Father would ask more questions if he didn't come than if he did. Dr Mackenzie has provided him with a drug, a stimulant, to mask Sherlock's symptoms while he is here. They tested it before he left Cambridge. It seems quite effective. It wore off just before we arrived at the house. I suspect he will seem much better at supper."

"I hope so. Father is already suspicious."

"There's another thing you should know. I suggested to Sherlock that he spend the Long Vacation in London with me."

"Indeed?"

"I think it would do him good."

"Perhaps it would."

"I'll suggest it to Father," Mycroft said.

"Well, I'll go now and allow you wash before supper."

In another room just down the hall Jonathan watched in silence as Sherlock dug the morocco case out of one of the bags he had been carrying. Sherlock had removed his jacket and rolled up his shirt sleeve. He took the needle out of the box and filled it as Dr Mackenzie had taught him. Watching this made Jonathan uneasy even though he understood its purpose. Sherlock lay back against the pillows, injected himself, and replaced the needle in its box. He rolled down his sleeve.

"Here's a fresh coat, sir. That one is rather rumpled. And here is your comb."

"Thank you," Sherlock said. "You should spend the rest of the holiday with your family."

"If you need me, sir, I am quite glad to stay with you here," Jonathan said.

"I will be fine. Go on."

"Yes, sir."

With mixed feelings Jonathan gathered up his belongings and headed down the back-stairs. After Jonathan left, Sherlock went downstairs to the dining room. He greeted his parents and Mycroft who were already there, and then turned and greeted Sherrinford and his wife Amanda, who came in behind him.

"You look much better, Sherlock!" his mother said.

"Thank you, mother," he said. "A little rest can do wonders."

Supper went well. Sherlock ate sparsely, but he held up his end of the conversation. He felt his father's scrutiny relax as the meal progressed and he knew the first hurdle was behind him. After supper Sherlock retired to his room even though he knew it would be sometime before he could sleep. Sherlock took the violin out its case and tuned it. Then he played until he tired and blew out the lamp and went to sleep.

Hours later Sherlock woke with a start. Some dream...he forced himself not to think about what it might have been. He looked about in the dark. This was his room in Yorkshire. Was he still dreaming? Then he remembered that he was indeed back in his room in Yorkshire for the holiday. Moonlight was peeping through a crack in the curtains and falling like a ghost on the floor. He rose and walked to the window and pulled the curtains closed.

He turned back and leaned against the bedpost. He was tired, so tired. He missed the energy and the enthusiasm the cocaine gave him and he looked with longing at the box upon his desk. But Dr Mackenzie had warned him that he had not given him enough to span the nights as well. He thought of lying down again. He was tired and somewhat foggy, but he was hungry as well. He lit a candle. The stuffed weasel on the mantel stared at him. The clock next to it said it was after 5 o'clock in the morning. He put on his dressing gown and padded down the stairs to the kitchen to see if there was something to be found.

Sherlock was startled in his inspection of the pantry by the sound of the kitchen door opening. He looked up. A lamp was shining in the doorway.

"Mr Sherlock," said Tessy, the cook, as she set the lamp on the table. "What can I be doin' for thee?"

"I was hungry," he said.

"Ah. Tis somethin' I can help with. Sit thyself down," Tessy said. "But let me warm it up a bit in here first," she said lighting the oven fire that she had laid the night before.

Then a wave of cold fought with the heat of the fire, as she opened the back door and brought in a covered stone pitcher.

"I've a wee bit of milk from yesterday. Today's won't be in for a mite yet."

With a wooden spoon she cracked the ice in the pitcher and poured some of the half frozen milk in a pot that she set to heating.

"I've some muffins from yesterday that I can toast up for thee, with some butter and jam," Tessy babbled on as she worked.

Sherlock watched in silence and Tessy did not seem to mind his silence. In some ways it was as if the last year, or the last dozen years even, had not happened. It was as if he was a small child again hiding in the kitchen with the cook. She seemed the same. It was he who was different. It was he who could not be that child again. But before he could follow this melancholy line of thought far, Tessy had set a steaming mug of warm milk before him with a plate of toasted muffins covered with jam and melting butter.

"Thank you," he said.

"Th'art welcome to stay, but the girls will be coming down soon," she said.

He took her meaning and picked up the plate and the mug. Tessy held the door open for him.

"Mr Sherlock," she said just before she shut the door.

He turned back to her.

"If thou be needin' Jonathan for onny reason, drop a word an' I'll send for 'im without disturbin' onnyone in the Hall," she said.

Sherlock suddenly realized who the butler had been speaking to when Jonathan overheard him repeat his father's threat to send him to an asylum.

"I'll be fine, thank you," he said and turned and headed for his room.

He finished his snack as the sky was beginning to lighten. He thought of picking up the violin and looked with longing at the morocco box. But it was still too early for either. So he crawled back under the quilts and fell asleep.

When he awoke again it was after 10 o'clock. They had let him sleep in. He reached for the box, filled the needle, and drove it home before washing and dressing.

The demands on Sherlock over the holiday were many and few. There were many that required him to play the role of the dutiful and contented son, and few that required much thought. For the most part his presence was enough.

Sherlock survived the Squire's Christmas Ball. He ate sparingly of the many delicacies offered him. He had no appetite, but he remembered Dr Mackenzie's warning. He begged off dancing, but at his mother's urging he played a few carols on his violin. He noticed then that the slight numbness in his left arm was interfering with his playing. It wasn't enough to be obvious to an undiscerning audience, but it bothered him. Even the influence of the cocaine was not sufficient to convince him that he was playing his best. As Sherlock was putting his violin away, his mother approached him.

"Thank you, Sherlock. Your music was beautiful."

"Thank you, Mother, but I am a bit rusty."

"Merry Christmas, Dr Thompkins," Mrs Holmes called over the hubbub as the doctor approached them.

"Merry Christmas, Mrs Holmes, Sherlock."

"Merry Christmas, Doctor," Sherlock said concentrating on wiping the rosin dust from the stick of his bow. He realized that he was now standing next to the only person in the dale who might recognize the cocaine symptoms.

"My son is such a perfectionist. He was claiming that his violin playing was less than it should be."

"It sounded lovely to me."

"A little slow on changing stops, I fear," Sherlock said as he closed the violin case. "I should take the violin back with me when I return to Cambridge so I may practice."

"See what I mean, Doctor. But that is a fine idea, Sherlock. It is good to keep in practice."

"Perhaps you can find others at the college to play with. Start a little quartet or something," Dr Thompkins suggested.

"Perhaps."

"Enjoy the party, Sherlock. You should relax yourself a bit before you return to your studies. I hope you will excuse me, doctor, while I attend to my other guests," Sherlock's mother said as she left them.

"You look like you've lost some weight again," Dr Thompkins said.

"I had a slight illness a few weeks ago, something I ate," Sherlock said dismissively, avoiding eye contact with the doctor.

"They have an excellent hospital there at Cambridge."

Just then Jonathan appeared at the doctor's elbow.

"Doctor, there is a woman complaining of feeling faint."

"Probably a bit too much punch and a bit too much dancing. But I'll see to her. Merry Christmas, Sherlock! Lead the way, Jonathan."

"Sherlock!" Andrew Goble cried as he approached and shook Sherlock's hand.

"It is good to have you back among us. How's life at Cambridge?" the curate asked.

"It takes some getting used to."

"It is very different from life around here."

"Yes."

"Did you find anyone to fence with?"

"No, I hadn't brought my gear, but I am thinking of taking it when I return."

"You should do that. There are always some men looking for a good bout."

"So far I've had enough to do to keep up with my reading."

"Don't work too hard. You need to take some exercise as well, and enjoy your holiday while you can!"

"Thank you. Merry Christmas."

"Merry Christmas!"

Even after the Squire's Ball was over the days were busy with preparations for Christmas and Boxing Day. His mother also had plans to celebrate Sherlock's birthday early since he had to be back in Cambridge before his real birthday on January 6th. The days were a whirlwind and the cocaine sustained him through them.

The nights were long and bleak. Sometimes Sherlock was so tired when the last dose of the cocaine faded away that he dropped right off to sleep and slept through the night. Other times he was awaken by nightmares and lay awake for hours afterwards longing for the comfort of the drug. But he knew if he were to exhaust his supply the only possible local source was Dr Thompkins. He could not be assured that the doctor would have any or would give it to him. He had to make it last. It was the only thought that stayed his hand some nights. There were too many ghosts here in this room, in this house, and on the moors beyond. Too many memories that he had to avoid. He needed to survive the holiday and make his way back to Cambridge. There he had the possibility of a future. Here he had only a past.

Sometimes at night he would lie on his bed concentrating on the ticking of the clock as each minute passed that he had to endure. Once he delved beyond that in his mind to listen to subtler sounds of the meshing of the gears and of the whirling of the wheels that made the clock work. Then he took the clock down from the mantel and opened the back and watched it work as he had as a child. As he watched, he wished it was as easy to look inside someone's head and see how it worked, but then he put the clock back and left those dangerous thoughts behind.

Sherlock took the epees off the wall and held them in his hands. It felt good. He laid them on the bed and dug through his closet and pulled out the rest of the fencing gear. In the morning he asked Thomas, the butler, to assist him in finding some boxes. They packed the fencing gear, his violin, and his boxing gloves to take back to Cambridge with him.

Sherlock interacted very little with his father over the holiday. He greeted him cordially at meals and described some of the lectures he had attended to him. He did not mention the number of lectures he had missed, or how far he was behind in his reading, or that he had been excused from the Previous Exam this term. But he wasn't asked either. Sometimes he felt the squire was watching him during the ball and other family events, but he knew he was presenting the image expected. All he had to do was maintain that image until he was away again.

Then the final day of Sherlock's holiday came. Jonathan returned to the manor house and helped Sherlock pack the rest of the luggage. They retired early. In the morning the bags and boxes were piled in the sleigh before dawn. The squire and Sherrinford and their wives bid Sherlock and Mycroft farewell in the foyer. The driver lashed the horses and they began the long, cold journey to the railway station. Sherlock felt a sense of relief and impatience as the sleigh pulled away from Holmes Hall.

The last dose wore off before they reached Cambridge and Sherlock fell asleep on the train. Jonathan woke him when they arrived. The cold night air rushed in as the door of the carriage opened. The cold stabbed at Sherlock like icy needles and he shivered. He felt tired and slow-witted. He allowed Jonathan to lead him. A porter helped them gather the luggage and find a cab. The cab took Sherlock and Jonathan to their rooms and the cabman helped them carry the luggage up the stairs. Mycroft bid them farewell there before having the cab-driver take him on to an inn in town for the night before travelling on to London in the morning.

126

Chapter 13

Back in Cambridge

"Followed by reactions of lethargy during which he would lie about with his violin and his books, hardly moving save from the sofa to the table."
Dr. Watson, The Musgrave Ritual

The following morning Dr Mackenzie came to visit.

"He's still asleep, doctor," Jonathan said quietly.

"Did things go well?"

"I believe so, sir. But you will have to ask him. He sent me off to visit my family for most of the holiday."

"He must have felt some self-confidence if he was willing to part with you."

Jonathan smiled.

"You seem more relaxed yourself, Jonathan," Dr Mackenzie said.

"It was good to see my family again and I am more confident that you will be able to help Mr Sherlock overcome his troubles," Jonathan responded.

"I hope so. But you might want to have a strong cup of coffee ready for him when he awakes. He might be a bit drowsy without some stimulant. Don't let him get in the doldrums. Tell him that I will call again in the evening to see how he is faring."

That evening Dr Mackenzie noted a peculiar whine emanating from the rooms as he knocked on the door. When he entered he found Sherlock Holmes lying upon the sofa in his dressing gown with bow in hand and a violin lying across his knees. Sherlock looked up.

"Good evening, Dr Mackenzie," Sherlock said.

"Good evening, Sherlock," he said as he took a seat in one of the chairs near the fire. "That is a rather unusual method of playing the violin."

"It takes less energy," Sherlock said.

"Excuse me, sir," said Jonathan, "but Mister Sherlock can play quite well when he wants."

"You have been excessively bold since your holiday," Sherlock said wiggling his bow at Jonathan.

But the glint in Jonathan's eye suggested that he was not taking the rebuff seriously.

"How are you, Sherlock?" Dr Mackenzie said.

"Limp as a rag," Sherlock replied. "You didn't bring any more of your wonder drug, did you?"

"No."

"Just having Jonathan ply me with coffee and tea?"

"It seems to have gotten you out of bed," Dr Mackenzie said.

"Yes, but I don't have any enthusiasm for much else."

"We'll work on that," Dr Mackenzie said.

"Excuse me again, sirs, but supper will be ready soon. Is Dr Mackenzie staying?" Jonathan asked.

"Stay, Dr Mackenzie. Then the two of you can unite and force me to eat," Sherlock said.

Dr Mackenzie smiled.

"I'll stay," he said.

"Very good, sir," Jonathan said.

"You may be limp, but you seem in a much better humour than before you left," Dr Mackenzie said.

"I was scared witless then. The very fact that I have returned here to Cambridge has lifted a great shadow from me. The drug was sufficiently invigorating to allow me to fool my father. Mycroft suggested that I spend the long vacation with him in London and my father seemed to think it was a good idea. He will not expect me to return to the estate for another year at least."

"So you have time."

"Yes."

"And the violin?"

"I'm glad I brought it back with me. I'm not sure my neighbours will agree," Sherlock said.

Dr Mackenzie laughed.

"It is a thick, old building. Perhaps the sound won't carry far," he said.

"I brought my fencing gear as well. The curate, Andrew Goble, once again urged me to find someone here to fence with."

Jonathan set down the last plate.

"Supper is ready," he said, and they came to the table and Jonathan served them.

After supper Dr Mackenzie looked at his watch.

"I must be going soon, but I was wondering if I could impose on you."

"How so?" Sherlock asked.

"Will you play something for me?"

"I suppose I could play a short piece if you wish. Do you have something in mind?"

"No. Anything. I would like very much to hear you play."

Without another word Sherlock sat up, lifted the violin from the case and tucked it under his chin. He closed his eyes and drew the bow across the strings, producing a haunting melody. Sherlock's whole being was transformed as he played. At the end he lay back again drained, setting both the violin and the bow across his lap. The music had woven a spell on them all and for a few minutes they sat in silence.

"That was quite lovely. Mozart's Adagio in E, was it not?" Dr Mackenzie said at last.

"Yes. Are you a musician?"

"No, but I come from a family of musicians and patrons of the arts. My father founded the Norwich Music Festival and my uncle founded the Norwich Philharmonic. So I have heard many talented violinists, but I don't know that I've ever heard anyone play a violin better."

"It was passable. I don't have the stamina at the moment for anything longer."

"That's just the counter-reaction to the cocaine. It should wear off and you should have more energy in a few days."

"Yes, your miracle drug did have that drawback. It also interfered with my violin playing while I was taking it."

"In what way?"

"My arm was slightly numb where the injections were made."

"Yes, I had not thought of that. I believe the violin will be far better medicine for you than the cocaine. I prescribe frequent doses of violin-playing. You can tell your neighbours that you are under doctor's orders if they object. But," he said taking out his watch again, "I must be getting back to the asylum. I will stop by again in a few days. Send for me if you have any problems. Good night, Sherlock."

"Good night, Doctor."

Sherlock followed Dr Mackenzie's prescription and the violin helped calm his nerves. The next day he began attending Chapel again and taking supper in Hall. He worked at catching up on his reading and tried to attend all of his lectures. It wasn't easy at first. He still felt fatigued and sometimes foggy, but Dr Mackenzie assured him that the only way to regain his ability to concentrate was to strive for it. Neither merely waiting for it, nor trying to artificially induce it, was the answer. Sherlock still had his black moods now and then, but he gradually improved.

One day in mid-January as he sat down for breakfast Sherlock noticed that the blind was still down on the window. He mentioned this to Jonathan.

"It's snowing, sir," Jonathan replied.

Sherlock closed his eyes and leaned his head on his hand. For a moment he sat there and Jonathan began to be concerned.

"Sir?"

Sherlock looked up.

"Then get your hat and coat and be prepared to come with me to Morning Prayers in fifteen minutes."

"Sir?"

"As you know, snow has been associated with my nervous attacks on at least three occasions. Dr Mackenzie believes that it may set off some reaction in my brain. I do not wish it to happen again. I do not know of any way I can prevent an attack, but you do. So I am taking you with me."

"Just to Chapel?"

"No, to lectures, too. We will stop back here briefly in-between. We will return for lunch. I will decide after lunch what we shall do after that."

"Yes, sir," Jonathan said, once more admiring his master's determination.

When Sherlock was ready Jonathan latched the door behind them and they descended the stairs together. Sherlock steeled himself as they stood before the front door.

"Open it," he said.

Jonathan opened the door. Sherlock grabbed him by the shoulder and pushed him through the doorway before him. Once committed, he did not wish to hesitate. Snowflakes fell about them as they ran to the curb and started across the street.

"Sir? Perhaps it would help if you spoke to me while we walked," Jonathan suggested.

"I believe at the moment that excessive conversation will result in us both being run down by a cab. Hurry on."

Once on the other side of the street they began walking to the gates of Sidney Sussex College.

"Good mornin', Mr Holmes," the head porter said as they entered. "I think you are just in time."

As he spoke the chapel bells began to ring announcing the service.

"Good morning to you, too. That was a well-timed prediction. Hurry on, Jonathan, the chapel is over that direction. I will sit near the back. You stay in the vestibule and we will join up again after the service."

Jonathan couldn't help looking around as they entered the chapel with gowned undergraduates on all sides of them. Just inside the door Sherlock pulled Jonathan to one side and doffed his coat. He handed it to Jonathan.

"Wait here," Sherlock whispered and then went forward to take a seat.

By now Sherlock had attended Morning Prayers at the Sidney Sussex Chapel dozens of times. He had also attended services at great cathedrals in York, London and the capitals of Europe. But

Jonathan had never seen anything more than the village church back in Yorkshire. The words were the same. When one of the scholars read a psalm, Jonathan knew he could recite it by heart himself. He had learned to read from the King James Bible and knew it cover-to-cover. But somehow the sensation was grander here. The chapel itself was not large, nor especially ornate. He knew that there were bigger, grander churches in Cambridge, some within a few blocks. It was the people he saw in the little church who impressed him. He had never seen the senior members of the college in their full regalia, nor had he seen this many undergraduates at one time. He was awed by the sight.

Jonathan was shorter than most of those in attendance and as the congregation stood at the end of the service, he lost all hope of being able to find Sherlock in the throng. But he stayed in the vestibule close to the stream of gowns flowing from the chapel and soon Sherlock's long thin fingers grabbed his shoulders and pulled him in line before him. Outside the chapel the snow was falling heavily. Jonathan handed Sherlock his coat. As he was putting it on, Jonathan saw a haughty-looking undergraduate smirk their direction and make a comment to one of his friends. Then Jonathan and Sherlock went on their way toward the gatehouse.

"Mr Holmes," a voice called just as they began.

Sherlock stopped and turned around and Jonathan followed suit. As he did he recognized the man who was addressing Sherlock.

"Mr Holmes," Dean Hoch said, "I am glad to see that you made it to Chapel this morning. I wasn't certain that you would come."

"I'm doing my best."

"Yes. Your attendance has been quite regular since the beginning of the term. I trust you are getting on with your reading?"

"Yes, sir."

"Very good. Well, I shouldn't keep you standing here in this weather. We don't want you becoming ill and missing more lectures."

"No, sir. We don't. Good day, sir."

Sherlock turned back towards the gates and grasped Jonathan by the shoulder again.

"Onward," he said.

Back in their rooms Sherlock tossed his cap on a chair and himself on the sofa. Jonathan fed the fire in the sitting room. He wondered if Sherlock was having doubts about his plan. It was working so far, but it seemed to be a strain on him. Sherlock hadn't yet removed his overcoat and in a few minutes he rose and headed towards his bedroom.

"I will retrieve my notebooks and we shall be off again."

It was still snowing heavily. Sherlock turned Jonathan northward keeping at least one hand on him at all times. Sherlock also did as Jonathan advised and maintained a running monologue as they wound their way through the university.

"I have lectures this morning at St. John's and at Trinity College. North here along Sidney Street to St. John's then down St. John's Street afterwards to Trinity.

"Good morning, Mr Jones," Sherlock said to the porter at St. John's.

"It's a white one, isn't it, Mr Holmes?"

"Yes, not really to my liking."

"Who's your little friend?"

"My servant, Jonathan."

"Well, you'd best hurry on."

"Here we are," Sherlock said. "Come inside the building. I don't want you to freeze. Wait inside here. If anyone asks what you are doing here simply tell them I asked you to wait for me here."

When they returned to their lodging after the lectures, Jonathan built up the fires and put the kettle on before removing his coat.

"Will you be ready for your lunch soon, sir?

"Yes, I am famished," Sherlock responded, much to Jonathan's delight.

"Then I shall set it out directly."

"We pulled it off," Sherlock said as Jonathan set the table. "I had my doubts that it would work. But Dr Mackenzie is correct. If I don't want to be locked in a cell then I have to find ways to keep going about my business."

"If you will be staying in for a while this afternoon, I would like to go out to the market."

"I'll be reading. I probably will want you to come with me to the Hall for supper."

"Certainly."

After Sherlock had eaten, Jonathan bundled up and headed out with the shopping basket. While he was gone there was a knock at the door. Sherlock set his book aside and opened the door himself.

"Good afternoon, Dr Mackenzie. Come in."

"Good afternoon, Sherlock. Where is Jonathan?"

"Running errands. I believe he wanted to lay in more provisions in case this blizzard continues. Take off your coat and find a warm spot by the fire. What brings you out on this snowy day?"

Dr Mackenzie gave Sherlock a puzzled look as he took off his coat.

"I was worried about you. Needlessly it seems. I know that you had trouble with snow in the past. Yet you seem in high spirits. Did you decide to stay in?"

"On the contrary, doctor, I went to Morning Prayers and lectures as usual this morning."

"Indeed? Without any difficulty?"

"I took Jonathan with me. I clung to him like a drowning man when we were out of doors."

"I think that is not quite accurate," Jonathan said as he closed the door behind him. "I felt more like a trained poodle."

"A trained poodle indeed," Sherlock snorted. "Where have you ever seen a trained poodle?"

"There was a man with one at the market once. He waved his arms and the dog hopped around on its hind legs," Jonathan said as he removed his coat before hurrying off to the kitchen.

"Doctor, you study human behaviour," Sherlock said. "Why is it that when I am in a good humour my servant gets cheeky?"

"He knows when you are in a good mood," Dr Mackenzie suggested.

"And thinks he can proceed with impunity?" Sherlock interrupted.

"Perhaps, but I think it is just an expression of his own relief."

"If he didn't have the most impeccable timing with his soft-boiled eggs, I'd give him notice."

"I don't think he believes that. I know I don't."

"The water is hot," Jonathan said, seemingly oblivious to their exchange about him, but they both knew he had heard. "Would you like a cup of tea, doctor?"

"Yes, that would be very nice. Thank you," Dr Mackenzie replied and then turned back to Sherlock. "Were you in as good a mood when you started out?"

"Not at all. I was petrified. I'm just beginning to restore some type of order to my thoughts. I live in constant fear of my brain being completely unravelled again by another nervous attack. I have not had one in over a month now and I'd rather not have another ever again. But if I hide from every snowstorm I could be a prisoner all winter for the rest of my life. I decided that I needed to find a way to deal with it. So we ran an experiment."

"And it worked."

"It may not be the most efficient method of proceeding, but it did prove that it was possible for me to get about in the snow."

"You faced your fear and triumphed. No wonder you are in high spirits! Well, I will let you to return to your reading. I should return to the asylum before the road to Fulbourn becomes impassable. My driver was not happy about coming up here. I am sure that he will be in much better spirits himself when he is home again. I will see you next week."

"Good day, Dr Mackenzie," Sherlock Holmes said.

136

Chapter 14

Dreams and Doubts

"He began to play some low, dreamy, melodious air,—his own,
no doubt, for he had a remarkable gift for improvisation."
Dr. Watson, *The Sign of Four*

Before dawn one morning in late February Sherlock cried out and sat up in bed gasping for air. His heart was pounding and shreds of a dream tugged at his mind. As his eyes focused in the dark he saw a candle flame before him at the end of the bed. He pushed the dream from his mind and watched the candle flame move around to the side of his bed. It was followed by soft footsteps. Then he heard the glass being lifted on the table lamp and the candle flame leaned towards the wick and light came forth from the lamp revealing the bearer of the candle to be a boy in his nightshirt with his yellow hair in disarray. Jonathan looked back at Sherlock for a moment but no words passed between them as Sherlock struggled with the pounding of his heart and the quieting of his mind. Sherlock shut out all thought, except his observations of the boy as he moved about the room. Jonathan turned toward the fireplace and knelt before it. Soon flames danced there as well. Then he stood and walked back to the bed. He set down his candle, poured a glass of water and held it out. Sherlock took it with trembling hands and gulped the cold water. As he did, Jonathan and his candle glided out of the bedroom again. In a moment Sherlock could see the glow from another lamp through the doorway to the sitting room. Sherlock set the glass down and leaned his head in his hands. Then he heard footsteps again and looked up. Jonathan stood next to his bed holding out his violin and bow. Sherlock reach up and took them.

"Thank you," Sherlock said, finding his voice at last. "You should go back to bed."

"It is nearly time for me to be up anyway, sir. I plan on dressing and proceeding with my routine, unless you object."

Sherlock shook his head.

"Can I be of any further service?"

"No."

Jonathan began to withdraw.

"Be sure to call me at the usual time," Sherlock called to him.

"Yes, sir," Jonathan responded from the doorway.

As Jonathan dressed in his closet off the kitchen he heard the whine of the violin from the bedroom. Then he lit the fire in the sitting room and the other lamps. He picked up the pitcher and went out for more water. When he returned the sound of the violin had stopped. He tiptoed to the bedroom door and peeked in. Sherlock had fallen back asleep with the violin across his knees and the bow beside him. Jonathan carefully removed them from the bed and went back to his work. Hours later he took Sherlock's breakfast to him on a tray and woke him. Sherlock ate and rose and dressed. He put on his academical gown and headed to the Sidney Chapel for Morning Prayers and then on to the day's lectures. When he returned about midday Sherlock saw another coat on the rack as he tossed his gown on the hook next to it. It was Thursday.

As Sherlock had settled into the routines of his studies, Dr Mackenzie's visits had become shorter and less frequent. Eventually it became his habit to stop by briefly on Tuesday and Thursday afternoons to check on Sherlock's progress.

"Good afternoon, Dr Mackenzie," Sherlock said as he entered the sitting room.

"Good afternoon, Sherlock. Jonathan says that you had a nightmare this morning."

"Yes."

"It is the first one in several weeks?"

"Yes."

"Tell me about it."

Sherlock walked over to the window and looked out at the grey day. Dr Mackenzie followed him with his eyes.

"No monsters or demons this time," Sherlock said. "I was with her and then she was simply gone and I was alone."

Dr Mackenzie waited in silence.

"Perhaps it was the simplicity of it that—" Sherlock said, "It seemed quite real."

Sherlock sighed.

"You feel haunted," Dr Mackenzie.

"Haunted?"

"Forced to suffer her loss over and over again."

"Yes," Sherlock said quietly.

Dr Mackenzie read his mood more from his body language than his words. Dr Mackenzie knew that Sherlock Holmes kept people at a distance. He could feel the distance between them even when he forced Sherlock to speak of things he would rather not. Right now he could see that Sherlock was struggling. He was at a crossroad where he could either make significant progress or slide backwards. Dr Mackenzie knew that his job was to push him forward.

"Let's say for the purpose of argument that there is something to this spiritual world that Sidgwick and his colleagues are investigating," Dr Mackenzie said. "If she were a spirit, would she torment you like that?"

"No," Sherlock responded.

"If we eliminate a literal haunting, what have we left?"

"That I'm losing my mind."

"That statement is far too broad to be useful," Dr Mackenzie responded. "Clearly whatever is happening is occurring in your own mind and the dreams are a sign of it. It is impeding your progress at the moment. But I think we need to turn it around and look at it from another angle. The problem isn't that she won't leave you, but that you won't leave her."

Sherlock turned and looked at the doctor quizzically.

"Was there any funeral service?" Dr Mackenzie asked.

"No. They never found—" Sherlock whispered.

Dr Mackenzie realized that Sherlock was dangerously close to having a nervous attack.

"Sherlock, come over here and sit down on the sofa."

Sherlock obeyed. Dr Mackenzie leaned forward and grasped him by the knee. His grip was almost painful. Sherlock looked down at the doctor's hand but made no complaint.

"No service of any kind?" Dr Mackenzie asked.

"No." Sherlock said shaking his head. "Her father died shortly after she disappeared. There was no other family. I-I was too ill to leave my room."

"You never had a chance to say goodbye to her."

"No," Sherlock said. "I try not to think about what happened. If I do—"

"It can precipitate one of your attacks."

"Yes. Sometimes thoughts of her come unbidden. I push them away. But I can't control my dreams."

"I think you can," Dr Mackenzie said releasing his hold on Sherlock's knee. "They have changed, haven't they?"

"Yes."

"In your waking mind you accept that she is gone, but I think on some level you are still searching for her."

Sherlock stood and walked away from Dr Mackenzie. His gaze fell upon the violin lying in its case on the table before him. He stared at it without touching it.

"She never heard me play," Sherlock said.

Sherlock turned from the violin and began pacing the sitting room floor.

"Must I banish all thoughts of her from my mind forever?" he asked.

"Do you want to?"

"What I want seems to be irrelevant, Doctor," Sherlock Holmes said dryly. "The question is: What do I need to do and can I do it?"

"Before you tried shutting all your pain inside and it didn't work. I'm not suggesting that you do that again. You need to bid her farewell, Sherlock," Dr Mackenzie said, "not for her sake, but for yours."

"I don't know if I can do that. The dreams make me think of her. Sometimes they are pleasant and sometimes they are not. Either way they seem to threaten my ability to function. I promised to— I-I wish to honour her memory and make the best I can of my life because she would want me to, but her very memory threatens that. How can I go on if the dreams continue to haunt me?"

"The dreams are a symptom of your illness."

"My illness...."

"Yes, it's an illness just as much as the measles or consumption. I don't hold with those who believe that a nervous condition is the result of some moral weakness. If a man breaks his leg or has a fever we don't blame him for not being able to stand. We simply do our best to help him. The same should be true of a nervous condition."

Sherlock paused in his pacing.

"A man may succumb to a physical illness if his body doesn't have the strength to fight it. The same is true of a nervous condition, is it not, Dr Mackenzie?"

"Yes. Sadly that is quite true."

Sherlock resumed his pacing.

"Sometimes I fear that I am not strong enough to survive it," Sherlock said.

"Nearly every person that I have treated with any kind of nervous condition has had similar fears and doubts at times. I believe the only ones who are never troubled by such fears are those whose mental condition has deteriorated so severely that they are incapable of rational thought."

"That is not terribly comforting. You yourself admit that few people are cured at the asylum."

"That is true. Part of the problem there is that we are dealing with a mix of patients who have terminal organic illnesses with nervous effects, incurable lunatics, and people with potentially curable nervous conditions. The members of the first group often die at the asylum within a short time. The second group live out their natural lives there. It is only the third group of patients that we have any chance of a 'cure.' Unfortunately the records kept at asylums in the past are inadequate to determine the true rate of success at helping such people. I've been trying to improve those records here. But Sherlock, if I thought you belonged in the asylum I would have arranged for it despite our crowded conditions. You said that you heard me arguing the point with Dr Burton."

"Yes."

"The order for admission to the asylum only requires the signature of two doctors. Obviously, Dr Burton would have signed, but I was unwilling. I believe you can overcome this. You are young, strong and clever. While your illness may mask or suppress your intellect at times, I know that Sidney Sussex would not have admitted you if they did not believe you were intelligent. You have survived some terrible shocks. Your condition is not a sign of weakness, but strength. You would not be here now if you were weak. I've seen others survive similar conditions, even worse ones. None of the people whom I have previously encountered with a condition similar to yours is currently in an asylum. They all are leading normal lives."

"Except Mary Ann."

"Well, yes, but I explained her circumstances to you. I don't know for a fact that her condition was like yours because additional injury was done before she was brought to the asylum. I probably shouldn't have introduced you to her when I did. It was premature. I didn't know enough about your case to fully understand the effect it would have on you."

"It wasn't your fault, Dr Mackenzie."

"I appreciate your generosity in saying so. I take my Hippocratic Oath quite seriously, though I am human and I stumble sometimes."

"You've done me far more good than harm."

"You have improved a great deal since November."

"Yes. But I thought the nightmares were gone."

"You will have set-backs sometimes. You need to remember how far you have come."

"What if I can't improve any more than I have? What if I can't maintain what I have gained?"

"You won't know that if you don't try. You are young. You have no idea what good you might do—"

"Or what harm," Sherlock said.

"Who have you harmed?"

"I draw death and destruction to those around me."

"Rubbish," Dr Mackenzie said.

Sherlock stopped pacing and stared at Dr Mackenzie.

"What?" Sherlock said.

"Nonsense. Call it what you will. I have seen no evidence of that whatsoever. In the three months I've known you, the only 'harm' that has been associated with you is that you attempted on yourself. You are feeling dispirited at the moment and are projecting your fears into reality when there is no basis for them."

Sherlock sat down and was silent for several minutes.

"I suppose there is truth in what you say," he said at last, "but it doesn't make it any easier."

"I never said it would be easy. You must find strength and comfort where you can."

Sherlock stood and walked back over to the violin and picked it up.

"The violin helps?" Dr Mackenzie asked.

"Yes. The violin seems to exorcise the darkest of my thoughts and lift my spirits," Sherlock said, bringing the violin with him to the sofa. He lay down with it across his knees. He drew the bow slowly across the G string causing the instrument to moan in response. He leaned his head back and sighed.

"I meant what I said," Dr Mackenzie said, drawing the conversation back to where it had started. "I think you need to tell her goodbye so that you may heal."

Sherlock looked up at him but said nothing.

Dr Mackenzie pulled out his watch.

"I must return to the asylum. Is there anything more I can do for you today?"

"No."

Dr Mackenzie stood up and headed for the door. Jonathan was already there with his coat, but the doctor turned back to where Sherlock lay on the sofa. He had another thought.

"You told me that you brought your fencing gear back from Yorkshire. Have you tried it since you returned?"

"No."

"You should," Dr Mackenzie said. "If nothing else the exercise would do you good."

Sherlock said nothing and Dr Mackenzie bid him good day.

Soon it was time for Sherlock to cross over to Sidney Sussex for supper. He picked up his cap and gown and coat and left in silence. When he returned he tossed them on the hook, walked into the bedroom and closed the door.

A chill went through Jonathan as he remembered the last time that door was closed between them. But as he walked towards it, the door opened again. Sherlock came out and placed his hand on Jonathan's shoulder for a moment. Then he removed it and picked up the violin from the table.

"I do not wish to be disturbed."

"Yes, sir."

Sherlock returned to his bedroom leaving the door ajar. Jonathan could hear him tuning the violin. Then Sherlock began to play. He played for hours. It was not the scratching and whining that resulted when the instrument lay upon his knees. The sounds that came forth were melodious and entrancing; sometimes fast; sometimes slow; sometimes happy; sometimes sad. Through the crack in the door Jonathan could see Sherlock standing before the window of his bedroom with the violin upon his shoulder and his eyes closed, united with the instrument as he let it speak for him. Jonathan sat down in the chair before the sitting room fire and listened to the music until he drifted off to sleep.

As dawn began to light the sky outside the windows, Jonathan snapped awake to silence. He jumped up and looked into the bedroom. There his master lay curled upon the bed asleep with one hand still grasping the neck of the violin. Jonathan smiled and went on about his chores. When the time came he woke Sherlock and sent him off to Chapel and lectures as usual.

That evening after supper Sherlock unboxed the epees, masks and gauntlets. He sat before the fire for some time with one of the epees in his hand. At last he put it aside and went to bed. For two weeks the fencing gear graced the sitting room. Now and then Sherlock would pick up an epee and stare at it for a while.

Dr Mackenzie saw them laying there the next three times he

came to visit.

"No," Sherlock said one day, anticipating his question from the direction of his gaze.

"Why not?"

"I haven't found the time."

"You have been going to your lectures?"

"Yes."

"And your supervisions?"

"Yes, and Chapel and Hall," Sherlock said.

"Doing your reading?"

"Yes."

"Surely you could go by the gymnasium some afternoon."

"I thought perhaps Jonathan and I would practice in college a bit before I—"

"Then why haven't you? Are you afraid of being beaten?" Dr Mackenzie interrupted.

"By Jonathan?" Sherlock asked. "No."

"By other students then?"

"No."

"Then why?"

"I just—" Sherlock began, but broke off. He didn't really know why.

"I think you are afraid of failing."

"That is absurd, Dr Mackenzie," Sherlock countered. He was becoming annoyed. He was quite proud of his skill at fencing. "You've never—"

"Not at fencing. It is merely a symbol."

"A symbol? You are talking nonsense, doctor," Sherlock snorted.

"Jonathan said fencing helped you improve before. But now you stall. You are afraid that if you reach that level again that it will get your hopes up as it did before. You are afraid to be well and to lose that again."

"Yes, damn it!" Sherlock yelled. "It didn't work before. I failed. If I do the same thing, I'm likely to have the same result. Do you know what it is like? It's like – It's like falling off a cliff and having every bone in your body broken! How many times do you think someone can endure that?"

"You've said that you don't want to stay as you are."

"I don't!"

"If you've lost your resolve—"

"No!"

"Then you must keep trying."

"I am continuing my studies."

"You are going through the motions."

"That is better than I was doing four months ago."

"You have made progress, but you must keep moving forward."

"And if I fail?"

"Then I will be here to catch you. I told you before: you aren't alone in this anymore. Do you still want my help?"

"Yes!"

"Prove it to me. Fence with Jonathan tomorrow."

Sherlock stared at him for a moment.

"I will," Sherlock agreed.

Chapter 15

Bouts and Bites

"Never in the delirious dream of a disordered brain could anything...more hellish be conceived than that... which broke upon us out of the wall of fog."
Dr. Watson, *The Hound of the Baskervilles*

The rain began mid-morning on Friday. When Sherlock returned from his lectures, Jonathan insisted that he change to dry clothes and have some hot tea. The boy would have towelled Sherlock's hair dry as he sat before the raging fire in the sitting room if Sherlock had not shooed him away.

Sherlock remembered his promise to Dr Mackenzie. The rain prevented him from fulfilling it, but he thought about it.

"Where did you put my fencing jacket?" he asked Jonathan.

"In the closet here, sir," Jonathan said as he pulled it out and handed it to him.

Sherlock tried it on. He was fortunate that in recent years he had grown more in leg than breadth of shoulder. It still fit and was in good shape. No tears; no lose seams. He examined the length of each epee with his fingers. The blades were smooth and free from spurs. The caps were firm, the guard solid, and the wrappings in place. He examined each gauntlet and each mask carefully. They were in good condition.

"Find your jacket," he told Jonathan before retiring to his room with his books. "We will have a go at it in the morning."

"Yes, sir," Jonathan said.

The next morning the March sun rose bright and warm and steamed away the last remnants of the rain. After Sherlock returned from Chapel, he and Jonathan crossed the street and entered through the gates of Sidney Sussex College carrying the epees, gauntlets and masks. They stopped in a corner of Hall Court, donned their masks and saluted each other.

"En garde," Sherlock called and advanced on Jonathan.

Jonathan's hopes rose as Sherlock scored against him. Jonathan had seen Sherlock at his best and his worse. He was doing well today. The bout was swiftly over. Sherlock scored again and then disarmed Jonathan by knocking his epee from his hand and into the air. Sherlock caught it in mid-air as he had the first time they had ever crossed swords two years before. Jonathan smiled beneath the mask and caught the epee as Sherlock tossed it back to him. They saluted again and engaged.

Jonathan did his best, but he was far more concerned with observing his master than scoring and far less adept than his master at both. But Jonathan could tell that it was different again from the way things had been the previous spring. Sherlock was physically stronger than he had been then and seemed less inhuman than he had been, but there was another aspect to Sherlock's execution that Jonathan did not understand at first. Gradually he realized what it was: they had an audience. Some members of the college had leaned out their windows to observe them. A few fellows and undergraduates passing by had stopped to watch as well. As Jonathan became aware of this, he became more self-conscious of his own limited skills, but he realized that it had the opposite effect on his master. Sherlock Holmes was performing for his peers at the college. It seemed to cause him no discomfort, but rather brought out an extra flair in his performance.

At the end of the third bout some of the spectators clapped their hands. Sherlock Holmes gave them a slight bow. One young man with a pale face, a high thin nose, and large eyes came languidly forward and addressed him.

"You seem to be quite a skilled swordsman, Holmes. Have you—"

"Musgrave," one of the others interrupted from further back, "I'm surprised that you condescend to speak to Holmes. He's far below your station even, a mere subscriber. Oh, but I forgot. Your family lost its titles 300 years ago."

Holmes and Musgrave turned toward the rude speaker. It was Lord Cecil, who was now sharing a chuckle with his followers. Musgrave did not seem the least bit angered by Lord Cecil's jibes. He merely looked bored. He turned back to Holmes and seemed about to make another attempt to speak when he was once again interrupted.

"I have heard that Mackenzie's been paying visits to Holmes' rooms," Lord Cecil said. "Perhaps Holmes'd feel more at home at the asylum than in college."

Sherlock felt himself turning red. It was the first time any of his fellow-students had mentioned anything about Dr Mackenzie within Sherlock's hearing. It wasn't something he was prepared to discuss and it angered him that it should be brought out in this insulting and public manner.

"No doubt you would feel much more at home in a gambling parlour," Sherlock retorted, "where you obviously spend a great deal of time, and most likely, a good deal of silver. I suppose you have forgotten undergraduates are prohibited from gaming? I understand your father has spoken out against gambling in the House of Lords and would outlaw it all if he had his way. I don't know what he would think of his own son's participation."

Lord Cecil turned pale.

"It's a lie," he shouted pushing through the crowd towards Sherlock Holmes.

"Your coat sleeves say otherwise. They didn't get those marks from study. I wonder when you have time for reading between the gambling and your participation in the Amateur Dramatics Club. What would the Duke think of having an actor in the family, Lord Cecil? Especially one who often plays the female roles?" Sherlock concluded as he turned away and squatted down to set his fencing mask on the ground.

Lord Cecil became red as beetroot during Holmes' second speech. As Sherlock turned away, Lord Cecil grabbed him by the shoulder to turn him back around prepared to swing at him. But Sherlock had expected that. He turned at his knees keeping his body low and bringing his left fist up into Lord Cecil's belly as he turned. Lord Cecil doubled up gasping and choking. His comrades hustled him away before the exchange drew the attention of the college officials.

"We should be going as well," Sherlock said to Jonathan. He

quickly picked up his mask and epee from the ground and began walking towards the gatehouse.

"I'm sorry if we created a bit of a scene, Musgrave. Perhaps we should find a more private spot to practice next time."

"It hardly could be considered your fault, Holmes," Musgrave responded as he followed them. "Lord Cecil's been looking for a fight since he arrived at the college. It looks like he finally found the wrong person to pick on."

"You don't seem to mind his taunting."

Musgrave shrugged.

"It is a very old story."

"Members of your family were Cavaliers?"

"Yes, and we are quite proud of it."

"It is odd that you would choose Sidney Sussex."

"Members of my family had been coming to Sidney long before Cromwell did and, of course, Sidney had no idea what type of scoundrel he would become later. But that's all history. It makes for interesting reading but what matter is it to us today? Lord Cecil seems especially fond of collecting twaddle and delving into personal matters that no gentleman should. I wouldn't pay him any mind."

"Holmes!" another student called breathlessly as Sherlock and Jonathan were about to leave Musgrave and exit the college gates. The three of them turned towards the newcomer. Sherlock recognized him as a third year man at Sidney.

"Holmes, I'm glad I caught you. I'm Maberley. I saw you and your boy fencing in the court. You have exceptional skills."

"Thank you."

"I wanted to tell you that there is a group of fencers that meets at the university gymnasium on Wednesday afternoons. Not quite a club yet. Just whoever drops by for a few bouts. I've been reading hard this term and haven't been able to make it. I'm going down shortly."

"You were reading for the Classical Tripos?" Sherlock asked.

"Yes. Thank God, that's over. But you should definitely go by the gymnasium and meet the other men who fence."

"I'll do that. Thank you," Sherlock said and bid farewell to Maberley and Musgrave before crossing to his lodgings.

Despite the fight with Lord Cecil, Sherlock was feeling good about the proceedings Saturday morning. As he mounted to his rooms he fully intended to meet with the fencers Maberley had mentioned.

But Sherlock Holmes was not destined to make it to the gymnasium that week. As he was going to chapel the following morning, he heard a voice cry "Stop!" behind him. When he looked around he saw another student, Victor Trevor, chasing a bull terrier across the court. As Sherlock turned, the dog launched itself at his ankle. Sherlock cried out in pain and fell to his knees as the dog's teeth tore into his flesh. He struck at the dog's nose with his fists in hopes of disengaging it, but the dog only ground its teeth into his leg more painfully. Trevor and several bystanders rushed to Sherlock's aid, but they could not dislodge the dog. Every attempt was both unsuccessful and excruciating for Sherlock. He writhed in pain. Then a groundskeeper ran up with a pistol and shot the bull terrier. Sherlock jumped with the proximity of the blast. Someone forced open the jaws of the dead animal and removed it. Fellows and undergraduates were drawn from Sidney's Chapel by the commotion and crowded around. Sherlock's ravaged ankle was bleeding profusely and everything was a blur of sound and colour and pain to him as he lay on the ground. Caps, gowns, black, red, gold, white, the blue of the sky. The chimes, a hubbub of voices, a voice asking someone to hail a four wheeler, and pain, and more pain as someone pulled at his ankle.

"Hold still, Mr Holmes," said Dean Hoch. "We need to bind the wound to stop the bleeding."

Sherlock was bundled into a cab and transported to the hospital. He moaned with each jolt of the vehicle. At the hospital there was the painful tumult of removing him from the cab and transporting him inside. Hands and faces came and went in a blur. Then he heard Dr Burton's gruff voice and he turned his face to look at the doctor.

"Stay with me, Sherlock. I have to see what we have here," Dr Burton said as he removed the bloody bandages. "Johnson, get over to Fulbourn quick and find Dr Mackenzie, wherever he is. Tell him I have Sherlock Holmes here."

"Nasty bite, a lot of tearing. Quite a bit of bleeding. Where's the animal that bit him?" Dr Burton said.

"A man shot and killed him," a voice said.

"Damn him," Dr Burton said. "Who are you?"

"Victor Trevor. It was my dog that bit him," he responded.

"Had your dog been acting strangely?" Dr Burton asked as he continued to examine the wound.

"Well, he broke his leash and ran off and bit this chap for no reason. He's never done that before. I admit I was impatient with him. I needed to get him back so I could go to Chapel, but that doesn't excuse him biting like that. Why are we discussing the dog rather than this fellow here?" Trevor said with some irritation.

"Damn it, Mr Trevor," cursed Dr Burton again. "I'm sorry, Sherlock. We need to bind you down. I know it hurts, but I can't have you moving like that. Thompson, the morphia."

Before Sherlock could protest he felt the bite of the needle in his leg and the straps being placed on his arms and legs.

"Smith, flood the wounds with iodioform. Don't suture," Dr Burton said as he washed Sherlock's blood from his hands.

Then he turned back to Victor Trevor and grabbed the young man roughly by the shoulders. He looked down at him and growled.

"Mr Trevor, it is very simple: If your dog was rabid, then there is a high probability that Mr Holmes here will die a horrible death. If the dog wasn't rabid, then Mr Holmes may limp around for a while. If I don't know, I have to treat him as if the dog was rabid and cauterize the wound which is far more painful method of treatment than I would use otherwise. I have to make the decision now before he bleeds to death."

"I'm sorry, doctor. I didn't understand the significance of your questions. Please ask me anything and I will do my best to answer."

"Was your dog acting strangely? Growling a lot? Thirsty? Afraid of water? Foaming at the mouth?" Dr Burton asked.

"I just bought him a week ago. He seemed a cute thing, but he has been rather irritable and growling and barking. They told me last night I had to remove him, but I couldn't take him home yet because there are no trains until after 5 o'clock today. I had not noticed any unusual thirst or foaming at the mouth."

"Inconclusive," growled Dr Burton. He spoke to one of his students for a moment before turning back to his patient. "Sherlock, do you understand me?"

"Yes," he replied.

"The dog may have been rabid. The safest course is to cauterize the wound. You are bleeding too much for me to wait for the morphia to take full effect. It will be very painful."

"Do it," Sherlock said.

"Open up, bite on this," Dr Burton said.

Sherlock obeyed.

"Hold him," Dr Burton told his students.

Sherlock was overwhelmed with the most searing pain shooting up through his leg. It belittled all he had felt before. He would have screamed if Dr Burton had not gagged him. The nauseating stench of burning flesh filled the room.

"Stay with us, Sherlock," came Dr Burton's voice through the wall of pain. "I need to do it again."

Pain shot through him again as they cauterized another part of the wound. Then a very distressed-looking Dr Mackenzie appeared. He was out of breath. The medical students parted to allow him through to Sherlock's side.

"Ah, Mac, dog bite, possibility of rabies. I've given him morphia but it has not reached full effect yet. I need to finish cauterizing the wound."

Dr Mackenzie took Sherlock's hand. Sherlock looked at him, but Dr Mackenzie could tell that he was barely conscious.

"This should be the last one," Dr Burton said.

Dr Mackenzie heard a small voice behind him say, "Oh my God," and he reached around with his free arm and pulled Jonathan to his side.

"Sherlock, hold on," Dr Mackenzie said. "Here it comes."

But at the next shock of burning pain the room dissolved in Sherlock's mind to a pit of hellfire populated by savage biting dogs.

"Burton, he's fainted," Dr Mackenzie said.

"Students, keep an eye on him. We don't want to lose him now," Dr Burton said.

Dr Mackenzie shifted his hand to feel for Sherlock's pulse. It was weak, but steady. One of the medical students removed the gag.

"What's happening?" Jonathan asked.

"I'll explain in a few minutes," Dr Mackenzie said.

"You might want to take the boy elsewhere and talk to him. I think we can take care of Mr Holmes now," Dr Burton said.

Dr Mackenzie agreed and he and Jonathan left the room.

"And you," Dr Burton said, turning to the stunned Victor Trevor who had witnessed the procedure from a corner. "You should leave."

"C-can I come back later and see how he is? I feel responsible," Trevor asked.

"You should feel responsible. Perhaps this will teach you to keep better control of your animals. Yes, you can come back. Mr Holmes can decide whether he will see you or not him once he's awake."

The medical students finished dressing Sherlock's ankle. Dr Burton allowed Jonathan come back in and sit with Sherlock while he spoke to Dr Mackenzie.

"How is his leg?" Dr Mackenzie asked.

"I don't think there is any permanent damage. He should stay off it a while and then he'll have a bit of a limp for some months at least. But he's young. I think it should heal well," Dr Burton said.

"You gave him morphia?" Dr Mackenzie asked.

"Yes," Dr Burton said.

"I should have warned you about that. It seems morphia aggravates his nervous condition. It causes him to have terrifying hallucinations. I am concerned about what the reaction to all this will be. It could be a serious setback."

"If I'm not to give him morphia, then what do you suggest I do?

He will be in a lot of pain for days, possibly weeks."

"We experimented with subcutaneous cocaine injections for his nerves. He did well with them. He said they caused his arm to be a numb. I did some research and discovered that Schroff and Demarle also reported that cocaine had anaesthetic properties. A Dr Fauvel in France began using a cocaine preparation as a local anaesthetic almost ten years ago."

"Hmmm. I have some, though I have not experimented with it yet. We could try injecting right into the calf muscle," Dr Burton said.

"That should work," Dr Mackenzie said.

"I'll let the morphia wear off first," Dr Burton said. "Mac, I know how you feel about it, but I had to bind him for the cauterization. If he'll react badly to the morphia then I don't want to release him yet. I don't want him to further damage that leg."

"I'll stay with him," Dr Mackenzie said.

Jonathan looked up as Dr Mackenzie returned to the bedside.

"He'd been doing better," Jonathan said.

"Yes?" Dr Mackenzie said as he sat down next to the unconscious Sherlock.

"We fenced yesterday morning. We couldn't Friday because of the rain."

"Did it go well?"

"He was in good form. Some of the other college students watched and he spoke to them afterwards."

"And?" Dr Mackenzie asked as Jonathan hesitated.

Jonathan told him of the words exchanged between Sherlock and Lord Cecil and the brief fight. Dr Mackenzie knew that there was a stigma attached to seeking help for a nervous condition, though a visit to an asylum seem to becoming fashionable in some artistic circles. Many people in Cambridge knew Dr Mackenzie by sight and knew what his position was. In a metropolis like London it might be possible to keep such visits confidential, but Cambridge was too small for that.

"This Lord Cecil is certainly no gentleman," Dr Mackenzie said. "I'm not surprised that Sherlock was offended, though whether fisticuffs was the appropriate way for either one to handle it—"

"He is treated with more respect by folks at home," Jonathan said. "The Holmes' are important people there."

"Here he must prove himself—a common enough circumstance of men of his age coming to the University, and a factor to keep in mind."

Dr Mackenzie found Jonathan more forthcoming than he had been when they first met and they discussed Sherlock's progress and set-backs while they sat by his side.

Later Sherlock stirred. He tossed about within the restraints and cried out. He was breathing heavily and his heart was racing. Dr Mackenzie took his hand and called his name. Sherlock's eyes shot open with a confused look in them. He closed them again. Dr Mackenzie called his name again. Sherlock half opened his eyes and looked at him. He pulled his arm up against the restraint.

"Why?" Sherlock asked.

"Dr Burton had to restrain you to cauterize the wound."

Sherlock stared at him and then nodded.

"I-I remember. The dog—"

"Yes. He gave you morphia before I arrived. It caused hallucinations again, didn't it?"

"Yes."

"How do you feel?" Dr Mackenzie asked as he felt his pulse.

"My head hurts. My leg feels on fire."

"Open your eyes, please," Dr Mackenzie requested.

He checked his pupils. They were normal and responding to light.

"The morphia is wearing off," Dr Mackenzie said. "Dr Burton will be back in a little while. We have decided to try an intramuscular cocaine injection into your leg instead to see if that will numb the pain without the hallucinogenic effects of the morphia. In the meantime, tell me what you saw."

Sherlock sighed and shut his eyes.

"It was the dog. At college. Chasing me. Biting. More dogs. People pulling and pushing. Fire everywhere. My leg on fire. A hound with fangs of fire. Gnawing at my leg. A gun shot. The hound fell. A horse fell. She was gone. Sandy biting. He kicked her off. Sandy growling. Keeping him from Violet. She was on her horse. She was so close. I could see her again. So close. Why didn't I call to her then? She was so close....Why I didn't I stop her?"

Dr Burton came up beside Dr Mackenzie during Sherlock's narration and heard it evolve from recent events to the fantastic to tortured memories and feelings of guilt. He didn't comprehend it all, but he understood the desire to avoid a repetition. As Sherlock became silent. Dr Mackenzie turned to Dr Burton.

"Help me hold him down," Dr Burton said.

He pulled back the blanket covering Sherlock's injured leg and stuck the needle into the calf muscle above the bandages and turned the plunger. Sherlock jumped as they touched his leg, but with the restraints and both of them holding him he was not able to move much. Dr Burton removed the needle and they released him.

"These can go," Dr Burton said unbuckling the restraints.

Dr Mackenzie helped him and then they settled the blanket back over Sherlock. The two doctors withdrew from the bedside to talk.

"It should not take long to take effect," Dr Burton said. "There is another problem, Mac. I need to send him home tomorrow. I have this influenza. I need the space."

"He will be most comfortable in his own rooms. Jonathan can keep an eye on him and let us know if he develops any other symptoms."

"Yes, I think his boy can handle that," Dr Burton said. "I have other patients to see. I'll be back later."

Dr Mackenzie approached the bed again.

"How is your leg now, Sherlock?" he asked.

Sherlock opened his eyes and looked at him.

"It is numb. Will I be able to walk on it again?"

"Dr Burton says you should regain full use of it. You'll need to stay off it a few weeks to allow it to heal. After that you'll have a limp for a little while and a scar forever. How are you feeling otherwise?" Dr Mackenzie

"Better," Sherlock said.

"Dr Burton needs to send you home tomorrow. There's an illness going around and he's starting to run out of space. He'll show you and Jonathan how to maintain the injections and get you up on a crutch later today."

"It is probably just as well," Sherlock said.

Hours later Dr Burton drove the needle home again.

"Are you feeling well enough for a visitor this afternoon?" Dr Burton asked. "The young man who owned the dog that bit you would like to visit. He feels bad about it. He's waiting now."

"Yes, send him in," Sherlock said.

"Sherlock, this is Victor Trevor," Dr Burton said.

"Yes, I know him. We are in the same year at Sidney."

"Hello, Holmes. I'm terribly sorry about what happened. The dog had never done anything like that before. But it seemed to me that the cure was worse than the bite," Trevor said with shiver.

"You were here for that?" Sherlock asked.

"Yes, it was horrible to watch. I'm sure it must have been much worse for you," Trevor said.

"I could have sent him away," Dr Burton explained, "but I thought it might teach him to keep his animals under control."

"Well, it certainly made me feel bad about it," Victor Trevor said. "Don't worry about a thing. I've wired my father and he'll pay for the doctor bills and everything. If there is anything you need, just let me know."

Victor and Sherlock spoke for a few more minutes before Victor said he had to leave. Jonathan came again later. He brought Sherlock's mail and read it to him. Eventually Jonathan noticed that Sherlock was growing quieter and shifting in his bed uncomfortably.

"Is something wrong, sir?" Jonathan asked.

"Yes, my ankle hurts," Sherlock said.

"I will find Dr Burton," Jonathan said.

Jonathan was back in a few minutes with the burly doctor and his entourage of medical students. One student held a syringe.

"Sorry for the delay. I had some emergency surgery. A child ran out in front of the wheel of a cab," Dr Burton explained.

Sherlock pulled back the blanket from his injured leg.

Dr Burton said, "This time we are will try something new. Jonathan, I want you to come here so I can show you how to do this. I suspect that Sherlock will often inject himself. But in case there is some reason he can't, I want you to know how. Insert the needle straight into his calf here. You need to press firmly enough to pierce through the skin and into the muscle, but not too hard."

Jonathan looked dubiously at Sherlock who nodded, and said "Go ahead." So Jonathan took the syringe and did as he was instructed.

"There now, just screw down the plunger."

Sherlock winced as he did it, but was glad of the relief that followed. Jonathan smiled.

"While we are here," Dr Burton said, "I'll have my students change the dressings. Watch them, Jonathan, and learn."

The medical students proceeded to cut off the old dressings, clean the wound and wrap Sherlock's ankle in new dressings.

"Here's something else that you can help Sherlock with," Dr Burton said holding out a crutch.

Jonathan took it. Sherlock slid himself over to the side of the bed and gingerly lowered his good leg to the floor. Jonathan handed him the crutch and helped him lift his weight up on it. Dr Burton and the medical students watched.

"Now bring the crutch forward and lean into it and bring your good leg forward," Dr Burton said.

Sherlock experimented at walking in circles with Jonathan following close behind. Finally Sherlock came back to the bed and sat down again.

"It is manageable for short distances," Sherlock said.

"It's meant for necessities. I mostly want you flat on your back for the next week or so. You are not to go beyond your lodgings without my approval. If anyone wants to speak to you, they'll need to come to you."

"Yes, Doctor."

"Come on, gentlemen, we have rounds to make," Dr Burton

said to his students.

Chapter 16

Victor Trevor

The following morning Dr Mackenzie brought his carriage around and took Sherlock back to his lodgings. He and Jonathan helped Sherlock tackle the stairs on the crutch. Sitting on a window-sill in a landing between flights of stairs, Sherlock was catching his breath.

"So what are the symptoms of rabies?" he asked.

"Well, the first ones are shortness of breath and dry mouth," Dr Mackenzie said.

"Like this?" Sherlock said with a grin.

"No, when you are not trying to climb three flights of stairs on a crutch."

"Go on," Sherlock said.

"Then fever, chills and aches followed by restlessness, agitation, hypersensitivity, feelings of terror, insomnia, anxiety, confusion, and hallucinations progressing to delirium."

"I already experience many of those symptoms," Sherlock Holmes said.

"I have discussed that problem with Dr Burton. There are distinguishing factors," Dr Mackenzie said.

"So if those symptoms develop I have rabies, and then what happens?" Sherlock asked.

"Are you certain you want to hear this?" Dr Mackenzie asked.

"Yes," Sherlock insisted, standing back up and facing upstairs again. "You tell me of the horrible death I may be destined for, and I'll work on some more stairs."

"The final stages are marked by unquenchable thirst, the inability to speak or swallow, and the production of large quantities of saliva and tears. There can be muscle spasms or paralysis, delirium, and irregularities in breathing and heartbeat."

"And?" Sherlock prompted him.

"Death usually occurs about a week after the first symptoms appear."

"How?"

"Sometimes death is due to the heart merely stopping. In other cases the patient experiences muscle spasms in the throat which effectively choked him to death."

"So it would make taking arsenic seem like fun," Sherlock said.

"No. Just because something is a more terrible way to die doesn't make poisoning yourself fun. You should know that," Dr Mackenzie responded with irritation.

"Haven't you ever been curious about what it's like to die?" Sherlock asked.

"I assume I'll find out soon enough. What is the purpose of this morbid talk? Are you trying to tell me something?" Dr Mackenzie asked.

"No," Sherlock said leaning against the wall and turning to face Dr Mackenzie. "I'm tired of climbing these stairs and am bored out of my mind. I don't know if I'll be alive in three weeks. So contemplating my future beyond then seems a little absurd, even though right at the moment I have no desire to die. Rabies and death are just the topics uppermost in my mind at the moment. So that's what I am talking about."

"That is understandable," Dr Mackenzie said, making a mental note that the drug might be impairing Sherlock's ability to judge what might be socially acceptable topics of conversation on a semi-public staircase. He wondered how far this conversation was carrying up and down the stairwell.

Just then Victor Trevor bounded up the stairs.

"Ah, Holmes, they said you had gone back to your rooms," Trevor said.

"'Going' is more accurate," said Sherlock, "since I am still one flight short."

"Well, here, Doctor, why don't you get his arm on one side and I on the other and we'll give the crutch to the boy. I think this way we can make faster going of it.”

It was much faster and they soon had Sherlock resting on his own bed.

“Thank you, Trevor, the stairs were quite tiresome,” Sherlock said. “Dr Mackenzie, have you been introduced to Victor Trevor?”

“I don’t believe so,” Dr Mackenzie said.

“Ah, he’s the one to whom credit is due for this adventure,” Sherlock Holmes said.

“I shan’t take ‘credit’ for it when ‘blame’ is more accurate,” Victor said.

“Dr Mackenzie, meet Victor Trevor, owner of the dog that froze upon my ankle yesterday morning. Though I suppose ‘former owner’ of the ‘former dog’ is more accurate since I was told the dog was unwisely shot. At least it seems unwise from my current perspective though it didn’t seem so at the time. Victor, meet my friend, Dr George Mackenzie. He is brilliant doctor, researcher, writer, lecturer, etc., etc., an astute observer and reasoner, but a poor conversationalist on staircases.”

“Is he right in the head, Doctor?” Victor asked.

“It is the pain medication,” Dr Mackenzie responded. “Dr Burton increased it for the journey here. It is catching up with him now that he is lying down. It will wear off.”

“Which is a pity since I feel positively brilliant at the moment,” Sherlock said.

“I can testify to the fact that you don’t sound as brilliant at this moment as you think you are,” Dr Mackenzie said.

Trevor laughed.

“Well, I need to be going. I just wanted to see how you were getting along. Good day, Holmes,” Trevor said.

“Good day, Trevor,” Sherlock Holmes responded.

“If I weren’t in such a good mood, doctor, I’d be offended by your contradicting me like that,” he said to Dr Mackenzie after Trevor left.

“Precisely. I think perhaps Dr Burton overdid it a bit. I think your judgment is impaired at the moment and you can’t tell a brilliant thought from a ridiculous one. They both seem equally good to you," Dr Mackenzie said.

Sherlock raised his eyebrows.

"And who is to know the difference?" he asked.

Dr Mackenzie laughed.

"Keep your remarks cryptic enough and no one will. But sometimes it is best to follow Pascal's advice and keep silent if you want people to think well of you. Enough philosophy though. Let's get you situated before it wears off."

Dr Mackenzie helped Sherlock off with his boot, his trousers and his coat, and into his dressing gown and under the blankets. Then he arranged the pillows until Sherlock was comfortable.

"Let me see the bandage," Dr Mackenzie said. "No, I don't see any oozing. I think it will do for now."

"Dr Mackenzie, are you staying for lunch?" Jonathan asked. "I can serve it in here."

"Yes, I think I should keep an eye on your master here a bit longer," Dr Mackenzie said.

"He wants to see if I start foaming at the mouth," Sherlock said.

Dr Mackenzie just shook his head. But he did notice that Sherlock began slowing down over lunch and he had an appetite for it which was another sign that the drug was wearing off. After lunch Sherlock fell asleep. The move from the hospital and up the stairs had exhausted him, but the cocaine had masked that fact.

"Let him sleep a while. Dr Burton said he showed you how to do the injections," Dr Mackenzie said.

"Yes, sir," Jonathan said.

"It will be times like this when you may need to do them. If Sherlock falls asleep it will often be because the cocaine has worn off. He needs to sleep though, too. So it may be best to let him do so until the pain becomes bad enough to wake him. If he asks, you can give him an injection when he wakes up and then he should be fine. His hands might be too unsteady due to the pain to do it himself. I've prepared the syringe. The dosage is lower this time. He'll be less lively, but it should be enough to numb the pain."

Hours later Sherlock Holmes awoke. Dr Mackenzie's prediction was true and he was in much pain. Jonathan pulled back the blankets from the injured leg. He took up the syringe and laid his other hand on Sherlock's calf. Sherlock jumped.

"I'm sorry," Sherlock said. "The whole leg seems aflame. Grip it tightly. I'll do better to hold still."

Jonathan reached out again and gripped Sherlock's lower leg more firmly and drew it towards his knee, bracing it tightly between his hand, his knee and the bed. He looked for a clear spot and drove the needle in. He twisted the plunger down and then withdrew the needle and set it aside. He replaced the blankets.

"Learning doctoring now, too?" Sherlock said.

"I'll learn whatever you need me to learn, sir," Jonathan said.

"My leg hurts less," Sherlock said struggling to sit up. "Help me with these pillows. There are some letters that I should be sending," Sherlock said. "If you will bring writing implements, I shall write the letters and send you out with them. Pile the books from my desk on this table here and I will study while you are gone."

When the letters were ready and Jonathan was about to set out, Sherlock asked him to leave the door open for anyone who might call. Some of the letters were to officials at the college and Jonathan delivered them in person. Then he took the letters addressed to Sherlock's family to the post office. Before Jonathan returned the Dean and the Senior Tutor from Sidney Sussex called upon Sherlock. He set his book aside.

"Good day, Mr Holmes, I received your note," said Rev. Clowe. "Rev. Hoch and I thought we would step across and see how you were."

"I know you were in a lot of pain yesterday when I bandaged the wound in the court," Dean Hoch said.

"That was you, sir? Thank you. It is still quite painful when the medication wears off."

"I received a note from Dr Burton yesterday. He explained that there is a risk that you could develop rabies. He wants you confined to your rooms until that can be determined. But he said you were free to have visitors and were not contagious regardless of the outcome."

"Yes, that's what he told me. He would have kept me there, but the hospital is quite busy."

"Yes, I know. We have a number of undergraduates who are ill at the moment," Dean Hoch said.

"I have informed the Master and the Vice Chancellor of your circumstances," Rev. Clowe said.

"Presuming that you do not show signs of rabies, will you be able to resume you studies next term?" Dean Hoch asked.

"I believe so," Sherlock said.

"And be prepared for the May exams?" Dean Hoch asked.

"I will do my best," Sherlock said.

"Mr Trevor told me that he was willing to help you get around, and carry books or take notes for you or whatever you might need when the new term begins," Rev. Clowe said.

"Will Trevor be disciplined for having the dog?" Sherlock asked. "He really feels bad about the whole thing. He's been to visit me and he helped me mount the stairs here this morning, which was challenging on one leg."

"I can imagine that would present some difficulties," Dean Hoch said. "I think that providing whatever assistance you may need to keep up with your studies will be sufficient discipline for Mr Trevor's share in this misadventure, seeing as the dog has already been destroyed."

"Please let me know if you need any tutoring. I can give you recommendations," Rev. Clowe offered.

"I will, sir."

"Very good. I wish you a speedy recovery, Mr Holmes," Dean Hoch said.

"Thank you, sir."

"Good day."

The following day Victor Trevor came by to visit again. This time he noticed the epees and the fencing masks stacked in a corner of Sherlock's bedroom.

"I heard about you and your boy fencing in Hall Court."

"Yes. We are not likely to be doing that for a while."

"No, I suppose not. Any other sports?"

"I've done some boxing in the past, but not recently."

"Ah, maybe after your leg gets better we can go a few rounds."

"Certainly."

"Of course, that explains it."

"Explains what?"

"The rumour about how you laid out Lord Cecil."

"I think 'laid out' is a bit of an exaggeration. He was still standing when he left."

"You know how rumours are. It doesn't matter anyway. He's an arrogant blighter. He deserved to get laid out. So it is just as well that's what people are saying. I heard it wasn't exactly Marquis of Queensbury rules."

"If you heard correctly then you heard that he grabbed me from behind, which certainly isn't Queensbury."

"They say he said some nasty things to you."

"The only thing he said about me was that Dr Mackenzie visits me sometimes, which, as you now know, is true."

"Dr Mackenzie seems like a nice man and you don't seem loony to me. But they say you said some remarkable things about Hamley, like you knew things that other people didn't. How did you know those things about Lord Cecil?"

Sherlock Holmes chuckled.

"You are from Norfolk though you are currently lodging in Hobson Street. Besides the boxing, which you already mentioned, you have done a bit of rowing, and took up rugger last term. You are reading Mathematicals, which you hate, and you are fond of chocolates. You are an only child."

"That is amazing! It is all true. Tell me how you know it."

"Callosities on your palms are characteristic of the rowing man. The pattern of bruises and the occasional stiffness of your neck and shoulders during the term suggested a team contact sport. These things together with the amount of mud you occasionally accumulated tell me that you are new at the game and spend a fair amount of time on the ground. Since we have a number of lectures together, the course of your study was obvious."

"And the chocolates?"

"Every time you've come to visit you've had a spot of it somewhere, like the one currently on the underside of your right thumb."

Victor Trevor turned his thumb over and looked. Then he licked off the spot of chocolate he found there.

"Can you do that with anyone? Just stand out on the street corner and tell things about people?"

"My brothers and I did it as a game."

"Remarkable! I wish I could do that. Well, I must be off. I have to meet with my tutor."

The following afternoon Trevor was back.

"Hullo, Holmes. How's your ankle?"

"It is still quite painful. It's hard to get in a comfortable position with it. How's your tutoring coming?"

"It is probably not as painful as your leg, but it is not pleasant either. I don't like his attitude. I admit that I need some help, but I don't care being treated like a complete idiot. I may have to find another tutor," Trevor said as he pulled a pipe and tobacco pouch out of his pocket. "Do you mind?"

"No, go ahead. Jonathan was about to bring my tea. Will you join me?"

"Certainly! It is rather neat that you have your own boy rather than the irascible gyps and sour-faced bedders in college. My landlady is nice enough but it's not the same as having a boy at your beck and call," Trevor said as he jammed a plug of tobacco in his pipe with his finger. "Is he a good cook?"

"Yes, if you are looking for basic Yorkshire fare and you don't mind a rather limited menu. He was taught by my father's cook, though I believe he had learned some from his mother before that."

"Yes, sir," Jonathan confirmed as he brought the tray in.

"You're from Yorkshire?" Trevor asked after Jonathan had gone.

"Yes, though I've lived in London and France as well, and visited a few other countries on the Continent."

"Never done much travelling myself. My father did when he was a young man. He doesn't talk about it much. I think he's afraid it might give me the urge to wander. I had an older sister. She died of diphtheria while she was visiting an aunt in Birmingham. It rather put the willies in my father about letting me travel any. He owns an estate near Donnithorpe and until I came here he kept me pretty close to home. If I don't drop him a note every day, he has a panic. But I suppose you know all that already. Probably given away by ink on my finger or a spot of dust on my nose, eh?" Trevor teased.

Sherlock Holmes smiled, and he and Victor Trevor went on talking for a while over the tea things. Later Trevor reluctantly confessed that he had to go.

"I should get to my reading. Not that it will make a lot of difference, but I should try."

"If there is anything you think I can help you with, let me know," Sherlock said. "I'm obviously not doing much else but studying myself."

"That is good of you. You wouldn't mind if I brought my books by tomorrow evening and picked your brain?"

"Not at all."

Trevor came by each evening and studied with Holmes. Sometimes they fell into talk of other things as well.

"Look, Holmes, I hate to say so," Trevor said at the end of the term, "and I hope you don't take it the wrong way, but I'm rather glad my dog bit you. You've helped me enormously. I'll never be a Wrangler, but it all makes a lot more sense to me. I've given the old tutor the boot. I've rather enjoyed our talks. I haven't gotten to know a lot of the other men here yet. I'm hoping you wouldn't mind if I drop by now and then during the break just to visit."

"I would like that. I'm not going anywhere myself. Since I'm not showing any symptoms of rabies, I'm going to accept your offer to assist me next term."

"I'd be glad to help you get around to lectures when you are up to it."

On the evening of the ninth day of his isolation Sherlock called Jonathan to his bedside. He was holding the syringe and the small bottle of cocaine.

"Have you heard from the doctors today?"

"No, sir."

"This is the last of the drug," he said as he filled the syringe and jabbed it into his leg. He closed his eyes for a moment as it took effect. "That will last a while, but I have none for tomorrow." He took up a pencil and a slip of paper and scribbled a note. "Take this to Dr Burton at the hospital.

"Yes, sir."

Jonathan returned a half hour later.

"Dr Burton said he would call upon you tomorrow morning."

"No other response?"

"No, sir."

The following morning Jonathan ushered the burly doctor into Sherlock's room.

"How are you feeling?" Dr Burton asked.

"My ankle hurts," Sherlock said.

"Not an unexpected result when a dog tries to have it for breakfast," Dr Burton said as he unwrapped the bandages. "It looks like the wound is healing nicely. You were lucky that your boot protected the Achilles tendon. Tears to the muscle will heal much faster than injury to that would have. No symptoms of rabies?"

"I have not noticed any."

"Neither Dr Mackenzie nor your boy report any either," the doctor said re-wrapping Sherlock's ankle. "You can start getting around with that crutch. Don't be afraid to put some weight on that leg sometimes. Have you tried standing on it?"

"No."

"Well, let's try it."

"It hurts already."

"As bad as a week ago?"

"No."

"Then stand on it."

"It is quite painful. I used the last of the cocaine last night."

"Dr Mackenzie asked me not to give you any more."

"Why?"

"He is concerned about continuing it too long. We know so little about how it works."

"But it does work."

"Don't waste your breath arguing with me about it," Dr Burton said. "Dr Mackenzie's the one you need to convince. I'll bow to his judgment on this and he can be mighty stubborn once his mind is made up. You'd be better off sending your boy down to the market for some ice or just bucking up and bearing with it."

"Dr Mackenzie was right."

"About what?"

"You don't dispense much pity."

"No. I don't have any time for it. My business is healing folks. Your business is studying."

"The new term starts in two weeks. Trevor has offered to help me hobble to lectures," Sherlock said.

"That's the ticket. I'll tell the Dean that you are free to come and go," Dr Burton said as he packed up his bag.

That afternoon when Victor Trevor came by he found Sherlock Holmes in the sitting room with his leg propped up on the sofa surrounded by towels packed with ice.

"Ah, you've abandoned the bedroom."

Sherlock told him the news.

"You don't seem terribly happy about it."

"My leg hurts and the doctors won't allow me any more of the drug I was taking."

"Then we'll just have to think of things to take your mind off it."

"Like what?"

"I'll think of something," Trevor said with a devious looking grin.

After supper Trevor returned with a basket. He set it on the floor of the sitting room and pulled a paper from his pocket.

"I have here the list of lectures for the Easter Term," he said handing the paper to Sherlock.

Sherlock glanced at the list briefly and set it aside.

"What's in the basket?" he asked.

"Do you mean to tell me that your psychic abilities have not allowed you to divine the contents of the basket? Sidgwick would be disappointed in you!" Trevor teased.

Sherlock laughed.

"Beyond the chocolate fingerprints on the handle which I can see from here, and which most likely are indicative of both the nature of some of the contents and the fact that they have been 'tested,' I can't determine anything further without inspecting the basket closer," he responded.

"Allow me do the examination," Trevor said pulling the cloth off the top of the basket and drawing things out of it. "Here we have the ingredients for a party, a small party, but a party nonetheless. We are celebrating your survival of the dog bite and your release from quarantine. I have blown my allowance on this and shall have to confess my sins to Dad, but I have no doubt that he will forgive me once he understands it was for a good cause. It is an international feast. We have here a bottle of champagne. That's French, isn't it? You said you have been to France. Here are the aforementioned chocolates, which I was told were imported from Belgium, and which are quite good, a bit of cheese from Switzerland, a sausage from Germany and a bag of walnuts for the domestic contribution. I did not forget the crackers and the picks; otherwise we'd have to smack the walnuts with mathematical texts, which are certainly dense enough to do the trick in my opinion. And here, a gift for you. I don't know if you shall like it, but it was all I could think of."

Victor Trevor handed Sherlock Holmes a small box with string tied around it. Sherlock untied the string and opened the lid. Inside wrapped in tissue paper was a briar pipe and a pouch filled with tobacco.

"I've never tried it, Trevor," Holmes said as he lifted it out.

"Well, try it and see if you like it. You need to inhale it slowly at first until you get the knack. Here let me show you how to pack it and light it. You have to draw the air and the flame into the tobacco to light it."

After a few tries Sherlock succeeded in lighting the pipe. He coughed the first time he inhaled the smoke.

"It's different once you master it. Well, set it aside for now. Let's open the champagne," Trevor said unwiring the cork and letting it fly.

Jonathan brought glasses for them and the two young men spent the evening drinking the champagne and eating the delicacies had Trevor brought. Later when the champagne bottle was empty and the floor of the sitting room littered with walnut shells and plates of crumbs, Sherlock tried lighting the pipe again. He had more luck with it this time and the two of them carried on talking, laughing and smoking their pipes for hours. Eventually Sherlock began to tire and Trevor looked up at the clock.

"Good heavens, it is hours past curfew. I shall be fined at the very least, probably gated."

"Is your landlady a strict one at keeping your times?"

"Oh, she's a motherly sort and seeing this is my first offense I can probably talk her in to putting me down as returning before twelve, if not before ten. It's the proctors I'm concerned about."

"I've heard they go to bed at midnight."

"I don't believe it."

"Stay here tonight then and square it with your landlady in the morning," Sherlock said. "You can have the sofa. We have an extra blanket. Jonathan will get it for you."

Victor Trevor agreed. He helped Sherlock hobble back to his bed and then he curled up on the sofa in the sitting room. In the morning Jonathan provided both young men with coffee before Trevor scurried off.

174

Chapter 17

College Life

"At first it was only a minute's chat, but soon his visits lengthened
Sherlock Holmes, The *Gloria Scott*

The first morning of the Easter Term Victor Trevor breakfasted with Sherlock Holmes again. Then they descended the stairs of Sherlock's lodging house and worked their way across the street to attend Morning Prayers in the Sidney Chapel before heading on to lectures. Sherlock manoeuvred gamely on his crutch but it slowed him considerably. Victor carried Sherlock's books and notes and opened doors for him as he carried on a nearly constant stream of babble. When Trevor did not have an anecdote or a joke to tell, he quizzed Holmes about his observations of people they passed on the streets. Sherlock Holmes found his company amusing and it distracted him from the pain in his leg and the difficulties in getting around.

After lectures they compared notes. Trevor was fascinated by Holmes' insights into the lectures and his occasional witty remarks about the lecturers themselves. Trevor's admiration and attention also inspired Sherlock to follow the lectures with greater concentration if for no other reason than to impress his friend.

The first evening the two young men arrived slightly late for supper at the Hall. Only two seats were open at the freshman table, one at the end and one on the side next to it. Holmes hobbled up to the end seat and sat down and pushed his crutch under the table. Trevor took the seat to his left. The scholar at the other end of the table welcomed Sherlock Holmes back. Holmes thanked him. Musgrave, who was sitting to his right hand, spoke up.

"While you were quarantined Trevor has been regaling the whole table with tales of your amazing deductive powers," Musgrave said.

"Merely the application of logic to observations," Sherlock Holmes said.

"He is far too modest," Trevor insisted. "Just today while trying to navigate across the street to the college with his bad leg he just casually remarks that a man doffing his hat for no particular reason was offering his services as an artist's model. Well, I just couldn't let that go. I had to run over and ask the man."

"Leaving me in the middle of the street with my crutch," Holmes said, earning a laugh from the other young men at the table.

"Holmes was right! The man pointed me to a painting of the patriarch Abraham on display in a shop in Green Street. He said he was currently available for sittings if I was an art student, to which I was forced to demur. I should not have doubted Holmes, but I find his skill at this a constant source of amazement."

As dinner was served, the other men at the table asked Sherlock Holmes how he had come to that conclusion. He explained and gave other examples of observable signs of other occupations. For the first time since Sherlock Holmes had come to Sidney Sussex, he felt like a member of the college rather than an outsider.

As Sherlock hobbled from the Hall with Victor Trevor the next day, Orford, a second-year man, approached.

"I say, Holmes, Trevor, I'm having a few men over to wine this evening at my rooms in college. You're welcome to join us."

Sherlock hesitated, but Victor responded with enthusiasm.

"Let's do it, Holmes. It sounds like fun. You can demonstrate your amazing deductive powers."

"You are beginning to make me sound like a street conjurer."

"Something like that," Victor Trevor said unabashedly.

Orford laughed.

"I'm sure there will be other interesting fellows there as well. I've invited quite a mix from several colleges and you never know who else might wander in."

Sherlock Holmes finally surrendered to Trevor's urging and the two of them joined the throng at Orford's rooms. The conversation was wide ranging. A group about the sandwiches was having a theological debate; at the cake it was politics. As Trevor and Holmes were exploring the punch bowl, one man said, "Richardson's going in for stinks, I believe."

"What on earth is that?" Trevor interjected.

"Don't you know? Chemistry and all that sort of thing. Natural Science, I believe they call it. You can take a degree in that, an eminently useful and interesting study for those whose minds incline towards such pursuits."

"Oh, but those scientific fellows are of some practical use," another said.

"How? They don't help us to live, except the mechanical part of them. They contribute a little to our comfort," a third said, setting off an argument among his fellows as Holmes and Trevor listened.

"But hydrostatics, and dynamics and all those things, come into practical use."

"Of course, all those minor branches are useful, but what's the use of all their complicated problems, differential calculus, and all those other things that one hears about, but doesn't even understand the meaning of?"

"Advantage of knowledge."

"Well, I suppose it amuses them, and doesn't do us any harm. But I must say I'm all for utility."

"I suppose you don't think much of geology then?"

"No, not much; it's curious, perhaps, to know that we began by being zoophytes, if we're to believe all these fellows tell us. But I think half the things they assert as undisputed facts are mere matters of surmise."

"Surmise! Not at all. They have certain facts they go by and deduce their inferences from perfectly legitimate sources."

"Oh, that's all very well for abstract reasoning. But when you have facts to go by—"

"When you find the same remains in the same relative position in all parts of the world, common sense shows that there's nothing strained in the arguments they deduce from their discoveries."

"Oh, I quite agree that their arguments may be very logical and very plausible, if you follow them in their own line."

"Enough twaddle, there's a game of whist starting up."

"That's logic I can follow."

With that the group adjourned to another room leaving Holmes and Trevor to wander about until another of their college called to them and began quizzing Holmes on this skill he had at determining the occupation of strangers.

"It begins," Sherlock Holmes said, "with the observation of trifles about the person and reasoning back to the source of those trifles." He proceeded to give some examples as others joined the group. It was an entirely different experience than the breakfast in the Michaelmas Term and by the end of the evening Holmes had to admit that he was glad Trevor had convinced him to go.

Trevor often stayed to study in the evenings after helping Holmes back to his rooms following supper. Much to Jonathan's dismay, Sherlock began to follow Victor's habit of lighting up his pipe as the two young men studied. With a scowl and a cough Jonathan threw open the window to release the smoke that filled the sitting room one evening. Sherlock looked up.

"You may retire, Jonathan," he said. "We'll see to things."

Jonathan lit the lamp in his little closet off the kitchen. He curled up with a book with one ear listening to the young men talking and laughing in the sitting room. Victor left for his own lodgings by quarter to ten to avoid the wrath of the proctors and Sherlock went off to his bedroom shortly thereafter. Then Jonathan crept out to make sure that everything was put away, the lamps were out, and the door latched before blowing out his own lamp and closing his eyes.

When Dr Mackenzie visited on Thursday, Sherlock was out.

"How is he?" Dr Mackenzie asked Jonathan.

"Quite well. He's eating and sleeping and his leg is improving, or at least he complains of it less," Jonathan said.

"No attacks? No nightmares?"

"None that I know of."

"Is he studying?"

"Yes. Mr Trevor helps him to the lectures and the two of them study together."

"Are they getting along?" Dr Mackenzie asked.

"Yes. I think Mr Trevor is good for him. Mr Sherlock is sounding a lot more like he did before — before things happened."

"It all sounds quite good. He had seemed in better spirits the last few times I was here. Perhaps more interaction with young men of his own age is exactly what he needs. I will suspend my visits for now. You both know where to find me if I'm needed."

"Yes, sir."

In a few weeks Sherlock Holmes was able to stand on his injured leg for short periods, but walking continued to be awkward and painful, and climbing stairs was still difficult. With Victor helping him, Sherlock managed to attend all his lectures in the Easter Term, and Victor's requests for assistance prompted Sherlock to keep up with his reading and distracted him from other thoughts. Trevor was in the Boat Club and Sherlock had some time to himself when Victor was rowing. Practice for the boat races increased as May Week approached. Victor invited him to watch, but Sherlock begged off claiming he needed some time to rest his leg. While that was true, it was also true that Sherlock wasn't much interested in team sports, a sentiment he had learned not to express around the university.

"You are coming to watch the May Week boat races, aren't you?" Victor said one day.

"Well, it is still rather a challenge for me get around," Sherlock responded.

But Victor Trevor wasn't taking no for an answer.

"Watching the boat races is obligatory! You must support Sidney! You don't need to follow along the tow path. Just watch from the shore. Take Jonathan with you to help you get around. It will be fun! You absolutely must come watch us!"

While Sherlock himself was not much interested in the May Week boat races or the surrounding spectacle which he had heard tales of from his brothers, it did seem to mean a lot to Trevor. So he agreed to watch the races.

Cambridge University and nearby parts of town were dominated by men, mostly young men. The company of so many men of his age had been a new experience for Sherlock Holmes, but it was something he was growing accustomed to, especially since Victor Trevor had drawn him more into college life. His mobility still being rather limited, most of his interactions with the other young men at the college revolved around Chapel, Hall, lectures and supervisions.

May Week was different. May Week included not only the boat races on the Cam between crews from the different colleges of the university, but a whole host of accompanying parties and events. The town and the university were festooned for the occasion, and friends and relatives of many of the graduates and undergraduates were expected to visit. But there was one aspect of May Week that Sherlock was not prepared for. Perhaps his brothers had intentionally failed to mention it and perhaps Victor Trevor was himself ignorant of it.

As Sherlock and Jonathan approached the shore of the Cam they saw it was lined with parasols, and the parasols were held by women. Some were older women, mothers and aunts of undergraduates; but the majority of them were young women who were no doubt using the event as an opportunity to attract suitors. As this thought crossed Sherlock's mind, Jonathan bumped his unencumbered arm. Sherlock looked around at him.

"I'm sorry, sir. I stumbled," Jonathan said.

Something out of the corner of Sherlock's eye caught his attention. It was Victor Trevor waving frantically from the opposite shore.

"There's Trevor," Sherlock said pointing. "It looks like he wants us to cross. Here, you precede me and be my pilot through the crowd. We need to cross that bridge."

Jonathan went ahead and Sherlock placed his free hand on Jonathan's shoulder and worked the crutch with the other hand. Slowly they wormed their way across to Victor Trevor.

"Ah, you made it! Holmes this is grand! I've talked the rest of the Boat Club into making you an honorary member for the week in compensation for your injury. You can watch from over here rather than being trampled by the crowd."

"Thank you."

The group near the Boat House consisted entirely of students. They included the current eight-man rowing team, and other rowers, as well as other members of the Boat Club who really weren't the rowing type, but didn't have out-of-town guests. Holmes joined this latter cluster.

Having delivered Sherlock to his destination, Jonathan found a spot out of the way to sit down and watch the goings-on. He was within sight of Sherlock, who could signal if he needed him. Jonathan was glad that Trevor had talked Holmes into bringing him. He had never seen anything like this. There were festivals in the dale back in Yorkshire, but none that reached this magnitude. He was amazed at the number of people he could see as he looked down the river and he knew there must be many more further down where the river meandered out of sight. These were not farmers and simple folk, but well-dressed ladies and gentlemen of means. There were more beautiful young women lining the opposite shore than he had ever seen anywhere in his life. He realized that was what made Sherlock pause, and he noticed now that his master avoided looking in that direction. But Jonathan wasn't worried about him. He could see that Sherlock was engaged in conversation with some of the other students. Listening to the people around him, Jonathan got the gist of the rules of the race and looked forward to the start.

The boat races at Cambridge were "bump" races. All the boats were started down the river at the same time with two lengths between them, the order determined by the previous year's races. When an aft boat overtakes or makes contact with a fore one, a "bump" was declared and both boats were removed from the river and the following day the order of the two boats was reversed. The first boat was called the "head of the river" and their goal was to keep in front of all the other boats. The goal of most of the boats was to bump a boat ahead of them on each of the four days of the races. Many of the supporters of a boat ran along the tow path next to the river during a race to keep the boat in sight until it had bumped or been bumped and then retired to picnics, dinners, balls and other forms of entertainment for the remainder of the day.

Jonathan watched as the first boat appeared round the corner, followed on the towing-path by a moving mass of parti-coloured supporters of different boats. The boats which had made their bumps rowed past with flags displayed in their sterns, and the multitude dispersed to return the next day after lectures. Sherlock begged off from the parties and balls due to his leg but he did come to the Boat House on each of the four days of the races.

There amongst the crowds of undergraduates, Sherlock Holmes had others inquiring about his deductions. One of the questioners was Sir Thomas Ripley, a son of a baronet, who was amongst Lord Cecil's entourage. Separated from Lord Cecil and his entourage Ripley seemed pleasant enough and quite intelligent. He found Holmes' conversation quite stimulating.

As Sherlock and Jonathan were on their way back to their lodgings after the last of the races, Sherlock suddenly made Jonathan stop and be silent. They could hear Thomas Ripley and Cecil Hamley talking around the corner of a building.

"You have to admit that he has talent," Ripley said.

"Oh, I do," Cecil Hamley yawned. "He is quite talented. For portions of the last two terms he has rested in the comfort of his lodgings and attended no lectures, Chapel or Hall, and yet he's not been sent down. That requires some talent."

"The bloody dog bit him!"

"Convenient, wasn't it? Staged right in front of the whole college. I wonder what kept him from the Little Go in the Michaelmas term? That seems to have been very hush-hush. But mind me, you can place your money that some occurrence will prevent Mr Sherlock Holmes from completing the Mays as well."

"Bosh!"

"Just remember I told you! But I've must hurry off now. I have an appointment at the Hoop."

"He was right about the ADC."

"Hush!"

"You are willing to say anything about someone else, but won't hear a word of truth about yourself."

"Truth? Truth is what I say it is."

"That cuts it for me, Hamley. Lord or no lord, I've had enough of your nonsense."

"So be it then. Go where you will. I'm off to the Hoop."

Then there were only footsteps going away and after a few minutes Sherlock and Jonathan continued on.

If Lord Cecil had placed the bet he had proposed, he would have lost. No new event prevented Sherlock from sitting for the May exams. He was still using the crutch by exam week, but he was walking nearly normally. He limped to his first exams, but he did well on them, ranking in the first class.

"Oh, Holmes, now you should be burned for witchcraft," Trevor told him on the last day of exams.

"They don't burn witches in England anymore," Holmes replied.

"Regardless, Lord Cecil says you couldn't possibly be deducing these things. Now he's decided it is some type of sorcery."

"Not reading for the Natural Science Tripos, is he?" Holmes snorted.

"No. Classics, I believe," Trevor said.

"That seems appropriate. He's a little behind the times. Will he convene a tribunal to condemn me?"

"Don't put it past him."

"Lord Cecil must be bored out of his mind if he has nothing better to do than make up stories about me."

"Oh, he spreads rumours about everyone. Some he hears. Some he makes up. But the ones about you are the most entertaining. The best one he told on me was that I threw a game of rugger by intentionally missing the ball. I know he didn't see the game. I swear that I did not intentionally slide ten feet with my face in the mud to avoid that ball. I slipped. But speaking of bored.... What are your plans for the Long Vacation?"

"I am going to visit my brother in London."

"You should come to visit me in Norfolk first!" Trevor said.

"Are you certain?" Holmes asked.

"Yes, yes. I insist you come for the first month! My mother died quite a few years ago. So it is just the two of us, my father and me. It would be jolly good to have you to visit. I can show you around the place. Donnithorpe is not a bustling town like Cambridge, but we have some fine hunting and fishing out there."

"That would be a capital idea."

"I shall wire my father and arrange it, but you should consider it settled."

Chapter 18

Donnithorpe

*"And that recommendation... was the very first thing which ever made me feel
that a profession might be made out of what had... been the merest hobby."*
Sherlock Holmes, The *Gloria Scott*

Donnithorpe was a little hamlet just to the north of Langmere,
in the country of the Broads. Victor Trevor went ahead a few days
early while Sherlock made arrangements with Mr Darley and
sent Jonathan back to Yorkshire on a train. Then abandoning the
crutch, Holmes limped onto a Great Eastern Railway carriage and
headed towards Donnithorpe. Victor met him at the station with a
cart and he pointed out the sights as they drove to the estate.

"We'll take the boat out tomorrow and do some fishing. As you
might have guessed, Dad and I are not the scholarly types who
collect postage stamps or some such. My father has a small library,
but we spend most of our time outdoors."

A fine avenue of lime trees led up to the wide old-fashioned
house made of brick and oak-beams. But Sherlock found Victor's
father more interesting than the house. He was a thick-set, burly
man with a shock of grizzled hair, a brown, weather-beaten face,
and blue eyes which were keen to the verge of fierceness. Yet that
fierceness of look was not reflected in his actions and he had a
reputation for kindness and charity on the countryside. Old Trevor
was a man of some wealth with extensive landholdings. He was
the local Justice of the Peace and was noted for the leniency of
his sentences from the bench. For all his accomplishments he was
a man of little culture who knew hardly any books, but he had
travelled far, had seen much of the world and had remembered all
that he had learned.

Sherlock Holmes learned many of these things over a pole and
a hook in a boat with the Trevors. But he learned many more things
than the old man's stories told him.

One evening shortly after Sherlock's arrival, they were having a glass of port in the library after dinner, and cracking and eating nuts. Victor Trevor began telling his father of Sherlock Holmes' skill at observation and inference.

"He can tell a man's trade by his hands and something of his history by his features and attire."

"Indeed?" asked Mr Trevor.

The old man evidently thought that his son was exaggerating in his description of one or two trivial demonstrations that Sherlock had performed for Victor.

"Come, now, Mr Holmes," said the elder Trevor, laughing good-humouredly. "I'm an excellent subject. See if you can deduce anything from me."

"I fear there is not very much," Sherlock answered. "I might suggest that you have gone about in fear of some personal attack within the last twelvemonth."

The laugh faded from old Trevor's lips and he stared at Sherlock in great surprise.

"Well, that's true enough. You know, Victor," he said turning to his son, "when we broke up that poaching gang they swore to knife us, and Sir Edward Hoby has actually been attacked. I've always been on my guard since then, though I have no idea how you know it."

"You have a very handsome stick," Sherlock answered. "By the inscription I observed that you had not had it more than a year. But you have taken some pains to bore the head of it and pour melted lead into the hole so as to make it a formidable weapon. I argued that you would not take such precautions unless you had some danger to fear."

"Anything else?" he asked, smiling.

"You have boxed a good deal in your youth."

"How did you know it? Is my nose knocked a little out of straight?"

"No. It is your ears. They have the peculiar flattening and thickening that marks a boxing man."

"Anything else?"

"You have done a good deal of digging by your callosities."

"Made all my money at the gold fields."

"You have been to New Zealand."

"Right again."

"You have visited Japan."

"Quite true."

"And you have been intimately associated with someone whose initials were J. A., and whom you afterwards were eager to entirely forget."

Mr Trevor stood slowly, fixed his large blue eyes on Sherlock Holmes with a wild stare, and then pitched forward in a dead faint, with his face among the nutshells which strewed the cloth. Victor and Sherlock were horrified. They quickly undid his collar and sprinkled water on his face. He gave a gasp or two and sat up.

"Ah, boys," Mr Trevor said, forcing a smile, "I hope I haven't frightened you. Strong as I look, there is a weak place in my heart, and it does not take much to knock me over. I don't know how you manage this, Mr Holmes, but it seems to me that all the detectives of fact and fancy would be children in your hands. That's your line of life, sir, and you may take the word of a man who has seen something of the world."

"I hope I have said nothing to pain you?" Sherlock Holmes said.

"Well, you certainly touched upon rather a tender point. Might I ask how you know and how much you know?" Mr Trevor said in a half-jesting fashion, but a look of terror still lurked at the back of his eyes.

"It is simplicity itself," Sherlock Holmes said. "When you bared your arm to draw that fish into the boat, I saw that J.A. had been tattooed in the bend of the elbow. The letters were still legible, but it was perfectly clear from their blurred appearance, and from the staining of the skin around them, that efforts had been made to obliterate them. It was obvious, then, that those initials had once been very familiar to you, and that you had afterwards wished to forget them."

"What an eye you have!" the elder Trevor cried with a sigh of relief. "It is just as you say. But we won't talk of it. Of all ghosts the ghosts of our old loves are the worst. Come into the billiard-room and have a quiet cigar."

Sherlock spoke of it no more. He knew well the ghosts of old loves and they haunted him that night. As he lay in the dark of his room old Trevor's words came back to him. He had not put much thought to them at the time, so concerned had he been about his host's health. But now they flooded back full of import.

"...all the detectives of fact and fancy would be children in your hands. That's your line of life, sir..." old Trevor had said.

The ghosts in Sherlock's own mind echoed a country constable's stinging declaration: "...there's no detective on earth who could find her now."

The old memories of joy and pain, the memories that he avoided and suppressed, came unlocked and they hit him now like a gigantic wave and submerged him. In his mind he once more looked out the study window and saw Violet fighting to free herself from Moriarty's grasp. Then she was riding away and he could not catch her and the snow was everywhere, but she was gone and he was lost, forever lost.

They had hidden it from him until they could hide it no more and then they said, "...there's no detective on earth who can find her now." The truth had rent his soul and fractured his nerves. It all lived for him again from beginning to end in his mind and tortured him.

This night he was alone, alone in a room in an old house with near-strangers. There was no one here who knew of the tragedy or the effect it had had on Sherlock Holmes. There was no Jonathan, or Sherrinford, or Dr Thompkins, or Dr Mackenzie to intercede. For the first time Sherlock experienced one of the nervous attacks when he was entirely alone.

He had no concept of time. It could have lasted minutes or hours. Finally trembling and gasping for breath, he clawed his way to the surface of the wave of hallucinations and emotions. He fought the wave back from whence it came. It subsided again with the words: "...there's no detective on earth who can find her now." The words reverberated through his mind like an aftershock as he lay trembling and staring into the dark room on the bed clothes wet with sweat and tears.

Then old Trevor's words resounded through his brain with the voice of sanity and clarity: "…That's your line of life, sir…"

"…There's no detective on earth who can find her now," the fading ghosts retorted.

"…That's your line of life, sir…" came back again like a spark in the dark and kindled a fire within his soul.

"…There's no detective on earth who can find her now," echoed again.

Sherlock sat up suddenly in bed.

"There will be!" he declared aloud.

As Violet's loss had left him empty and at sea, old Trevor's words now filled him with determination and direction.

"There will be such a detective as the world has never known," Sherlock Holmes swore to the darkness.

Still shaken by the attack, Sherlock lay on the bed for a while. But he was too excited to sleep, so finally he lit a candle and stepped out into the hall. He had not gone far when he encountered Victor Trevor.

"I say, Holmes. You, too?" Victor said as they met. "Perhaps it is a trick of the light, but you are looking ghastly. Are you sure you are well?"

"Just a nightmare," Sherlock said.

"Well, come on then," Victor said and Sherlock followed him. "I was a bit shaken by the goings-on this evening and having trouble sleeping myself. I thought I'd try a bit more of the port," Trevor said extracting the decanter and a pair of glasses from a cabinet.

"What about you?" Victor said as he poured.

"It certainly was unnerving," Sherlock said. "I've never had anyone react to my observations and deductions like that. People are sometimes surprised, but never has anyone fallen over in a dead faint. Has your father ever had a fit like that before?"

"No, never," Victor said.

"I've been thinking about what he said concerning me being a detective and all. Maybe there's something to that," Sherlock said.

"You think?" Trevor asked.

"It makes sense," Sherlock said taking the glass.

"You certainly have the skills for it."

"I'd need to learn a lot more."

"But that's true of any line you go for."

"Yes."

"I suppose now would be the time to make up your mind about such a thing before you get too far along."

"That's true," Sherlock said thoughtfully.

"What would your father think of it?"

"He wouldn't like it."

"That's something to think about."

"Yes."

"Well, the port is hitting me," Trevor said. "I think I'll be wandering back to bed."

"So will I," said Sherlock.

"Then I will walk that way with you."

The following day Sherlock Holmes was excited and impatient to explore this new career, but his visit had hardly begun. He resigned himself to making the best of it. However, there had developed a touch of suspicion in Mr Trevor's manner towards him. Old Trevor did not mean to show it, but it was so strongly in his mind that it peeped out at every action. Victor remarked on it.

"You've given the governor such a turn," said Victor Trevor, "that he'll never be sure again of what you know and what you don't know."

"I should leave. I'm making your father uneasy," Sherlock said.

Victor tried to argue, but he finally had to concede that it would probably be best. He convinced Sherlock to stay two more days. Sherlock wired to Mycroft that he would be coming up early.

The day before he was to leave Sherlock Holmes and the two Trevors were sitting out upon the lawn on garden chairs basking in the sun and admiring the view across the Broads, when a maid came out to say that there was a man at the door who wanted to see Mr Trevor.

"What is his name?" asked old Trevor.

"He would not give any."

"What does he want, then?"

"He says that you know him, and that he only wants a moment's conversation."

"Show him round here."

An instant afterwards there appeared a little wizened fellow with a cringing manner and a shambling style of walking. He wore an open jacket, with a splotch of tar on the sleeve, a red-and-black check shirt, dungaree trousers, and heavy boots which were badly worn. His face was thin and brown and crafty, with a perpetual smile upon it, which showed an irregular line of yellow teeth, and his crinkled hands were half closed in a way that is distinctive of sailors. As he came slouching across the lawn Sherlock heard Mr Trevor make a sort of hiccoughing noise in his throat. He jumped out of his chair and ran into the house. He was back in a moment, and Sherlock smelled a strong reek of brandy as he passed him.

"Well, my man," said he. "What can I do for you?"

The sailor stood looking at him with puckered eyes, and with the same loose-lipped smile upon his face.

"You don't know me?" he asked.

"Why, dear me, it is surely Hudson," said Mr Trevor in a tone of surprise.

"Hudson it is, sir," said the seaman. "Why, it's thirty year and more since I saw you last. Here you are in your house, and me still picking my salt meat out of the harness cask."

"Tut, you will find that I have not forgotten old times," cried Mr Trevor, and, walking towards the sailor, he said something in a low voice. "Go into the kitchen," he continued out loud, "and you will get food and drink. I have no doubt that I shall find you a situation."

"Thank you, sir," said the seaman, touching his fore-lock. "I'm just off a two-yearer in an eight-knot tramp, short-handed at that, and I wants a rest. I thought I'd get it either with Mr Beddoes or with you."

"Ah!" cried Mr Trevor. "You know where Mr Beddoes is?"

"Bless you, sir, I know where all my old friends are," said the fellow with a sinister smile, and he slouched off after the maid to the kitchen.

Mr Trevor mumbled something to Sherlock and Victor about having been shipmate with the man when he was going back to the diggings, and then, leaving them on the lawn, he went indoors. When they entered the house an hour later, they found him stretched dead drunk upon the sofa. The whole incident left a most ugly impression upon Sherlock's mind, and he was not sorry the next day to leave Donnithorpe behind.

Chapter 19

The *Gloria Scott*

"Because it was the first [case] in which I was ever engaged."
Sherlock Holmes, The *Gloria Scott*

When he joined Mycroft in London, Sherlock said little of what had occurred at the Trevor estate or why he had left early, but he excitedly explained to his brother his determination to become a detective.

"Are you certain of this, Sherlock?" Mycroft asked.

"As I have been certain of nothing else in my life," Sherlock responded. "I will need to alter my studies radically. I have been making a list of the things I need to learn so that I may cover the subjects in a thorough fashion. It goes without saying that I need to study past crimes and the habits of criminals—"

Sherlock stopped and frowned at his brother.

"Stop looking at me like I am a specimen in a museum," he said.

"I believe that is the way I look at everyone," Mycroft said. "However, since it is rather difficult to watch myself while I am looking at other people—"

"Stop," Sherlock said waving his hand at his older brother. He jumped up and began pacing the floor. "I don't know who I would have been if things had been different. Perhaps I would have been the engineer Father hoped for, or perhaps I would have ended up as—as a bee farmer. I don't know. All I know now is that this is what I am meant to do. It feels so right that it seems impossible to me that the thought never occurred to me before.

"It is true that events of the past few years encourage this direction. However, I have no delusions that I can change the past or solve the mysteries it holds. I hope to unravel the mysteries of the future so that missing people are found and criminals pay for their crimes. And I set my course well aware that Father will most likely oppose it. I will deal with that when the time comes."

Sherlock stopped pacing and looked at his brother again.

"Does that answer all your questions?" he asked.

"It does," Mycroft said. "I believe that you will be a formidable detective."

Sherlock smiled in response.

"Then put that massive intellect of yours to work and help me plan what I need to study," Sherlock said.

"I could no doubt conjure up topics to be researched from my brain alone. However, I suggest that we consult that daily compendium of crime called *The Times*," Mycroft said.

"Ah! An excellent idea," Sherlock said.

Together the two Holmes brothers pored over *The Times* reading crime stories and analysing what information would be most useful for solving each one. When they had finished with *The Times*, Sherlock rushed out and came back with the *Daily Telegraph*, the *Police Gazette* and other newspapers. They spent the rest of the evening studying those. When they were done they looked at the list.

"So what do you already know of these things?" Mycroft asked.

"History of crime, some, biology, some, botany, a little, geology, some, physical mechanics, a great deal, chemistry, not a thing."

"Then that looks like a place to start."

"It does indeed," Sherlock said.

The following day Mycroft set off to his employment with the government as usual. Upon his return Sherlock greeted him excitedly.

"I have made some inquiries. I can immediately begin an introductory course in chemistry at St. Bartholomew's Hospital. I have wired to Father for the funds. I am sure that he will approve of my taking on additional studies during the vacation. If I do well it will provide me with an argument to change my course at Cambridge to the Natural Science Tripos. However—"

"However, you need the funds right now," Mycroft said.

"Yes, tomorrow," Sherlock said.

"I will advance you the funds and you can repay me when the

draft comes from Father," Mycroft said.

"Thank you," Sherlock said.

For the next seven weeks Sherlock studied chemistry at Bart's. There he learned the basics of the atomic theory and the periodic law and became familiar with the methods of quantitative analysis, but he also met an interesting young man by the name of Charles Stamford. Stamford was a fixture at Bart's. He had seen many medical students come and go, and yet he was the youngest student there.

Stamford's mother was a charwoman who cleaned offices at the hospital. His father had died when he was young and his mother had been afraid to leave him home while she worked lest he fall in with evil companions. So the boy had grown up within hospital walls, first silently following at his mother's heel and later being trusted to sweep floors and do other small jobs. As he grew he began to assist with cleaning the laboratories and the dissection rooms. He had no formal schooling. He knew nothing of classics or higher mathematics, but there was no one who had more exposure to medicine than he. His reading primers were discarded pharmaceutical solicitations. He learned math in the lab washing instruments and glassware. Officials at the hospital had grown fond of the lad and they were impressed by his intelligence despite his background. When he reached 13 years old they accepted him as a medical student. It was arranged that part of his fees would be waived and the remainder would be exchanged for his labour. He took a few lectures at a time. He studied by day and worked cleaning the hospital by night. This meant that his medical training proceeded slower than normal, but given his tender years that seemed reasonable.

Despite his abnormal upbringing Stamford was the most amiable, conventional fellow. He could be as curious and mischievous as any 13-year-old. His primary goal was to complete his medical training and obtain a position so that he could provide for his mother. He knew precisely how hard she had worked to raise him and the opportunities that her work had laid open to him. He was intent on repaying her.

But the upshot now was that if there was anything anyone wanted to know about Bart's, Stamford was the one to ask. He knew every nook and cranny of the building. He knew everyone who worked there, and most who had worked or studied there in the past five years. He knew all the rules and regulations. He knew what one could get away with and what one didn't dare, and whom to ask concerning what. He knew where all the equipment was and where it was supposed to be, and he definitely knew where all the bodies were buried and where to find the ones that weren't buried yet.

Stamford's age was obvious to anyone who caught sight of him in classes and many of the medical students treated him like a younger brother. Some teased him and some merely humoured him. Stamford took it all in good turn. Bart's was more than his school or his employer, it was his family.

Sherlock Holmes soon realized Stamford's special knowledge and sought to make him an ally. It would be an exaggeration to call them friends for there were no confidences between them, but Holmes knew Stamford to be a reliable source of information and respected that. It was Stamford who helped Sherlock Holmes arrange to use the laboratory for his own researches when they were not being used by medical students.

When Sherlock was not at the laboratory he could be found at the Reading Room of the British Museum around the corner from Mycroft's rooms on Montague Street. Mycroft sometimes heard Sherlock come in very late at night and often he was gone in the morning before Mycroft arose. But when the brothers did meet Mycroft found Sherlock in the highest of spirits.

One day in autumn when the Cambridge Long Vacation was drawing to a close, Sherlock received a telegram from Victor Trevor imploring him to come to Donnithorpe. Sherlock had completed his course at Bart's some weeks before and he was spending most of his time at the Reading Room of the British Museum. But he dropped everything and set out for Norfolk at once. Victor met him with the dog-cart at the station. Victor had grown thin and careworn. He had lost his loud, cheery manner.

"The governor is dying," were the first words Victor Trevor said to Sherlock.

"Impossible!" Sherlock cried. "What is the matter?"

"Apoplexy. Nervous shock. He's been on the verge all day. I doubt if we shall find him alive," Victor said.

"What has caused it?" Sherlock asked.

"Ah, that is the point," Victor said. "Jump in and we can talk it over while we drive. You remember that fellow who came upon the evening before you left us?"

"Perfectly," Sherlock said.

"Do you know who it was that we let into the house that day?"

"I have no idea."

"It was the devil, Holmes," Trevor cried.

Sherlock stared at him in astonishment.

"Yes, it was the devil himself. We have not had a peaceful hour since—not one. The governor has never held up his head from that evening, and now the life has been crushed out of him and his heart broken, all through this accursed Hudson."

"What power had he, then?"

"Ah, that is what I would give so much to know. The kindly, charitable, good old governor—how could he have fallen into the clutches of such a ruffian! But I am so glad that you have come, Holmes. I trust very much to your judgment and discretion, and I know that you will advise me for the best."

They were dashing along the smooth white country road, with the long stretch of the Broads in front of them glimmering in the red light of the setting sun. From a grove upon the left they could already see the high chimneys and the flag-staff which marked the squire's dwelling.

"My father made the fellow gardener," said Victor, "and then, as that did not satisfy him, he was promoted to be butler. The house seemed to be at his mercy, and he wandered about and did what he chose in it. The maids complained of his drunken habits and his vile language. Then dad raised their wages all round to recompense them for the annoyance. The fellow would take the boat and my father's best gun and treat himself to little shooting trips. And all this with such a sneering, leering, insolent face that I would have knocked him down twenty times over if he had been a man of my own age. I tell you, Holmes, I have had to keep a tight hold upon myself all this time; and now I am asking myself whether, if I had let myself go a little more, I might not have been a wiser man.

"Well, matters went from bad to worse with us, and this animal Hudson became more and more intrusive, until at last, on making some insolent reply to my father in my presence one day, I took him by the shoulders and turned him out of the room. He slunk away with a livid face and two venomous eyes which uttered more threats than his tongue could do. I don't know what passed between Dad and him after that, but Dad came to me next day and asked me whether I would mind apologizing to Hudson. I refused, as you can imagine, and asked my father how he could allow such a wretch to take such liberties with himself and his household.

"'Ah, my boy,' said he, 'it is all very well to talk, but you don't know how I am placed. But you shall know, Victor. I'll see that you shall know, come what may. You wouldn't believe harm of your poor old father, would you, lad?'"

"He was very much moved, and shut himself up in the study all day, where I could see through the window that he was writing busily."

"That evening there came what seemed to me to be a grand release, for Hudson told us that he was going to leave us. He walked into the dining-room as we sat after dinner, and announced his intention in the thick voice of a half-drunken man."

"'I've had enough of Norfolk,' he said. 'I'll run down to Mr Beddoes in Hampshire. He'll be as glad to see me as you were, I dare say.'"

"'You're not going away in an unkind spirit, Hudson, I hope,' said my father, with a tameness which made my blood boil."

"'I've not had my 'pology,' said he sulkily, glancing in my direction."

"'Victor, you will acknowledge that you have used this worthy fellow rather roughly,' said Dad, turning to me."

"'On the contrary, I think that we have both shown extraordinary patience towards him,' I answered."

"'Oh, you do, do you?' he snarled. 'Very good, mate. We'll see about that!'"

"He slouched out of the room, and half an hour afterwards left the house, leaving my father in a state of pitiable nervousness. Night after night I heard him pacing his room, and it was just as he was recovering his confidence that the blow did at last fall."

"And how?' Sherlock asked.

"In a most extraordinary fashion. A letter arrived for my father yesterday evening, bearing the Fordingbridge postmark. My father read it, clapped both his hands to his head, and began running round the room in little circles like a man who has been driven out of his senses. When I at last drew him down on to the sofa, his mouth and eyelids were all puckered on one side, and I saw that he'd had a stroke. Dr Fordham came over at once. We put him to bed; but the paralysis has spread, he has shown no sign of returning consciousness, and I think that we shall hardly find him alive."

"You horrify me, Trevor!" Sherlock cried. "What then could have been in this letter to cause so dreadful a result?"

"Nothing. There lies the inexplicable part of it. The message was absurd and trivial. Oh, my God, it is as I feared!"

As he spoke they came round the curve of the avenue, and saw in the fading light that every blind in the house had been drawn down. As they dashed up to the door, Victor's face convulsed with grief, a gentleman in black emerged from it.

"When did it happen, doctor?" asked Trevor.

"Almost immediately after you left."

"Did he recover consciousness?"

"For an instant before the end."

"Any message for me?"

"Only that the papers were in the back drawer of the Japanese cabinet."

Victor ascended with the doctor to the chamber of death, while Sherlock remained in the study, turning the whole matter over and over in his head. He wanted to see the letter that had frightened old Trevor so badly. If there were a hidden meaning in it, he was confident that he could pluck it forth. For an hour he sat pondering over it in the gloom, until at last a weeping maid brought in a lamp, and close at her heels came Victor Trevor, pale, but composed, with papers in his grasp. He sat down opposite Sherlock, drew the lamp to the edge of the table, and handed him a short note scribbled upon a single sheet of grey paper.

"The supply of game for London is going steadily up," it ran. "Head-keeper Hudson, we believe, has been now told to receive all orders for fly-paper and for preservation of your hen-pheasant's life."

Sherlock was bewildered at first. Then in an instant he saw that every third word, beginning with the first, would give a message which might well drive old Trevor to despair. He read the new message to Victor.

"The game is up. Hudson has told all. Fly for your life."

Victor Trevor sank his face into his shaking hands.

"It must be that, I suppose," said he. "This is worse than death, for it means disgrace as well. But what is the meaning of these 'head-keepers' and 'hen-pheasants'?"

"It means nothing to the message," Sherlock Holmes said, "but it might mean a good deal to us if we had no other means of discovering the sender. You see that he has begun by writing 'The... game...is,' and so on. Afterwards he had, to fulfil the prearranged cipher, to fill in any two words in each space. He would naturally use the first words which came to his mind, and if there were so many which referred to sport among them, you may be tolerably sure that he is either an ardent shot or interested in breeding. Do you know anything of this Beddoes?"

"Why, now that you mention it," said Trevor, "I remember that my poor father used to have an invitation from him to shoot over his preserves every autumn."

"Then it is undoubtedly from him that the note comes," said Holmes. "It only remains for us to find out what this secret was which the sailor Hudson seems to have held over the heads of these two wealthy and respected men."

"Alas, Holmes, I fear that it is one of sin and shame!' cried Victor Trevor. "But from you I shall have no secrets. Here is the statement which was drawn up by my father when he knew that the danger from Hudson had become imminent. I found it in the Japanese cabinet, as he told the doctor. Take it and read it to me, for I have neither the strength nor the courage to do it myself."

Holmes read the papers to Victor. The papers were endorsed outside: "Some particulars of the voyage of the bark Gloria Scott." On the inside was written: "My dear, dear son, now that approaching disgrace begins to darken the closing years of my life, I can write with all truth and honesty that it is not the terror of the law, it is not the loss of my position in the county, nor is it my fall in the eyes of all who have known me, which cuts me to the heart; but it is the thought that you should come to blush for me—you who love me and who have seldom, I hope, had reason to do other than respect me. But if the blow falls which is forever hanging over me, then I should wish you to read this, that you may know straight from me how far I have been to blame. On the other hand, if all should go well (which may kind God Almighty grant!), then if by any chance this paper should be still undestroyed and should fall into your hands, I conjure you, by all you hold sacred, by the memory of your dear mother, and by the love which had been between us, to hurl it into the fire and to never give one thought to it again.

"If then your eye goes on to read this line, I know that I shall already have been exposed and dragged from my home, or as is more likely, for you know that my heart is weak, be lying with my tongue sealed forever in death. In either case the time for suppression is past, and every word which I tell you is the naked truth, and this I swear as I hope for mercy.

"My name, dear lad, is not Trevor. I was James Armitage in my younger days, and you can understand now the shock that it was to me a few weeks ago when your college friend addressed me in words which seemed to imply that he had surprised my secret. As Armitage it was that I entered a London banking-house, and as Armitage I was convicted of breaking my country's laws, and was sentenced to transportation. Do not think very harshly of me, laddie. It was a debt of honour, so called, which I had to pay, and I used money which was not my own to do it, in the certainty that I could replace it before there could be any possibility of its being missed. But the most dreadful ill-luck pursued me. The money which I had reckoned upon never came to hand, and a premature examination of accounts exposed my deficit. The case might have been dealt leniently with, but the laws were more harshly administered in those days and on my twenty-third birthday I found myself chained as a felon with thirty-seven other convicts in 'tween-decks of the bark Gloria Scott, bound for Australia.

"The Gloria Scott had been in the Chinese tea-trade, but she was an old-fashioned, heavy-bowed, broad-beamed craft, and the new clippers had cut her out. She was a five-hundred-ton boat; and besides her thirty-eight gaol-birds, she carried twenty-six of a crew, eighteen soldiers, a captain, three mates, a doctor, a chaplain, and four warders. Nearly a hundred souls were in her, all told, when we set sail from Falmouth.

"The man next to me, upon the aft side, was one whom I had particularly noticed when we were led down the quay. He was a young man with a clear, hairless face, a long, thin nose, and rather nut-cracker jaws. He carried his head very jauntily in the air, had a swaggering style of walking, and was, above all else, remarkable for his extraordinary height. I don't think any of our heads would have come up to his shoulder, and I am sure that he could not have measured less than six and a half feet. It was strange among so many sad and weary faces to see one which was full of energy and resolution. The sight of it was to me like a fire in a snowstorm. I was glad, then, to find that he was my neighbour, and gladder still when, in the dead of the night, I heard a whisper close to my ear.

"'Hullo, chummy!' said he, "what's your name, and what are you here for?"

"I answered him, and asked in turn who I was talking with. 'I'm Jack Prendergast,' said he, 'and by God! You'll learn to bless my name before you've done with me.'

"I remembered hearing of his case, for it was one which had

made an immense sensation throughout the country some time before my own arrest. He was a man of good family and of great ability, but of incurably vicious habits, who had by an ingenious system of fraud obtained huge sums of money from the leading London merchants.

"'Ha, ha! You remember my case!' said he proudly.

"'Very well, indeed.'"

"'Then maybe you remember something queer about it?'"

"'What was that, then?'"

"'I'd had nearly a quarter of a million, hadn't I?'"

"'So it was said.'"

"'But none was recovered, eh?'"

"'No.'"

"'Well, where d'ye suppose the balance is?" he asked.

"'I have no idea,' said I."

"'Right between my finger and thumb,' he cried. 'By God! I've got more pounds to my name than you've hairs on your head. And if you've money, my son, and know how to handle it and spread it, you can do anything. Now, you don't think it likely that a man who could do anything is going to wear his breeches out sitting in the stinking hold of a rat-gutted, beetle-ridden, mouldy old coffin of a Chin China coaster. No, sir, such a man will look after himself and will look after his chums. You may lay to that! You hold on to him, and you may kiss the book that he'll haul you through.'

"That was his style of talk, and at first I thought it meant nothing; but after a while, when he had tested me and sworn me in with all possible solemnity, he let me understand that there really was a plot to gain command of the vessel. A dozen of the prisoners had hatched it before they came aboard, Prendergast was the leader, and his money was the motive power.

"'I'd a partner,' said he, 'a rare good man, as true as a stock to a barrel. He's got the dibbs, he has, and where do you think he is at this moment? Why, he's the chaplain of this ship—the chaplain, no less! He came aboard with a black coat, and his papers right, and money enough in his box to buy the thing right up from keel to main-truck. The crew are his, body and soul. He could buy 'em at so much a gross with a cash discount, and he did it before ever they signed on. He's got two of the warders and Mereer, the second mate, and he'd get the captain himself, if he thought him worth it.'

"'What are we to do, then?' I asked.

"'What do you think?' said he. 'We'll make the coats of some of these soldiers redder than ever the tailor did.'

"'But they are armed,' said I.

"'And so shall we be, my boy. There's a brace of pistols for every mother's son of us, and if we can't carry this ship, with the crew at our back, it's time we were all sent to a young misses' boarding-school. You speak to your mate upon the left to-night, and see if he is to be trusted.'

"'I did so, and found my other neighbour to be a young fellow in much the same position as myself, whose crime had been forgery. His name was Evans, but he afterwards changed it, like myself, and he is now a rich and prosperous man in the south of England. He was ready enough to join the conspiracy, as the only means of saving ourselves, and before we had crossed the Bay there were only two of the prisoners who were not in the secret. One of these was of weak mind, and we did not dare to trust him, and the other was suffering from jaundice, and could not be of any use to us.

"'From the beginning there was really nothing to prevent us from taking possession of the ship. The crew were a set of ruffians, specially picked for the job. The sham chaplain came into our cells to exhort us, carrying a black bag, supposed to be full of tracts, and so often did he come that by the third day we had each stowed away at the foot of our beds a file, a brace of pistols, a pound of powder, and twenty slugs. Two of the warders were agents of Prendergast, and the second mate was his right-hand man. The captain, the two mates, two warders, Lieutenant Martin, his eighteen soldiers, and the doctor were all that we had against us. Yet, safe as it was, we determined to neglect no precaution, and to make our attack suddenly by night. It came, however, more quickly than we expected, and in this way.

"'One evening, about the third week after our start, the doctor had come down to see one of the prisoners who was ill, and putting his hand down on the bottom of his bunk he felt the outline of the pistols. If he had been silent he might have blown the whole thing, but he was a nervous little chap, so he gave a cry of surprise and turned so pale that the man knew what was up in an instant and seized him. He was gagged before he could give the alarm, and tied down upon the bed. He had unlocked the door that led to the deck, and we were through it in a rush. The two sentries were shot down, and so was a corporal who came running to see what was the matter. There were two more soldiers at the door of the state-room, and their muskets seemed not to be loaded, for they never fired upon us, and they were shot while trying to fix their bayonets. Then we rushed on into the captain's cabin, but as we pushed open the door there was an explosion from within, and there he lay with his brains smeared over the chart of the Atlantic which was pinned upon the table, while the chaplain stood with a smoking pistol in his hand at his elbow. The two mates had both been seized by the crew, and the whole business seemed to be settled.

"The state room was next the cabin, and we flocked in there and flopped down on the settees, all speaking together, for we were just mad with the feeling that we were free once more. There were lockers all round, and Wilson, the sham chaplain, knocked one of them in, and pulled out a dozen of brown sherry. We cracked off the necks of the bottles, poured the stuff out into tumblers, and were just tossing them off, when in an instant without warning there came the roar of muskets in our ears, and the saloon was so full of smoke that we could not see across the table.

"When it cleared again the place was a shambles. Wilson and eight others were wriggling on the top of each other on the floor, and the blood and the brown sherry on that table turn me sick now when I think of it. We were so cowed by the sight that I think we should have given the job up if it had not been for Prendergast. He bellowed like a bull and rushed for the door with all that were left alive at his heels. Out we ran, and there on the poop were the lieutenant and ten of his men. The swing skylights above the saloon table had been a bit open, and they had fired on us through the slit. We got on them before they could load, and they stood to it like men; but we had the upper hand of them, and in five minutes it was all over. My God! Was there ever a slaughter-house like that ship! Prendergast was like a raging devil, and he picked the soldiers up as if they had been children and threw them overboard alive or dead. There was one sergeant that was horribly wounded and yet kept on swimming for a surprising time, until someone in mercy blew out his brains. When the fighting was over there was no one left of our enemies except just the warders, the mates, and the doctor.

"It was over them that the great quarrel arose. There were many of us who were glad enough to win back our freedom, and yet who had no wish to have murder on our souls. It was one thing to knock the soldiers over with their muskets in their hands, and it was another to stand by while men were being killed in cold blood. Eight of us, five convicts and three sailors, said that we would not see it done. But there was no moving Prendergast and those who were with him. Our only chance of safety lay in making a clean job of it, said he, and he would not leave a tongue with power to wag in a witness-box. It nearly came to our sharing the fate of the prisoners, but at last he said that if we wished we might take a boat and go. We jumped at the offer, for we were already sick of these bloodthirsty doings, and we saw that there would be worse before it was done. We were given a suit of sailor togs each, a barrel of water, two casks, one of junk and one of biscuits, and a compass. Prendergast threw us over a chart, told us that we were shipwrecked mariners whose ship had foundered in Lat. 15 degrees and Long 25 degrees west, and then cut the painter and let us go.

"And now I come to the most surprising part of my story, my dear son. The seamen had hauled the fore-yard aback during the rising, but now as we left them they brought it square again, and as there was a light wind from the north and east the bark began to draw slowly away from us. Our boat lay, rising and falling, upon the long, smooth rollers, and Evans and I, who were the most educated of the party, were sitting in the sheets working out our position and planning what coast we should make for. It was a nice question, for the Cape de Verdes were about five hundred miles to the north of us, and the African coast about seven hundred to the east. On the whole, as the wind was coming round to the north, we thought that Sierra Leone might be best, and turned our head in that direction, the bark being at that time nearly hull down on our starboard quarter. Suddenly as we looked at her we saw a dense black cloud of smoke shoot up from her, which hung like a monstrous tree upon the sky line. A few seconds later a roar like thunder burst upon our ears, and as the smoke thinned away there was no sign left of the Gloria Scott. In an instant we swept the boat's head round again and pulled with all our strength for the place where the haze still trailing over the water marked the scene of this catastrophe.

"It was a long hour before we reached it, and at first we feared that we had come too late to save any one. A splintered boat and a number of crates and fragments of spars rising and falling on the waves showed us where the vessel had foundered; but there was no sign of life, and we had turned away in despair when we heard a cry for help, and saw at some distance a piece of wreckage with a man lying stretched across it. When we pulled him aboard the boat he proved to be a young seaman of the name of Hudson, who was so burned and exhausted that he could give us no account of what had happened until the following morning.

"It seemed that after we had left, Prendergast and his gang had proceeded to put to death the five remaining prisoners. The two warders had been shot and thrown overboard, and so also had the third mate. Prendergast then descended into the 'tween-decks and with his own hands cut the throat of the unfortunate surgeon. There only remained the first mate, who was a bold and active man. When he saw the convict approaching him with the bloody knife in his hand he kicked off his bonds, which he had somehow contrived to loosen, and rushing down the deck he plunged into the after-hold. A dozen convicts, who descended with their pistols in search of him, found him with a match-box in his hand seated beside an open powder-barrel, which was one of a hundred carried on board, and swearing that he would blow all hands up if he were in any way molested. An instant later the explosion occurred, though Hudson thought it was caused by the misdirected bullet of one of the convicts rather than the mate's match. Be the cause what it may, it was the end of the Gloria Scott and of the rabble who held command of her.

"Such, in a few words, my dear boy, is the history of this terrible business in which I was involved. Next day we were picked up by the brig Hotspur, bound for Australia, whose captain found no difficulty in believing that we were the survivors of a passenger ship which had foundered. After an excellent voyage the Hotspur landed us at Sidney, where Evans and I changed our names and made our way to the diggings, where, among the crowds who were gathered from all nations, we had no difficulty in losing our former identities. We came back as rich colonials to England, and we bought country estates. For many years we have led peaceful and useful lives, and we hoped that our past was forever buried. Imagine, then, my feelings when in the seaman who came to us I recognized instantly the man who had been picked off the wreck. He had tracked us down somehow, and had set himself to live upon our fears."

"Oh, my God, Holmes, what tainted blood runs through my veins!" Victor Trevor cried and sank his head into his hands.

Sherlock Holmes tried to comfort his friend and stayed on through the funeral. But it soon became clear that Trevor needed to some time to himself. When Sherlock suggested that they meet back at the college, Victor told him that he wasn't going back.

"I have the money, but not the stomach for it. My whole life has been built on a lie and I need to find out who I am," Victor Trevor said.

Chapter 20

Changes

"Studying all those branches of science which might make me more efficient"
Sherlock Holmes, The Musgrave Ritual

While Victor Trevor was devastated by the lie his father had lived, and overwhelmed by the need to discover who he was, Sherlock Holmes was grateful to the old man for the light he had shed on his own future. Armed with letters from his instructors at Bart's, Sherlock headed to the North Riding of Yorkshire.

Life at Mycroft Manor had continued in both its sameness and its changes. The autumn skies were grey and the moors were purple and gold when he arrived. The grouse were fattening and the last of the harvest was coming in. In Holmes Hall, Sherrinford's son, Arthur, was toddling about with his nurse as Sherlock entered.

"Agnes," he heard his brother call, "Please keep the child in the nursery."

"Yes, sir."

"Your mother will be pleased to see you, Mister Sherlock," Thomas said. "She is in the sitting room."

"Thank you, Thomas," Sherlock said accepting the butler's hint that he should pay his respects to his mother.

She was in the sitting room working on a bit of needle work.

"Hello, Mother," Sherlock said as he entered the room.

"Oh, Sherlock, it is so good to see you! You should have written that you were coming home."

"I wasn't certain of it myself until I boarded the train. I was staying with another man from my college in Norfolk whose father just passed away. I didn't know whether I could get away before the term began."

"How is the boy taking it?"

"Very hard, unfortunately. I don't know that I was much comfort at all."

"But you tried. That's what is important. You are looking much better than you did at Christmas. How is your ankle? I noticed you were limping a little when you came in the room."

"Just a bit stiff, though it aches sometimes. I believe it will continue to improve."

"That's good. Well, you must be tired from your journey. You rest and I will tell Tessy that we have another for supper. We can talk more later."

"Yes, Mother."

Sherlock mounted the grand staircase and headed for his room, but as he reached the door he saw his brother coming from the direction of the nursery with a scowl upon his face.

"Hello, Sherrinford," he said.

"Oh, Sherlock! I didn't know you were back."

"I arrived a short time ago," Sherlock said. "You seem a bit harried."

"Just a lot on my mind," Sherrinford said. "The harvest was very busy, but not as good as I had hoped. Amanda seems to be having more problems with this second child. Dr Thompkins has insisted on complete bed rest. Arthur is wonderful, but he requires much patience. But I know you didn't come home to discuss my troubles. Tell me why you are here. I thought you weren't returning until Christmas."

"I came back to discuss something with Father before I return to Cambridge. I want to change from the Mathematics Tripos to the Natural Science Tripos. I spent most of the summer in London studying chemistry and I am far more adept at that than mathematics."

"That could delay your degree," Sherrinford said

"Perhaps. But I may have time enough. I had to cancel my first attempt at the Previous Exam—"

Sherlock stopped when Sherrinford frowned.

"Mycroft told you about the first term, didn't he?"

"Yes."

"But I intend to try again this coming term. With that out of the way I could concentrate on the new subjects. Now is the best time to change to avoid delays."

"Yes, that makes sense. Is that what you came to tell Father?" Sherrinford asked.

"In part. I'll talk with him after supper. I need to be back in Cambridge in a few days. But I should wash for supper."

The squire greeted Sherlock cordially as he entered the dining room.

"It is good to see you again, Sherlock. How are your studies progressing?"

"My course at St. Bartholomew's Hospital went very well. I would like to discuss my education with you in more detail after supper, if you have the time."

"Yes, certainly."

Then as dinner was served Sherlock shifted the conversation to some exhibits that he had seen at the British Museum during the summer.

As the meal concluded the squire stood and said, "Come, Sherlock, we will retire to my study to discuss those matters."

The squire picked up his cane and limped from the dining room. Sherlock followed, noting the irony that his own slight limp was on the opposite leg than his father's. But he also knew that the squire was the one person in the world who would not ask him about his ankle. As his father settled himself behind his desk, Sherlock sat in one of the chairs before it.

"Now what is it you would like to discuss?" Squire Holmes asked.

"I have been thinking a great deal about my education since I've been at Cambridge. After some consideration I have decided that I would like to change my course to the Natural Science Tripos. I have here letters from my instructors at St. Bartholomew's Hospital," he said drawing them out of his pocket and handing them to his father. "I believe, based on my work there, that I have more natural aptitude for science than mathematics."

Squire Holmes opened the letters and read them. A look of surprise spread over his face.

"These are quite glowing reports," he said.

"Yes, sir," Sherlock responded. "I am sitting for the Previous

Exam at Cambridge this term. I believe that now would be the most appropriate time for a change to prevent any delays in obtaining my degree."

"I can see the logic in that argument, but I think far more weight has to be given to these recommendations. I was surprised when you took the initiative during the Long Vacation. You had not shown an inclination toward additional study in the past. But these letters indicate that it was a wise decision and that your prowess may indeed lie more in the direction of science. It would be foolish to ignore their advice. As you may know, I have long had an interest in the sciences myself as a mere follower. I would be proud to have a scientist in the family. You have my blessing to switch Tripos."

"Thank you, Father," Sherlock said, and left the room with some qualms about his deception. Some small voice inside said that perhaps he could truly fulfil his father's expectations and earn his respect. But his whole soul opposed the idea of once again suppressing his own will and his own instincts in attempt to meet his father's expectations. It was the one thing in his life he had always failed at. No. He had found his own path and he would follow it.

Sherlock spent the next day sorting through the things in his room. He boxed up most of his books and some other odds and ends. He packed his collection of rocks and fossils. He extracted the case of the magnifying lens his grandfather had given him from the desk drawer. He dared not open the case, but gingerly wrapped it in wool and packed it as well. He packed more of his clothes from his closet. He left the stuffed weasel that Sherman had given him on the mantel. It seemed to belong there and taking it would make the depth of his evacuation more obvious. He didn't expect anyone to search through the drawers and closets in his room to see what he had taken. But the weasel had been a fixture for so long that it would be easily missed by anyone entering the room.

That evening after supper Sherlock walked down the road behind the manor house. As he passed the stables he paused for a moment before walking on. Always in the past he would have been greeted by his dog, Sandy, when he walked this way. But Sherrinford had written to him the previous autumn that the intrepid Sandy had been killed in an encounter with a bull. So many things had happened last autumn that it had not really registered, but now the silence did. He walked on.

When he reached the cottages, Sherlock walked down the row and knocked on the door of one. A surprised Jonathan opened the door.

"Sir! I did not know you were coming back."

"Pearl did not tell you I arrived yesterday? I thought she always knew all the news from the Hall."

"My sister married and left the manor a few weeks back. I spoke to your brother a week ago, but he hadn't heard from you."

"I was in Norfolk again. I didn't warn anyone that I was coming up."

"You could have sent for me when you arrived. I would have come up to the Hall."

"I have managed. Will you be ready to come with me tomorrow?"

"Yes, sir. I was merely awaiting your summons."

"First we will be going down to London to pick up some of my things, then on to Cambridge."

"Yes, sir," Jonathan said. "I could be packed and at the Hall within the hour."

"The morning will be fine. I will see you then," Sherlock said.

"Good evening, sir," Jonathan said.

"Good evening."

Jonathan Beckwith was a more experienced railway traveller when he boarded the southbound carriage with Sherlock Holmes the following morning than he had been the previous autumn. His experience was still very limited, but he had been quite proud to have successfully made the return trip to Yorkshire by himself at the end of the Easter Term. But as jaded as he may feel about railway travel at the ripe old age of fourteen, he had to admit to being excited at the prospect of going to London.

His expectations of actually seeing some small portion of London while he was there were thwarted by the thick fog that was enshrouding the city when they arrived. The air was dense and oily like wet wool but the smell was different. The fog trapped the smoke from coal fireplaces and factory smokestacks, and the reek of horse manure and human waste, and mixed it with the stench of commerce and manufacturing of every kind to create a porridge that the boy gagged on with his first lung-full.

Sherlock chuckled.

"Welcome to London, Jonathan."

Sherlock arranged for their luggage to be sent on to Bishopsgate station then engaged a hansom to Mycroft's rooms.

There was little to be seen as the cab wound its way through the streets. Gas lamps loomed up and faded away in the fog. The lit windows of buildings they passed were mere blurs of light in the night. Horse and driver must have found their way by instinct because street signs and landmarks were hardly visible.

Sherlock had wired a few days before that they were coming and would be spending the night before going on to Cambridge. The ever-watchful Mrs Nugent, Mycroft's landlady, intercepted them on the stairs as Sherlock was paying the driver.

"Mr Sherlock, I'm glad to see you found your way in this pea-souper. This your boy? A smart looking lad, isn't he? What's your name, boy?"

"Jonathan," he replied.

"Then come along to the kitchen, Jonathan, and we will find you something to eat and show you where you'll sleep tonight. Mr Sherlock, we'll have supper up for you and your brother shortly. Tis a miracle that your brother was willing to wait for you but he's like to be starved now."

Over supper Sherlock told his brother Mycroft about what had transpired in Norfolk and his discussion with their Father in Yorkshire.

"He approved my studying science though I have no delusions that he would approve the use I intend to make of that knowledge."

"Are you prepared to accept the consequences when he finds

out?"

"Yes."

Sherlock had left hurriedly for Norfolk when Trevor's wire had arrived. After supper he packed his belongings and then tumbled into bed. It had been a long day. But Sherlock and Jonathan were up at dawn, or at least what the clocks said was dawn. It took some time to find a cab in the fog, but at last they secured a four-wheeler and soon they and their bags were on their way to rendezvous with the luggage at the station and take the next train to Cambridge.

On Monday morning Sherlock had a meeting with Rev. Clowe and expressed his desire for the change of course. Sherlock had brought the letters from his instructors at Bart's and one from his father. He also knew that the Senior Tutor himself was a chemistry enthusiast and speculated that might help his cause.

"This is somewhat unusual," the Senior Tutor said.

"But not totally unheard of," Sherlock said.

"No. You are correct. I am quite pleased to see you turn your talents in this direction. I myself find unravelling the mysteries of science far more engaging than mathematics and I think you have the potential to make a name for yourself as a scientist. I will need to submit the change to the Vice Chancellor for approval, but with these testimonials I am confident that he will agree to it."

"Thank you very much, sir."

"How are you on accommodations? Usually second year we bring undergraduates in college, but we are rather pressed at the moment."

"I'm fine in the same rooms as last year, sir," Sherlock said.

"Good, good. Well, I'll need to assign you to a new supervisor. Come back in a few days and I will have sorted that out."

"Thank you, sir."

There was a new group of freshmen at dinner at the Sidney Sussex Hall as Sherlock and others of his year gathered.

"Looks like your ankle is doing better," Musgrave noted.

"Yes," Sherlock responded before taking a bite of whatever it was on the plate.

"Where's Trevor? You two were inseparable in the spring," Blankton asked.

"He's not coming back," Sherlock said.

"No? I thought he'd done well enough to keep on."

"He had."

"What then?"

"His father died a few weeks ago," Sherlock responded.

"Oh, my."

"He found it rather unsettling."

"Were you there?"

"Yes."

"That leaves a hole in our teams," Blankton said.

"There's always the Freshmen," suggested Hackstead.

Jonathan was disappointed to hear that Victor Trevor was not returning to the college. While Jonathan had not approved of all Trevor's habits, he felt Trevor had been good for Sherlock. Now Sherlock returned to spending most of his hours in solitude.

Yet it was different. Jonathan noticed that Sherlock seemed much more absorbed in his new studies, often doodling out his own problems, or pacing the floor talking to himself as he tried to come to a deeper understanding of the material. He still smoked the pipe Trevor had given him. He smoked almost constantly as he studied, forcing Jonathan to retire to his closet to avoid the tobacco smoke. But Sherlock seemed more focused and more intrigued by the subject matter, sometimes springing up and shouting for joy when he solved something to his satisfaction. If Sherlock Holmes was sometimes negligent about eating or sleeping it was because he was concentrating on something. Still Jonathan worried that overwork might cause a relapse and send him once more into the darkness. He soon learned that one threat could make Sherlock maintain regular habits.

"Sir," he said, "If you don't sleep, I shall send a note to Dr Mackenzie."

Sherlock would scowl at him, slap his book shut, and go off to his bedroom.

Chapter 21

House of Mourning

*"I had never heard him refer to his relations
and hardly ever to his own early life."*
Dr. Watson, The Greek Interpreter

In early November Sherlock lay on the sofa in the sitting room reading a chemistry treatise as smoke curled up about his head from his pipe. There was a knock on the door and Jonathan went to open it. It was rare for them to have visitors this term and Sherlock looked up as Jonathan returned.

"Mycroft!" Sherlock exclaimed with surprise as he sat up. "What brings—" he began, but cut himself off as he observed his brother's demeanour. "Who died?" he asked instead.

Mycroft sat down across from him.

"Mother died last night," Mycroft said.

"Good heavens, I have heard nothing!"

"According to Sherrinford's wire it was quite sudden. She took ill just the day before. He asked me to tell you. I thought it best to come in person."

"This is quite shocking."

"Yes, it is," Mycroft said watching his brother carefully.

"We were never really close," Sherlock said.

"The funeral is Saturday. Will you come?"

"Yes, of course."

"You won't have any difficulty with it?"

"No, I think not."

"Good. If you would be prepared to do so, I would like to take the first train in the morning."

"Yes. I can do that."

"Then I'll find a hotel for the night. I will come round for you with a cab in the morning," Mycroft said rising.

Jonathan handed Mycroft Holmes his hat and coat and saw him out the door then turned back to his master.

"You will stay here," Sherlock said.

"Sir?"

"I will only be gone a few days and I need you to take notes to the Dean and the Senior Tutor tomorrow to explain my absence."

"Yes, sir," Jonathan said, consoling himself that Sherlock had survived the whole summer without him. And yet, he knew if it had been his own mother that he would not be as unaffected as his master seemed. But the decision had been made and he had no rational argument to oppose it. He kept his tongue and helped Sherlock pack and saw him off with his brother in the morning.

Holmes Hall was shuttered and draped with black when Mycroft and Sherlock Holmes arrived there the following evening. Thomas, the butler, ushered them into their father's study. Squire Holmes looked up from the pile of papers he was working at as they entered. There seemed to be more grey in his hair than Sherlock remembered, but the squire seemed more distracted than mourning.

"Mycroft, Sherlock, have a seat. It is good of you to come. You will have to excuse me, but there are many details to attend to, and etiquette was always more your mother's forte than mine. And, well—"

"I'm sorry, Father," Mycroft said.

"As we all are. It is a great loss. I'm sure Sherrinford would like to speak to you both and I have much work to do, arrangements to make."

Sherlock and Mycroft took the hint and left the study. As they approached the grand staircase Sherrinford met them coming down. He was looking haggard.

"Sherlock! Mycroft! Thank you both for coming. You will have to excuse us if things are a bit disorganized. Amanda has been ill since Edward's birth late last month and then both Arthur and Edward came down with scarlet fever. The nurse had her hands quite full with the three of them even with the maids' assistance. Dr Thompkins had several illnesses throughout the dale to attend to. So he was stretched quite thin. Mother was helping tend Amanda and the boys when she became ill herself. And now - now we have lost her organizing skills and we are in utter chaos. I brought Mrs Beckwith in to sit with Amanda. Amanda blames herself quite needlessly and I fear it is preventing her from getting well. Amanda's mother should arrive tomorrow. Her father and brother are coming, too. Father has made most of the funeral arrangements himself while I try to care for my family. It has been very difficult for us all."

"Oh, quite understandable, Sherrinford," Mycroft said. "Do not concern yourself on our behalf. If there is anything that Sherlock or I can do to ease your burdens, please do not hesitate to ask."

"Thank you," Sherrinford responded.

Sherlock had brought his violin from Cambridge and spent any free time he had in his room practicing his mother's favourite pieces. Saturday morning lowering clouds and a light rain dampened spirits further as the carriages drove to the village church. It was a simple service which was concluded by Sherlock's violin.

Members of the Holmes family were not buried in the churchyard, but in a private cemetery within the manor gates. After the funeral, the vicar, the curate and the family proceeded to the cemetery for the interment. The rain was falling steadily as the squire's carriage halted at the cemetery. Siger Holmes stopped his youngest son from exiting the carriage.

"Sherlock, I want you to return to the house," the squire said. "The driver can come back for us."

"Why?" Sherlock asked, startled.

"Because your mother would not approve of your standing in the rain, even if it was to see her in her grave."

After a moment's thought, Sherlock nodded. He could not deny the truth of his father's statement, nor did he want to argue with his father over his mother's grave. He sat back in the carriage clutching his violin case and allowed the driver to take him to the manor house ahead of the rest of the party.

When his brothers returned they heard the sound of the violin through his bedroom door and knocked. They entered when invited and found Sherlock upon his bed in his dressing gown with the violin upon his lap. He looked up at them through hooded eyes.

"He was right, you know," Sherrinford said.

"There is no need to discuss it," Sherlock replied.

"There will be visitors stopping in to express their condolences."

"I will be down."

"Then we will leave you to your violin," Mycroft said.

Outside in the hall Sherrinford stopped Mycroft.

"Is he going to be all right?"

Mycroft paused.

"I believe so."

"You hesitated."

"Despite what you may think, Sherrinford, I can neither read his mind, nor predict the future."

"He seems more closed off than he was a month ago."

"It has been as much of a shock to him as to the rest of us. He just can't safely allow those feelings to surface. So he denies their existence. Leave him to his violin and I believe he will manage well enough."

On Monday Sherlock returned to Cambridge and threw himself into his studies once more.

One evening a week later Dr Mackenzie paid Sherlock a visit. Sherlock gave Jonathan an accusatory look as he ushered the doctor in the room.

"Good evening, Dr Mackenzie. Did Jonathan send for you?" Sherlock asked.

"No. Should he have?"

"No."

"I apologize if I am intruding. I was in town for another purpose and thought I would see how you were doing. I have not seen or heard from you since spring," Dr Mackenzie said.

"I've had no problems recently."

"And your ankle?"

"It is a bit stiff still. It aches now and then, but nothing excessive," Sherlock said as he put his books aside and retrieved his pipe from the mantel. He packed it thoughtfully.

"When did you start that?" Dr Mackenzie asked.

"Trevor gave it to me. I find it helps me concentrate."

"I heard that Victor Trevor did not return to Sidney this term."

"That's true," Sherlock confirmed.

"His father died?"

"Yes. I was with him at the time."

"That was probably a comfort to him."

"Perhaps. But he needed to sort some things out afterward."

As Sherlock lit his pipe, Dr Mackenzie looked at the books Sherlock had set aside.

"Paley. So you are sitting for the Previous Exam this term?"

"Yes."

"But the other books. You are studying chemistry now, not mathematics."

"Yes. I switched to the Natural Science Tripos at the beginning of the term."

"Any particular reason?" Dr Mackenzie asked.

"I have chosen a new direction for my career. Victor's father pointed the way for me back in June. I examined the skills I would need and felt that I was most lacking in chemistry. So I spent the Long Vacation studying chemistry at Bart's and changed to the Natural Science Tripos when I returned to Cambridge."

"What is your goal?"

"The scientific study of crime," Sherlock Holmes said.

"That sounds very interesting from an academic point of view."

"Oh, I plan to put it to very practical use. I shall be the world's first consulting detective."

"And what exactly is a consulting detective?" Dr Mackenzie asked.

"Individuals and professional detectives will lay their cases before me and I will give them my opinion for a fee."

"Interesting. Do you believe that you can make a living at this?"

"Yes. That is my expectation."

Dr Mackenzie looked thoughtful.

"You haven't had any more attacks, hallucinations or nightmares?" he asked.

"None since the night I made my decision," Sherlock said.

"But you did then?"

"Yes."

"Would you tell me about it?" Dr Mackenzie said.

Sherlock sat down and explained the visit to the Trevor estate and what occurred there.

"I can understand how you might be drawn to such a pursuit, and I find his assessment believable. I've seen some of your skills at observation and inference. I just had no idea what you could make of them beyond parlour tricks or medical diagnosis.

"I've put a great deal of thought into it since," Sherlock said.

"It certainly sounds like you have. I wish you luck with your endeavour."

"Thank you."

"Everything has been going well this term?"

"Yes."

"Then why is Jonathan scowling at you?" Dr Mackenzie asked.

Sherlock frowned at Jonathan who retreated to the kitchen.

"Because he thinks I should tell you that my mother died."

"When did this happen?" Dr Mackenzie said with surprise.

"A little over a week ago. I went up for the funeral and came back down directly afterwards."

"What did you feel about that?"

"Not much of anything."

"No?"

"I suppose I should feel more about it than I do, but we were never close."

"No nightmares?"

"Actually I don't remember having any dreams at all recently," Holmes said.

Dr Mackenzie found this somewhat disturbing. Dreams sometimes reflected the inner workings of the mind. Not remembering dreams was not necessarily the same thing as not having them. It could mean that he was refusing to remember them. While Sherlock may have found some of his dreams disturbing before, pretending that they did not exist was not the solution. Was Sherlock shutting everything inside as he had done before? Would it explode again sometime in the future? His behaviour now seemed quite normal despite Jonathan's concerns. All of his responses were quite calm and rational. It was also clear to Dr Mackenzie that while Sherlock had honoured his prior agreement with him by recounting the events at Donnithorpe, Sherlock himself did not feel the need for Dr Mackenzie's assistance at the moment and he would rather return to his book.

"You find this new course of study engaging?" Dr Mackenzie asked.

"Very much so."

"Well, then I shall leave you to your studies. Please send for me if you need my assistance. Good evening."

"Good evening."

Sherlock continued with his plans to take the Previous Exam in the Michaelmas Term. It was an experience much different from the Mays. Names were printed on little pieces of paper arranged in alphabetical order down long lines of tables in the Senate House. The examiners, gowned and hooded, walked up and down the rows to prevent any cribbing or copying. Some young men seemed fearless of the result, but the majority were anxious and earnest. For the first three days there were papers morning and afternoon. These were followed by the examination viva voce. But Sherlock had found little in Paley's outlines that he had not already known when he matriculated. He returned to the manor afterwards confident that he could please his father with the results of his exam.

The holiday in Yorkshire was bleak and lacking the usual festivities. Thick clouds overhung the moors as Mycroft, Sherlock and Jonathan descended from the railway carriage at the Thirsk station once more. The sleigh was waiting for them. As they climbed aboard, the driver addressed them.

"Sirs, it will be dark before we reach the Hall."

"Then light the lamps, Henry, and loose the bells," Mycroft said. "Mother would forgive us for our attention to safety."

Darkness fell swiftly as they slid into the bosom of the dale. Candles stood in the windows of many cottages and farmhouses, but Holmes Hall was still shuttered and black-draped. The Squire's Ball had been cancelled for the second time in three years and wassailers kept their distance from the Hall. While other houses in the dale might be celebrating the yuletide, no merriment would breach the mourning at the manor house.

Sherlock sent Jonathan off to visit his family for the holiday. It was rare that Sherlock and his brothers saw their father outside of mealtimes and meals were solemn and silent as none of the young men was willing to break with their father's example. Sherlock spent most of his time in his room reading his chemistry books.

One evening Sherlock set them aside when someone knocked at his door.

"Come in, Mycroft," Sherlock called.

Mycroft entered carrying a wooden box with marble squares inlaid in the top.

"Would you care for a game?" Mycroft asked.

"You mean: would I care to be beaten?"

"Come now, Sherlock, it has been years since we last played. Surely your analytic and strategic powers have improved since then."

"I would hope so. Well, let's set it up," Sherlock said walking over and sitting in one of the chairs by the small table.

Mycroft set the box on the table and claimed one of the other chairs. The brothers slid out drawers on either side of the box. They extracted the chess pieces from the drawers and began setting them on the board on the top of the box.

"A courier came from London for you last night with a pouch of files," Sherlock observed as he set pieces on the board.

"Yes. He was sent by my superiors," Mycroft said.

"Is anyone actually your superior, Mycroft?"

"Anyone I have met? No."

"You sent him off again this morning?"

"Yes, with my response," Mycroft said moving his pawn.

The initial plays went swiftly.

"It seems a bit odd that they would have a man travel for the better part of two days to obtain your response," Sherlock said.

"They value my analysis of the data."

"They must. No one currently in London could do as well?"

"No," Mycroft replied, moving his knight.

"Why didn't they just send a telegram recalling you to London?" Sherlock said shifting a bishop.

"I explained the circumstances before I left," Mycroft said, as if his explanation were the final word.

"You are not just a clerk, are you?" Sherlock asked.

"No."

"You aren't going to tell me what you really do, are you?"

"No."

"I'll figure it out some day," Sherlock said as he studied Mycroft's move.

"I'm sure you will."

"You are trying to distract me with your queen," Sherlock said.

"Queens are useful for things like that," Mycroft responded.

Sherlock stared at Mycroft trying to plumb the import of that cryptic remark. Was Mycroft merely talking about chess? Sherlock's thoughts were broken by another knock at the bedroom door.

Sherrinford entered and pulled up another chair.

"I hope I am not interrupting your game."

"What is troubling you, Sherrinford?" Sherlock asked.

"A disagreement with Father?" Mycroft asked, moving his queen again.

Sherrinford shook his head. He had forgotten how well his brothers could read him. They had delved right to the heart of the matter even though they had barely glanced up from their chess pieces.

"Not precisely. I haven't confronted him about it. Under the circumstances it doesn't seem appropriate."

"Out with it," Sherlock said as he took Mycroft's final rook.

"I believe that Father no longer trusts me," Sherrinford said.

"Has he said anything to that effect?" Mycroft asked.

"No."

"Based on my experience," Sherlock said somewhat bitterly, "I think if Father did not trust you he would make it abundantly clear."

"I believe Sherlock is correct," Mycroft agreed.

"He seems to want to manage the estate entirely by himself now," Sherrinford said. "I know that the harvest this year was less than we had hoped—"

"And you should also know that the harvest yield is affected by many variables over which you have no control, such as the weather," Mycroft interrupted.

"Well, yes, but there have been other incidents over the years that I think have made him doubt my judgment."

"Oh, come now, I think you are being hard on yourself," Sherlock said getting up from his chair and hunting for his pipe.

"I am sure that if there had been any mismanagement of the estate we would have heard of it," Mycroft added.

"I think there must be some other explanation," Sherlock said as he struck a vesta and held it to the bowl of his pipe.

"Perhaps he is trying to relieve some of the strain on you while your family is convalescing," Mycroft suggested.

"He may be looking for ways to keep himself busy," Sherlock said. "He may find the mourning period excessively tedious."

"Do you intend to finish this game?" Mycroft asked Sherlock.

"Yes," Sherlock said and sat back down to stare at the board.

"Or perhaps Father is trying to prove that he is still useful," Mycroft said casually moving a piece after Sherlock finally played. "He has trained you in the running of the estate. You have two sons. The succession is assured. I have my own career and he has little hand now in Sherlock's education. You know that he was never a terribly social person. It was Mother who impressed upon him the importance of maintaining their social circle, and etiquette now says that is improper. So what is there left for him to do?"

"And perhaps he is somewhat motivated by guilt for spending

so little time with his own family," Sherlock said moving a bishop.

"He was younger than you are, Sherrinford, when his brother died and he inherited the estate," Mycroft said. "Mother's death may have reminded him of the early days of his marriage and how much he gave up. Perhaps he now sees his younger self in you and realizes that there is no need for you to make the same sacrifice."

"I hadn't considered any of that," Sherrinford said thoughtfully.

"Tend to your family," Mycroft suggested. "Let him take back the reins for now. They will be yours in time regardless."

"Yes. I will do that," Sherrinford said. "Thank you. Thank you both for coming. I don't know if Father appreciates it, but it has been a great comfort to me."

"Checkmate," Mycroft said.

"Bah. Someday I shall beat you at chess, Mycroft," Sherlock said.

"Perhaps, my dear boy, perhaps!" Mycroft responded with chuckle. "But tonight I shall take my win and retire. I shall see you both in the morning."

"Good night."

"Good night."

228

Chapter 22

Circumstantial Evidence

"Circumstantial evidence is a very tricky thing."
Sherlock Holmes, The Boscombe Valley Mystery

Sherlock was glad to return to Cambridge after the holiday. He was anxious to resume his studies and be away from distractions. With the Previous Exam behind him he could concentrate on the subjects for the Natural Science Tripos. But even after the Lent Term began he was not satisfied with the pace of his courses. They proceeded too slowly. The lectures were covering much less material than he wished. His instructors quickly became impatient with the questions he asked and they were easily offended if he challenged their answers. He devoured the recommended reading and read more. While initially he had concentrated on the chemistry that he was lacking, he now was reading geology and botany as well. He devoured the books on the subjects at the University Library and for a time they kept him satisfied.

Henry Bradshaw, the University Librarian, was an invaluable resource and an intriguing fellow with his own keen powers of observation. Sherlock would have enjoyed having him as a mentor, but there were many demands upon his time. Sherlock accepted what help he could get and proceeded to absorb all knowledge that he felt would be useful to him.

One evening in late winter Sherlock came out of his room to find Jonathan sitting at the table carefully picking stitches from his fencing jacket.

"May I help you, sir?" Jonathan asked.

"No, I just came looking for a book. What are you doing there?"

"Letting it out again."

"Ah. Yes. You keep growing, don't you?"

"Yes, sir. And my respect for my mother's wisdom grows as well."

"How so?"

"She was not only wise enough not to cut the material when she first took it up, but she stitched it in stages. I found when I removed the first seam last spring that there was already a second seam underneath. Now that it is too tight again and I am removing that seam. In another year I shall need to buy a new one. I have saved up enough for it—"

Jonathan stopped and frowned.

"Or I had, but the money went over to my sister Pearl to help her set up housekeeping with her new husband. So I had to begin again."

"I would increase your wages if my allowance weren't fixed. But you are welcome to any little savings you can eke out," Sherlock said.

"We have a small reserve, but I wouldn't want to touch that, sir. We might need it for emergencies."

"Yes, that is prudent. And you are wise to be preparing your fencing jacket. My leg is much better than it was. Perhaps fencing is what I need to loosen it up."

On a bright March morning, Sherlock stretched out his ankle as he lay in bed. Yes, he thought, it was still a little stiff, but it no longer pained him as it had. He jumped out of bed and startled Jonathan who was brewing coffee in the kitchen.

"Change your clothes. We shall go over to Sidney to do some fencing."

"Before breakfast?"

"Yes."

Jonathan asked no further questions and fifteen minutes later the two of them stood en garde in Hall Court of Sidney Sussex College. They practiced forms and had a brief bout before returning to their rooms so Sherlock could wash and change for Chapel. Sherlock found that the fencing not only helped loosen his ankle but it was an invigorating way to begin the day.

"We shall do this every day," he told Jonathan.

"As you wish, sir," Jonathan replied. He was pleased with

Sherlock's new enthusiasm, but wondered if he could keep up with his energy.

The next morning they had just taken up their en garde positions when a scream pierced the air at Sidney Sussex College. Sherlock dropped his epee and threw his mask aside.

"Stay here," he commanded Jonathan before running across the court into the hall from which the scream had come.

A few other undergraduates, obviously shaken from their beds, joined him as he ran up the stairs. At the top level one of the bedders stood screaming in a doorway. He pushed past her and saw a body hanging by a rope. Its face was bloated and discoloured.

"Oh, my God," cried one of the other students behind him. The remainder stopped at the doorway and stared silently. Sherlock walked to the bed, reached out a hand and touched the body. It was cold.

"Go and tell the Dean, and take her out of here," he said.

The other students obeyed; glad to have someone taking charge. They led the hysterical servant downstairs. Sherlock Holmes shut the door and swept his gaze about the room. It looked like any other undergraduate's room in college. There seemed to be little disturbance in it beyond the corpse hanging from the bedpost. He turned back to it. The "rope" had been made from torn bed linens. Below the body was an overturned chair. On the desk beyond there was some correspondence on the stationery of the university. In the centre of the blotter there was a page of white paper freshly written upon. The inkwell was still open and the pen lay on the blotter with a dried splotch of ink below it. Sherlock glanced up at the corpse again. There was a small ink mark on the right middle finger of the corpse. He stepped toward the desk and glanced at the paper.

"Mr Holmes," a voice called behind him.

Sherlock turned back towards the doorway. Dean Hoch stood there. Several of the Fellows and many more students had gathered behind him in the hall.

"Please come away. The police have been sent for," the Dean

said.

Sherlock walked towards the door.

"We need to clear the hall. All of you have other matters to attend to," Dean Hoch said.

The undergraduates began to turn reluctantly from the room. Sherlock listened to the buzz of voices in the hall as he joined the others heading down the stairs. He heard several overlapping conversations.

"Who is it?"

"Hostler, a third year man."

"Did you get a look?"

"Hostler? Why Hostler? He's just gotten a first class degree."

"Yes, it was hideous. I'm going see it in my dreams."

"Has he? His name wasn't on the Classics Tripos list."

"You are mistaken. It was read."

"It isn't on the printed lists."

As the students dispersed into the court, constables ran past them towards the building they had left. Jonathan sat guarding the fencing gear in the court where he had left him. He rose as Sherlock approached.

"There is something I must do," he told Jonathan.

"Yes, sir. I will take the gear back to our lodgings."

"Thank you," Sherlock Holmes said.

Sherlock walked swiftly to the Senate House where the Tripos lists hung. He read over them rapidly. Hostler's name wasn't there. Sherlock turned when he heard someone come up behind him. It was Lord Cecil. He leaned against a column and looked bored.

"You had to see for yourself, didn't you?" Lord Cecil said.

"Yes."

"It's not there," he yawned.

"No."

"It was," Lord Cecil said.

"I heard you say that in the hall. How do you know?"

"Because it is here," Lord Cecil said pulling a paper from his waistcoat pocket, unfolding it leisurely and holding it out. As Sherlock reached for it he pulled it back and smiled impishly, then held it out again. Sherlock took it the second time. The paper contained the same list of names with the addition of Hostler in its proper place.

"What is this?" Sherlock asked.

"Oh, so you can't deduce where that list came from?"

"I can deduce several things about it, including that is was written with a short pencil while the writer was leaning the paper against cut stone, one of these steps or the wall there perhaps, but it would be simpler if you just told me where you got it from."

Lord Cecil shrugged. He seemed to be enjoying the moment.

"My gyp copies the entire list when it is read," he said offhandedly. "If you've ever attended the announcement of Tripos results you know that at the end of the reading of the list they usually toss down printed copies. He tries to get one of the printed lists but there is always a scramble for them. That's why he writes the names down for me. This time there was some whispering with the Senior Examiner as he neared the bottom of the list and when he finished he announced that the printer had made an error in the printed lists and they had to be destroyed. New ones were being printed and would be available later in the day. It caused a bit of grumbling but those present had already heard the results that they were most interested in."

"So you are saying that they read off Hostler's name, but it wasn't on the list that was handed out later in the day."

"Precisely."

The bells began to ring for Morning Prayers.

"A pretty puzzle, isn't it?" Cecil Hamley tossed off as he turned and left.

Sherlock ran back to his lodging house. Jonathan stood on the front steps with his cap and gown. Sherlock took them and headed back across the street to Sidney Sussex as he put them on. There was much suppressed excitement and murmuring amongst the members of the college as they filed into the chapel. Sherlock Holmes joined the throng and took a seat near the back. He saw Lord Cecil find a seat as the service began. Dean Hoch took the rostrum.

"As I am sure many of you are aware, there was an unfortunate accident this morning at the college. I hope out of respect for the family and the sake of the college that all of you will refrain from focusing unwanted attention on the incident. We must not allow it to distract us from our studies," the Dean said before he led them in prayer.

As everyone filed out of the chapel afterwards, Sherlock heard Lord Cecil whisper to one of his friends: "What are they hiding?" which echoed Sherlock's thoughts exactly.

Sherlock Holmes had very mixed feelings about the incident. He knew all too well the type of feelings that could drive a man to do such a thing. He also knew from his own experience that the college would make an effort to keep it quiet. But if a number of students had seen the room why would the college officials pretend it was an accident? There were too many voices that would contradict such an assertion.

Sherlock was contemplating these thoughts as he headed for the college gate to return to his lodgings. In the gatehouse he saw Dr Mackenzie exiting to Sidney Street ahead of him. Sherlock caught up with him as he reached his carriage.

"Dr Mackenzie!" Sherlock called.

Dr Mackenzie turned.

"Good morning, Sherlock," Dr Mackenzie replied.

"What are you doing at Sidney?" Sherlock asked.

"The police asked me to look at a paper."

"The suicide note?"

Dr Mackenzie looked about the busy street.

"Here, let's just step into my carriage for a moment," he said.

Sherlock climbed in after him and sat down.

"What do you know of it?" Dr Mackenzie asked.

"I was the first person to enter the room after the bedder screamed. Most of the college was just rising. Jonathan and I had come over to fence before breakfast."

"Ah. And you saw the note?"

"I only read the first sentence before the Dean arrived and asked me to leave the room. Why did the police want you to read it?"

"They wanted my opinion on the state of mind of the writer."

"Your conclusions?"

"That I can't say just yet. If there is an inquest, it will all come out then."

"If?"

"I can't say any more. I'm sorry."

"I understand. But it was clearly suicide from everything I saw."

"I don't know of anything to contradict what you saw. I'm just hoping this is the end of it."

"What do you mean?" Sherlock asked.

"A suicide among students at a university sometimes spawns others, even among students who seem to have no connection with the first. It is not something we entirely understand."

"Perhaps hopelessness is contagious."

"An interesting theory. Regardless of the cause, I hope there are no more."

"Perhaps it would help if they understood what drove him to it," Sherlock suggested.

"Do you believe that anyone can truly comprehend what goes through a person's mind at such times?" Dr Mackenzie asked.

"Not if they haven't been there. But perhaps they can understand the stresses that drove him over the edge of reason."

"Perhaps, though I doubt that would stop an impending suicide," Dr Mackenzie said.

"Why was his name taken off the Tripos list?" Sherlock asked.

"You know of that?"

"Half the college knows of it by now and I suspect the other half will know by tomorrow. It won't be long before it is all over the university. Do you know why?"

"I can't tell you that," Dr Mackenzie responded.

"Then I am holding you up to no purpose. Good day, Dr Mackenzie," Sherlock said starting to leave the carriage.

Dr Mackenzie touched his arm to stop him.

"Sherlock, I would if I could. I must respect the confidences of others as I do yours."

"I understand that, doctor," Sherlock said.

"Perhaps it is not good for you to dwell on this incident too much."

"For me it is a case study of a human death, merely a lesson in my studies."

"Well, try not to tread on any toes. It is a sensitive subject."

"I will heed your advice, Dr Mackenzie."

"Good day, Sherlock."

"Good day, Doctor," Sherlock responded as he climbed down from the carriage.

Thoughtfully Sherlock crossed the street and climbed the steps to his rooms. He had several theories that would connect a student's suicide with his name being removed from the Tripos list, but he lacked the data to decide amongst them. He hadn't known Hostler personally. Sherlock's instinctive observations of him at Chapel and Hall had yielded nothing remarkable. He had no evidence that it was other than a suicide and Dr Mackenzie seemed to agree with that. Was there any crime here? And if there was, hadn't the perpetrator punished himself? Then why did it keep gnawing at him?

Understanding what motivates humans to extreme actions beyond the social norm was important for understanding why people committed crimes, or at least that's what Sherlock told himself as he lit his pipe and opened one of his books and began reading. From time to time his mind wandered back to the image of the body hanging in the room. He wished he'd had time to read more of the note. It might have answered his questions. He didn't expect that the college officials would tell him any more than Dr Mackenzie had. In fact, it was probable that they would be less forthcoming. He wondered how much Lord Cecil could tell him about the matter and how much of it would be true. After several attempts to keep his mind on the book, Sherlock tossed it aside and headed to the college library.

At Sidney Sussex students were clustered in the court staring up at the closed shutters of the window where the body had been found. The body had been removed hours before and yet they still gathered. Was it a vigil or merely morbid fascination? Several men of Sherlock's year separated from the group and questioned him as he passed.

"I heard you were in the room."

"Yes."

"What did you see, Holmes?" Mickleby asked.

"The same thing everyone else saw," Sherlock responded.

"Ah, but you managed a ring-side seat. No great deductions?" Lord Cecil asked sarcastically.

"Only the obvious ones."

"It was no accident," Lord Cecil said.

"No."

"And you don't have any theory about why someone would do such a thing after receiving their degree?"

"As you know, there seems to be some doubt about whether he had actually passed the Tripos," Sherlock said.

"Or perhaps passed by questionable means?" Lord Cecil said.

"Is that possible?" another student asked.

"There are ways," Lord Cecil said cryptically.

"The note suggests—" Sherlock began.

One of the dons interrupted.

"Gentlemen, the Dean made it quite clear that he wants no speculation on this topic. I'm sure that all of you have better things to do than stand here and stare up at that window. Be about your business."

The undergraduates glanced at each other and began to move away in silence. Sherlock Holmes tried to intercept Lord Cecil after they were out of sight of the don.

"Do you know something?" Holmes asked.

"Perhaps," Lord Cecil tossed over his shoulder and kept walking towards his residence hall.

Holmes followed. Several of Lord Cecil's group fell in between him and Holmes. In the middle of the court, Lord Cecil turned around to face Holmes again. His followers parted.

"Are you going to follow me home like a lost puppy?"

"I want to know what you know."

"Ah, doesn't everybody?" Lord Cecil said smiling at his companions. "I am flattered that the mysterious Sherlock Holmes feels he can learn something from me without the use of his crystal ball. Go on," he said to his companions. "We can meet later. I'm not afraid of Holmes."

Lord Cecil watched his companions enter the building, and then turned back to Holmes.

"Perhaps we can exchange some information," he suggested.

"What do you want to know?" Sherlock Holmes asked.

"You saw a note?"

"Yes."

"What did it say?" Lord Cecil asked.

"It was addressed to his father. I didn't have time to read it all."

"But you read part of it."

"Yes. He wrote that he was sorry, but that he could not live with the disgrace of the accusations."

"Is that all?"

"That's all that I read."

"Hmm. I wonder if he actually did it."

"Cheated on the Tripos?"

"Yes."

"Do you know for a fact that he was accused of that?"

"Perhaps. Oh, the boy was under a great deal of pressure from his father to succeed. Aren't we all? The question is whether that caused him to actually cheat, or if it was a false accusation that drove him to his death."

"How do you know he was accused?"

"I have my ways."

"I think you have ways of being annoying," Holmes said.

"The feeling is mutual. Why should I tell you?" Lord Cecil retorted.

"Because I might be able to answer your question."

"Ha! You know that I don't believe your deductive nonsense. You are just a busybody like me. I am curious about what you were doing in Mackenzie's carriage this morning after his meeting with the police and the Master."

"We were talking."

"About the suicide?"

"Yes, but he wouldn't tell me anything."

"My dear boy, you seem to be stymied at every turn," Lord Cecil jeered.

"You said that we could exchange information," Sherlock Holmes reminded him.

"I did, didn't I? It is very simple: servants talk. When people talk, I listen. The word on the back-stairs is that Hostler was seen with the exam papers in his hands after the examination period, but before the papers were graded. He was accused of substituting new answers after the exam."

"After the exam?"

"Yes, after the exam."

Sherlock Holmes was silent.

Lord Cecil's companions reappeared.

"Ha ha! Well, you seem to have got more information from me than I from you. As enjoyable as this discussion has been, Holmes, I've been invited to a lunch over at Peterhouse and I need to be getting on."

Holmes stood for a moment after Cecil Hamley and his friends departed. How would one change the answers afterwards? He contemplated this question as he continued on to the college library. It had nothing useful on the topic he was interested in. So he walked over to the University Library.

The assistant librarian helped him find a few references on chirography, graphology, forgery and questioned documents. There weren't very many and they did not contain a lot of information. Sherlock absorbed them quickly. But the author of one book on handwriting intrigued him. He reviewed it carefully. He would pursue that later.

The library was near the Senate House. He stopped there again. For a moment he stood staring at the Classical Tripos list. Then he copied down some names and started walking south along King's Parade and Trumpington to some of the other colleges of the University. He looked up several of the students on the list he had made. Some of them had left town. Some of those who remained had heard of Hostler's death. Others had not. He asked them questions.

"Did anyone seem especially nervous?" Sherlock Holmes asked.

"God, we were all incredibly nervous."

"Anyone any more so?"

"Well, no, why?"

"Did anything unusual happen?"

"No. Has someone been accused of cheating?"

"I need you to think."

"This is preposterous. I've given up thinking. I don't plan to do it again the rest of my life."

"Benjamin seemed shaky but he's always been a nervous chap."

"I heard about Hostler. I'll tell you what's really creepy. Hostler broke his pen a few pages in. He had a spare but he said afterwards that it was his lucky pen and so he was doomed. I never believed in such things but now...."

He shivered.

"Do you remember one of the undergraduates breaking his pen?"

"Well, yes, now that you mention it."

"Do you remember which one?"

"Well, it was the unfortunate Mr Hostler, wasn't it?"

"Why are you asking all these questions? God if only I had Hostler's brains! If my pen had broken I'd have been a puddle. He just went back to it."

"Hostler was always underrating his own ability. Sharp as a tack."

Chapter 23

A Closer Examination

*"If you shift your own point of view a little, you may find it pointing in
an equally uncompromising manner to something entirely different."*
Sherlock Holmes, The Boscombe Valley Mystery

After talking to a couple of students at Pembroke and looking
up one in Downing College, Sherlock Holmes continued walking
southeast to Hill Street and east along Cherry Hinton. He was
soon beyond the town and surrounded by countryside. In another
mile great stone walls loomed up on the north side of the lane. The
gatekeeper asked his business and Sherlock told him he was here
to see Dr Mackenzie.

"Ah, one of the University students?"

"Yes, sir."

"Follow the drive around past the trees there until it curves to
the right before the main building. You'll know when you get to the
entrance. There's a big circle in front. He's most likely in his office
at this hour. If not, they can find him for you."

Sherlock continued his walk within the gated grounds. He
passed two smaller buildings within the trees and could hear voices
of people somewhere to the right. It sounded like a game of cricket.
Soon a large Elizabethan brick building loomed before him. He
remembered coming here with Dr Mackenzie over a year ago.
He had been afraid of the building and what it represented then.
He wasn't now. He was on a mission. He walked up the steps and
entered. He was directed to the Medical Superintendent's office.

He knocked and entered when invited.

"Hello, Dr Mackenzie," Sherlock said.

Dr Mackenzie looked up from the papers on his desk.

"Come in, Sherlock. Sit down. This is a surprise. What can I do
for you?" he said.

"You've written a book and some papers on handwriting
analysis," Sherlock Holmes said.

"Yes. I've used it as a tool in studying different forms of insanity."

"That's why the police called you in."

"Yes," Dr Mackenzie admitted.

"Did they show you the examination papers or just the suicide note?"

Dr Mackenzie observed Sherlock Holmes very carefully. He wasn't sure at this moment what their respective roles were. Were they still doctor and patient, or something else? Why exactly was this twenty-year-old young man interrogating him?

"Just the note. But I told you I couldn't speak of that," Dr Mackenzie said.

"I'm not interested in your conclusions regarding the suicide note. I don't think they would tell me anything I don't already know. In the part that I read he stated that he could not bear the disgrace of the accusations. As I told you this morning, it is well-known at Sidney that his name was first included on the Classics Tripos list and then stricken from it. I have heard that he had been accused of cheating on the Tripos."

"I cannot confirm or deny any of this," Dr Mackenzie said.

"Just listen then," Sherlock said. "He was not accused of having learned the exam questions in advance or having brought the answers into the exam room, but rather of having changed his answers after the exam was over. Why would anyone take that risk? Why especially would Hostler? I have talked with some of his fellow-students in the Classics Tripos and they all say that he was a first rate student, a nervous one, who might underestimate his own abilities, but one who did well despite his concerns. They also said that he was an honourable man. I believe a mistake has been made, a mistake that drove an innocent young man to take his own life. I wish to clear his name and restore his honour."

"How do you propose to do that?" Dr Mackenzie asked.

"I have read everything that the university library has on authenticating documents, forgeries, counterfeits, chirography, graphology, etc.—"

Dr Mackenzie leaned back in his chair.

"Good heavens! Today?"

"Yes. There is less than you would imagine. I came upon your own works related to handwriting. I was somewhat intrigued by Mr Ransom's attempts at writing in code on plate II."

Dr Mackenzie furrowed his brow. He turned in his chair and found his own copy of the book in the bookcases behind him and thumbed through to the relevant plate. He looked at it and then back up at Sherlock Holmes.

"Code?" he asked.

"The inverted words. It is a very crude code but he may have made later attempts which were more effective."

"How do you know this?"

"You wrote in the book that he had written another letter with every second or third word all in capitals in which the subject was incoherent and two other letters composed wholly of unmeaning marks and strokes."

"Are you saying that those could have been in code?" Dr Mackenzie asked.

"It is possible. A few months back I decrypted a code in which the true message was extracted from every third word. The message otherwise seemed to make no sense. The other letters could have been using some form of substitution code, substituting marks for letters," Sherlock said.

"Why would he write in code?"

"Of course, I don't know anything other than what you wrote in the book," Sherlock responded, "but even that is suggestive. You wrote that he had delusions about certain groups and thought he was commanding an army."

"Yes."

"Paranoia seems the most obvious answer. He thought people were reading his letters to his wife, which wasn't really paranoid because obviously you were. But how much of this might have been part of his illness may depend on something I don't know the answer to."

"What is that?"

"Did his wife understand what he had written to her?"

"Do you think she might have? I suppose it is possible."

"You never asked?"

"No. I assumed it was gibberish."

"It might be, just encoded gibberish," Sherlock said.

"It never entered my mind. But you didn't really come here to discuss my book."

"No."

"What do you want?"

"I want to look at Hostler's exam papers. I am perfectly willing to do it here or at any other location under your eye and with your guidance."

Dr Mackenzie laughed. He knew now that this young man was no longer his patient.

"My guidance!" he cried with a smile. "You've just shown me the shortcomings of my analysis in my own book. I may learn more from you than you from me!"

"Regardless," Sherlock Holmes said with a wave of his hand, "it is extremely doubtful that either the family or the university would allow a fellow undergraduate to study the exam papers. However, if approached by the medical superintendent of the county asylum who has some expertise in studying writings, and who expresses an interest in restoring the young man's honour...."

"That's all you are interested in: restoring his honour?" Dr Mackenzie asked.

"Yes."

"Then I will ask, and if they are willing, then you can be my student assistant in this project."

"Thank you, Dr Mackenzie," Sherlock said.

Dr Mackenzie pulled out his watch.

"How did you come here?" he asked.

"I walked."

"You will be late for supper at the Hall if you walk back. Come, I'll drive you to Sidney Sussex."

Back in his rooms after supper, Sherlock tossed his academical gown on a chair and took up his violin. He threw himself on the sofa as Jonathan silently retrieved and hung up the gown. Holmes laid the violin upon his knees and drew the bow across it. The strings whined in response. He lifted the violin by the neck and began to tune it.

He had set one line of inquiry in motion, but something else was still nagging at him. There were treacherous gaps in his data. As he plucked at the strings and adjusted them, he considered how best to fill those gaps. He could try asking Lord Cecil, but he doubted the thoroughness and accuracy of the man's information. He needed confirmation of what Lord Cecil had already told him as well as more complete facts. He set the violin down on the sofa and watched Jonathan building up the fire. It was a cool evening. Then Sherlock walked to his desk and took up a piece of foolscap and a pencil. He wrote a few words on the paper and drew a map below them.

"Jonathan, I need you to do something for me early next morning. I need you to talk to the servants of one of the examiners and find out who accused Hostler of cheating and why. I've written down the examiner's name and drawn a map so you can find his office."

"Hostler is the man who hanged himself?" Jonathan asked as he took the paper.

"Yes. I've been told that someone saw him in the room with the exam papers after the examination period, but before the papers were graded, and that he had been accused of changing his answers. I need to know more about the accusation. Who made it? Did they see Hostler? Did they know him? How did they claim he made the switch? Anything."

"You want me to learn what I can from the servants?" Jonathan asked.

"Yes."

"I'll do my best, sir."

"Don't worry about my breakfast," Sherlock said. "This is more important. They may speak more freely before their masters arrive."

"Yes, sir."

Sherlock then retired to his room with the violin, and Jonathan heard its whine late into the night. At first light Jonathan peeped into Sherlock's bedroom before setting out on his mission. He found his master asleep upon his bed fully-clothed, the bow still in his hand and the violin upon his knees. Jonathan left quietly.

Sherlock awoke hours later to the pounding on the door in the sitting room. As he became conscious, he remembered that he had sent Jonathan out. He rose and answered the door himself. It was Dr Mackenzie.

"Good heavens. It looks like you slept in your clothes."

"Very astute, doctor," Sherlock said as he closed the door behind him.

"I suppose that is better than the alternative," Dr Mackenzie said.

"Not having slept at all?"

"Yes. Where is Jonathan?"

"Out on an errand. Let me put the kettle on and see if we can't manage to make ourselves some tea without his assistance."

After he had done so, Sherlock found his pipe and lit it.

"I happened to arrive at a most opportune time," Dr Mackenzie began. "Hostler's father was berating several University officials for falsely accusing his son of cheating and thus driving him to his death. He quickly took up my offer to examine the papers and the University had no choice but to agree. I have the papers here."

Sherlock held out his hand and Dr Mackenzie handed him a portfolio. Sherlock spread it open upon the table and looked at the examination papers one by one.

"I have also brought some tools with me," Dr Mackenzie said and drew from his bag a wooden box which he set upon the table. He manipulated a latch upon the box and slid it open. Inside was a brass microscope.

"Ah, that could be useful," Sherlock said as he looked up.

"The university is very anxious that the whole matter be laid to rest as quickly as possible. They tried to keep the death quiet and present it as an accident, but somehow the papers got wind that it was a suicide and the newspapers are full of it this morning."

"I haven't seen them yet," Holmes said. His pipe had gone out.

He set it aside.

"Have you eaten?" Dr Mackenzie asked.

"No, I was asleep when you knocked."

The kettle whistled.

"I'll take care of that," Dr Mackenzie said. It did not take him long to find the tea, the pot and the cups.

Sherlock continued examining the papers. The first two pages were neatly written with a thin J pen. Then at the bottom of the second page there was an ink blotch. The following pages where written with a broader pen.

"These later pages were written with the same pen as the suicide note."

"Yes, that was my impression, though the note was written in a much more agitated mood than the exam was."

"But these were written more hurriedly than the first two pages."

"It is those later pages that they claim were inserted," Dr Mackenzie said as he gathered some fruit and bread and butter.

Sherlock took each piece of paper and held them up to the window in turn and stared at them. Then he piled them back in the portfolio. Dr Mackenzie closed it and pushed it to the other side of the table. He set the plate and the cup of tea before Sherlock and sat across from him with his own cup.

"I don't understand it," Sherlock said.

"Understand what?" Dr Mackenzie asked.

"Why they think these were inserted. I see no irregularities. No indication that these pages have ever been separated or modified."

Sherlock wrapped his cold hands about the teacup. It felt good. He drank some. It was weaker than Jonathan usually made it, but the warmth felt good.

"Perhaps there are more minute signs that the microscope will show," Dr Mackenzie suggested.

"Perhaps, but we are not talking about a professional forger here. Furthermore, my question is: why did they accuse him if there is nothing suspicious visible to the naked eye?"

Sherlock downed the rest of the tea. The room was cold.

Jonathan was obsessive about keeping their rooms warm. Sherlock looked towards the fireplace. The last fire was long dead.

"What time is it, Dr Mackenzie?" he asked.

"Shortly after ten o'clock, why?"

"Where is that boy?" Sherlock asked.

"Jonathan? You said that he had gone out on an errand."

"I presumed so since he was not here when I woke."

"He left while you were asleep?"

"Yes."

"Is that unusual?"

"Not necessarily. But today was not routine. Last night I asked him to run a special errand early this morning."

"When would he have gone?"

"Dawn, I would have expected," Sherlock said.

"That's over four hours ago. Do you think something has happened to him?"

"I certainly didn't foresee any danger in the errand I sent him on. I think it is premature to start the hue and cry," Sherlock said retrieving his pipe and knocking the old dottle into the fireplace, "especially because that might interfere with his mission if he is still about it."

"Is that possible?"

"If he was being thorough, yes."

Sherlock paused to light his pipe.

"I would appreciate it, Doctor," he continued, "if you would go over the papers with your microscope to see if there have been any erasures or modifications. Thinness in the paper, bits of rubber, disruptions in the grain, etc."

Dr Mackenzie examined the papers while Sherlock Holmes paced the floor.

"I see nothing that suggests that any modifications were made. The only disturbance in the grain is here where the blotch of ink is."

"May I?" Sherlock asked.

"Yes."

Sherlock looked through the microscope at the ink blotch on

the second page. There was a disruption in the grain. There was nearly, but not quite, a hole through the paper.

"What would you interpret that as?" Sherlock asked.

"A pen malfunction, especially since he changed pens afterwards," Dr Mackenzie answered.

"Would you believe the pen broke?" Sherlock asked.

"Oh, yes. The broken part could have caused this disruption."

"Several others taking the exam at the same time told me that his pen broke while he was taking the exam."

Sherlock then slid the edges of two of the sheets of paper under the microscope at the same time edge to edge.

"What do you think of this?" Sherlock said.

Dr Mackenzie looked at them through the microscope.

"I think they were once one sheet of paper, a piece of foolscap folded over and torn along the fold."

"And yet one is written with one pen and the other with the other. If you were to substitute other work would you do that?"

"If the other students saw my pen break, possibly."

"Look at the ink of both parts. Do you see any difference in their age?"

"No, but a difference of a day or less may be difficult to determine."

"Now tell me about the psychological characteristics you see in the writing," Sherlock said as he took up his pacing once again.

"He's very intelligent, though somewhat unsure of himself. Perhaps he has an overly critical parent. That would not be inconsistent with what I saw of his father. The writing with the J pen is very neat, copybook neat. This was written by a person who aims to please. After the blotch, his fist shows the same characteristics, but it is more rushed as if he was afraid that he would run out of time."

"Does that seem consistent with having one's pen break during an exam?

"Certainly."

"But is it consistent with a writing made in one's rooms and swapped in later?"

"No, certainly not. I think everything points to the fact that this is his original exam."

Just then the door opened hurriedly and Jonathan entered closing it a bit more quickly than usual.

"I'm sorry, sir," Jonathan said breathlessly as he removed his coat. "I was much longer than I expected. It took quite a while to gain their confidence and once they started talking it was hard to get them to stop. But I — Oh, excuse me, Dr Mackenzie, I hadn't noticed you there. I'm sorry, sir, if I interrupted anything."

"No, Jonathan, Dr Mackenzie and I had just completed our study of Hostler's examination papers. Sit down and tell us what you have learned."

"I spent time with several of the servants in that particular building. The best way to gain their confidence seemed to be to offer to help them with their work. One fact that I believe may be important, which was pressed upon me by several of them, is that Espersen, the examiner, is very absentminded. He loses his keys, his glasses; He misses appointments. So when the charwoman found his door unlocked she was not terribly surprised. She was surprised when she saw a young man standing there in the dark room with a stack of papers in his hand. She says he dropped them when he saw her and knocked her down on the floor in his rush to get past her and through the door."

"So she merely saw him in the darkened room and as he rushed past?"

"Yes, sir."

"But she recognized him as Hostler?"

"No, she said she wouldn't know one of the students from the other."

"Then how—"

"If I may continue?" Jonathan said.

"Yes, yes," Sherlock Holmes said impatiently.

"She picked up the papers from the floor and placed them back on the desk and went on about her work. When Espersen next came in the office he was in a temper about his papers being disarranged. He asked his manservant about it but he knew nothing. He went ahead and graded the papers. The Tripos list was drawn up. Shortly thereafter he encountered the charwoman who said that she hoped nothing had been amiss with his papers, and that she had tried to pick them up the best she could. This suddenly called to mind the jumbled exam papers and he gave her a tongue lashing for disturbing his things. She defended herself by explaining about the young man she had seen with the papers. This threw him in frenzy and he demanded to know what the young man looked like. She said all she knew was he was a thin lad with blond hair."

"And Hostler had blond hair."

"Espersen became convinced that he was the one. He said they must re-examine the papers. There was nothing unusual about any of the papers except Hostler's. The Tripos list was in the process of being read, but they withdrew the printed lists. In a short period of time they had Hostler in and accused him of entering the room and swapping in new sheets for his exam. He denied having been in there or having done anything with the exam papers. But they pulled his name from the Tripos list and notified his father. A committee was to be appointed," Jonathan concluded.

"They created a mountain of vague suspicions and circumstantial evidence that would never had held up under any kind of scrutiny," Sherlock said in disgust.

"But it was enough to send Hostler over the edge," Dr Mackenzie said shaking his head sadly. "It was just too much on top of the stress he was already under. His suicide was a rash decision made in solitude. If he had waited another day his father would have been here."

"Perhaps his father was the very person he could not face," Sherlock said.

"Yet his father immediately challenged this cobweb of suspicion upon arrival, only he is now defending his dead son's honour."

"Which I think is completely vindicated," Sherlock said.

"Yes."

"And if they saw nothing wrong with the other exam papers—"

Sherlock Holmes stopped pacing and stood dead still in the middle of the sitting room. A dramatic change came over his face.

"What is it?" Dr Mackenzie asked.

"If none of the papers were changed, then what was the man the charwoman saw doing with the papers?"

"Perhaps he was just looking at them?"

"But if he wasn't Hostler, who was he? The newspapers! Dr Mackenzie! You said that it was all over the papers this morning. Did they mention that Hostler had been accused of cheating?"

"They mentioned rumours that he had been seen with the exam papers. Unconfirmed, of course."

Sherlock grabbed Dr Mackenzie's arm. There was a wild look in his eye.

"Is your carriage out front?"

"Yes, but—" Dr Mackenzie replied becoming concerned about the sudden change in Sherlock's behaviour.

"Quickly, then. Bring your bag. I can only hope that we are not too late," he cried.

Sherlock Holmes threw open the door and ran down the stairs with Dr Mackenzie and Jonathan in his wake. Neither was sure whether Sherlock was reacting to a deduction, a flash of intuition, or a fit of some kind. But they weren't going to let him out of their sight in any case. They piled into the carriage and Sherlock gave the driver directions. In a few minutes they tumbled out again and raced through the gate of Downing College.

"This way. I was in his rooms yesterday."

The three of them ran up the stairs, drawing startled looks. The oak was sported. Sherlock knocked at the outer door. When there was no answer, he tried the knob. It was locked. He got down on his knees and looked through the key hole. The key was in the lock.

"Doctor, do you have some long thin instrument in your bag?"

"Yes," Dr Mackenzie said as he dug into his medical bag.

"I need a piece of paper," Sherlock said.

Jonathan drew from his pocket the piece of foolscap that Sherlock had given him the night before. Sherlock unfolded it and slid it under the door. He then probed in the keyhole until he heard the key fall on the paper. He pulled the paper back out, picked up the key and unlocked the door. And there, much like he had seen in the room at Sidney Sussex College the day before, a body hung from the bed post by a rope made of torn bed linens.

"Quickly! We must cut him down," Sherlock cried as he grasped the young man about the waist and lifted him. Dr Mackenzie used a scalpel to slice away at the rope tied around his neck. Then they laid him out on the bed.

"He's still warm," Sherlock said.

"There's a pulse. It's weak, but it is there," Dr Mackenzie said.

"Close the door, Jonathan," Sherlock said as he noticed the sound of the students gathering in the hall.

"Bring some water," Dr Mackenzie said.

Sherlock fetched a glass of water from the pitcher on the desk. As he did so he spotted the paper lying there.

"There is a note," he said.

Dr Mackenzie sprinkled water on the student's face. He flinched.

"I think he will make it."

Sherlock picked up the end of the sheet hanging from the bedpost.

"Fortunately, his lack of skill at noose-tying saved his life. You may have observed that the knot was up against his chin rather than pressing against his windpipe. There wasn't enough of a drop to break his neck and the air passage was not completely blocked. He might have still suffocated eventually due to the unnatural position but it gave us time."

Just then there was a knock at the door and it opened.

"What is this?" an older man asked.

"It is a medical emergency. I am Dr Mackenzie. May I ask who you are?"

"Paton, the head porter here, sir. I know who you are, Dr Mackenzie, and these two?"

"My assistants."

Just then Lucas Pritchett gasped and coughed and Dr Mackenzie handed him the glass of water and urged him to drink.

"What's the matter with him?"

"We cut him down from this," Sherlock said holding up the

would-be noose next to him.

"Oh, my God, not another one. Thank God you came. How did you know?"

"You can thank the young man by the bedpost for that," Dr Mackenzie said. "I think longer explanations had best wait."

Pritchett had his eyes open and he was trying to speak. Dr Mackenzie shushed him. The young man grasped the doctor's hand.

"Do you think you can stand?" Dr Mackenzie said.

He nodded.

"I think he is recovered enough to be moved. If you can clear the hall, I think it would be best for all concerned if I took him with me."

"Yes, of course, doctor."

"The college officials know where to find me."

Chapter 24

New Studies

"Have you ever had occasion to study character in handwriting?"
Sherlock Holmes, *The Sign of Four*

"You saved a man's life," Dr Mackenzie said a week later.

"It was a near thing," Sherlock said. "I should have realized sooner that if it hadn't been Hostler in the room, it must have been another undergraduate who might feel guilt over Hostler's suicide once they knew the cause."

"You are being hard on yourself. No one else could have come to that conclusion sooner."

"That is no excuse," Sherlock said.

"Regardless, he is grateful. He said that he didn't do anything but look at the exam papers. When he found the door open he just became curious about how well he had done. The charwoman came in before he had even noticed that the papers hadn't been graded."

"How is he now?" Sherlock ask.

"His parents took him home a few days ago. I think he will be fine. The university concluded that the entire incident was a horrible mistake. They conferred BAs on both of them."

"And otherwise are trying to bury the whole affair."

"Well, yes. You can't blame them. You have benefited from that tendency yourself."

Sherlock was silent for a moment.

"Dr Mackenzie," he said at last, "I have to admit that I enjoyed working with you on this. I was wondering if you might have time to teach me more."

"About handwriting?"

"That and other things."

"Aren't they giving you enough to study at the university?" Dr Mackenzie asked.

"Not enough that is relevant. I have been studying additional subjects on my own."

"I can see that handwriting analysis would be useful in the study of crime."

"If it is truly possible to identify the personality or state of mind of the writer it could be invaluable."

"Some people are sceptical."

"And yet your description of Hostler tallied with those of his fellow-students."

"It requires some practice."

"I assumed so. You said that you had other samples. Perhaps we could review those together."

"I think I could find time for that. I generally have a little time to spare Tuesday and Thursday afternoons."

"Yes, that would be fine."

So Sherlock began walking down to the asylum twice a week to study with Dr Mackenzie. They reviewed handwriting samples that Dr Mackenzie had collected from patients and staff at the asylum. They analysed each other's handwriting. Sherlock Holmes also taught Dr Mackenzie some of things he knew of cryptography.

"In case you encounter any other patients writing in code," he explained.

Together they reviewed the finer details of document examination and the detection of forgeries. Dr Mackenzie found Sherlock Holmes to be both an excellent student and teacher. Sherlock's studies with Dr Mackenzie seemed to cool Sherlock's impatience with his university studies. But they piqued the curiosity of others.

One evening as Sherlock was walking back from Fulbourn he encountered Lord Cecil leaning against a tree along the road.

"Taking up tree worship?" Sherlock asked.

"No, not really a nature person myself. I'd heard you'd taken to walking out here and I thought I'd see what was so attractive."

"Is it unusual for a man to take some exercise in the afternoon?"

"Not at all. Many of men at the university do. But not you.

At least not previously. Suddenly this term you are much more physically active: fencing in the mornings and taking constitutionals in the afternoon."

"It has resulted in a significant improvement in my health."

"Yes, I've noticed that you seem to have overcome your earlier problems in that regard."

"Do you keep track of all the members of the college?" Sherlock asked.

"Why, yes, I do. It's a hobby of mine," Lord Cecil said with a smirk.

"That and spreading lies," Sherlock retorted.

"Oh, I admit that I embellish sometimes."

"And sometimes you feed information to the newspapers."

"Well, yes. But let's not talk about me. The county asylum is out this way, isn't it?"

"Yes."

"What are you doing out there?"

"Studying."

"With Mackenzie?"

"Yes."

"I understand that he gives clinical lectures to medical students, but you aren't studying medicine."

"No, I'm not, but I really don't think it is any of your affair," Sherlock said as he started walking again towards Cambridge.

Lord Cecil followed.

"Hostler's name was restored to the Classics Tripos list," he said.

"Perhaps its removal was a clerical error," Sherlock replied without turning around.

"I heard that Dr Mackenzie convinced the university officials that it was all a mistake and there hadn't been any cheating."

"Good for him."

"Do you know anything about that?" Lord Cecil said struggling to keep up.

"Perhaps."

"I thought we agreed to share information."

Sherlock turned on him angrily.

"That was before you carelessly leaked information to the newspapers and nearly cost another student his life."

"What? What kind of lies are these?" Lord Cecil cried.

"It's true. You claim to have your sources. Check with them. It is one thing to be curious and quite another to spread what you hear with total disregard for the effect it has on others," Holmes spat out before turning on his heels and continuing.

Lord Cecil stopped walking.

"That is an outrageous accusation! You are mad! I don't think you are studying out there! I think you are being studied!" he called to Holmes' back.

Sherlock Holmes ignored him and kept walking until he reached the gates of Sidney Sussex College. He was not dissuaded from his study sessions at the asylum by Lord Cecil's probing or insinuations, even when the insinuations began to spread as rumours through the college. Sherlock was determined to learn all he could despite what others might think. He was fascinated by the wide range of subjects that Dr Mackenzie had studied and the contributions he had made to many professional publications.

Dr Mackenzie was flattered that Sherlock wished to read through the rest of his own works. They had interesting conversations ranging from causes of irrational behaviour to whether a madman should be legally responsible for what was really an unconscious act. There were times that Dr Mackenzie doubted that this Sherlock Holmes could be the same young man who had tried to poison himself sixteen months before. He was astounded by how Sherlock's determination to be a detective had helped him focus his thoughts, not only to steady his nerves and control his turbulent emotions, but to allow him to absorb knowledge with such speed and enthusiasm. When Dr Mackenzie had been treating Sherlock, he had hoped and expected that Sherlock would reach a level of stability, but the results had been greater than he expected and had come despite additional shocks and challenges.

Dr Mackenzie now realized that some of the characteristics

which he had attributed to the cocaine in their first experiment had really been part of Sherlock Holmes' normal personality asserting itself when the stress of his nervous condition had been relieved. Sherlock was extremely quick-witted, physically active and impulsive without the drug. While the drug may have magnified those characteristics to ridiculous, or even dangerous, extremes, it had not created them. Dr Mackenzie could see how someone with such talents might find a diminished capacity intolerable, and he understood Sherlock's prior impatience with his condition.

"Sherlock, I wonder if you would do me a favour," Dr Mackenzie said after one of their study sessions. "We have a new patient at the asylum this morning and we can't identify her. She was found wandering around by a constable. She has not spoken at all nor does she seem to understand our words. I was wondering if you might give us some clues to her identity as you did with that boxer."

"Certainly," Sherlock said.

Dr Mackenzie led Sherlock through the wards. But as they were approaching the woman in question, Sherlock suddenly froze. Dr Mackenzie looked back at him and then remembering what Jonathan had done, he grabbed Sherlock firmly by the arm and called his name. Sherlock shook his head and looked at him. Dr Mackenzie turned him around and led him back to his office quickly. He directed Sherlock into a chair and sat next to him.

"What happened there? Did you nearly have an attack?" Dr Mackenzie asked.

"Yes. But I'm fine. Thank you."

"What provoked it?"

"It was her. From the back she looks like—But she can't be."

"I'm sorry. I did not realize. Let's forget it," Dr Mackenzie said.

"No. No. Now I must see her. Uncertainty will just make matters worse. I have to know," Sherlock insisted.

"Are you sure?"

"Yes."

They went back again with Dr Mackenzie watching Sherlock carefully. The last thing he wanted to do was to unravel all the progress Sherlock had made. They approached the woman from behind again. A matron was still trying to comb the tangles out of her long dark hair without pulling it too badly.

Sherlock slowly circled her concentrating on examining details of her hair, her dress, her posture and at last her face without touching the woman. The matron looked up at Dr Mackenzie who nodded his assent to Sherlock's examination. Then Sherlock squatted down before the woman and gently reached for her hands. He turned them over lightly in his own, noting their callouses.

"This dress is not what she was wearing when she came to you?"

"No, sir," the matron answered. "What she was wearing was hardly a rag. All shredded, it was."

"Could you show me her forearms?"

"Here, deary, let's show the man your arms?"

The woman look at Sherlock as the matron gently pushed up the long sleeves of the gown to reveal her forearms but he avoided making eye contact with her and merely noted that her forearms were marked with scratches and bruises and there were red rings about her wrists.

"Thank you," Sherlock said.

He looked down at the slippers on her feet.

"She was barefoot, wasn't she?"

"Yes, sir."

"And the bottoms of her feet were red and raw. There were longer scrapes and scratches on her legs and red rings about her ankles like those on her wrists."

"Yes."

"Suffering from malnutrition and dehydration?"

"Yes, indeed! How did you know?" the matron answered wide-eyed.

"I've seen enough."

Sherlock and Dr Mackenzie returned to Mackenzie's office.

"No resemblance really. Older. A domestic for some time, probably since childhood. She may not have any family or any family that may notice her missing. The house that employed her was probably in the country. They are unlikely to come looking for her or even admit that she worked there if you inquire. You might try the agencies. One of them may have placed her at some time if she had not grown up in service to that house.

"Explain, please."

"You can see from her hands and arms that she worked hard all her life, cleaning and scrubbing, but subject to much abuse as well. If the house she worked for had been in the city it is likely they would have brought her to your door themselves when they found she was losing her wits. But these people bound her and gagged her. Perhaps to hide her from someone visiting the house, perhaps for some other purpose. But she was afraid and the fear was enough to make her strong with desperation. She knocked over the chair they had bound her to. The legs broke and she managed to free herself from her bonds though not without taking away some splinters from the chair in her arms and most likely her legs. She must have escaped from the house, but if she had worked there all her life she probably knew the ways in and out better than the owners. She ran and hid for several days before someone found her and brought her here. I suspect she covered some distance but it could not be too far, probably within the county."

"Why the country?"

"There are numerous thorn scratches on her arms, as if she had forced her way through a thorn hedge. That's unlikely in the city."

"Thank you, if what you say is true then we would not want her to return there even if we found the house."

"Quite true."

Shortly after the start of the Easter Term Sherlock was once again invited to join the other fencers at the university gymnasium on Wednesday afternoons. This time no marauding bull terriers prevented him from doing so. He began going there every week.

"Touché," Sherlock Holmes said.

"By Jove, Holmes, you are a magician with that thing. It seems to be at two places at once!" Drake said.

"Again?"

"No, I've been beaten enough today, thank you. Sometime

when I'm fresh I'll try you again."

George Rowland of Trinity College came in just then carrying two wooden sticks and two bowls or baskets of leather.

"Ever played singlestick, Holmes?" Rowland asked.

"No. I've heard of it. The play is much like the sabre, correct?"

"Yes. It was originally a training sword for the sabre. Some follow the same rules as sabre fencing, but many use broader rules allowing the use of the point as well as a cutting touch. Thigh and mask hits are allowed."

"May I?" Sherlock Holmes asked holding out his hands. Rowland handed him one of the sticks. Sherlock hefted the single stick. It was about an inch in diameter and a yard long.

"Ash?" he asked.

"Yes, and the baskets are buffalo hide," Rowland said.

"I did some training with a sabre a number of years ago. This is much lighter than a fencing sabre," Sherlock said.

Rowland offered one of the baskets. Holmes transferred the stick to his left hand, placed the basket over his right hand and stuck the end of the stick through the hole in the basket so he could grasp it from the inside.

"Want to give it a try?" Rowland said.

"Certainly."

"I want to see this," Drake said. He knew the fresher Rowland was obsessed with swordplay and had voiced his frustration with being unable to best Holmes.

Three drubbings later Drake laughed from the side-lines as Rowland conceded.

"It was a clever idea, Rowland, bringing in a weapon that Holmes had probably never used before. But I don't think the weapon matters. Holmes could probably thrash any of us with a teaspoon."

"Thank you," Holmes said with a bow in Drake's direction. He turned back to Rowland. "Thank you. I appreciate the opportunity to try it."

"He seems to go into a trance of some kind," Buckley said as the young men picked up their gear and began heading out of the gymnasium.

"Merely a form of concentration that my fencing master taught me," Holmes said.

"No. No. You are on to something," Rowland said. "It must be some sort of wizardry. That would explain why none of us can beat him."

"Then Lord Cecil was right."

"Nonsense," Sherlock said.

"He certainly likes to throw it your way. No wonder you took a poke at him."

"He attacked me first," Sherlock replied.

"His Lordship was rather foolish to attack anyone who can fence like that," another undergraduate said to Sherlock. "You should have smacked him with your gauntlet and met him at dawn with real swords. It would have saved a lot of us from grief at his tongue."

Sherlock chuckled.

"You slew him well enough with words and that left hook, but it's not quite as permanent a solution as running him through would be. Well, here's where we part. Drake, Rowland, Holmes, next week?" Buckley said.

"Yes."

"Rowland," Holmes said as they parted to go to their respective colleges. "Bring your singlesticks again next week and I'll give you a chance to get your revenge."

"I'll do that."

As they walked down Sidney Street toward the college, Darnell said. "You're pretty light on your feet. Even done any night climbing?"

"No."

"We are going up the Library tonight. We have a third year man from King's leading us who knows all the tricks. Want to join us?"

"When?"

"A quarter to 10 at the Senate House passage."

As Holmes joined them near the Senate House that night, Darnell and Bensen, both third year men at Sidney, introduced him to Vaughn from Jesus College and Walters, the Kingsman. No one else was around.

They walked past the Senate House until they came to some iron railings which connected to the highest part of the Library. The railings looked like a row of iron javelins. Walters walked halfway down them and stood under the glare of a lamp-post. He spoke softly but firmly and in the stillness of the night his words were easy to hear.

"Before we can do some real climbing we must cross these railings," he said, "This is the easiest place to cross. That projection there makes the balance easy. Just grasp it here like this and push yourself up on your arms. When your hands are level with your hips, raise your foot and place it on to the narrow horizontal bar here. Then just step over like this and drop down on the other side."

Sherlock and the other students followed Walters over the fence. It was no more challenging than any fence any of them had scaled as boys. Then they stood on the Library grounds. On their right was a large double doorway. Above the doorway the word BIBLIOTHECA was carved in stone. A ledge projected out above it about ten feet from the ground. Immediately in front of them was a drain-pipe. It ran up the wall twenty-five to thirty feet to the roof.

"This is the best place to start," Walters said. "It is not the easiest drainpipe because of the recess, but it has the advantage of privacy. The caretaker lives in the south-west corner on the opposite side. Some refer to this as the 'sunken drainpipe' because of its position between the other wall and the buttress."

Walters began removing his boots.

"You climb barefoot?" Sherlock Holmes asked.

"I do. Most men wear rubber-soled shoes. I feel that I get better holds this way. I spent a year at sea before I came to the university. I learned to climb the masts barefoot. I wouldn't do it any other way."

"I think I will try it," Holmes said taking off his boots and tying them to his belt by their laces.

"You can't place both feet on the drain-pipe at once," Walters said. There is just enough room to wedge your right foot on the pipe and you grip it with your right hand like this. Then you stretch your left foot out to the side, to the edge of the projecting blocks of stone. Get your foot as high as possible, press hard on it, at the same time shove hard with the right foot, pull outwards with the right arm, and to the right with the left hand against the edge eighteen inches away. It is a lot easier than it sounds. The recess widens near the top and you can get both feet beside the pipe and then you can walk straight up. Watch out for the loose corner-stone at the top."

Walters began to scramble up as he described. In minutes he had gained the roof edge. Darnell followed with Walters coaching from above. Vaughn was next followed by Bensen. Holmes carefully observed the others as they climbed and followed swiftly behind them. The insect-like crawl up the drainpipe was easy for anyone who had scaled craggy tors. Sherlock hoped there were greater challenges to come.

"As you can see once the roof is reached it is possible to wander at will in all directions because the different roof-levels are connected with iron ladders. The most interesting climb remaining on the Library is this way," he said turning right and leading them.

In a short time he reached an iron ladder that was about fifteen feet high. He ascended the ladder and turned left walking along the foot of the roof. The others followed close behind. They descended into a sunken well and emerged from the well on a broad, flat roof with a pinnacle at its near left-hand corner standing about twenty-five feet high. From the roof of the Library there was a good view of the town. Even this high up King's Chapel seem to loom over them disapprovingly and glowered at them in the moonless night. St. John's Chapel stood out in the distance against the racing clouds.

"I've heard it's haunted," Darnell said as they all looked out at St. John's Chapel.

"I heard someone fell climbing it once," another said.

"That's what it was. He was climbing and fell to his death. Now he warns other climbers away.”

“Just as likely a rumour perpetuated by the officials at St. John’s to scare climbers off.”

Walters was silent.

“Have you been up St. John’s Chapel?” Sherlock asked him.

“Part way. Then a thunderstorm came out of nowhere and the rain and the lightning drove us down.”

“Do you plan to try it again?” Sherlock asked him.

“Perhaps.”

Just then they were startled by the sound of steps below. The five of them crept to the edge of the Library roof next to the Senate House Passage and peeped over the edge to watch silently as a proctor passed below. Their fear of being discovered by the proctor was far greater than any fear of the drop below them. After the proctor was gone Walters drew back from the edge and spoke.

“We should be going down.”

“Have you ever climbed any of the town buildings?” Sherlock asked as they came to earth again.

“No,” Vaughn said.

“I’ve a done a few,” Walters said. “Too easy to get up and uninteresting once you get there. I like a challenge. I only climb the Library as a guide to the uninitiated.”

“If the weather holds up we might try King’s Chapel before the end of the term,” Vaughn said.

“That is a more worthy climb,” Walters said.

“It would have to be after May Week because we promised to wait for Cahill,” Bensen said. “He’s rowing for Trinity Hall and won’t break his training before then. Are you interested, Holmes?”

“Just tell me when,” Sherlock Holmes said.

Chapter 25

New Heights

"Now I must kick off my boots and stockings.
I am going to do a little climbing."
Sherlock Holmes, *The Sign of Four*

Sherlock had just returned from Fulbourn late one afternoon a few weeks later. He had intended to go directly to dinner at the Hall before returning to his rooms, but Jonathan intercepted him at the gatehouse to Sidney Sussex College. He held a twisted piece of paper in his hands.

"Sir, a gyp from Jesus College just delivered this. He said that you must see it as soon as possible."

Sherlock took the note and untwisted it.

"Tonight, half past nine," was all it said.

"Ah."

Sherlock tore a piece of paper from one of his notebooks and wrote a response. He twisted the paper like the note he had received and handed it to Jonathan.

"Do you know your way to Chapel Court at Jesus College?"

"I can find it, sir."

"Third staircase second floor. Give this to Vaughn. If he is not there leave it with his bedder or gyp. If the oak is sported—"

"Excuse me?" Jonathan said.

"If the outer oak door of the room is latched, leave the note stuck in the door."

"Yes, sir."

"I will see you after supper."

"Yes, sir."

"I was beginning to doubt that we'd get this in before the Mays with all the rain we've been having," Walters said as they met just outside the walls of King's College. "Wet roof tiles are suicidal. But the weather's holding today and we have a moon to guide us."

"A full moon no less," Cahill said.

"That's the best kind. Not going to be superstitious are you?" Vaughn asked.

"No. Not me, but some would say it was sacrilegious to do it on a Sunday."

"We're attending Chapel, aren't we?" Darnell joked.

"Been twice already today, but the services would have been far more interesting if they had been given on the rooftop," Bensen said.

But Walters was serious.

"This is the tallest building in Cambridge," he reminded them. "It is 160 feet tall and much more difficult to climb than the library. If any of you wants to change your mind, there is no strike against you. I don't want anyone getting the jim-jams once we are up there. It could be disaster for all of us."

"No, I'm in," Cahill said.

"Me, too," The others echoed.

"First you need to get into college. There are probably over 40 ways to get into King's without going through the gatehouse, but I'll show you my favourite. There's no night porter prowling the grounds here at King's. So that's an advantage."

They entered the college and reached King's Chapel without incident. They stole silently past the lamp-post near the main entrance, then walked around to the north-east turret opposite the Library. In that corner there were blocks of stone with toe-holds between them that made it an easy climb for the first few feet. Beyond that they had to use the lightning-conductor, a narrow strip of metal running up the side of the building attached to the building with metal clamps. The lightning-conductor was not strong enough to hold more than one man at a time. Walters went first to show them how to climb it. Holmes followed Walters, gripping the lightning-conductor with his fingers and moving his feet from clamp-to-clamp as he climbed. The clamps were cold against his bare feet. It took more concentration than strength, but a lag in either would result in a dangerous fall. Above the lightning-conductor was the chimney proper with better grips between the bricks for fingers and toes. Holmes made quick work of the next 60 feet.

At last all six of them were on the roof. With gestures Walters showed them how to attack the turrets. Holmes started up one by stepping on the sloping slab of stone on the side and gripping the clover-leaf shaped holes in the turret with his hands.

Near the top of the turret was a drain pipe that ended in a bowl that was firmly clamped to the wall. Holmes grasped this bowl to anchor himself for the final ascent to the parapet. Suddenly there was burst of sound and feathers as a flock of pigeons took off from their roost as Walters reached the parapet before him. Holmes clung to the bowl of the drainpipe waiting and listening for any sign that anyone below had noticed the flight of the birds. After a few seconds of silence he continued on. After he gained the parapet Holmes found himself in a forest of gargoyles.

Once they were through the gargoyles, Walters told Holmes that he was going to climb the north-east spire as the others were coming up the turrets. Before Walters reached the top of the spire he began signalling to Holmes to look at the ground below. Sherlock Holmes moved to a suitable vantage point and looked down to where Walters was pointing. He saw a policeman approach the door of the porters' lodge and ring the bell. The lights came on in the lodge. Holmes drew the attention of the other climbers and they all realized they would soon be surrounded. They began to descend but it seemed certain that the porters would catch them. The third year students were especially desperate to avoid apprehension which would mean the loss of their degrees. As he neared the base of the turret he was descending, Sherlock Holmes tried the turret door and found it unbolted. He signalled to the others to follow him. They all quickly tumbled through the door and bolted it from the inside. The wire door above them inside the turret was not shut, and they went up higher to avoid meeting any porters coming up the spiral staircase. No one came. After fifteen minutes they summoned their courage and went down the stairs. The door below was locked but Walters knew where the key was hidden. They opened it and entered the chapel and hid for half an hour. At last deciding that the porters had abandoned the search they left by the north-west door and stole across the grounds of King's College. A clock was striking half past 11 as they did and they knew there might be proctors patrolling outside the college.

"Come, there is another way out of college here," Walters hissed. "Good luck!" he whispered as they departed and he returned to his room at King's College.

The Trinity Hall man was gone in an instant. Sherlock Holmes, the two third-year Sidney men, and the man from Jesus College sprinted across King's Parade, skirted the marketplace and dived down back streets on their way back to Sidney Street. The clock was striking a quarter to midnight as Sherlock Holmes reached his lodging house. He paid his pence to Mr Darley, tiptoed past Jonathan sleeping in a chair before the fire and tossed himself upon his bed and was soon asleep.

The post did not bring a great many letters to their rooms. Sherlock received two or three letters from each of his brothers every month. Sherrinford's letters were usually filled with the antics of his sons or the general news of the dale. Mycroft's letters varied from politics to an intriguing chess gambit. Mycroft had also begun clipping crime stories that he thought Sherlock might find interesting from the London papers and sending them along with his letters.

Prior to her death Sherlock's mother had written to him weekly and his father less often. Afterwards his father's letters diminished in frequency to a monthly missive containing a draft for Sherlock's allowance and a perfunctory query as to how Sherlock's studies were proceeding. They had little else to say to each other.

The most well-travelled letter had been the one that arrived that spring from Victor Trevor postmarked from India. The letter made Sherlock smile, if but briefly, and Jonathan was glad Trevor was keeping in touch with his master.

All of these letters passed through Jonathan's hands, so he knew their frequency, if not their contents. Sometimes he thought he could guess their contents by the timing of them. For example, when a letter came from the squire a few weeks before the end of the Easter Term when no draft was due, Jonathan assumed that the purpose was to inquire as to Sherlock's plans for the Long Vacation. Since Mr Sherlock had not yet told him of his plans, Jonathan himself had not known the answer.

But the day after the ascent of the King's College Chapel Mr Darley delivered into Jonathan's hands a letter purporting to be from St. Bartholomew's Hospital in London. Jonathan interpreted that to mean that his master intended to study at Bart's over the Long Vacation as he had the previous year. Jonathan's suspicions were borne out that evening after Sherlock opened it. Sherlock spent a while at his desk examining the contents of the letter, staring at the calendar and writing before he called Jonathan to him and presented him with three envelopes addressed to the hospital, the squire and his brother Mycroft.

"Post these tomorrow," Sherlock said.

"Yes, sir."

"We should be prepared to close up the rooms for the Long Vacation on the 19th. I will be going up to London and sending you back to Yorkshire."

"Yes, sir. Will there be anything else, sir?"

"You may lock up for the night and retire. I'll be reading in here a bit before going to bed."

Shortly thereafter Jonathan retired to his closet and wrote a letter to his mother, telling her that he would be coming home for the summer in a few weeks. He knew that meant a summer making repairs to her cottage and helping her with the garden and canning and carding wool and so on. But that was indeed a holiday for him.

The weeks passed quickly. Between his regular chores Jonathan packed the books he was taking back with him to Yorkshire and did some extra cleaning to prepare the rooms to be vacant for some time.

Sherlock did well on his May exams again, but paid little attention to his ranking beyond writing a hurried note to his father regarding the results. Then he and Jonathan turned custody of the rooms over to Mr Darley until they returned, and headed to the railway station. At the station Jonathan boarded the train which would take him on the long journey west and north to Yorkshire and Sherlock boarded another to London. Mrs Nugent spotted Sherlock as he descended from a cab before the building in Montague Street and greeted him at the door.

"Ah, Mr Sherlock, your brother warned me that you were coming back to visit us again. Let me unlatch the door there. Mr Mycroft will be back at the usual time. Will you be wanting your tea?"

"Yes, Mrs Nugent. Thank you very much."

"Good evening, Sherlock," Mycroft said as he doffed his hat and coat. "How was your journey?"

"Unremarkable."

"And the May exams?"

"They went well."

"You wrote that you found the pace of academia a bit slow."

"Well, yes, the information content of the readings and the lectures is not as dense as I would like, but the lecturers were rather impatient when I questioned them about practical applications. I suspect most of them didn't know the answers. The Senior Tutor was very helpful, but he has many calls upon his time. I had some fascinating discussions with Dr Mackenzie, but they are keeping him quite busy at the asylum these days as well. So it will be good to be back at Bart's. I've enrolled in another course in chemistry, plus one in human anatomy and again they have agreed to allow me to use their facilities for my own experiments when they are not being used by the medical students. I appreciate being given the freedom to learn what I feel is important without being constrained by someone else's expectations."

So while other undergraduates from Cambridge were out punting, shooting or socializing during the Long Vacation, Sherlock Holmes divided his time between the lectures and the labs at Bart's. Each morning with his eggs and coffee he examined the latest crime news in the London newspapers and clipped articles. Sherlock had begun collecting these clippings in books and organizing them by type.

The human anatomy course at Bart's was different from anything Holmes had studied at Cambridge and dealing with the cadavers was a new experience as well. He did not shrink from it as some medical students did. Many of the cadavers that the hospital received were criminals who had been hanged. Others were paupers who had died in hospital of disease or violence on the streets. Still others came from the asylums, lunatics who had died of natural causes and not been claimed by relatives. Sherlock spent much more time with the cadavers who died by violence, making minute examinations of the injuries that led to death. It earned him a rather grisly reputation among the medical students who were just as happy to leave him alone with those corpses and concentrate on the others until he was done. He once bemoaned the use of the embalming fluid which he said interfered with studying the rate of decomposition, which comment earned him an even wider berth from the medical students. None of the students disliked Holmes. They just didn't know what to make of his obsession with violent death, and none of them dared ask. Sherlock Holmes paid little mind to their sideways glances, so absorbed was he in learning all he could from the cadavers themselves.

His studies at Bart's were invigorating and Sherlock was sorry when his courses ended in August. He divided his remaining time in London between reading about historic crimes at the British Museum and watching criminal trials at Old Bailey.

It was at Old Bailey that Sherlock met P. C. Randall and he learned of the existence of the collection of weapons, tools and other artefacts of crime at the Central Prisoners Property Store at No. 1 Great Scotland Yard. One night Randall invited him to view the collection.

"It is not open to the public. It is intended for study, but as you seem a serious student of crime, I think it can be permitted."

In late September Sherlock began packing to return to

Cambridge. His commonplace books contained substantially more notes and articles on crime than they had in the spring.

"I am wondering about the usefulness of these clippings, Mycroft," he said to his brother as he thumbed through his books prior to packing them for the journey. "I believe knowledge of past crimes and trends in crime will be invaluable to the work I propose to do."

"But you doubt the accuracy of the newspaper accounts?"

"Precisely. I've read the news reports of the deaths of some of the cadavers that came through my hands and I realized how much is missing from such accounts. Reporters tend to gloss over the details and write sensational conclusions which may have no factual basis."

"Have you ever found enough to contradict the news reports?"

"No. Not enough to say who was responsible. I merely had the cadavers out of context. But I certainly found indications enough to say that the newspapers were not completely accurate."

"Enough to warrant talking to the police?"

"Sadly, no," Sherlock said.

"Are the court records you have read any better?"

"They supplement the newspaper accounts and sometimes contradict them. But they aren't accurate reflections of what occurred either. In a trial you have two sides espousing different theories of the case. Sometimes the facts are entirely lost in the process."

"And without the facts there is no means to test the theories."

"Exactly. I need more data than any of these sources provide if I am to understand the means and the methods used by criminals sufficiently to reason from effect back to cause. Even my visits to the police crime collection were of limited use. While it was fascinating to examine the weapons and other memorabilia, I need to study actual crime scenes, fresh crime scenes," Sherlock Holmes concluded as he closed the commonplace book and placed it in his bag.

Chapter 26

Science of Detection

"He was still, as ever, deeply attracted by the study of crime."
Dr Watson, A Scandal in Bohemia

Jonathan returned to Cambridge a few days before the Michaelmas Term was to begin in accordance with Sherlock's instructions which had arrived in Yorkshire by letter in mid-September. Jonathan retrieved the latchkeys from Mr Darley. He aired the rooms out, washed the linens, and stocked the larder. The shopkeepers and the merchants all welcomed him back, most especially his favourite bookseller, who recommended several of the latest tomes to him. Jonathan chose instead a used volume by Dickens to while away the time until his master returned. So it was that Jonathan was physically sitting before the fire in Cambridge lost in a boy's adventures in London when the door opened and Sherlock Holmes strode in. Jonathan jumped up, dropping the book beside the chair.

"Welcome back, sir," Jonathan said.

"You may return to your book, Jonathan," Sherlock said as he deposited his bags in his room. "I will be going out again directly."

"Yes, sir, will you be dining at the Hall this evening?"

"Perhaps, but I won't be here at any rate," Sherlock responded heading for the door again.

"Sir—"

"Yes?"

"Your cap and gown?"

"Oh, yes, one of the drawbacks of being at the University," Sherlock said as he retrieved them. "I've grown accustomed to walking about London without such regalia."

Jonathan winced as Sherlock rolled the gown up and stuffed it in a travelling sack.

"Jonathan, you have walked about town more than I have. Where would you say the most dangerous part of Cambridge is?"

"Dangerous?"

"Where the brigands and the ruffians hang about."

"Down Newmarket Road towards Barnwell, so I've been told. I haven't been there."

"That's where I'll be," Sherlock said.

The door closed behind him before Jonathan could say anything more. Somewhat puzzled, Jonathan went back to reading about the rogues in London while his master sought their kind in Cambridge. Sherlock reappeared shortly before curfew, tossed his cap upon the table and removed his gown before throwing himself upon the sofa.

"You were wise to remind me to take my cap and gown. The proctors were swarming everywhere. Other than that I've had a frightfully uneventful evening. I trust your summer went well."

"Yes, sir."

"Good. I'll be retiring shortly. There is Chapel to attend in the morning and the obligatory meetings and arrangements to be made before the official start of the term. None of it is interesting, but it must be done."

"Will you be wanting to fence before breakfast this term?"

"I think not. Perhaps again in the spring."

"Very good, sir."

"I would like to read the morning dailies if that won't strain our budget."

"It should be manageable."

"Oh, and I don't expect to be eating lunch here this term. So you can economize there."

"Yes, sir."

The following morning Jonathan ran out at dawn to retrieve the papers before brewing Sherlock's coffee and preparing his eggs. The timing of the eggs was always crucial. If they were cooked too early, then they risked either getting cold or being hard boiled. If cooked too late, then Sherlock would not have time to eat them before leaving for Morning Prayers. Having accomplished that feat and seen his master off to Chapel, Jonathan began cleaning up the breakfast things.

He noticed that the papers strewn across the table had pencil markings on them. There were circles on articles about local crimes. Jonathan remembered that Sherlock had started collecting such articles during the Lent Term. He wouldn't want the newspapers thrown away until he could cut out the articles that he wished to save. Jonathan carefully refolded the newspapers and stacked them in a corner of the sitting room before setting about his other chores. By afternoon he had finished with the shopping and cleaning for the day. Knowing that his master would be having dinner in Hall at Sidney Sussex and would mostly likely not be back before evening, Jonathan sat down once more with Dickens. Supper time came and went and curfew was approaching before Sherlock Holmes burst in the door again.

"Either there are no more criminals in this town, or my timing is atrocious," Sherlock exclaimed casting off his cap and gown. "I have some reading to do before I retire. Be sure to call me in the morning."

"Yes, sir," Jonathan said.

As he banked the fire and blew out the lamps he wondered what Sherlock had been about these last two evenings.

In the morning Sherlock Holmes laughed at the newspapers.

"See," he said pointing his egg spoon at the paper, "I am in one place and crimes are committed somewhere else. I suppose there must be a limit to this bad luck. I will try to the south this evening."

After Hall that evening as Sherlock Holmes walked down a street he saw a cluster of people, including a few police constables. Sherlock moved closer for a look. Constables began to push the crowds back.

"Nothing to see here, folks. Move along."

When Sherlock did not immediately move aside, a senior official present looked at him more directly.

"You, you're the boy I spoke to in hospital," Chief Constable Bevans said. "Holmes it was."

"Yes, sir."

"Well, I'm glad to see you've taken to observing rather than participating, but you need to move along now."

"I was hoping to study the scene of the crime."

Chief Constable Bevans squinted at him.

"This is police business here, not some laboratory experiment. A man's been killed and we've got work to do. This is no place for students. Just take yourself back over to your college."

A man poked his head past Sherlock's shoulder for a look. The other constables spread their arms wide and pushed back the whole crowd surrounding Sherlock as a stretcher was brought in. Tangled in the crowd Sherlock Holmes could not see much. He thought of waiting until the police left and the crowd dispersed, to examine the scene, but it was dark and he didn't have a lantern or even a candle to see with. He would be better prepared next time. At least this time he had been on the correct street. As he walked back to his rooms he made a mental list of the kit he should assemble.

When he returned he found Jonathan once more buried in the book. The boy began to rise, but Sherlock waved him down and threw himself on the sofa across from him.

"We have notebooks and pencils aplenty," Sherlock said.

"Yes, sir," Jonathan responded.

"And candles and vestas?"

"Yes, sir," Jonathan responded.

"Do we have a dark lantern?"

"No, sir."

"Do you think one can be obtained at a reasonable price?"

"I will inquire, sir."

"Do we have a measuring tape?"

"No, sir."

"Any little bags or envelopes, like one might collect stamps in?"

"No, sir," Jonathan said picking up one of the pencils and note pads and began making a shopping list.

"String. And chalk," Sherlock said thoughtfully. Then he became silent staring at the ceiling.

"Is there anything else you need, sir?" Jonathan said after a few minutes.

Sherlock blinked and faced him.

"Sleep," he said rubbing his eyes, "I think I shall have to handle that myself after I spend a little time with my books. Good night, Jonathan."

"Good night, sir."

Gradually Jonathan began to understand that Sherlock was spending his mornings attending lectures and supervisions on chemistry, geology and botany and his afternoons and evenings searching for crime. While there were constantly numerous small thefts about the city, the average smash-and-grab or pickpocket leaves little evidence. Larger robberies were more interesting to study, but they were few in number in Cambridge. It was homicide which provided the most opportunities and the greatest frustrations.

"You again," Chief Constable Bevans said when he noticed Sherlock Holmes among the crowd of onlookers. "Have you developed some depraved fascination with death?"

"I'm doing a scientific study of crime."

"Science ain't got nothin' to do with it. Just the act of some callous criminal here."

"Not the heat of passion?" Sherlock asked.

"No, not this one. Robbery, most like."

"Ah, but that's science right there. You've obviously come to that conclusion based on your observations combined with your years of experience. If—"

"I don't have time for this nonsense. Move along."

Sherlock turned away, but he did not go far. Less than a block away he sat down and waited until the police left and the crowds sought other amusements. Then he lit his dark lantern, stuffed his cap and gown in his bag and approached the scene of the crime again.

The first thing he learned was that there was no hope of tracing footprints after the police were done. They had so thoroughly trampled the scene by then that little, if anything, was left of the footprints of either victim or perpetrator. But he found other things: blood splatters, match sticks, cigar butts, and, at this scene, a watch. It was off in a corner mostly covered by debris but there was fresh blood on it and splatters on the wall above. A rock not far away was drenched in blood at the edge of the congealing pool. Perhaps this watch was the treasure that cost a man his life. Sherlock opened the back and inside were scratched several numbers, pawn ticket numbers. A poor man's watch, probably the only valuable he had. So he fought to keep it and lost. Sherlock could imagine the encounter as if he had seen it.

But the clock was ringing the third quarter. He hardly had time to return to his lodgings before curfew. Mr Darley had been eying him of late and was unlikely to give him any grace. Sherlock doused the light and pulled on his gown as he made his way back through the streets of Cambridge. The last chime of curfew was ringing as he closed the front door behind him.

"Good evening, Mr Holmes," Mr Darley said. "That was a close one."

"Yes, indeed."

"Out studying were you?"

"Yes," Sherlock replied, but noticed as he did that Mr Darley was staring at the knees of his trousers that were covered with dirt. The knees! How many times had Mycroft stressed the importance of the knees? And now Sherlock found himself at the wrong end of such an observation.

"Studying geology is such a dirty business," Sherlock said, and slung his pack up against his back allowing the lantern inside it to issue a metallic clang as it hit. Then he turned and headed for the stairs. In the sitting room Sherlock found Jonathan asleep in the chair before the fire with Nancy, Fagan and dear little Oliver nestled in his lap. He left the boy there and headed for his bedroom.

"Chief Constable, it is him again," a constable said a few nights later.

Bevans approached Sherlock Holmes and scowled at him.

"Mr Holmes, I've half a mind to haul you over to see that mad doctor friend of yours."

"He fully approves of my study of crime," Sherlock replied.

"Shows you're both mad. But I think that's a requirement to work at one of those places. I know his predecessor there went balmy and they had to practically drag him out of his office. I don't know whether they start mad or working there makes them go that way, but you won't get me sleepin' around a bunch of loonies like that. I'd be afraid that one would slit my throat."

"I believe that Dr Mackenzie practices the obvious precaution of locking his door at night."

"Just the same. As for you, I want you to keep your nose out of police business or I will be talking to your Dean."

Frustrated with how little he managed to discover at scenes and mindful of Bevans' threat Sherlock decided to try a different tact. He began watching people in the market square. Once he spotted his victim he set up the bait. Sherlock spun around and grabbed the young man by the arm when he took it.

"You won't find much in there anyway," he said as he retrieved his wallet.

"Blimey, you're quick."

"I've been watching you. I set you up for the snatch."

"You ain't a copper, are you?"

"No, but give me a reason why I shouldn't turn you in?"

"Give a bloke a chance. I gotta eat. Anyway, I ain't really took nothin' from you."

"Only because I stopped you. Tell you what, you show me the tricks of your trade and I'll let you go."

"Oh, is that how it is? Planning on horning in on my territory? Well, I've been thinkin' this town is too small anyway. Might head to London."

"Get on with it."

"Well, there are different philosophies. A beginner'll need a distraction, a bump to disguise the snatch. Then some of us develop such a delicatsy of touch that the bloke don't feel a thing. Ask for directions to an address and by the time the fellow explains it I have his purse, his hanky and perhaps even his watch chain."

"I've done a bit of sleight of hand, magic tricks. I understand misdirection."

Sherlock studied carefully the methods and techniques of the young pickpocket as he demonstrated them to him. Suddenly the two young men found themselves surrounded by three constables who grabbed them by the arms.

"Gorr! You said you weren't with the police."

"Oh, you have my assurance he isn't. Jacobson, Michaels, you take that one down to the station and search him well. You'll be lucky if he doesn't have your watch by the time you get there."

"Mr Holmes, you are coming with me. We are going to pay a visit to your Dean."

"I haven't broken any law, Chief Constable," Sherlock said.

"Maybe not, but your behaviour is peculiar enough make me think you're working up to it. Besides students are supposed to be studying, not getting in my way. Never can find a proctor in this town when you need one," Bevans grumbled.

Without another word Chief Constable Bevans marched Sherlock Holmes across to Sidney Street and into the college. He nodded to the porter in the gatehouse, but he obviously knew his way to the Dean's office. The Dean did not keep them waiting long.

"What can I do for you, Chief Constable Bevans?" Dean Hoch said.

"I came upon Mr Holmes here with Danny the Dip, a pretty notorious pickpocket, and it looked for all the world like Danny was teaching Mr Holmes the trade."

"The trade?"

"How to pick pockets."

"Mr Holmes, is this true?"

"Yes, sir."

"This is rather unseemly behaviour, Mr Holmes."

"Unfortunately, this isn't the first time I've encountered Mr Holmes recently."

"No?"

"Several times now I've run into him poking around where there's been a murder or a robbery. Starts makin' one suspicious.

Either he's got criminal leanings, or he ain't right in the head."

"Can you explain yourself, Mr Holmes?" Dean Hoch said.

"I am making a scientific study of crime," Sherlock said. "I've been examining crime scenes to learn how crimes develop and what kind of traces the criminals leave behind. Chief Constable Bevans has not been encouraging."

"That's entirely understandable. The police don't need people interfering in their business. But learning to pick pockets, Mr Holmes?"

"He was showing me his tricks," Sherlock Holmes said. "He only agreed to do it after I threatened to turn him in for picking my own pocket."

"Why, Mr Holmes? Why would you want him to teach his 'tricks' to you?" the Dean pressed him.

"If you want to learn the methods of criminals who better to ask than a criminal?" Sherlock responded.

Dean Hoch scowled at him.

"Mr Holmes, to the best my knowledge you haven't violated any specific rules of the college, but this type of behaviour in an undergraduate could reflect badly on the college and the university. I will give you a warning this time, but you are to handle yourself with a bit more decorum and to stay away from criminals and places where the police are working."

"Yes, sir."

But two weeks later Sherlock Holmes was brought before Dean Hoch once again.

"Mr Holmes, this time the proctor caught you at a pub after curfew without your cap and gown on."

"Yes, sir."

"What were you doing there?"

"Playing chess."

The Dean lifted his eyebrows and looked up at the proctor.

"That is what he was doing, sir, playing chess with an old gent."

"Were you aware of the time?"

"Yes, sir. I told Mr Blake that I should be going but he was in the middle of a story and wanted one more game of chess. He wouldn't finish the story unless I agreed to another game."

"A story?"

"Yes, sir."

"What type of story?"

"About a burglary. Mr Blake is a retired cracksman. Gave it up after prison. He mends shoes for a living now. But he was telling me about the old days."

"Of breaking into houses?"

"Yes, sir."

"Still learning about crime, Mr Holmes?"

"Yes, sir," Sherlock said.

"I've never heard of anyone with such an interest in crime who didn't end up committing it," the Dean said.

"That is not my intent, sir. I aim to solve crimes."

Dean Hoch shook his head.

"You do know that you weren't supposed to be in the pub?"

"Yes, sir."

"Were you drinking?"

"No, sir."

"No sign of it, sir," the proctor said.

"Where was your gown?"

"In my bag, sir."

"Mr Holmes, this is a fairly minor infraction of the rules. You will need to pay the proctor and your landlord their fines, and we will be sending a letter to your father. What concerns me most is the direction your activities are taking. You have been doing well in your studies since you overcame your health problems and switched to the Natural Science Tripos. I do not understand why you would threaten your academic career with these extracurricular activities."

"I am training myself to be a detective," Sherlock Holmes said.

"You can be a scientist, Mr Holmes, or a detective, not both."

"I disagree, sir—"

"And now you are being insolent. There will be no further discussion. You know the rules of the college. We expect you to follow them. We also expect you to act like a gentleman. You are to do nothing and to consort with no one which would reflect badly on the college or the university. Understood?"

"Yes, sir."

As he left Chapel the next morning, Sherlock was intercepted by the Senior Tutor.

"Come by my office after your lectures. We need to talk."

"Yes, sir."

"While I don't precisely understand your intent," Rev. Clowe said to Sherlock Holmes when they met later in the day. "I do understand the way scientific enquiry drives a man. Most of the stories you've heard about my exploits as an undergraduate are true. I certainly did carry out some experiments under conditions that were less than ideal. But I managed to just toe the line and never quite go over it. Sometimes it was mere luck that disaster didn't strike or the authorities didn't catch us. Either you are having a phenomenal stroke of bad luck this term or you are pushing the boundaries too far.

"I will tell you now, Mr Holmes, that Dean Hoch has had doubts about you from the beginning. He wanted to know why we were making an exception for a sickly boy when we had turned other young men away. But I was the one who had spoken to you and the Master put weight on that. I had seen something at that time, a spark of brilliance that I thought we could fan into flame. That — incident — the first term just furthered the Dean's argument that we were wasting a seat on you. I stuck my neck out and argued on your behalf. I still believe I was right. I think you are showing signs of being a first rate chemist that this college could be proud of. However, to attain that goal you must reign in your behaviour. After I've stood up for you as I have, I would be severely disappointed if you were sent down due to your non-academic behaviour."

"I have merely been trying to learn what I need to pursue my chosen occupation," Sherlock protested. "I don't see how anything I have done has harmed anyone."

Rev. Clowe sighed. He remembered well being an earnest twenty-year-old feeling constrained by the contradictory rules of society. He ran his fingers through his hair.

"Mr Holmes, you will be eligible to sit for the Natural Science Tripos next term. What you decide to do after you receive your degree is up to you. But if you desire to obtain that degree you must be careful to avoid drawing the Dean's attention until then. I'm just asking you to keep your extracurricular activities out of the spotlight. Could you give that a try?"

"Yes, sir."

Chapter 27

Criminal Pursuits

The botany book sailed through the air and hit the wall with a thwack. Jonathan rose to retrieve it.

"Leave it there," Sherlock said. "The author is still living in the Dark Ages. Hardly an advance on the Doctrine of Signatures. Why should I waste my time with it?"

He rose from the couch and cleaned out his pipe. Jonathan wondered if the book would have made a better impression if it had concentrated on tobacco plants. He didn't dare chuckle at the thought. After a frustrating week of trying to stick to his academic studies, Sherlock Holmes was in a foul mood. Jonathan watched as he refilled the pipe and lit it. Sherlock began pacing the sitting room floor.

"I shouldn't be required to waste my time reading irrelevant and outdated material that I will merely have to unlearn," Sherlock ranted. "I have only so much space in my brain. I'd prefer to fill it with things that are practical and useful."

Jonathan was silent. He knew that his master was talking more to himself than to him. But the soliloquy was cut short by a knock on the door. Jonathan glanced at the clock as he rose to answer it. It was shortly after curfew. When Jonathan opened the door he recognized the man standing there as a freshman who lived two floors below in the same lodging house. He was a short, round fellow and was obviously winded.

"Good heavens, I don't know how you stand the stairs. They'd be the death of me. Is Holmes in?"

"Yes—"

"Just give him this then. I said I would bring it. Didn't know I'd be climbing Everest. I'm going to go collapse now."

Jonathan took the twisted piece of paper from the undergraduate who turned and shuffled off. He took the note to Sherlock.

"I heard," Sherlock said as he untwisted the note and read it.

It was from Walters. They were going to attempt the dreaded St. John's Cathedral the following night and he was invited to join them. It was tempting, but as he considered it another idea came to mind. He scribbled out a response.

"Here. Take this tomorrow morning."

Then Sherlock Holmes disappeared into his bedroom. Jonathan heard him open the window and make several sounds. Jonathan walked into the room and looked towards the window, and then towards the wardrobe and then towards the bed, but there was no one there. Sherlock's boots and stockings lay on the floor. The window was open still, but Sherlock was nowhere to be seen. With a thrill of fear Jonathan rushed to window and looked down. Below he saw Sherlock Holmes jumping free of the drainpipe that ran down next to the row of windows. Sherlock looked up at him with a self-satisfied smirk and grasped the drainpipe again and began to climb. Jonathan drew back as Sherlock reached the window and climbed in. Sherlock closed the window behind him.

"It is a bit sharp out there for climbing barefoot, but it was tolerable for testing the theory. Can we spare enough from my allowance buy some rubber-soled shoes tomorrow?"

"I think it quite likely," Jonathan said.

"Good. Then I shall get my kit together again tomorrow and see if I can't observe the criminal mischief of this town and keep out of the limelight as the Senior Tutor requested."

Jonathan didn't know whether he should be glad that Sherlock was going to quit moping about the rooms throwing books and tantrums, or concerned about the new mischief he was obviously planning.

The following morning as Sherlock was finishing his eggs, Jonathan brought a stack of notes and silver and laid it before him.

"This is what remains of your November allowance," Jonathan said.

"There are still three weeks left in the month."

"Yes, sir. We'll need money for food, coals and sundries. This is the reserve we've saved up."

"With any luck the shoes will cost substantially less than the reserve and we can eat for the rest of the month," Sherlock said, but he pocketed all the money before heading off to Chapel. "Don't forget to take that note!" he reminded Jonathan.

"I won't, sir."

Jonathan cleaned up after breakfast then hurried off to King's College to deliver the twisted note. He was back before noon. He made Sherlock's bed and tidied up bit before making his lunch. In the afternoon a delivery boy brought a package which Jonathan set upon the table. An hour later Sherlock himself followed.

"Ah, good, they arrived. Here," he said handing over the remaining notes and coins. "I believe we still have enough for food and coals."

Sherlock tore open the package and inspected the black rubber-soled shoes. Then he removed his boots and tried them on.

"Excellent. They still need a bit of breaking in, but I think they will do quite well."

Then he went to the wardrobe in his room and extracted the travelling sack. He sat upon the floor inspecting the contents of his kit and preparing for the night ahead. He had sent his regrets to the climbers attacking St. John's Chapel. He was going to do some climbing, but for a very different purpose.

He took to the rooftops of Cambridge on his own to observe the activities on the streets below. He did not bother with the buildings surrounding the marketplace because there was nearly always a policeman there which tended to discourage criminal activity. However, the roof of the Corn Exchange a few blocks away was a fine vantage point for observing many of the backstreets nearby. The climb is a difficult one. The drainpipe ran close to the wall and the slots in the stone behind it were narrow so he could only fit one finger behind it at a time.

Other buildings in Cambridge were easier to climb. Smaller buildings offered fewer choices of views but allowed for closer observation. He found that he could easily observe the activities of criminals and the police from above without their notice.

Hardly a week later Sherlock Holmes was heading back to his lodgings as curfew approached after an evening of climbing and observing. He stopped in an alley and listened when he heard a familiar voice through a window.

"This is all that I have for now," Cecil Hamley said.

"It is not enough."

"I've paid the debt thrice over."

"'Tis 'interest'," the man said.

"Usurious interest then," Lord Cecil said.

"If you can't pay it then we shall have to apply to your father, the Duke."

"No, no. You'll ruin me."

"Just collecting a debt."

"He'll insist on knowing what for. He'll disown me! I'll be sent down from the University in shame. Don't do it. I beg of you. I'll arrange something."

"Very good, your Lordship," the man said in a mocking tone.

Cecil Hamley exited the building cautiously looking around and then dodging through the very alley where Sherlock was hiding. Sherlock Holmes followed him back to Sidney Sussex College. In the court Sherlock grabbed him by the shoulders. Lord Cecil spun around white as a ghost.

"You! My God, you gave me a start. I thought you were a garroter! So it is true. You have been spying on me."

Despite his attempts at bravado, Lord Cecil was obviously shaken. He was having difficulty maintaining his usual level of arrogance. He seemed instead to be a vibrating mass of fear and anger.

"Not before tonight," Sherlock said.

"I don't believe it. You may have the others fooled, but I don't believe this deductive nonsense. It's a sham! You are a faker! An illusionist using cheap conjurer's tricks!" Lord Cecil spat, turning away and continuing to walk towards his hall.

Sherlock followed him and grabbed his arm to stop him as he

opened the door.

"It's not nonsense. I do really deduce things. I can do more as well. Let me help," Sherlock whispered.

"Get your hand off me. I want none of your tricks! Stay away from me or I will report you to the Dean," Lord Cecil cried.

"Aren't you afraid I will tell him what I know?"

"There! See! I knew it! Blackmail! We'll just see if I know a few things about you that he doesn't then!"

"No, that's not what I meant," Sherlock insisted. "I heard what that man said to you. You should go to the police."

"The police! My God! And become embroiled in a scandal! You don't understand at all!"

"I think I do."

"Just stay away from me and keep your nose out of my affairs!" Lord Cecil hissed and shut the door behind him.

Sherlock dared stay no longer. He made his way out of college and back to his lodgings across the street. He went to bed soon after, but he did not sleep well that night. His mind would not leave what he had heard alone.

Sherlock Holmes began watching that gambling house with regularity. They seemed to encourage undergraduates from the university to participate despite the fact that it violated the university rules. They especially encouraged freshmen from aristocratic families. They had a special room at the back with another door to the mews. If any proctors from the colleges came in the front they were greeted politely, but saw no sign of any of their charges. The undergraduates didn't dare report each other for fear of being fined or sent down themselves. But it wasn't as simple as catering to the forbidden gambling urges of undergraduates. The proprietors were also cheating them and as their losses ran up and their funds became short, the proprietors would offer to lend them money until their luck turned. With the gambling fever upon them they took the offer and signed note after note and went deeper and deeper into debt. If they tried to stop gambling and just pay off their debt, they found it impossible to break free. The debt seemed to never be paid and they were pressed with threats to tell their families as Lord Cecil had been. He was far from alone. Holmes recognized many other undergraduates from the university. He was appalled at the injustice of it, but he knew that if he went to any of the undergraduates and proposed they go to the police they would react like Lord Cecil had. They were trapped. He decided to put an end to it himself. Sherlock Holmes decided to find and destroy the loan notes.

"I seem to remember that you did a bit of climbing back in Yorkshire," Sherlock said to Jonathan late one night.

"Yes, sir, fences and trees mostly."

"Do you think you could climb this drainpipe?" he said pointed to the one outside his bedroom window.

"Yes, sir."

"Good. I need you to come with me tonight."

"Sir, if I may, isn't it after curfew?"

"Yes, it is, which is why we cannot go down the stairs."

When Jonathan arrived in the alley below, he found Sherlock donning his gown as some concession to the rules of the university. They wound through a series of mews, alleys and streets keeping an eye out for proctors. Finally they arrived near the rather seedy looking establishment that Sherlock had been watching for several weeks. Sherlock removed his academical gown, rolled it up and tossed it to Jonathan.

"Here, hold this until I get back," Sherlock whispered.

"Sir?"

"I suggest that you stay out of the lamplight. One of the proctors might recognize you if they come this way and I'll pay for your mischief."

"Yes, sir," accepting Sherlock's strange bit of humour without comment.

"I believe I can do this alone, but I brought you as a precaution. If I'm not back in an hour go for the police," Sherlock said before leaving him.

Jonathan sighed, backed into the alley and sat upon a crate. He unwadded the gown and folded it neatly. He thought back to his mother in Yorkshire who had always wanted him to go into service. He didn't think this was what she had in mind. Four years ago he was a country lad dreaming of adventure and now he was hiding in an alley in Cambridge at his master's bidding. Jonathan had to admit it was exciting. It certainly was more interesting than making beds or serving tea. He was not quite sure what Sherlock was about. Jonathan just hoped whatever he was doing tonight was legal. He had seen the inside of the Cambridge gaol once and that was sufficient.

As the minutes passed Jonathan became increasingly uneasy. Sherlock's last comment had suggested there might be an element of danger. The second quarter rang out from the clock tower. Had he meant that if he wasn't back in an hour that he wasn't coming back? A sudden crash next door did not increase Jonathan's ease. He glanced around and armed himself with a good stout stick from the alley. Just then he heard his name being called hoarsely and ran in the direction of the voice certain that it was Sherlock's.

Dashing to the front of the building and through the door Jonathan found two large men bending over Sherlock. Without thinking that each of the men individually outweighed him two to one, Jonathan swung his stick at the head of the nearest one. It was enough of a blow to attract the man's attention and he immediately turned to Jonathan cursing. Jonathan called upon his fencing skills to keep the man at bay. Being unable to reach past Jonathan's stick without being struck in the forearm, the man picked up a chair and swung it at Jonathan. The man swung wildly in rage and Jonathan managed to dodge or parry the chair several times. Then the man made a savage low swing which Jonathan blocked by holding his stick with both hands before him and shutting his eyes. The chair hit the stick fiercely and splintered in a thousand pieces that sprayed about the room. Then he began throwing everything he could get hold of at Jonathan as the boy ducked and dodged.

Sherlock was now on his feet bloodying the face of his other attacker. When he had that man down Sherlock threw a chair out a front window for no apparent reason. Shortly afterwards a constable's whistle blew outside and the two men suddenly lost interest in Sherlock and Jonathan and headed towards a back door. Sherlock threw another chair out the side window and grabbed the bewildered Jonathan. The two of them dived out the window into the same alley where Jonathan had been waiting. Sherlock started down an adjoining alley, but Jonathan ran back despite Sherlock's hissing. He caught up Sherlock's academical cap and gown from the crate where he had left them and hurried back after him. Several twists and turns later, Sherlock forced Jonathan into a dark corner and whispered "silence" in his ear. They stood frozen while footsteps scurried around and voices shouted. Finally it grew quiet. Then Sherlock led him down a few more passages until they came to the alley behind their lodgings.

Sherlock scrambled up the drainpipe, pushed the window open with one hand and crawled in. He directed Jonathan to follow and helped pull him in the window and shut it after him. Jonathan sat for a moment on the floor after he tumbled in but one look at Sherlock as he sat across from him leaning his head against the wall had him up and after soap and water and bandages.

The following morning Sherlock received a summons to the office of Dean Hoch. He responded with a note that he was ill. But that only served to earn him a personal visit from the Dean and Chief Constable Bevans.

When they were ushered into Sherlock's room, the nature of Sherlock's illness was quite evident. Despite Jonathan's ministrations of the night before, Sherlock had two black eyes, lacerations on his face and hands, and distinctive bruises on his throat. Jonathan had come away mainly with bruises and splinters on his hands and a few stray scratches on his face.

"Do you care to explain your condition, Mr Holmes, or shall I deduce its cause? We've had a complaint from the constabulary that some of their men saw what they believe was one of our undergraduates and a young boy running from a gambling house where a fight had broken out. The descriptions sounded suspiciously like you and your servant, Jonathan, and from the looks of the two of you I would say that our suspicions were confirmed."

"There is no doubt in my mind that it was them," Chief Constable Bevans said looking at Sherlock and Jonathan. "I've seen far too much of you the last couple of years," Bevans said waggling his finger at Sherlock. "This one has seen the inside of our gaol before," he said approaching Jonathan, who backed away from him, "and he will do so again if we catch him at any further mischief."

"They were trying to kill him, sir," Jonathan protested.

"Quiet, Jonathan," Sherlock said. "Leave him alone," he said addressing the Chief Constable. "Jonathan was merely trying to defend me. He had no idea why I went there. I will answer for anything he did."

"Indeed you will," the Dean said. "I strongly suggest that you explain to me why you broke curfew and were fighting with those gamblers."

"I found out that they were taking advantage of undergraduates with a weakness for gambling. They were enticing them into breaking the college rules and then cheating them. Once they gathered up notes against them, they were blackmailing them with threats to expose them to the college or their families. I went there to stop them at the only time the establishment was not full of gamblers. When they discovered what I knew they attacked me."

"Oddly enough we found no records of gambling debts in the place, just some ashes," Bevans said.

"Perhaps they destroyed the evidence when they heard the police coming," Sherlock suggested.

"Perhaps. Regardless, it was a police matter and you had no business interfering. I don't wish to see your face about Cambridge or hear your name ever again."

"Mr Holmes," Dean Hoch said, "A room in one of the halls has recently become vacant. You must move into college by the end of the week and limit your activities to the college grounds unless attending a lecture at one of the other colleges. You are not to set foot elsewhere in the town without my leave. Is that understood?"

"Yes, sir."

"If you violate that stricture, the sanctions will be harsh," Dean

Hoch said.

"Yes, sir. May I take Jonathan with me?"

"Yes, but he must confine his movements to the college grounds. If he makes any wrong step he will be removed."

"Yes, sir."

Dr Mackenzie arrived shortly after the Dean and the Chief Constable left.

"So the rumours are true," he said looking at Jonathan as he opened the door. "You do look like you were in a fight. Dr Burton sent a note to me that police had come to the hospital looking for two boys who had been in a fight. No one had been there but he said that the descriptions sounded a lot like the two of you. How is Sherlock?"

Jonathan ushered him into Sherlock's bedroom.

"Goodness, you look awful. I trust no permanent damage was done," Dr Mackenzie said.

"No, I'll be sore for a while. But I accomplished what I set out to do," Sherlock said.

"Which is?" Dr Mackenzie asked.

"Better left unsaid," Sherlock said. "It was a mistake to get Jonathan tangled in it and I shouldn't involve anyone else."

Dr Mackenzie looked at him quizzically.

"Are you sure that you aren't getting in over your head?" he asked.

"Since I've now been banned from the town, I will have to confine my future studies to the nefarious deeds of chemicals in test tubes," Sherlock said.

"Perhaps it is for the best," Dr Mackenzie said.

"Perhaps," Sherlock said, "I need to be better prepared before I tackle real criminals again."

"So you aren't dissuaded by this?"

"Not at all," Sherlock responded.

"Your determination is admirable. I just hope you will be careful."

He wished Sherlock a speedy recovery and bid him good day.

An hour later there was another knock on the door and Jonathan came into Sherlock's bedroom to announce another visitor.

"Lord Cecil would like a word with you," Jonathan said.

"Send him in," Sherlock said curious as to the outcome of this visit. At least he found this stream of visitors distracted him from his aches and pains.

"Good heavens, you look a sight," Lord Cecil said very excitedly. "I heard what happened. I couldn't believe it! I know those two. You could have been killed!"

"I probably would have been if Jonathan had not come to distract one of them. In the end it was the constables drawn by the row who probably saved us both."

"They say that all the notes were destroyed. All evidence of my gambling debt is gone. I can't believe that is just a coincidence. Why did you do it? You have no reason to like me."

"I admit that you have not given me any, but that doesn't matter. What they were doing was wrong. You weren't the only one in their clutches. Who knows how many lives they had ruined and how many more they would have ruined in the future? They needed to be stopped."

"Well, I've heard they've left town now. You saved my neck. My father would have probably done worse than disown me. He hates gambling. Perhaps that's why I do it. I don't know."

"Perhaps you'll want to lay off it in the future," Sherlock suggested.

"Yes, I'm not very good at it. Now I'd be terrified to get into another jam."

Lord Cecil examined his fingernails nervously.

"I heard the Dean was over here. You aren't being sent down, are you?"

"No," Sherlock said. "They want me in college where they can keep an eye on me. I'm being gated. It is not my first infraction."

"You didn't mention me, did you?"

"No."

Lord Cecil looked thoughtful.

"I don't understand it. I've tried to start fights with you. I've harassed you. I've spread gossip about you. Then last night you had me at your mercy. You could have taken those proofs yourself and held them over my head. You merely destroyed them. You've been sanctioned yourself by the college for what you did and yet you have not mentioned my name. Your average man would have taken his revenge when he could."

"Then perhaps I am not your average man," Sherlock Holmes said. "I brought nothing away from that den of thieves except cuts and bruises. I have nothing to hold over your head and I do not intend to mention your name in connection with it at all."

"Then I have grossly misjudged you and treated you very unfairly," Lord Cecil said offering his hand. "I apologize. I want to thank you, not only for getting me out of this jam, but for teaching me that there are still men of integrity in the world."

Sherlock took his hand and shook it.

Chapter 28

The Final Stroke

"I had come to believe that he was an orphan with no relatives living."
Dr Watson, The Greek Interpreter

Sherlock and Jonathan were quite busy for the next few days moving their things into the rooms at Sidney Sussex College. Living in college required some adaptation. Smoking is not allowed inside the precincts of the college though many an undergraduate did it on the sly during the hours when there was no itinerant porter to object. Jonathan appreciated the rule. Sherlock Holmes did not, but he quickly learned the times and places that one could get away with lighting up a pipe.

The rooms they were assigned in college were on the second floor not far from the Porter's Lodge. The sitting-room was smaller than they had in private lodgings. It had a single window that faced out across Hall Court. There was a reading-desk, a few chairs, a table, and a carpet. Two doors opened from the sitting-room; one into Sherlock's bedroom, large enough for a bed and a bath, and only large enough, and the other into the gyp's closet. The quarters were a bit more cramped, especially for Jonathan who would have make do with the little gyp's room for a pantry, closet and bedroom. He had full use of the sitting room when Sherlock was out. Jonathan appreciated the view out the window across Hall Court. Sometimes he would put crumbs on the window-sill and birds would come to peck at them. That gave him a few entertaining minutes between his chores. He was no longer allowed to make his daily trips to the shops and the market in Cambridge. He missed his conversations with the merchants and the chance to look over the goods and visit the bookstores. Fortunately he had bought a couple of books just before this happened. They would keep him for a while. There were bookshops quite near the college. Perhaps in a few months' time he could obtain leave to visit them.

Sherlock attended dinner in Hall as before. They didn't have the little stove they had in lodgings. Jonathan could still make tea and coffee by putting the kettle upon the hook in the fireplace. Jonathan retrieved Sherlock's "commons" of bread and butter from the college buttery each morning and lunch from the commissary. It was more expensive than what he had been able to bargain for in town, but they managed. Often Sherlock stayed at the library or the laboratory through lunch.

Jonathan met the other servants who worked in the building and still more who worked elsewhere at the college when he went to the buttery and the commissary.

The bedmaker on the stair was a heavy, wheezy woman named Harriet who seemed to appreciate not having to climb the extra flight of stairs to tend to Sherlock's room, though Jonathan once heard her grumble about folks stealing coin from her pocket by invading her stair. She lived in town and left at 6 o'clock each day. Jonathan wasn't exactly sure where she was most of the time when she was there. She was not at all a handsome woman. Jonathan had heard the rumour that all bedders at the university were chosen for their ugliness so that the college men would not be tempted to indiscretions.

The other men on the stair also shared a gyp named Jacob to brush their clothes, wait at breakfast, and do any other work of a valet kind, but like many gyps Jacob seemed to vanish about mid-day and not reappear until shortly before Hall. One morning in the buttery Jonathan heard Jacob whispering to another gyp.

"I feel sorry for that boy, wouldn't want his position."

"Why not? Just one man to see to. Seems a light job."

"That might be, but I hear his master's a bit cracked in the head."

"Hah. I think all these college men are crazy."

It was the end of the following week when they were beginning to settle into their new routine that the telegram came from Yorkshire. It arrived while Sherlock was attending his lectures. Jonathan took it from the college porter with some trepidation and placed it on the table. When Sherlock returned he drew his attention to it. Sherlock scowled, but wasted no time ripping it open and reading it. Then he tossed it aside.

"My father demands my presence in Yorkshire to discuss some matters in person. I'm going to request leave from the Dean to go this weekend. I won't be in Yorkshire long. I want you to remain here."

"Sir—"

"It won't be pleasant, but it is something I have been expecting. I must go alone."

"Yes, sir."

Sherlock ate supper at the Hall as usual Friday evening then took the last express out of Cambridge for Ely. The rail connections were not the best but it could not be helped for no trains left Cambridge on Saturday. Sherlock stepped off the train at the Thirsk railway station early Saturday afternoon, walked into the village and hired a ride to the manor.

Sherrinford heard the sound of a wagon drawing up before the door. Visitors to Holmes Hall were rare these days. The squire had discouraged guests since the death of his wife nearly a year ago and the only people who visited regularly were Sherrinford's in-laws. But even they did not arrive unannounced.

"What have we here, Thomas?" Sherrinford asked the butler.

"It seems to be your brother, sir," Thomas said.

Sherrinford threw open the door as Sherlock was thanking the driver.

"To what do we owe this pleasure?" Sherrinford asked his brother after the driver pulled away.

"I was summoned," Sherlock said as they entered the house.

Sherrinford frowned.

"That does not bode well. Do you know why?"

"I believe so," Sherlock said. "Sherrinford, remember that talk we had long ago about leaving me to my fate?"

"Yes," Sherrinford said warily.

"The moment has come. I owe you much I can never repay. But today may be the last time Father allows me to pass the threshold."

Sherrinford scowled.

"At least tell me what is going on," Sherrinford said.

"Not now. I want to get this over," Sherlock said.

Sherlock knocked and entered his father's study. He walked past the two chairs facing the desk. He could feel his father's eyes upon him as he did so. He stopped near the far corner of the desk and turned his back to the window. He faced his father.

"You summoned me," Sherlock said.

"I have received these notices of sanctions from Sidney Sussex. Explain them," the squire rumbled.

Sherlock was not intimidated by his father's gruff manner. He had expected it. He had been expecting this moment to come for over a year. Sherlock stood straight with his head held high and his hands clasped behind his back as he explained what he had done to incur the sanctions and why. Then he explained to his father his plan of study and his intent to become a consulting detective.

"So this why you changed to the Natural Science Tripos?"

"Yes."

"But you didn't feel it necessary to inform me of this plan?"

"I told you that I had more natural aptitude for chemistry than for mathematics, which is true."

"Why didn't you tell me the whole truth?"

"I didn't think you would approve."

"I don't." Squire Holmes shook his head. "I thought you had reformed. You had recovered from your illness and seemed to be doing well at the university — until this. Or perhaps you have been deceiving us all along."

Sherlock did not respond. His father shook his head again.

"I am glad that your mother is not alive to witness this. You have no idea how many times she took your part."

Siger Holmes rose slowly. He circled the desk on the side nearest the door — the side farthest from where Sherlock stood — and limped across the room. He stopped and scowled at the globe in the corner. Sherlock turned in place to observe his father's perambulations, but he did not move otherwise. He had not shown any reaction to his father's accusations, nor made any attempt to deny them. He waited silently for his father to continue.

Siger Holmes pulled himself up to his full height and turned back to face Sherlock eye-to-eye. In height and breadth he dwarfed his son. But Sherlock's steel grey eyes met Siger's blue-grey ones steadily: two strong wills locked in silent combat. Siger Holmes knew that this person before him was neither the obedient child, the rebellious youth, nor the shattered young man of only two years before. Yet he was the sum of all of them, and something more.

This Sherlock Holmes stood sword-straight prepared to cut the umbilical cord with a cold, unflinching stroke. Siger had watched Sherlock fence with M. Bencin in France many times. He had not been able see Sherlock's eyes behind the fencing mask, but the aura had been similar: concentration, control, and singularity of purpose. He could admire that strength and determination even as he was certain in his own mind of the inappropriateness of his son's charted course, and of his own unwillingness to be associated with it. If Sherlock would no longer accept his guidance and his judgment, if his defiance was that complete, then there was but one outcome.

"What would you do if I told you to cease in this course?" Siger Holmes asked his son.

"I would continue with it anyway," Sherlock said firmly.

"And if I were to cut off your funds?" his father asked.

"I would find a way to continue my studies," Sherlock Holmes said.

Then there was silence between them, but the silence did not frighten Sherlock as such silences in this study had frightened him in the past. He no longer felt that his future depended upon his father's will. Instead the silence fed his determination to control his own fate and no longer be at the mercy of another. It was Sherlock who broke the silence.

"I am determined to follow this course and I will do it with, or without, your assistance," Sherlock Holmes said.

"To become a consulting detective?" his father said with a grimace as if he had bitten something distasteful.

"Yes," Sherlock said.

"That is no career for a gentleman," Squire Holmes said, and Sherlock understood the import of that statement as it came from his father.

"It is who I am meant to be," Sherlock Holmes said without hesitation.

"Then you are no son of mine," Siger Holmes said firmly. He returned to his desk and sat down like a judge approaching the bench to sentence the accused. He looked up at his son and spoke his judgment.

"I will not shame you before the college and the university, as you have shamed me and your entire family by your behaviour. I will continue paying your fees while you are at Sidney Sussex College and provide you with the allowance you are now receiving while you remain there. But if you continue on your current path," Siger Holmes said grasping the sanction letters in his hand, his anger rising, "I don't anticipate that will be for very long. Once you leave there you are on your own." He paused. "I never wish to set eyes on you again."

"As you wish," Sherlock Holmes said and left the room, shutting the door to the study behind him.

Sherrinford intercepted him in the foyer.

"It is as I predicted," Sherlock said.

"We need to talk," Sherrinford said.

"No. I shall not stay. I am not welcome here. I need to return to the railway station. I must be back in Cambridge tomorrow."

"Then we'll get one of the wagons and I'll drive you to the station. We can talk on the way."

Sherlock agreed.

On the way to Thirsk Sherlock explained to Sherrinford the cause of his summons and what had transpired in the study. He was resigned to his split with his father and had expected it before he arrived. Whatever bitterness he felt towards his father long predated the encounter this afternoon. Sherlock explained his plans for the future to his brother. Sherrinford could sense Sherlock's excitement and determination when he spoke of his plans to be a detective. He was glad to see his youngest brother once more enthusiastic about life.

"If you need anything, let me know," Sherrinford said. "Remember what I told you before: You will always be welcome here when I am squire."

The two brothers clasped hands and bid each other farewell not knowing when, if ever, they would see each other again.

Sherlock Holmes returned to Cambridge and his rooms at Sidney Sussex College, making certain that the head porter knew he was back as the Dean had requested. Then he took up his books as if he had not been gone at all.

Sherlock was silent for a few days about what had transpired, and there were times when Jonathan caught him watching him thoughtfully.

"Jonathan," Sherlock said finally one day.

"Yes, sir."

"When I returned to Yorkshire, my father and I argued as I had expected we would. He has disowned me and told me never to return. He said that he would continue my allowance as long as I was at Sidney Sussex. But I want you to know that you may return to Yorkshire if you wish. I'm sure my brother—"

"I would to prefer to remain here, sir," Jonathan responded.

"I've seen you with the birds. I know that you miss Yorkshire."

"I've been content here in Cambridge."

"But now you can't even visit the shops in town."

"I talk to the gyps and the bedders when I go the buttery and commissary."

"Yes, you talk to their face and they talk behind your back."

"Yes, sir. I am aware of it," Jonathan said.

"They talk about me," Sherlock said.

"Yes, sir. I have no regrets about serving you. They don't understand."

"Do you understand?" Sherlock asked.

"I understand enough. Your journey had been difficult. But I believe you will do great things."

Sherlock Holmes smiled. It was rare since Trevor had left

college that Sherlock smiled.

"Then you may stay," Sherlock said.

He started to turn away, then turned back to Jonathan.

"The holidays aren't far off. I am willing to pay for you to return to visit your mother from my allowance."

"I would prefer to remain here with you for the holiday."

"You know that most of the undergraduates will leave and thus most of the gyps and the bedders will take the time off. It will be rather quiet around here."

"Just the same—"

"Stay if you wish."

Sherlock Holmes had no further conflicts with the college officials during the remainder of the Michaelmas term. He spent most of it studying for the exams and attending lectures and reading what other books he found at the library that might be useful. He followed the expected routine and the Senior Tutor breathed a sigh of relief.

Once Dr Mackenzie stopped in for a visit.

"He is at the library, sir," Jonathan told him.

"Studying hard, is he?"

"Yes, sir,"

"But doing well otherwise?"

"Yes, sir."

"I am sure you both will be glad of a bit more freedom when you go home for the holidays."

"We are staying here for the holidays."

Dr Mackenzie was startled.

"But surely the Dean—" Dr Mackenzie began and stopped. "It isn't the Dean, is it?" he asked giving Jonathan a piercing stare.

Jonathan was silent. Dr Mackenzie recalled the reason for his prior visit and the current restrictions. He thought of all he had learned of Sherlock's family relations. It wasn't much, but it was enough.

"He had a split with his father," he concluded.

Jonathan said nothing, but he didn't have to say anything.

Dr Mackenzie paced the floor.

"Three years ago he suffered a traumatic event which almost killed him and drove him near to suicide; two years ago he suffered a relapse and tried to poison himself; a year ago his mother died and he seemed little affected; and now he's been disowned by his father, and sanctioned and restricted by his college and you tell me he is fine."

Jonathan remained silent. Dr Mackenzie threw up his arms.

"And I pretend some little understanding of the human mind," he said.

Another thought cross his mind.

"He's not taking any stimulants."

"I am not certain what you mean, sir. He drinks coffee and sometimes tea. In Trevor's time there was sometimes wine about, but not now. Tobacco is prohibited in college. He finds that rule quite irksome and I think he finds ways to indulge sometimes."

"Nothing else?"

"No, sir."

"And you would know."

"Yes, sir."

"Yes, you would," Dr Mackenzie admitted. He had seen how Jonathan watched his master. The very fact that Jonathan was calm and unconcerned was testimony to his master's state of mind.

"He's just obsessed with becoming a detective and little else matters."

"Yes, sir."

Dr Mackenzie shook his head.

"I wish all my patients could be cured by an obsession like that. I wish him well," Dr Mackenzie said pulling out his watch. "I must be getting back. Tell him I called."

Chapter 29

Confessions

"I think that he has behaved most kindly and honorably throughout."
Mary Morstan, *The Sign of Four*

When Sherlock failed to appear for an exeat at the end of the term, Dean Hoch sent for him and told him that he was free to leave for the holiday. Sherlock informed him that he was staying in college without explaining why.

Undergraduates began abandoning town. As Sherlock Holmes was leaving Chapel one morning someone called out to him.

"Holmes!"

He turned around to face Lord Cecil.

"I wanted to talk to you before I left town. Could we go up to your rooms?" Lord Cecil said.

"Certainly," Sherlock Holmes replied.

"Would you mind sporting the oak?" Cecil Hamley asked. "I would rather that we not be disturbed."

"I doubt there is any danger of that," Sherlock said, but he closed the heavy outer door just the same.

The two young men tossed off their caps and gowns.

"Have a seat," Sherlock said.

Sherlock Holmes was proceeding courteously, but cautiously. They had not spoken since he had moved into college and he was uncertain of the state of relations between them. Holmes had noticed that Lord Cecil had approached without the loud arrogant manner he had formerly adopted. He had also noticed in the past few days that Lord Cecil had been going about the college without his followers.

"No one comes by, do they?" Lord Cecil asked.

"No."

"Well, they still talk about you. Many are awed by your talents and envious of your daring. I suppose they've just been busy with their own affairs."

"I know better than that," Sherlock said. "They don't even speak to me at dinner. They fear that the trouble I've gotten into is contagious and they don't want to put their degrees in jeopardy when they are so close."

"Yes, you are probably right. Look here, I just wanted to say that I haven't forgotten what you did. I know that all this is a consequence of that. I'm — I'm sorry. If there is anything I could—"

"I don't think there is," Sherlock said.

"I am grateful—"

"And for that you risked talking to the pariah. That's quite a departure," Sherlock said somewhat cynically.

"Yes, I deserved that," Lord Cecil said. "Over the past few weeks I've been thinking a great deal about what you did and the things you said and it has changed my perspective. The change didn't sit well with everyone. I'm afraid my previous circle didn't find me quite as entertaining as formerly."

"Didn't?"

"We had a falling out when I defended you. It lifted the scales from my eyes. I realized none of my supposed friends would have ever done what you did. I was either a stepping stool or a side-show to them. We had some words. I ended it by telling them all to leave. It is just as well. I have had a lot on my mind. I haven't been in the mood to entertain them. I've been doing a lot of thinking over the last few weeks." Lord Cecil continued, "I know it is no excuse, but the world I was raised in always seemed to me to be a sham of gentility and generosity with an undercurrent of intrigue and greed. I hated it, and yet in rebelling against it, I suppose I became exactly what I hated. No one that I knew seemed genuine. But you are, aren't you? You really can do the things you say and when you offer to help someone you mean it."

"Yes."

"Perhaps my own demeanour was repelling the good men from me."

"I think it likely," Sherlock said.

Lord Cecil threw up his arms.

"Frankness! Honesty! I need bigger doses of that!" he cried.

"I've always lived among hypocrites. You were right when you said that the Duke has spoken out against gambling and several other vices and abominations in the House of Lords. I don't know if anyone takes him seriously because he certainly has his own preferred vices. He's had at least a dozen mistresses over the last twenty years. No one talks about it. Certainly not the Duchess, she's had her own flings. I wonder who strayed first: the goose or the gander? Not that it matters. Now that I think of it there may be some question as to whether I'm the Duke's son at all. Maybe that's why he's always hated me. I don't know that there is a way to prove it. So we are stuck with each other. In any case, being a third son I am superfluous. He's always made that abundantly clear."

Lord Cecil sighed.

"I never meant any harm," he continued. "I just didn't think that there were any innocent parties. I thought everyone was after their own game. But I also didn't imagine that anyone could be seriously harmed by anything I did.

"I was shocked by what you said to me on the road from Fulbourn that day. At first I was convinced you were lying because I hadn't heard of the other suicide attempt. You and Dr Mackenzie handled it so swiftly that hardly a whisper got out. From all reports the student walked from his room with the doctor. So no one thought it could be anything that serious, just a post-Tripos breakdown. They're common enough. But I finally managed to piece enough together to make sense of what you said. Then I was angry because you were right. It was partially my fault. I did pass the information to the newspapers. The only reason I don't have blood on my hands is because you saved his life.

"The world isn't supposed to work that way. No one is supposed to die because of me! That was far too close to rest easy on my conscience. In essence you saved me then as well. I was angry at you for lying — when I lie all the time — then I was angry at you for not lying, and then I was angry at you when you saved me from being a murderer! I've accused you of being mad! I'm the one who has been acting like a lunatic!"

"You can change that," Sherlock said.

"Yes. Yes. I know. But I don't know who to be," Lord Cecil said, then suddenly he changed the subject. "I heard that you are staying here over the holiday."

"Yes."

"I know that the math questionists are staying to cram for three more weeks, but you are reading for the Natural Science Tripos. That's several months away."

"That's correct."

"Then why are you staying?"

"I don't know that it is any concern of yours."

"Quite correct, Holmes. It is none of my affair, but would you at least tell me if these sanctions have caused you trouble at home?"

"Yes."

"I'm sorry—"

"It is not your fault. I chose to do what I did and it turned out to be the proverbial last straw. I knew the break was coming eventually. I don't regret it."

"That's some comfort, I suppose. I have much to think about," Lord Cecil said distractedly. "Well, I hope that you have a pleasant holiday despite all that."

"And you as well," Holmes said.

Lord Cecil picked up his cap and gown and wandered out. Holmes watched out the window as Lord Cecil crossed the court still deep in thought.

Several of the dons stopped in to chat when they heard Holmes was staying. It was awkward on both sides and he was just as glad when they left. Rev. Clowe brought by a tiny potted sapling of a fir tree not two feet high, nor a foot around. Jonathan decorated it with waxed string and pictures cut from old calendars.

"Rev. Clowe," Sherlock said as the Senior Tutor was preparing to leave, "I was wondering I might have a key to the college laboratory so that I may run experiments over the holidays."

"I don't see how there could be any harm in that," Rev. Clowe said. "I'll have a copy sent over."

"Thank you."

Dr Mackenzie stopped by on Christmas Eve. Sherlock was away at the laboratory. It was a cold night and the doctor was tempted by Jonathan's offer of a cup of tea and a spot by the fire. As he warmed himself he admired Jonathan's holiday decorations.

"You've made it quite cheery in here," Dr Mackenzie said.

"Oh, just a few things I scraped up. I have less to do, less I can do. So I keep things very clean and do a little extra to brighten things."

"Does he appreciate it?"

"He has been very busy."

"No problems?"

"No. It almost seems like that must have been a different person."

"I understand. When he was studying with me I felt the same thing. I've seen it before in others. People can appear very different when they are well. We can hope he has seen the last of it."

"Yes."

"Thank you for the tea. I can wait a little bit longer, but—"

"But what, Doctor?" Sherlock Holmes asked as he entered the door and tossed his coat, scarf, cap and gown upon a chair.

"But I will have to go back soon. There is a party tonight," Dr Mackenzie said.

"A party?"

"Oh, yes, they have a band at the asylum and there will be dancing and much gayety. They act quite crazy on Christmas Eve."

"You live at a lunatic asylum, Dr Mackenzie," Sherlock Holmes observed as he waved Jonathan back to his seat when he made a move to pick up Sherlock's things to put them away.

"Well, yes, but on Christmas Eve even the staff members act like lunatics. I have to be there to keep them sorted out. I would invite you to see for yourself. However—"

"The Dean is unlikely to allow me to go to the asylum unless it is a one-way trip," Sherlock finished for him. "I did manage to obtain authorization to cross the street to make a purchase this afternoon, but I dare say they had the assistant porter watching me the whole time."

"You would think you were a dangerous criminal," Dr Mackenzie said.

"Yes. It is rather preposterous."

"I don't understand why they would go to such an effort. Why not send you down and be done with it?" Dr Mackenzie asked.

"I think they haven't quite made up their minds as to whether I'm genius or a rogue."

Dr Mackenzie laughed.

"You are probably right. But they err in believing that it must be one or the other, and that being a rogue is necessarily bad."

"Such opinions wouldn't make you popular, Doctor."

"Sometimes they don't. But here, I brought this," Dr Mackenzie said handing a thick packet to Sherlock. "I thought perhaps you would find it useful."

Sherlock unwrapped the package and looked at the book inside.

"*Medical Jurisprudence* by Alfred S. Taylor. I have heard of him. He testified in several cases that I have read."

"I attended some of his lectures when I was taking my degree at Guy's Hospital," Dr Mackenzie said.

"Poisons, wounds, blood stains," Sherlock read as he flipped through the table of contents. "Thank you, Doctor, it looks extremely useful. Unfortunately, I haven't anything for you."

"Just seeing you well is gift enough."

Sherlock Holmes paused for a moment and looked intently at Dr Mackenzie. Then he turned to his coat on the chair and pulled a package from its pocket.

"Well, I suppose while we are giving gifts I could deliver this one. It may be a bit more traditional to wait until Boxing Day, but it might be good to open it now. Merry Christmas, Jonathan," he said handing a rectangular object wrapped in brown paper to him.

Jonathan beamed as he took it and began removing the wrapping. He had not expected a gift and he was flattered that Sherlock had gone to the trouble of seeking a variance from the college restrictions for the purpose of making the purchase. As the paper fell away Jonathan saw that inside was a book entitled *The Moonstone*.

"I noticed that you had finished Dickens' *A Christmas Carol* a few days ago."

"Yes, sir. It was the last that I had. Thank you, sir!"

Sherlock dismissed his thanks with a wave. Jonathan retrieved another package from the table and handed it to Sherlock Holmes.

"This came in the post today."

"From brother Mycroft," Sherlock said examining the package. "Well, let's see what it is."

Sherlock tore off the brown paper and opened the box inside. The box was filled with tissue paper which was wrapped around a leather-bound case. Sherlock drew the case out and opened it. He stared at the contents for a moment and then ran his long thin fingers up the smooth, gently curved walnut handle. He lifted it out and set the box aside. He ran his other hand around the brass rim. It was a large and powerful lens. The glass was flawless. Sherlock Holmes looked up from the magnifying lens to see Dr Mackenzie observing him carefully.

"It means a great deal to you, doesn't it?" Dr Mackenzie said softly, looking him in the eye.

"Yes," Sherlock responded returning the gaze.

Then Sherlock Holmes looked back at the magnifying lens. It was wood, metal, and glass, a tool of excellent construction.

"Yes. It will be quite useful in my work," Sherlock said restoring it to its case. "My brother is very perceptive."

Dr Mackenzie watched him a moment longer then stood up.

"Well, I should go to maintain some semblance of order at the asylum," Dr Mackenzie said. "Merry Christmas, Sherlock, and to you, Jonathan."

Both of them returned the greetings to Dr Mackenzie and saw him out the door.

Chapter 30

An East Wind

*"I was myself somewhat uneasy when through the long night
I still from time to time heard the dull sound of his tread"*
Dr Watson, *The Sign of Four*

The holidays passed quickly and quietly. Holmes spent the majority of them in the laboratory. Jonathan was correct in his belief that his master still found ways to indulge in tobacco. While most of his time at the laboratory was spent working through experiments, sometimes Sherlock went there merely so he could light his pipe with less danger of attracting unwanted attention. He enjoyed having the college laboratory to himself as he sometimes had at Bart's. He disliked being interrupted by conversation from the laboratory supervisor or other students when he was in the midst of a complex experiment, and as much as he appreciated Jonathan's service and devotion, Sherlock sometimes felt to the need to be away from even his scrutiny. But as he walked back to his rooms after dinner at the Hall on the second of January, he knew that it would not last much longer. The undergraduate members of the college were already returning. Lectures would begin again in a couple of days. Sherlock knew that it was time to turn his attention once more to the regular course of study. With a sigh of resignation, Sherlock Holmes tossed himself upon a chair and took up his books.

But a wind was rising from the east that night, and whether it was the wind buffeting the college, or the frustration of having to study subjects that he felt would be of little use to him, Sherlock Holmes was restless. He tossed his books aside and took up his violin instead, and then tossed it aside and paced the floor before disappearing into his room for the night.

Jonathan sensed Sherlock's agitation and heard him moving about in his room later. When he heard Sherlock in the sitting room long before dawn, Jonathan rose and lit a candle and joined him there. Sherlock was dressed and from the state of his attire, Jonathan was not sure that he had ever undressed. He was just finishing tying his boots as Jonathan appeared.

"May I be of service, sir?" Jonathan asked.

"No, Jonathan," Sherlock said as he picked up his cap and gown, "Go back to your bed. I'm going to the laboratory to see if I can complete one last project before the college becomes entirely overrun again. I'll be back when I'm done."

"Yes, sir," Jonathan said.

Jonathan saw Sherlock out the door and made sure that the outer oak door was latched behind him.

Jonathan thought it just as well that Sherlock had decided to go to the laboratory. It was best that he keep busy rather than sitting about and brooding. Jonathan had no doubt that Sherlock could absorb the information in the books with great speed once he set his mind to it. Another few hours would not matter much.

Jonathan lay down again, but sleep did not come. Soon he rose, dressed, lit the lamps and built up the fire. He made Sherlock's bed and dusted the rooms before preparing himself a cup of tea and some toast upon the fire. He drew a chair up to the window and set his plate and cup upon the window-sill to watch the sunrise.

The sun rose lazily in the sky and made little attempt to warm the air at Sidney Sussex College. The wind from the east was still rising and it tugged at the gowns of a few Fellows and undergraduates as they trickled towards the chapel for Morning Prayers.

The wind made Jonathan restless as well. Change was in the air. He could feel it. He spread the leftover crumbs from his toast upon the window-sill, but no birds came. Not even the pigeons. The birds were restless as well.

As Jonathan understood it, Sherlock would receive his degree at the end of the next term if he passed the Natural Science Tripos. After Sherlock received his degree, he —they— would be free to leave this place. Sherlock would obtain a position somewhere. Jonathan presumed he would take him with him. That would be another change.

As Jonathan sat there at the window looking across the court he realized that some of these young men were only a year or two older than himself. He was sixteen now and as tall as many of them.

He thought back to growing up on Mycroft Manor in Yorkshire. Nothing much seemed to change there; each year came and went much the same as the ones before. Oh, some winters were harsher than others and some harvests thinner; folks were born and died, but more was the same than was different. That's how his life had been until that winter....

He leaned his face in his hands trying to recall the whirlwind of events of the last four years, and as he did the morning was shattered by a roar that shook the building. Jonathan jumped and looked up to see people diving to the ground and glass flying into the court. He couldn't see the grounds around the laboratory from the window. Just a portion of its roof was visible over the top of the other hall. Fear filled him as dark clouds of smoke billowed up from the laboratory roof. He jumped up from his chair, ran out the door and down the stairs, but he was intercepted by one of the dons in the court and ordered back to the rooms without a word of explanation. With much trepidation Jonathan obeyed. He sat back down next to the window and waited, not knowing if Sherlock was alive or dead.

At the other side of the college near the laboratory, the young men were picking themselves up from the ground. Porters, caretakers and Fellows ran towards the laboratory as dust and smoke poured from the windows. A crowd gathered as the fellows and the caretakers scurried around putting out a fire in the laboratory and surveying the damage.

Undergraduates stood watching and whispering at a distance. A short time later one of the porters came out leading a figure much blackened by the smoke from the building. A ripple went through the undergraduates as they saw who it was, but before any dared approach, the porter and his companion were met by the Dean and the Senior Tutor who were already dressed for Chapel. The Dean squinted with disapproval.

"Are you injured, Mr Holmes?" Rev. Clowe asked.

"Not badly, a few minor cuts and burns, perhaps," said Sherlock, producing a handkerchief from a pocket and endeavouring to wipe his face.

"You are bleeding, Mr Holmes," said Dean Hoch.

"From the glass most likely," Sherlock said looking down at his left sleeve that was soaked with blood.

"Come to my office so I may take a look at it," the Dean said.

Dean Hoch led the way to his office and Rev. Clowe followed the two of them.

The Dean took out his medical bag and sent his servant for some hot water while Rev. Clowe helped Sherlock removed his jacket and shirt.

"What were you doing in the laboratory this early?" Dean Hoch asked as he cleaned the wound.

"I was performing an experiment," Sherlock said.

"A rather dangerous experiment it seems," the Dean said as he began to bind up Sherlock's arm.

Just then a college servant entered with a note.

"A message for you, sir," the servant said to the Dean.

"Just a moment," he said as he finished tying off the bandage. "You may want to go to the hospital and have a few stitches put in that later. But this will do for now."

He took the note from the servant. After he read it he handed it to Rev. Clowe.

"From the Master. Will you stay with Mr Holmes while I obtain the information the master requests?" Dean Hoch asked.

"Of course," Rev. Clowe replied.

"You might attempt to clean yourself up," the Dean said to Sherlock before leaving the room.

After the Dean left, the Senior Tutor waved the note.

"This does not bode well, Sherlock. The Master has summoned the three of us to appear before him. I warned you that you were pushing too close to the edge."

"I know," Sherlock said as he attempted to scrub the smoke, dust and yellow stains from his hands and face.

"I don't believe there is anything more I can do," Rev. Clowe said with a sigh.

Sherlock said nothing as he donned his shirt and jacket again. He sat silently until the Dean returned.

"If you gentlemen are ready, I don't think we should keep the Master waiting any longer," Dean Hoch said.

They followed him silently across the court to the Master's Lodge. They wound their way up the stairs in silence and a servant escorted them into the Master's chamber. Dean Hoch and the Senior Tutor stood before the Master's desk with Sherlock Holmes between them.

Rev. Philip Roberts looked up at them as they entered, his stern eyes glowering over his hooked nose and white beard. The Master glared at Holmes for a moment and then turned to the Dean.

"I understand that there was an explosion at the laboratory?" the college master said.

"Yes, sir," Dean Hoch responded.

"And you believe Mr Holmes here is responsible?"

"Yes, sir."

The Master turned his gaze back to Sherlock Holmes.

"Is this true?"

"Yes, sir," Sherlock said.

"Where is your gown, Mr Holmes?" the Master asked.

"It caught fire when—," Sherlock said.

The Master held up his hand.

"Start from the beginning and explain to me exactly what happened."

"I wanted to make tri-nitro toluene—"

"You look rather puzzled Rev. Clowe," the master interrupted.

"I did not know that the laboratory had any toluene in stock."

"It didn't," Sherlock admitted. "I used ethyl alcohol instead.

"Continue."

"I was using very small quantities. I had successfully mixed 4 millilitres of 95% sulphuric acid with 3 millilitres of 75% nitric acid and was adding that mixture to the ethylene in a 50 millilitre beaker when it exploded with a flash of light. The concussion shattered the beaker and knocked me back from the table. Dust filled the air and at first it seemed deathly quiet after the roar of the explosion. Then I heard the crackle of flames. Through the dust I could see that the spirit lamp had been shattered and the spirits had caught fire. The flames were spreading over the table and the floor. I attempted to smother the fire with my gown but it caught fire itself. Then one of the porters came to me through the dust and smoke and insisted that I leave the building. I believe they put out the fire shortly thereafter."

"Was the laboratory supervisor in attendance when you performed this experiment?"

"No, sir."

"Mr Niles is out of town for the holiday," Rev. Clowe added. "He will be back tomorrow."

The Master turned to the Senior Tutor.

"Rev. Clowe, does Mr Holmes' explanation sound plausible?"

"Yes, sir. The nitrating process is very sensitive and exceedingly exothermic. The substitution of ethyl alcohol for toluene might make the process more unstable. It is also possible that the explosion was due to the mixture overheating. A salt-ice bath is essential. It is extremely important to control the temperature while mixing the acids. Patience is also very necessary because the acids must be added very slowly while stirring rapidly. Each step could take 30-60 minutes. Any attempt to rush the process could cause the experiment to overheat and fail catastrophically."

"Did you sanction this experiment, Rev. Clowe?"

"Not precisely, sir," Rev. Clowe said. "I did provide Mr Holmes with a key to the laboratory so that he could run some experiments during the break. Mr Holmes has a very active and restless mind. I hoped that having access to the laboratory between terms would keep him from being idle and thus tempted to mischief. However, he did not consult with me about the type of experiments that he wished to perform. I should have inquired. I take full responsibility for failing to do so before I provided him with access to the facility."

"We will discuss that later, Rev. Clowe."

The Master returned his gaze to Sherlock Holmes.

"Did you consult any of the Fellows of the college before attempting this experiment?"

"No, sir."

The master tapped his fingers on the desk and scowled. He

looked over at Dean Hoch.

"The nature of the damage?"

"Twenty-eight windows were blown out, sir," the Dean said. "The glass in the cabinet doors in the laboratory was shattered. Much of the glassware and the scientific apparatus in the cabinets were damaged or destroyed. The fire was contained by Mr Holmes' efforts and quickly put out after he left. It did little damage beyond some scarring of the table and the floor, though Mr Holmes' gown is quite beyond repair."

"Estimated cost of repairs?"

"It is still too early for an accurate assessment. However, I believe it will cost the college at least a thousand pounds to replace the glass and the equipment."

"Any personal injuries?"

"Mainly cuts from flying glass. Mr Holmes himself seems to have had the most severe."

"And you cancelled Morning Prayers?"

"Yes, sir, the porters and the senior Fellows are instructing all undergraduates to remain in their rooms until the glass and debris can be removed and the damage fully assessed."

The Master shook his head. He adjusted his glasses and consulted some notes before him. Then he looked up at Sherlock Holmes with a piercing glare.

"Mr Holmes, while I rarely interact with the junior members of the college myself, I do receive reports of them. I am aware of all that goes on at Sidney Sussex College. When you first arrived you were quiet and studious. There were some health problems, but we had high hopes that you would take a first despite them. You postponed your initial attempt at the Previous Exam, but did quite well on your Mays. Then you requested a change of course from the Mathematical Tripos to the Natural Science Tripos. You performed well on the Previous Exam that term and seemed to be applying yourself diligently to your new course. I understand that you have taken two terms at St. Bartholomew's Hospital in London during the Long Vacations as well. However, since the commencement of the Michaelmas Term there has been a distinct change in your habits. Your academic work has continued to be excellent. It is your "extracurricular activities" which have repeatedly called you in censure. I see here that you received a warning in October after you were found loitering about police investigations and keeping company with a well-known pick-pocket."

"Yes, sir."

"After that you were fined for violating curfew, being about town without your academical gown after dark, and being found in a pub with a burglar."

"He was retired," Sherlock said.

"Excuse me, Mr Holmes?"

"He was a former cracksman."

The Master scowled at him and continued.

"Then you were sanctioned for violating curfew, brawling and interfering with police business."

"Yes, sir. I was trying stop—"

"It was none of your affair, Mr Holmes. You have no business interfering with the police and you have no business wandering about the town in the company of robbers, thieves and other known criminals."

"It was research, sir."

"Research? What kind of research is that?"

"I am studying crime so that I may embark on a career as a consulting detective."

The Master glared at him.

"I have no idea what a consulting detective may in truth be, but if it requires these types of behaviours then I believe it would be an unfortunate choice of career for someone of your intelligence, Mr Holmes. If you persist in that folly you will have to continue your researches elsewhere."

Sherlock was silent in the face of this condemnation. The Master looked back at the notes.

"At that time the constabulary requested that you be kept out of town. We could have sent you down then. We thought bringing you into college might provide you with better role-models and help you learn self-discipline. However, it only seems to have changed the nature of your activities without improving your discretion. Last month an experiment of your own initiative produced such noxious fumes about the college that classes had to be moved to another college. At that time you were warned to practice more caution in your experiments. Now this. Is there anything you have to say for yourself?"

"I'm sorry, sir. I misjudged the results."

"Unfortunately, being sorry is not good enough this time. Some small breaches of discipline might be undesirable, though not unexpected, of young men still learning the ways of the world. When such happens those young men must be called to account and taught the error of their ways. But you have gone beyond that. Your chemical experiments pose a very real danger to the persons and property of this college. Families may hesitate to send their sons to us if they feel it is not safe here. Your "researches" in town have brought Sidney Sussex College into disrepute as a community that harbours those of criminal tendencies. That harms not only our present graduates and undergraduates, but our alumni and those who may come to us in the future. The physical damage done can be more easily repaired than the reputation of the college, but we cannot ignore the magnitude of either. We have been extremely patient with you, Mr Holmes, but you have left us no choice. For the good of Sidney Sussex College, we must dismiss you from the college and strike your name from our rolls. You will have until the end of the week to remove yourself and your belongings."

"Yes, sir," Sherlock said, and turned to leave. Then he turned back again.

"There will be a bill for the damages, will there not, sir?"

"Yes, Mr Holmes."

"Don't send it to my father. I am going to my brother's rooms in London. Send the bill to me there. I will pay it myself."

"Leave the proper address with the bursar."

"I will do so."

Sherlock turned and walked out the door and down the stairs. His mind was racing. The dismissal from the college did not surprise him. But struck off the rolls? Was he such an embarrassment that they weren't willing to acknowledge he had ever been here? That stung far more than the slivers of glass he was still picking out of his hands. He had been banned from the town of Cambridge at the request of the constabulary and now he had been dismissed from Sidney Sussex College. He wouldn't wait until the end of the week. He was leaving this inhospitable town forthwith. He would continue with his "folly" elsewhere.

Jonathan was startled and immensely relieved when the door suddenly opened and Sherlock walked briskly in and slammed both doors behind him. His clothes were dirty and blood stained and he had a few cuts and some yellow stains on his hands.

"Are you all right, sir?"

"Yes."

Sherlock went directly to his desk and dug out a telegraph form.

He wrote upon it and then held it out to Jonathan.

"Take this to the post office. This should be enough to pay for it. Don't wait for a reply."

"But, sir?"

"The restrictions have been lifted. The porter will not stop you. Go."

"Yes, sir."

Jonathan did not feel the elation he would have expected to feel to be once more free on the streets of Cambridge. Instead he was filled with a sense of dread. Something bad had obviously happened so why had the sanctions been lifted? What was in the telegram he carried? His unease was not improved as he returned to the college grounds and noticed the careful way in which heads turned away from him and voices whispered. It was worse than it had ever been. Other servants at the college scurried away without a good morning or even an acknowledgement of his presence. It was as if he had some loathsome disease that no one had told him about.

When Jonathan entered their rooms, he was surprised to find their bags packed and waiting by the door. Sherlock was hurriedly packing the remainder of his belongings in the trunk which stood in the sitting room.

"I've arranged for the porter to see to the trunk. We will have to manage the rest."

"Where are we going, sir?" Jonathan asked.

"To the railway station," Sherlock Holmes answered cryptically. Jonathan knew better to press him when he spoke like that.

Jonathan and Sherlock hauled the bags downstairs and across the court to the gatehouse. In Sidney Street Sherlock hailed a passing four wheeler and they piled in. At the station a puzzled Jonathan waited while Sherlock bought tickets. Then Sherlock led him to a waiting train and pressed three of the bags on him.

"Take these. Here is your ticket. Here's enough silver to get a ride from the railway station to the manor."

"Aren't you coming, sir?" Jonathan asked.

"No. You know I am not welcome there. You are going back to Yorkshire. I am going to London."

Jonathan suddenly realized that this was not like their partings before. This was not meant to be a temporary separation. A million emotions flooded through him. Dr Mackenzie had been right when he said that their relationship was more than that of master and servant. Even though Sherlock was only five years older, he was the closest thing to a father that Jonathan could remember. He was the older brother Jonathan would never have. When Jonathan had been thrust into the role of Sherlock's caretaker, it was a role he had taken on with affection. Sometimes that job had terrified him, but the terror had always risen from the potential loss. He had gained much in return. Now he realized Sherlock was sending him away, forever.

"Have I done something to displease you, sir?" Jonathan asked, the hurt edging his voice.

"No, Jonathan. No one has been more faithful. But they dismissed me from the college, which means the end of my allowance. At the moment I haven't the resources to keep myself, much less you. There is a letter in one of your bags addressed to my brother Sherrinford. Give it to him in person and I have no doubt that he will take care of you."

"But what of you? Sir, I would rather—"

"Don't argue with me, Jonathan. Quickly now, you need to board," Sherlock said pushing the boy towards the train.

"Sherlock! Please—" Jonathan pleaded.

Sherlock took Jonathan by the shoulders and looked him in the eye.

"Trust me, Jonathan. This is best for both of us," Sherlock said.

It was not a command. It was an appeal to friendship, the one appeal that had always swayed Jonathan even when he wasn't sure Sherlock had his wits about him.

"Will you be all right?" Jonathan asked.

"Yes."

Jonathan dropped the bags and threw his arms around Sherlock. Just then the guard appeared.

"Look sharp, boys, I can't hold the train for you," the guard said.

Sherlock gently unpeeled Jonathan's arms and turned him towards the train again.

"Go on," Sherlock said.

This time Jonathan obeyed. He grabbed the bags and leaped through the door the guard was holding open. The guard slammed the door behind him and signalled the engine driver. Jonathan stared out the window of the carriage as the train began to move.

Sherlock Holmes stood on the platform and watched the train pull away, taking Jonathan and his past with it. Then he turned his face towards the train to London and his future.

Acknowledgments

I am grateful to Sir Arthur Conan Doyle for introducing the world to the greatest detective of fact or fancy. I strongly urge anyone reading this book to read the original four novellas and fifty-six short stories written by Sir Arthur Conan Doyle about Sherlock Holmes, for you cannot truly appreciate this book or any other imitation until you have read the original stories.

I used countless reference books and websites to recreate Yorkshire, Cambridge and London, England of December 1871 through January 1875. Numerous Victorian novels, biographies, autobiographies and other books in the public domain by or about Cambridge graduates helped me understand and recreate the language and habits of graduates and undergraduates of the time period, including *Charlie Villars at Cambridge* and *Harry Edgarton or The Younger Son of the Day* by George L. Tottenham, *The Memoirs of Arthur Hamilton, B.A. of Trinity College Cambridge University* by Christopher Carr (pseud. for Arthur Christopher Benson), *The Cambridge Freshman or Memoirs of Mr Golightly* by Martin Legrand, *Students Guide to the University of Cambridge*, 4th Ed. 1880, *Annals of Cambridge* by Charles Henry Cooper, *Cambridge Trifles: Splutterings from an Undergraduate Pen* by George Nugent-Bankes, and *Random Reminiscences* by Charles H.E. Brookfield. Some portions of this book are based on the *Round the Red Lamp* and *The Stark Munro Letters* by Sir Arthur Conan Doyle, which are also in the public domain.

Portions of chapters 16 through 19 are based on Sir Arthur Conan Doyle's short story, "The Gloria Scott," (currently in the public domain) compiled in *The Memoirs of Sherlock Holmes*, and the character of Victor Trevor originates there. I extrapolated Victor Trevor's character into other scenes. The character of Reginald Musgrave comes from "The Musgrave Ritual" also from *The Memoirs of Sherlock Holmes*. Stamford was mentioned briefly in *A Study in Scarlet* as the man who introduced Holmes and Watson. The backstory for Stamford described here is a figment of my imagination based on Watson's referring to Stamford as "young Stamford." Lord Cecil Hamley and Maberley are based on characters mentioned in Doyle's "The Adventure of the Three

Gables."

The Senior Tutor, Reverend Clowe, Dean Reverend James Hoch, supervisor Reverend Douglas Healy and the College Master Reverend Philip Roberts were also loosely based on the equivalent persons at Sydney Sussex College at the time. Some tales of Reverend Clowe's exploits are based on stories told by Rev. J. Clough Williams Ellis (on whom he was based) in the *Life of Robert Machray, Archbishop of Rupert's Land* by Robert Machray. George Rowland is very loosely based on Rowland George Allanson-Winn who would later co-author several books on swordplay and single-stick play.

Some of the descriptions of Victorians and their occupations which are recited by Sherlock Holmes are based on *London Characters and The Humorous Side of London Life*, a collection of public domain works by London sketch artists which has been collected on a website that can be found at http://www.angelfire.com/ks/landzastanza/london.html

Tales of night climbing at Cambridge University come from a variety of different sources most of whom prefer to remain anonymous. Their veracity cannot be proven. Since I left out portions of the climbing route information that I had, and what I had was rather dated and of questionable provenance, I would not recommend that anyone try to use this book as a climbing guide. The result could be most unfortunate.

The majority of the incidents reported herein are not based on any written record of any similar incidence in the City of Cambridge, at Sydney Sussex College or any other college of the University of Cambridge occurring between 1872 and 1875. The laboratory incident in the final chapter is based loosely on a similar experiment performed by my own father at his high school in Tulsa, Oklahoma, USA.

Dr George Mackenzie was loosely based on Dr George Mackenzie Bacon who was the medical superintendent of the Fulbourn Asylum (aka Cambridgeshire Pauper Asylum) at that time. I appreciate Karen Murdoch's assistance in retrieving some of Dr G. M. Bacon's publications from the University of Minnesota Library and other libraries. Dr George Mackenzie Bacon did indeed write *Handwriting Analysis of the Insane* mentioned in Chapter 23 and curious readers can seek it out and read the section discussed. However, there is no record of Dr Bacon ever treating a patient with cocaine, though papers from that time period do record

ACKNOWLEDGEMENTS

that many doctors tried using it to treat many different things.

I did extensive research on Victorian medicine and psychiatry as well as some reading on our current knowledge of these fields. I attempted to use the medical terminology in use at the time and place of the event in the book while being aware of more up-to-date research. It must be remembered that this book is set very early in the days of scientific pharmacology, and the dangers and addictiveness of cocaine or opium derivatives such as morphine were not yet known. In those days doctors often experimented on their patients or on themselves in an effort to better understand the effects of new drugs and to find new ways to help their patients. There was no system in place at that time for controlled testing of new drugs. The primary source of information that doctors had available (other that advertisements from the companies selling the drugs) were anecdotal case notes published in professional journals. The cases notes mentioned by Dr Mackenzie in this book are real.

No competent doctor today would give cocaine to a patient suffering from Post-Traumatic Stress Disorder (as Holmes was). The risk of addiction and damage to the nervous system is too great. Sherlock Holmes is lucky that Dr Mackenzie and Dr Watson both feared the long term effects of the drug and discouraged his use of it. There is no evidence in the Canon that Sherlock Holmes ever used it for long periods of time.

I owe a debt to William S. Baring-Gould for his biography, *Sherlock Holmes of Baker Street,* because that book first taught me to look upon Sherlock Holmes as a dynamic, living human being, and introduced me to the Sherlockian world beyond the Canon. I also thank Sherlockians everywhere for keeping green the memory of Sherlock Holmes. Without them I would never have been inspired to take this journey. I am grateful to those who have been willing to take the journey with me. I am hopeful that they will continue on with me as I follow Sherlock Holmes through his short acting career and the early days of his career as a detective in Parts II & III of *The Consulting Detective Trilogy.*

I am especially grateful to Larry Feldman, Leah Guinn, Ron Lies, Jeffrey McGraw, Frank Mentzel, Michael Procter, Steve Scott, Mark Stratton and Diane Zike for critiquing and commenting on the manuscript.

About the Author

Darlene became an avid follower of Sherlock Holmes when she was in high school. Since then she has corresponded with a number of Sherlockians around the world. She is a member and former "Chief Surgeon" of *Dr. Watson's Neglected Patients*, a scion of the *Baker Street Irregulars* located in Denver, Colorado. She is also a member of the *Hounds of the Internet* and the *Hudson Valley Sciontists*. She has had four articles published in the *Baker Street Journal*.

9 781938 143472